# ALWAYS ON MY MIND

BETH MORAN

Boldwood

First published in Great Britain in 2023 by Boldwood Books Ltd.

Copyright © Beth Moran, 2023

Cover Design by Debbie Clement Design

Cover Photography: Shutterstock

A CIP catalogue record for this book is available from the British Library.

Paperback ISBN 978-1-80483-355-1

Large Print ISBN 978-1-80483-351-3

Hardback ISBN 978-1-80483-350-6

Ebook ISBN 978-1-80483-348-3

Kindle ISBN 978-1-80483-349-0

Audio CD ISBN 978-1-80483-356-8

MP3 CD ISBN 978-1-80483-353-7

Digital audio download ISBN 978-1-80483-347-6

Boldwood Books Ltd
23 Bowerdean Street
London SW6 3TN
www.boldwoodbooks.com

*For Sophie Steele, who loves stories, and is sure to have a great one of her own*

# PROLOGUE

## TEN YEARS AGO

I might have felt this nervous before – heart racing, my stomach twisted up in knots – but right then I couldn't remember it.

This was one of those nights that I would surely never forget. Given that my prom date was my twin brother, my hopes perhaps shouldn't have been that high. But then again, his best friend Elliot Ollerton was arriving any minute, and that had the potential to change everything.

'Jessie, come on!' Isaac, my brother, called up the stairs. It was all right for him; all he'd had to do was put on a suit and rub some gel through his hair. My preparation for this evening had started a month ago, with trying on every party dress in Meadowhall. The shopping centre was in Sheffield, a decent drive away, but it was a rite of passage for every sixth form girl in Brooksby Academy. I wondered how many of them had thought about Elliot Ollerton the whole time.

I wasn't the only one who'd dreamed about being his date tonight. Having joined our school at the start of A levels, Elliot had not quite lost the frisson of interest that a city boy arriving at a village school stirs up. It helped, of course, that he was affable and at ease with himself. He was the fastest cross-country runner in the county, and had floppy blond hair and a smile that flipped hearts upside down.

What I lacked in terms of looks or any of the other, as yet mysterious, elements that caught a popular boy's attention, I made up for by being Isaac's twin. With the three of us catching the school bus from Houghton, an even more boring village than Brooksby, twice a day we spent twenty glorious minutes discussing everything from our English coursework to the likelihood of our driving instructor being an alien.

Tucked away inside my tender teenage heart, I knew that Elliot liked me. We were interested in the same things – social justice and mysterious crime stories. We would discuss food preferences until Isaac begged us to change the subject. Once, when he was playing Xbox with Isaac, I made him laugh so hard he snorted lemonade out of his nose.

What I had no clue about was whether he liked me just as a friend. Or, even worse, his best friend's sister who, Isaac had made clear, was completely Out of Bounds to any of his mates (I did point out that this only left people he didn't like as potential boyfriends, but his solution to that was I stay single).

But when Elliot looked at me, eyes crinkling with humour, or his forehead furrowed with concentration as we debated an issue, I couldn't help wondering if he felt the same as me. Which was utter infatuation. I was about as in love with Elliot Ollerton as a seventeen-year-old living in a tiny village who'd never been kissed can be in love.

So, as I inspected myself in the mirror for one last time, I knew that if this was going to be like the movies, I had to look right. So perfect that Elliot suddenly saw, not his friend's perpetually disorganised and amusing sister, but the Woman of His Dreams. As I adjusted the ice blue, floor-length dress, I felt a flutter of hope that it might be enough.

'Finally!' Isaac took one look at my hand gripping the banister and adjusted his tone. 'Hey, you look good though, sis. I like the... sparkly bits.'

'You've managed to look not quite so ugly yourself, for once.' Isaac and I shared the same black hair and pale grey eyes, with a smattering of tiny freckles. While his open features and bold bone structure had created a face that earned almost as many Valentine's Day DMs as Elliot, on me they prompted grandparents to declare me 'handsome'. And had earned me one Valentine's Day card to date. Which I suspected was from my dad.

'Come on then. Elliot's waiting.'

To everyone's surprise, Isaac had decided to go with me to the prom. As he'd patiently explained to our parents, he'd rather spend the evening with his mates than hanging about with a random girl pretending she was special. I was thrilled, as that meant we'd be going with Elliot. Rather than choosing the unimaginative (and expensive) option of hiring a limo or a tractor (this was the countryside; a lot of kids chugged to prom on farm machinery) Isaac had hired a tandem bike to cycle the mile and a half to the venue. When I pointed out that I wasn't spending a fortune on a dress only to arrive sweaty and dishevelled after cycling up the hill to the Houghton Country Club, he invited Elliot to ride tandem and added a kid's bike trailer on the back for me.

'Hey.' Elliot was attempting to prop the bike against a tree when Isaac and I stepped out onto the front path of our tiny terrace. He gave Isaac a complicated fist-bump then turned to look at me, where I was still hovering nervously half-way down the path.

And I mean, he *looked* at me. At my stubbornly messy hair tamed into a sleek twist for once, a few artful tendrils curled around flaming cheeks. Mum had insisted on doing my make-up and I don't know what kind of spell she weaved with that smoky eyeliner wand, but it had worked.

'Wow.' Elliot's eyebrows disappeared beneath his floppy fringe. For a second he appeared genuinely stunned, and my heart thumped so hard I was surprised the beading on my bodice didn't ping off. 'You look... I mean, you always look...' He stopped, cleared his throat, and tried again. 'Jess, you look beautiful.'

Before I could remember how to speak, Isaac had flung an arm around Elliot's neck and dragged him towards the tiny square of grass that made up our front garden. 'Photos, before Mum starts crying again.'

We did the obligatory poses while my parents cooed and clucked and made embarrassing comments about what they'd got up to at their school prom. Standing there, in between two of the people I loved most in the whole world, it felt as though all my dreams were about to come true.

For the next few hours I sailed along on a cloud of awestruck happiness. Once we'd safely locked the bike up, Elliot had waited for Isaac to go and say hello to another group of friends, then turned to me, face serious.

'I'm counting on you to protect me tonight.' He swivelled his eyes towards a group of girls loitering a few metres away, and gave a brief shudder.

'So I'm a shield to ward off all your admirers?' I folded my arms. 'I'm not sure how I feel about that. I thought we'd genuinely bonded over cheese and ketchup paninis. Now I find out you only want to hang out with me as a decoy date so Macy MacDonald won't jump you.'

'Come on, Jessie. You know that's not the only reason.'

The stomach fluttering started up again.

'There's Gabby Stephens and Serena Curtis... that girl with the weird eyebrows...'

I swiped him with my clutch bag just as Isaac strolled back over. 'What's this?' His eyes narrowed suspiciously.

'Elliot's freaking out about being sexually harassed. He's begging me to be his bodyguard.'

Isaac scowled. 'My sister is not guarding anyone's body this evening. Least of all yours.'

I bit back the retort that I'd do whatever I damn well liked, instead ducking my eyes to hide my frustration.

As it turned out, after the first few minutes, Isaac wasn't around to play protective brother. There was a pretend casino set up on one side of the room and he was quickly sucked into the blackjack table. Elliot showed no interest in joining him, instead finding us a bench in a shadowy corner.

The rest of the evening was utter bliss. I didn't care that I ended up ignoring most of my friends, that instead of getting tipsy and dancing my heart out I spent the next two hours with one person. As we laughed and talked, our knees somehow ended up touching. My arm had come to rest against his and our heads were bent so close together I could feel the warmth of his breath. Every millimetre of contact was like connecting a circuit that sent electricity humming between us.

I'd next to no experience when it came to flirting, but when Elliot nudged me with his elbow, eyes glinting, I knew it wasn't my imagination. Meandering through gentle teasing, earnest soul-baring, loaded comments that made my heart pound in my throat, it was as if we were the only two people in the room. I'd never felt so alive.

When he asked if I wanted to go for a walk, I couldn't help glancing over at the roulette wheel, where Isaac was cheering along with a small crowd of onlookers, a girl he'd gone out with a few times hanging off his arm.

'Forget him,' Elliot muttered, taking my hand in a seemingly innocent gesture that took my breath away. 'He doesn't get to decide this any more.'

*Decide what?* I squeaked inside my head. Was this a *this*? What sort of a *this*?

We walked across the patio and slipped through a gate leading to the golf course. Elliot's hand was clammy in mine, and it thrilled me beyond words to think that he might be nervous about *this*. The sun was setting behind a hill in the distance, and the light glowed red, orange and magenta across the ridge of the forest, as though the treetops were on fire. I knew how they felt.

'Are you cold?' Elliot asked, once we'd settled on a patch of grass out of sight on the far side of a hillock. He ran his hand along my bare forearm, which only made the goosebumps even bigger.

I took a trembling breath, shaking my head. 'I'm... maybe nervous?'

*Nervous... elated... wondering when I'm going to wake up and find I've overslept for school again.*

'Nervous?' Elliot pulled his hand back, brow creasing. 'Jessie, you know you don't have to worry about me trying anything.'

I shook my head, my voice a whisper. 'I'm more worried you might not try.'

After the longest silence, he placed a tentative hand against my cheek, leant in and kissed me. I felt like I'd come home.

Well, if home was like the best, most exciting, delicious place ever. Like the world's greatest theme park and music festival and restaurant all condensed into a couple of square centimetres of soft, fervent flesh.

*Is it possible to faint from being kissed?*

'What are you thinking?' Elliot whispered against my forehead when we'd finally managed to break apart and take a long, breathless moment for our brains to unscramble.

'I'm thinking I should have asked Mum to do my make-up ages ago.'

The fading sunlight cast his face in shadow as he broke into a grin, hand confident this time as his thumb stroked my cheek. 'I miss your freckles.'

'Oh! Okay, so is it the dress?'

Elliot lowered his eyebrows, confused.

'Well something made you decide you wanted to... do *this*.'

'You mean this?' He leant in and kissed me again. Softly this time, so that my bones melted into liquid gold. 'I've wanted to do that for ages.'

'Then why haven't you?' I shook my head, disbelieving. 'If that's true, why didn't you invite me to the prom, so I didn't have to ride in a kiddie seat behind my brother?'

'Because I promised him I wouldn't.'

'What?' I sat back, feeling the familiar prickle of fraternal irritation. 'My brother doesn't own me. This isn't medieval times. Why would you promise that?'

Elliot sighed, but he held tight to my reluctant hand. 'It was ages ago. We were drinking on the hilltop. I asked a question about you. I'd probably asked way too many questions, and he got suspicious. It wasn't a hard promise to make to a new friend, considering I didn't know you, then.'

'I can't believe he made you do that. Has he asked all the boys in school to stay away?' I gave a bitter laugh. 'And here I was thinking it was because I was so unattractive.'

'I don't know about anyone else. But it's definitely not that. Not that I want to think about anyone else finding you attractive. But, with Isaac... You can understand him thinking that if we get together, it could mess things up.'

I said nothing, still too busy seething at my brother.

'How many real friends does Isaac have? Not people he hangs out with, but real friends. The kind who've got his back.'

I shrugged. 'He's got me. He's never needed loads of friends.'

'He's always had you. And then he met me.' He paused, waiting for me to catch up. 'So, what happens if we have each other? Or we end up hating each other?'

'He'd take my side.' I released a slow sigh. 'And he'd lose you. His only actual friend.'

'Back then, it was an obvious promise to make.'

'But now you've broken it. What happens?'

Elliot took my other hand, his eyes fixed on mine in the twilight. 'I'll talk to him. Make him understand. If he knows how we – well, how *I* – feel, he'll understand that keeping the promise will only cause more problems.'

My breath had got trapped behind my rapidly expanding heart. It was the kind of question I wouldn't have dared to ask anyone apart from him. 'How *do* you feel?'

He laughed, ducked his head and took two eternally long breaths before looking up again. 'I love you, Jessica Brown. So much it hurts.'

\* \* \*

Once it grew cold, we wandered back inside, dropping hands so that no one would suspect anything before we'd had a chance to speak to Isaac. My brother, however, was nowhere to be seen. The crowd at the blackjack table told us that he'd gone to an afterparty with Brittney, yet another girl he'd dated once or twice. Elliot and I decided to walk home, stopping by the tandem to remove a bottle of screw-top wine from the trailer with the intention of drinking as we walked.

We drifted down the hill, entwined together, and it was close to midnight by the time we reached the junction at the bottom. There was a steady stream of cars going up and down the hill, picking people up, and every time we spotted headlights approaching we ducked into the undergrowth at the side of the road to avoid being seen.

'There's people there.' Elliot came to an abrupt stop as the sound of voices floated around the last corner.

'It's Isaac,' I whispered, heart pounding. I instinctively dropped Elliot's hand and moved away. 'It's fine, we can say we couldn't find him so you offered to walk me home. There's nothing suspicious about that.'

'Hey, Danny.' Isaac's voice was overloud, a sure sign he'd been drinking. 'Have you seen my sister?'

'Nah mate,' Danny called back. 'But Keisha saw her with some guy on the golf course. They were kind of busy, you know what I'm saying?'

In the midst of the jeers and whoops I heard Isaac demanding to know who it was, swearing with frustration when Keisha insisted she couldn't tell in the darkness.

'I'm going to find her.' Isaac's voice was rough with anger. 'And him.'

Elliot grabbed my arm and we ran to the side of the lane, ducking behind a tree that in daylight would have been a comically bad hiding place, but in the darkness offered sufficient cover that a furious, alcohol-fuelled brother would storm straight past.

We waited another five minutes, but while some of the group ambled back up the hill after Isaac, others were happy to wait where they were. The general consensus was that he was going to go ballistic.

'I have to go and find him.'

Elliot stepped away from me. 'If any of them see us together, they'll message Isaac straight away.'

I nodded. 'I'll go up the hill, you go down?'

'I'm not leaving you on your own in the dark.'

I shook my head. 'There are people everywhere. I'll be fine.'

'It's the people I'm worried about.'

'Don't be silly. No one would dare touch Isaac Brown's sister!' I placed my hand on his chest and he grabbed it, a grin flashing across his face. 'It's a ten-minute walk without you distracting me every five steps. I've got my phone.'

'Okay. Message me when you find him. And once you're home. And in bed. And as soon as you wake up... while eating breakfast...'

'I thought we were being discreet?'

Elliot's smile disappeared. 'Swear you won't say anything, Jessie. Not until I've had a chance to speak to him.'

I nodded. 'As long as you do it soon. I'm not good at keeping secrets from him.'

'You have to be, this time.' He placed both hands on either side of my face. His touch was gentle, but his eyes burned into mine. 'Swear to me you won't say anything.'

'I said I'll try!' I rolled my eyes, annoyed at my brother all over again, the wine making me bolshy.

'No. Say it. If you love me, then swear on my life that you won't say a word about us until I've explained everything.'

'Okay! If it means that much, I swear on your life I won't say anything.'

He pulled me up against his chest, bending his head to kiss me again. 'It's not that I don't trust you, just... I know how strong that twin thing is.'

After another hurried kiss, I insisted I had to go. I tucked the earbuds that we'd been sharing into his ears and clicked through his phone to the song that had been wafting across the golf course when he first kissed me, turning the volume up to ear-splitting.

'There. Now you can think about me all the way home.'

He laughed. 'I don't need a song for that.'

We crept back out onto the lane, me first, then Elliot once I'd gestured that the coast was clear. He then insisted on waiting until I'd gone. Maybe it was the wine, perhaps I was high on love, but I started to sway, adding in silly dance moves and spins as I walked, flinging my hands in the air as I felt the thrill of knowing he was watching.

I twirled around just in time to see it.

The deafening music must have muffled the sound of the engine.

His black suit must have made him invisible where he hovered by the side of the road.

But it was because I distracted him that he stumbled.

So, when the car hit, tossing Elliot into the air like a stuffed toy, I was the one to blame.

# 1

When Isaac and I left home, exactly one month after our eighteenth birthday, I swore to myself I'd never live with him again.

Not simply due to his constant pestering, concealer theft or post-sport stink. Isaac had been the other half of me since before we were born. Getting some space from him was how I hoped to get space from myself. Or at least the me I used to be, before.

I couldn't run away from me, but I could hide from the person who knew me better than anyone.

Only now, nearly eleven years later, I'd run all the way out of options.

I took a deep breath and picked up my phone. After all, it wouldn't be forever.

Hey bro. That spare room still available?

Instantly my phone rang. I braced myself before answering with as cheery a hello as I could muster.

'It's yours,' he said, not bothering with a greeting. 'Funnily enough, there aren't that many singletons looking for a house share in the metropolis of Houghton. When Mum said you might be moving back, I was hoping you'd be interested. When do you want it?'

Hearing my brother's voice for the first time in months made my stomach cramp. I started to mentally backtrack, thoughts scrabbling through alternative options, despite knowing full well that if there were any, I'd have found them by now.

'I have to be out of here by the weekend.'

There was a brief silence while I could hear Isaac holding back from asking me why on earth I'd waited to contact him until two days before being made homeless.

'If it's not ready that's fine, I can crash with a friend for a few days. Or weeks. However long, it's not a problem.'

It was a big problem. I didn't have many friends of my own here in Brighton. Not the kind who'd let me stay with them rent free, anyway. Besides, I was supposed to be starting my new job on Monday and I needed the money.

'No, it's ready. Arthur's been keeping some stuff in there, but that can go in the garage.'

'Arthur?'

'Arthur Wood.'

'You live with Arthur?'

Isaac huffed with impatience. 'We're not twelve any more, Jessie. You should be past being freaked out by the Woods.'

Arthur's family had provided the village with funeral services for three generations. Four, if you count Arthur.

'Does he still work there?'

'Why wouldn't he?'

'Because not everyone wants to end up working for their parents?' Said me, who was about to come home and do precisely that.

Another pause. 'Do you need picking up? I'm working on Saturday, but can do Sunday afternoon.'

'No, it's fine. Dad said he can give me a lift. On Friday, if that's okay?' I squeezed my eyes shut. 'And, well, thanks Isaac.'

It was only after we'd hung up that I remembered the most important question.

How much is the rent?

It was a couple of hours before he replied to my message.

100 a week including bills

Any chance of a twin discount?

This time he replied straight away.

That IS the twin discount!

A hundred pounds a week would hurt. My parents had been beyond generous in offering me the role of Activities Coordinator at the day centre they ran in a converted barn, which everyone simply called the Barn. Particularly as I strongly suspected the role hadn't existed until I'd mentioned I needed a new job. However, despite managing to allegedly get my life together in the three years I'd been living with my boyfriend, Seb, my bank account was still in recovery from the time that went before it. The compulsion to avoid settling too long in one place had led to years of flitting from one city to another, picking up crappy work and making impulsive decisions that had resulted in a somewhat precarious debt situation. The Debt Swamp, I called it. I'd finally made some real progress in dragging myself towards the edge of said swamp when everything got flipped upside down again.

I'd half wondered if Seb was going to propose when he'd taken me out for dinner. The coffee shop he managed had been wobbling on a knife edge since the start of the pandemic, but lately he'd seemed to shake off the despair and feel hopeful again.

It turned out that what he'd been feeling was mostly relief that the struggle was over.

'Klara's decided to cut her losses. We're closing at the end of the month.'

'Wow.' I sat back, the news ricocheting about my head. I was the only other remaining employee, so both of us would be out of a job. Although, unlike Seb, I was no stranger to sudden unemployment. 'You don't seem devastated.'

He shrugged. 'I knew it was coming, and I've been considering other options.' A smile curled at the edge of his mouth. 'I thought, why not take the opportunity to do some travelling?'

'Oh. That's a fantastic idea.' I sat back, the surprise now tinged with a glimmer of excitement. 'I've never been further than Spain. Have you thought about where we'll go?'

He'd had the decency to look contrite when he put down his slice of pizza and explained that this was a voyage he needed to take alone. 'You know I love you, Jess, and I'll miss you. But the past couple of years have been a nightmare. I need some space to recover. I'll be back, I promise, but this is something I have to do, before, well, before I commit to making things permanent. I mean, if that's what you want?'

'To make things permanent?'

He shrugged. 'We love each other, don't we?'

'Is that a proposal?'

He laughed. I'd missed Seb's laugh. 'It's a proposal to propose once I'm back. Let's do this properly, yeah?'

'How long will you be gone for?'

A few months at the most, he hoped. Long enough that it wasn't worth him finding a new place to live. The manager's role had included a one-bedroom apartment above the coffee shop, so we were losing our home as well as our livelihoods.

Seb offered to help me find somewhere else, but even without the secret Debt Swamp and disastrous credit rating, I couldn't afford a place of my own in Brighton, and without a steady income, no one was going to offer me a house share.

I could hardly complain – Seb had let me stay rent free for three years.

I could, however, secretly cry in the shower about how, just when I dared to think I might have a normal life, it had all gone wrong again.

Then I'd remember that someone would never have a normal life again, partly thanks to me, and I'd cry even harder before stuffing it all away deep down inside my sullied heart where it belonged.

And now, here I sat, surrounded by three bin bags and one tatty rucksack, waiting for my dad to come and take me home.

\* \* \*

It took five hours to get to Houghton, nestled on the edge of Sherwood Forest in Nottinghamshire. It would have been four, except Dad insisted he needed to stop off at a supermarket to get some 'bits and bobs', and while we were there decided I might as well pick up some essentials, which of course he then ended up paying for. My dad, like my mum, was about a whisker away from perfect.

Warm and thoughtful, unfailingly supportive since acciden-tally-on-purpose getting pregnant at eighteen, they'd refused to see us as anything less than wonderful. Now forty-six, with faces starting to bear the creases of love, laughter and a daughter who'd caused them countless sleepless nights, they'd been delighted that with Seb I might have found the happy ending they'd always believed was right around the corner.

Keeping up the pretence that I was now a healthy, functioning, financially stable adult would be exhausting, but at least I'd had plenty of practice.

## 2

Isaac called Dad's phone just as we stopped at the end of a winding lane that branched off Houghton's modest Main Street.

It was clear from Dad's responses that it wasn't great news. As his frown deepened, I took the opportunity to have a good look at my new home.

The cottage was larger than I'd expected. Variously sized windows were dotted in seemingly random positions, including a tiny one tucked under the eaves near to a wonky chimney. Brambles dangled over the fence like neighbours eager for a gossip, and the flowerbeds were full of weeds. The word that sprang to mind as I took in a broken weathervane, was *ramshackle*. It was the last place I'd expect my brother to call home, but it looked like the perfect place for his twin sister, as did the location. Having passed a row of terraces and a couple of swish new builds, this was the last dwelling before the village gave way to miles of open countryside.

It was nearly nine, and the sun had disappeared behind the treetops, casting the red bricks in shadow. The late April air carried the faint promise of summertime, and I'd forgotten how quiet it was on the edge of the forest. Apart from Dad's one-sided phone conversation, the only sounds were the birds' evensong, and the distant hubbub of youths playing football at the recreation ground. Closing my eyes for a brief moment, I absorbed the stillness and sent up a prayer that against all odds, I might find some peace here.

'There's a leak in the Barn kitchen,' Dad informed me, once he'd hung up. 'Isaac's not sure where it's coming from so could do with a hand. He's got a wedding tomorrow.'

One February, just over three and half years ago, in a stroke of bizarre luck, a reality TV star who'd grown up in Houghton and once worked part time for my parents had got married in the local church. Struggling to find a reception venue she liked nearby, Mum had offered the newly refurbished Barn. Mum and Dad extended their bank loan and quickly converted an out-building into a honeymoon suite. They hired a local joiner to construct a bar out of an oak tree felled in a recent storm, and bought a dance floor.

The Robin Hood themed wedding was a huge hit on the reality show, prompting a flood of enquiries that convinced Isaac to resign from his job as an accountant and create Robin Hood's Barn Weddings. With the day centre running Monday to Thursdays, that left Fridays to set up and Saturdays for celebrations. In the strange world of popularity culture, the limited availability only added to the appeal, and after hiring a creative director, Isaac charged a small fortune for people hoping to emulate the celebrity wedding, while offering a bargain rate to any Houghton locals throwing a party. The substantial profits were then used to help fund the day centre.

I could see by Dad's tense expression that he was torn between staying to help me settle in and rushing to the Barn. 'Just drop the bags at the door and I'll sort myself out. I'm an expert at moving house,' I said, heaving two bin bags out of the boot.

Dad swung my rucksack onto his shoulder and grabbed the shopping bags. 'If you're sure?'

'Of course! Oh – do I need to come with you to get Isaac's key?'

Dad smiled. 'You've been living in cities too long. If neither of the others are there to let you in, the key's under the squirrel.'

'Original.' It was only once the bags were all on the doorstep and Dad had enfolded me in his arms, repeating for the trillionth time how happy he was to have me back before hurrying off, that I processed what he'd said.

The others?

Shouldn't that have been *other*? As in, Arthur?

Was there someone else here that Isaac hadn't bothered to tell me about?

I gave a tentative tap on the door, and when no one answered, I quickly found the key inside a hollow plastic squirrel squatting under a bush, then took a moment to breathe in and remind myself how grateful I was to be here, and stepped inside.

Flicking a light on revealed a corridor containing a bike and a mini mountain of men's shoes. Stairs headed up on one side, but ignoring those, I grabbed the shopping bags and went to the open door at the end of the hallway, through which I could spy cupboards.

In here I discovered a large kitchen-diner, so I dumped the bags on the table and took a moment to look around before fetching the rest.

My trepidation grew as I took in the room. The dark-blue kitchen units and chrome appliances seemed clean enough, as I'd expect from Isaac, although the worktops were bare apart from a kettle and a toaster, so I hoped there were some cooking utensils hidden away somewhere. What threw me were the sticky notes. They were all over the place, including the cabinets, enormous fridge and the back door, in a variety of colours and written on in blocky black letters.

I felt another prickle of unease as I read the notes nearest to me:

*EAT THE CAKE*

*WODGER FULL BACK?*

*CHECK SIDE FOR PENNY POO*

As soon as I'd brought everything inside, I called Isaac.

'Is Arthur even stranger than I remembered?' I asked, after a quick hello.

'Dad's sorted the leak. Once we've finished clearing up I'll be straight home. Can we discuss your prejudice against undertakers then?'

'I'm talking about the sticky notes,' I replied, stress vibrating in my voice.

'Oh! No, they're Elliot's,' he answered, clearly distracted.

'What?' My uneasy thoughts tumbled into freefall. 'Who's Elliot?'

I didn't need to ask. Which other Elliot would it be than my brother's best friend from sixth form? But I had to ask. How could it be him? And why was Isaac's kitchen covered in his random notes?

Before Isaac could answer, the door leading from the kitchen into the back garden opened and a huge dog with a curly golden coat trotted in, panting.

'I'll speak to you later.' I hung up the phone.

Right behind him, his messy hair the exact same colour as the dog, chest heaving and dripping with perspiration, was Elliot Ollerton.

For a lurching second, I could have sworn planet Earth stopped spinning.

'Wait,' Elliot said, holding up one hand to the dog in a stop gesture. He carefully took off his trainers and placed them on the door mat, stuck a key in the back door and locked it. He then took a tatty towel from a hook beside the door and wiped each of the dog's paws. Finally, he took a glass out of a cupboard, filled it at the sink and drained every last drop before placing the glass in the dishwasher and turning around to look at me.

We stood there, staring at each other, my heart hanging precariously between beats, until the dog ambled over and pushed its nose into the pocket of my denim shorts, tail wagging like a helicopter blade.

'Hey, hi,' I managed to mumble, stroking the dog's floppy ear. Seeing him there, almost filling up the kitchen with his broad shoulders and dark eyes, running shorts showing far too much of his athlete's legs, was like being thrown back to that night. I could almost hear the sound of sirens wailing as I blinked to clear the image of his unconscious body being wheeled into the back of an ambulance. It was only the dog sniffing at my belt loop that stopped me from tumbling back in time completely.

'Penny,' Elliot said, with a note of warning. 'Say hello nicely.'

She instantly backed off, sitting down on the dark red tiles and offering me a giant paw, her tongue dangling out from one side of her mouth.

*Penny.*

So that explained the note about the poo.

Although not why anyone would put a reminder about that in their friend's kitchen. Unless she was Isaac's dog, something else I would know if I wasn't a pathetic excuse for a sister.

I shook Penny's paw before braving a glance back at Elliot as I straightened up. He hadn't moved. His eyes were darting around the kitchen, a furrow between his eyebrows.

*Come on, Jess. Get it together.*

'It's Jess. Isaac's sister? I'm moving in with him but he's got an emergency at the Barn, so said to let myself in.'

'Yes, of course.' He nodded stiffly. 'I knew you were coming. I just forgot it was today.'

'Oh. Right. Well it is!' I offered a shaky smile, instructed my lungs to keep breathing and willed my legs not to turn and run. 'I... um, did you want Isaac? I can tell him you called round.'

*Please go away now, because it feels as though my internal organs are seizing up.*

Elliot gave a slight shake of his head, the furrow deepening. His face was leaner than it had been ten years ago, more serious, but those dark eyes, that wide mouth, were exactly the same.

'I live here.'

*Oh no.*

On one level, I'd figured it out the second he'd walked in the door holding a key. But I'd needed it not to be true, so had chosen to deny the obvious.

'I'm sorry! Isaac never mentioned you were housemates.'

Or even plain old mates any more, come to think of it.

Elliot shrugged. 'He started renting off me when he moved back to start the business.'

'This is your house?' I asked, hoping he didn't hear the tremble in my voice.

'Yes.'

I was living in Elliot Ollerton's house. This couldn't be happening. I had to grab my things and go. Now. This minute. As soon as I'd figured out where I was going and how I was going to get there.

'Can I get you a drink?' Elliot asked, the frown easing into a cautious smile. 'Or something to eat?'

My mouth answered on autopilot. 'Tea would be great, thanks. Black is fine.'

I'd have preferred whisky, but it was probably best to wait until I was alone before I started on alcohol. I couldn't quite believe I'd said yes to a drink at all, but it was like I'd slipped into survival mode, and had no idea what else to do. I watched Elliot carefully filling up the kettle, his expression blank as he took mugs out of a cupboard and added teabags.

I knew he didn't remember what had happened. Isaac had said Elliot had woken up with no memory of the time around prom. What we'd said. How we'd kissed. That the accident – weeks in a coma, months in hospital, the rest of his life overshadowed by a traumatic brain injury – was mostly my fault.

Did he remember that back then, he'd loved me?

Traumatised and wracked with guilt, in my distressed, teenage mind, it somehow made sense to keep my vow to Elliot. I'd sworn *on his life* that I wouldn't tell anyone about us being together that night. He was in a coma. What if I said something, and then he died? In my panic, I'd convinced myself that the only reason to confess was in the hope that it might make me feel better. It would do nothing to help Elliot. And I didn't deserve to feel better, so I kept my promise. It was the only thing I could do for him, now.

I'd kept my secret for nearly seven years. Then, just over three years ago, almost out of their mind with worry, my parents had tracked me down to a rat-infested squat in Manchester. They'd pleaded with me to come home, confused and heartbroken about whatever it was that had caused me to spiral so far down, and to resist their attempts to help. Instead, we'd reached the compromise that they'd set me up in a studio flat and pay for a therapist. I chose Brighton, because I thought that walking on the beach and watching the sea might be a tiny reason to keep on living.

After a few agonising therapy sessions, I'd finally accepted that telling my secret to this woman with a kind smile might be my only hope. I kept it anonymous, no names mentioned, and of course she'd responded as I knew she would, with penetrating questions about whether or not I was really to blame, or whether it was in fact a horrible accident. If blame was required, then what about the car driver? The boy who wasn't watching the road behind him? How about my brother; did he not have a part to play? The school, for holding a prom in the first place?

This had the intended effect of making me confront how futile it was to apportion blame, how vital it was to process the trauma so I could move on. How I would never be free until I found a way to forgive myself.

Simply telling someone helped more than I could have imagined.

It would probably have helped more if I'd dared go back for another session.

## 3

*Okay, what now?* I tried to take a slow, steadying breath as Elliot continued making the drinks. The shame that during therapy had slunk off to make a home in the deepest, darkest parts of me stirred and stretched, abruptly awoken from its slumber.

If I ran away now, it would mean diving straight back into the chaos I'd worked so hard to leave behind. And it would crush my parents and Isaac. Elliot living here would be excruciating, but I could keep up the pretence for a few months. Or at least a few days, while I came up with an emergency plan to evacuate. Until then, all I had to do was avoid him as much as possible and hang onto enough of my sanity to appear normal.

I stuffed the memories back down, found the easy, breezy, couldn't care less mask I'd got so used to wearing and accepted the mug of tea.

'How long have you lived here?' I asked, my voice almost back to normal as I concentrated on Penny, now resting her head against my thigh.

'Four years,' Elliot answered.

'I'm sorry I just presumed it was Isaac's house.'

Elliot tilted his head. 'I'm not sure he's got enough reserves to buy his own place yet.'

'No. Of course not.' I flushed with embarrassment at revealing how little I knew about my own twin, and tried to move the conversation on. 'Is it just the three of you living here, you, Isaac and Arthur? There're no other housemates he's forgotten to tell me about?'

He smiled, and I tried to ignore how it tugged at my heart. 'Four of us, including you.'

At that point, the front door banged open, causing Penny to scamper out of the room to investigate. A few seconds later, Isaac burst into the kitchen, and the second I put my mug down he threw his arms around me and lifted me clean off the floor.

'Sis!' He puffed. At five foot three, I was eight inches shorter than him, but where he was still wiry, I'd gained curves that made me far harder to swing about than when I'd been a skinny teenager. 'This is so good. It's perfect. I've even cleaned your room.'

'Thanks Isaac, but maybe you could put me down, now?'

He dropped me with an oomph, followed by a laugh, and stepped back so we could size each other up properly. Isaac looked amazing, despite his navy trousers being dotted with stains and damp patches. The sleeves rolled up on his white shirt revealed toned forearms, and he'd changed his hair since I'd seen him at our aunt's house on New Year's Day. The shorter cut, coupled with the businessman style, suited him.

'Look at you, all sleek and handsome. I bet the brides love you.'

He pulled a face. 'Not so much when I'm covered in drain water. But occasionally bridesmaids can get overfriendly. And once they've had a few drinks, the mothers can be worse.' His eyes crinkled in a smile. 'You're looking well yourself. I was worried after hearing about Seb disappearing.'

'You're always worried,' I brushed him off. 'And Seb didn't disappear; he's taking a much-needed holiday. He knows I'm a big girl; I'll cope perfectly fine without him for a couple of months.'

'I need a shower. Nice to see you, Jessie.' Elliot offered a crooked smile as he walked past me into the corridor, Penny trotting after him, and the second he'd gone, I pawed through the carrier bags for the bottle of wine Dad had bought as a housewarming gift, pouring two glasses while Isaac chatted.

'You should have told me this was Elliot's house,' I said once we'd sat at the table. I tried to act casual, but my knuckles were white where they gripped the stem of my glass.

Isaac took a large sip. 'I guess in our twice-yearly text conversations, it never came up.'

That was an exaggeration. I replied to his texts at least every other month, and I'd seen him at New Year and our traditional birthday meet-up in August.

'Why, is it a problem? You two always got on.'

'No... but I would have appreciated knowing it was his house before I decided to live here.'

He shrugged. 'I don't see that it makes much difference.'

I took a long gulp of wine. 'When did he move back?'

'You know his parents relocated to be near the rehab centre?'

I nodded. I'd picked that much up in the nightmare summer following the prom.

'He moved in with them after he left rehab, but it wasn't exactly easy. He's a lot better now, but that's partly because he has his own space. He used the accident pay-out to buy this place as soon as he could.' He stopped abruptly, eyes narrowing. 'That isn't why you have an issue with him living here, because of his disability?'

'No! No. Isaac. Of course not! I don't have an issue. It just made me jump when he appeared in the kitchen.'

'Good. Okay. Some people can be... ignorant.'

'Hello, am I an ignorant person?'

Isaac grinned and took another drink.

'So the notes are to help him remember stuff? He said he knew who I was, but had forgotten I was moving in today.'

Isaac nodded. 'We barely notice it most of the time, but he still struggles with a change in routine, or remembering appointments, that kind of thing. The notes are mostly just precautionary these days. I'm impressed he remembered you, though. When I first moved in there was a note saying, "the housemate with black hair is Isaac, he's still a waster, ignore everything he says".'

I arched one eyebrow, pointing at a shelf by the kettle. 'I had spotted *that* one.'

The note read:

*If there's a woman you don't recognise, she's with Isaac*

He shifted on his chair. 'That's out of date.'

'What, so you've ended your womanising ways? Or is there just one woman now?'

His shoulder twitched.

'Hey, you know I'm not about to judge anybody for their relationship choices. Or lack of.'

'There's no woman.'

'That sounds quite final. Even if you've run out of single ladies in the village, what about all those bridesmaids?'

'I'm done with all that. I'm ready for more than the odd night with someone I hardly know.' He drained the last of his wine. 'The problem is, the "single lady" I want to commit to has decided I've got a terrible reputation. So.' He stood up, stretching until his fingers brushed the ceiling beam. 'I'm a woman-free zone, until I can prove her wrong.'

'Wow.' I sat back. While I'd missed these conversations with my brother – there wasn't another person on the planet I could talk to like him – hearing about his drastic change of heart was almost as unsettling as my surprise landlord. 'All I can say is I hope it works. That is, if I like her, and she's right for you. Ooh – is it someone I know?'

'Nope. I'm not having you turn this into a mission to fix Isaac. This is grown-up stuff, not anything for you to start poking your meddling fingers into.'

My initial annoyance at Isaac suggesting he was the grown-up, with me being the immature twin, quickly evaporated as I watched him clear the glasses and had to admit that it was true.

'I've got to be at the Barn at eight in the morning,' he said, once satisfied everything was tidied away. 'I'll show you around and then I'm heading to bed.'

The brief tour of my new home included Isaac pointing out the door to Elliot's en-suite bedroom on the ground floor, plus his and Arthur's bedrooms and the main bathroom on the first floor, but before then I had the pleasure of stepping inside the living room.

'Is this what living with boys is going to be like?' I asked, screwing my nose up at the leather gaming chairs, giant screen and spider-webs of wiring. There was a stack of weights in one corner, and what Isaac casually informed me was a 'multi-games table', near to a whiteboard displaying several charts underneath the title 'Chimney Cup 2022'. Isaac proudly showed me the mini fridge full of neon-coloured drinks and snack bags of ultra-processed meat.

'Where am I supposed to sit?' I asked, with a laugh tinged with apprehension. 'Am I allowed in here or is it men only?'

He pointed to a beanbag covered in dog hairs, squashed behind the door. 'We brought that in for you.'

'How very thoughtful.'

Isaac glanced at the chipped woodwork, beige walls and thread-bare carpet as if taking it all in for the first time. 'I'll show you your room. You can do what you like up there. Add some fairy lights and cushions.'

My bedroom turned out to be the one with the tiny attic window. Beneath the sloping ceiling was a bed, a wardrobe with drawers and a wonky side table. Once we'd added my bags, that left just about enough space for us to both stand on the green rug taking up the rest of the floor. To my relief, the bed was made up with a clean-looking duvet and pillows. There was also a pretty pink jug containing a sprig of wild flowers on the table.

'Mum?' I asked, nodding at the jug.

'I cleaned it first!'

'Thank you.' I nudged him with my hip. 'And thanks for letting me stay here, with a twin discount.'

Twin discount? How would that work if I was paying Elliot, rather than Isaac? Ugh. Something to worry about later, like when I actually had some money to pay someone. Isaac gave my hair a ruffle and left me to a night haunted by memories.

# 4

I'd planned to spend Saturday morning hiding in the attic, but my mother had different ideas, messaging me at ten on the dot to say that she was at the front door. I shrugged into a pair of grey joggers and soft blue hoodie, stuck my hair in a bun and braced myself.

'Jessie!' She beamed, once she'd squeezed every last air molecule out of my lungs. 'You're here!'

'Yep.' I stepped back to let her in.

'You look really well.'

'Isaac said the same thing. What were you expecting?'

'Well, it is a big blow. Losing your job, home and boyfriend in one go.'

I paused to look at her.

'I know! You haven't *lost* him. But you must miss him not being here.'

If I looked well, Mum was radiant. Her light-brown hair swung just above her shoulders, and she wore patterned dungarees and a chunky cardigan that would make some forty-somethings appear ridiculous, but on her youthful frame looked fun and funky. I suspected the glow on her cheeks was due to having both her babies living within the village boundary, enabling her to bombard me with compliments in person instead of down a phone line.

When she suggested we went out for brunch I leaped at the chance. Not so much because it would save me the cost of a meal – I did have a full cupboard for now – but it meant avoiding bumping into Elliot. We walked down the lane and along Main Street to the little row of shops, entering a small café that hadn't been here ten years ago.

'I'm so pleased you're staying with Isaac,' Mum said, while we waited for our eggs benedict and a giant pot of tea.

'I know.' I managed to smile. 'I'm happy to be home for a while, too.'

'For a while?' she asked, sitting back as the waiter put our food on the table.

'You know it's just while Seb's travelling.'

'You don't think he might join you here, once he's finished?'

I poured us both some tea, trying not to shudder at the very thought. 'We haven't really talked about it.'

'You haven't discussed any future plans? If you're getting married it's important to cover these things.' She waved a fork bearing a chunk of toast. 'I'm sure that a wonderful man like Seb understands you've got a fantastic career opportunity in Houghton. We could always find work for someone with his experience too. Isaac will be needing a bigger team soon. It would be so lovely, having you both settle here...'

This was exactly the type of conversation that made me let her calls go to answerphone more often than not. I made a mental note to ensure she never got hold of Seb's contact details. She'd be offering him a job the first chance she got, and then he'd either end up staying away longer to avoid the pressure, or decide it was a great idea, and a few months in Houghton would turn into forever.

'Are you having second thoughts about him? Is that why you've avoided talking about it?' She screwed up her nose in anticipation of my answer.

It said a lot that she didn't even question that the man who'd left the country might be having second thoughts about me.

'It's not that.' I sighed. 'I told you why he's gone. Badgering him with questions about what happens when he's back is the last thing he needs. It's hard enough us being apart without you second-guessing our relationship because we've not signed off on a ten-year plan. Not everyone's like you and Dad.'

'I know, I'm sorry. We like Seb. He seems good for you.'

'Good as in he offered me a job and asked me to move in with him?'

Mum raised one eyebrow, but she smiled to soften her words. 'Good as in, unlike some exes we won't mention, he doesn't live like a pig, treat you like a pig or, even better, keep a pig in his bedroom.' Her smile disappeared. 'He also doesn't move into empty properties without the owner's permission.'

'I'm glad you like Seb. I like him too. But I took the job on a three-month contract for a reason. We enjoy living in a bigger town, especially on the coast.'

'I know. I'll try not to get my hopes up. You know we just want you to be... I won't say happy. Life has too many ups and downs for that.' She took a thoughtful sip of tea. 'We hope that one day, wherever you are, you can be content.'

It took me a few blinks and painful swallows before I could reply. 'I hope so, too.'

We chatted a bit more about what she and Dad had been up to, and my new job, which of course she knew I'd be brilliant at, before she returned to the previous topic. 'Anyway, thank goodness Pete got married so you could have his room.'

I nodded. 'I couldn't handle sleeping on your sofa. No offence,

Mum.' My parents had sold their three-bedroom terrace to help fund the Barn, and bought a tiny one-bedroom flat with an open plan living area. 'Although I'm planning on moving out as soon as I've saved up enough.'

'Oh, no. Don't do that!' she exclaimed around her final mouthful of egg. 'Those boys need you!'

I sat back, wondering where on earth this was heading. 'They might resent that suggestion. And you calling them boys.'

'When they start acting like men, I'll stop calling them that.'

'Is there something I should know? How do they need me? I'm not going to be their stand-in housekeeper just because I'm female.'

Mum squinted out the window for a worryingly long moment. 'Oh no, it's nothing like that. They've just grown a bit... institutionalised.'

'What? They aren't in prison.'

'I don't know how else to put it. They spend nearly all their free time together, in that man-cave they call a living room, playing their endless competitions and swapping in-jokes that no one else finds funny. It's none of my business, but not one has had a serious relationship. Which is fine, of course, if none of them want one.' She held up her hands as if in surrender. 'But I'm convinced Isaac has his eye on someone, and Arthur does all the dating apps but it never goes anywhere. Would *you* want a date who serves up reheated chicken bites and baked beans before handing you a joystick?' She shook her head. 'It's a slippery slope to a pet pig.'

'Maybe they need to find girlfriends who like gaming. And chicken.' I ignored the comment about Isaac's secret crush. 'I don't think you're giving them much credit, either. Just because that's what they like to do together, I'm sure they wouldn't do it on a date. And I don't see how me living there will make any difference.'

She shrugged. 'Honestly, Jessie, I think they just need reminding that not everyone – in fact, *no one* apart from them – lives or dies by the Chimney Cup. All you need to do is change the subject every now and then, and the consequences could be monumental.'

* * *

Knowing Isaac would be at the wedding until late, I spent the next few hours sorting out my meagre possessions in my bedroom. My heart stuttered inside my chest when someone walked in the kitchen while I was sneaking a sandwich, but it was only Arthur. Although, it had to be said, there was never an *only* when it came to Arthur Wood.

'Jessica.' He offered me his hand, which, after a brief hesitation, I decided would be easier to shake than try to ignore. 'Making a sandwich I see.'

'Hi, Arthur. How's it going?'

'Now that would depend on what you mean by "it",' he replied, pointing a finger at me as though he'd made a genius comeback.

I resumed chopping my tomato, but one glance at his face showed that he was genuinely waiting for me to clarify the question. 'Um, I just meant your life in general. Like, how are you? How's work, any other stuff going on at the moment?'

'Right. Okay! Of course. Work is excellent, thank you. As for other stuff, I trounced Elliot at air hockey this morning, but I've not played Isaac and he's the reigning champ, so I don't want to count my chickens. Having said that, I'm top of the leader board for darts, despite a slight thumb injury thanks to a lapse of concentration by an emotional pallbearer. Now table tennis, hmm, that's another story...'

It took maybe two minutes for me to realise that, when it came to Arthur at least, Mum might have a point.

'Have you been out anywhere lately?' I asked, diving in when he paused to take a breath. 'I've no idea where's good to hang out these days.'

Arthur blinked as though I'd asked him to describe his favourite restaurant on the moon. He scratched his head, although it would have been hard to reach through the mass of ginger curls, and frowned. 'There's a funeral director's conference next month, but I don't suppose that would interest you. Apart from that I mostly go grave hunting.'

'Go where?' I'd been about to take a bite of my sandwich, but dropped it back on the plate, sure that whatever Arthur said next would put me off my lunch.

'You know, visiting graveyards and looking for the memorials of significant people.'

'Right. Like famous people?'

Arthur pulled a face. He was only a couple of inches taller than me, and in his baggy shirt and even bigger cotton trousers, he looked about twelve.

'People who should be famous, in my opinion. For example.' He took a step closer, eyes lighting up, and I steeled myself for another lecture. 'You probably haven't heard of Elspeth Tickle, born no more than six miles from here, in Middlebeck. When her husband fell in a ditch and died the day her fifteenth child was born, she took on running the farm single handed. Everyone was certain she would fail, but fail she did not. Instead, she not only became the biggest asparagus grower in the county, she bred not one but *two* new breeds of turkey, the first being the notable—'

The front door opened and Isaac called down the hallway, 'Hey! I forgot my phone charger. Has anyone seen it?'

'I'd better help him look,' I said, taking my lunch with me.

* * *

For the rest of the day I stayed in my room, a notebook on my lap as I tried to figure out a moving out plan. I'd done my best to shove all the ugly memories and feelings that seeing Elliot had churned up back down into my subconscious, but my horrible dreams and the way my breath jammed in my throat every time I ventured down the stairs showed how closely they hovered below the surface.

I had to get out of there.

There were several things standing in the way of that.

Firstly, my new job was in Houghton.

If I was going to live somewhere else, I needed money, so I needed that job. The chances of anywhere else offering me the generous hours and pay that my parents provided in the role they'd invented for me were a solid zero per cent.

Secondly, there were about a hundred other houses in the entire village, precisely one of which was currently available to rent: a three-bedroom house costing a thousand pounds a month, which for me might as well be a million, thanks to the Debt Swamp.

Thirdly, to rent a house you needed things like references and a deposit or at least a decent credit rating and I had none of those thanks to living like a human wreck for most of my adult life.

Fourthly, even if I did manage to find a rot-infested cubbyhole that someone decided to rent to me out of the kindness of their own heart, how could I possibly explain to my family that I was leaving a perfectly nice cottage, with family and old friends, for somewhere a zillion times worse?

I went round and round, poring over job sites and estate agents. Quite honestly, by the end of it I felt grateful to have a home at all. Even if it did threaten to send me spinning back into the pit of shame, at least I'd have hot water and a lovely kitchen to host my nervous breakdown.

*You could tell someone. Isaac, or your parents.*

*It would probably help.*

The soft, insistent voice that sounded a bit like my mother murmured in my head.

*No. I can't. It's hard enough living with myself when I know what I've done. How will I be able to handle knowing that every time they look at me they see the person who helped ruin Elliot's life? Or that, even worse, I kept it to myself all this time because of a vow? I'm not brave enough for that.*

My conclusion at the end of an afternoon spent scheming and plotting and drowning in self-loathing was simple.

I'd ask Isaac if I could pick up any wedding work. It had the double benefit of keeping me out of the house as well as earning more. I'd save pennies wherever I could and, in the meantime, I'd do what I'd been doing for the past ten years: stick on a smile and pretend to be fine. Oh, and I'd pray that Seb would hurry up and re-find himself, so this would all be over.

\* \* \*

At precisely 8 p.m. I heard two excited barks from the back garden. Looking out the window I saw Elliot doing warm-up stretches while Penny skipped around him. Somehow unable to move away, I watched as he opened the back gate into the field beyond and joined a footpath leading towards a stretch of forest in the distance, soon picking up the pace as he jogged between the rows of bright-yellow oilseed rape flowers.

He ran like the star he should have become. Head upright, arms pumping, his whole body a symphony of grace and power.

Only if you'd been looking for it, if you'd once gazed obsessively at how he'd run before and were desperately searching for any comparison, might you have spotted the slight list to the left, the occasional wobble, the hesitancy when he hit a patch of uneven ground.

I watched until he disappeared into the shadow of the trees, my tears dripping onto the windowsill.

## 5

The following morning, Isaac tapped on my door just before ten.

'Hey, Jessie, are you awake?'

'I am now!' It had been another rough night.

'We're all off out, but will be back around twelve. How about a welcome lunch, if you're not busy?'

I spent a few seconds trying really, really hard to come up with a valid excuse for being busy, but my brain was still half asleep. 'Okay.'

'Fab. See you then.'

I yanked the duvet back over my head, muffling the sound of his feet thudding down the stairs.

When I emerged from another restless snooze, it was past eleven. Time for a shower and tea in a Hufflepuff mug, which was about all I could stomach right then. I'd found Penny waiting at the bottom of the stairs, and she then followed me into the back garden where four plastic chairs covered in mildew and bird droppings lined up facing an overgrown hedge. I considered retreating inside but it was a gorgeous morning, with clear skies and gentle sunshine, and I appreciated having birds and butterflies to focus on rather than all those sticky notes. By the time I'd given a chair a good wipe with kitchen roll, reheated my tea in the microwave and sat down, Penny bumping beside me at every step, it was nearly twelve.

'He didn't say who he meant by "we",' I explained, my leg jiggling nervously on the chair. 'Is Elliot having lunch, or will he leave me and Isaac to have some twin time?'

Penny dropped her head onto my other thigh with a noisy sigh.

'You're right. They clearly do spend all their time together. And I know he's a nice guy. Believe me, I know. But it's complicated.' I sipped my tea and gave her ear a scratch, causing her eyes to close in ecstasy. 'That's a fair point, though. If we're living in the same house, I can't avoid him forever. Might as well get it over with and see if I can cope.'

Instead of replying, Penny jumped up and scampered back inside, which I would have thought quite rude until the front door opened a moment later.

Isaac found me finishing the last of my tea and trying to pretend I wasn't on the brink of a panic attack.

'Okay?' He looked far more like the old Isaac, in scruffy jeans and a T-shirt. In fact, I was fairly sure I'd given him that T-shirt on our seventeenth birthday.

'Mmhmm.'

'Settling in?'

'Yep.'

'Get up to much yesterday?'

'You know, unpacking, sorting stuff out. I had brunch with Mum.'

'Nice.' He nodded a few times. 'Are you going to join us while we cook or stay out here?'

*Us.*

My stomach shrivelled like a deflating balloon. But busying

myself with food prep would be an easier way to do this than facing each other at the table.

'I'll come and help.'

I was very glad I did. For the preservation of my stomach health as much as anything.

'What is that?' I asked, incredulous, standing beside Isaac at the worktop.

'It's my multicooker,' he said, with a hint of pride. 'It's great, you can cook anything in here.'

'Yes, I can tell.' I fought back a gag. 'There's bits of *anything* still in there.'

'Nah, I just use it for eggs most days.'

I peered closer, but not too close, due to the gagging urge. The pan was covered in a thick, blackened layer of what was clearly old egg remains. 'Isaac, you're supposed to clean it in between.'

He glanced at me, eyebrows creasing with puzzlement. 'Why would I do that if I'm just going to put more egg in it?'

'Because it's disgusting and unhygienic? How have you not got food poisoning?'

Arthur glanced up from where he was frying sausages and bacon at the hob, as if wanting to say, *duh!*. 'Jessica, it heats up to 160 degrees centigrade. Any bacteria will be destroyed every time it's used.'

Isaac flicked the multicooker on while we were talking, the cloying stink of rancid old egg starting to rise as it heated up.

'Okay, no,' I wheezed, pressing one hand against my mouth and stepping back. 'That is so rank. You have to wash it. Can't you smell it? *Or see it*? Your business caters for hundreds of people, you know that this breaches countless health and safety rules.'

Isaac stuck his chin out like a toddler being told off. 'I already said, it's—'

'Clean it, now!' I turned to Arthur. 'Were you going to eat eggs cooked in this thing?'

He shrugged. 'None of us have ever got ill.'

'And none of you have ever vomited due to the repulsive stench, and I presume taste, of whatever's cooked in there?'

'Not me. Elliot?'

Elliot was slicing mushrooms and tomatoes. 'I wouldn't eat anything that had touched Isaac's multi-germ-factory if it was the last meal on earth.'

He nodded to a note stuck on a cabinet that read:

*Do not eat Isaac's eggs under any circumstances.*

Arthur got out a clean pan.

\* \* \*

'Mum was right,' I mused, as I helped myself to the last hash brown (that I'd cooked myself while adhering to appropriate hygiene standards) using an ice-cream scoop because their spoons had 'gone'. 'You do need help.'

'What?' Arthur and Isaac both looked up sharply. Elliot carried on eating, but I caught the twitch of a smile.

'You're eating out of a pan and a mug, because you're allowing me the privilege of one of your three plates. These sausages aren't cooked, they're cremated. And this stool is the most uncomfortable thing I've ever sat on, even if it wasn't held together by duct tape.'

'Okay, so our kitchen skills aren't amazing. It hardly warrants Mum slagging me off behind my back,' Isaac huffed.

'It's not only that. You spent most of my welcome lunch discussing sub-clause three of clause four point five of rule thirteen in some made-up game.'

'Clause four point six,' Arthur said, stuffing a chunk of toast he'd double-dipped in the pot of baked beans into his mouth. 'Four point five is regarding the permitted diameter of the playing counters, nothing at all to do with the size of the goal!'

He shook his head, smothering laughter at my ignorance about the rules of death-ball, or kill-the-ball or be-bored-to-death-using-a-ball or whatever they called it.

'That's precisely my point. Given that someone who doesn't know what on earth you're going on about is here, supposedly being made to feel welcome, maybe include a minute or two of conversation that she can take part in?'

'Oh. I see. I think.' Arthur furrowed his brow.

Isaac, never one to back down if he could help it, hunched his shoulders in irritation. 'You're perfectly capable of changing the subject if it's boring you.'

'It's one of my ongoing side-effects.' I automatically froze in response to Elliot speaking. He was sitting diagonally opposite me at the table (they'd wanted to eat in the living room but I'd refused to balance a plate of food on my lap while wobbling on a hairy beanbag) and I'd done a reasonable job of ignoring him so far, keeping my body tilted so he stayed just outside my eyeline. His words were soft and deep, and long-buried memories rippled through my nervous system. 'I get stuck on a topic and don't pick up the cues that other people aren't interested. I can't remember day to day basics but for some reason have automatically memorised the entire Chimney Cup rule book, so it's easy for me to talk about. I'm sorry for being rude at your welcome lunch. That was the last thing we wanted.'

'Thank you,' I managed to stumble out after a slightly too long silence. 'I appreciate that none of you intended to leave me out. That was Mum's point.'

'So we can't cook and we make terrible conversation,' Isaac said.

'Any other criticisms picked up in the two whole days you've spent here that you feel the need to put out there?'

I looked at the scowl darkening my twin's face then let my gaze drift to his friend, hunched on a chair with a garish shirt buttoned up wrong. I sneaked a peek at Elliot, sitting bolt upright, his eyes darting over the table, gripping his knife and fork as if preparing to defend himself.

'No. And I'm sorry. I've been really ungrateful. I'm sorry for swanning in here and being disrespectful about how you live. Compared to some of the places I've ended up, this is brilliant. You're all brilliant.' I pressed my juice glass against one cheek, hoping to ease the burning embarrassment. 'Apart from the multi-cooker. That's utterly gross and needs binning as soon as possible. Anyway, if you've all finished eating, I'll wash up while you sort clause four thousand and five.'

'Four *point* five,' Arthur replied.

'I know. I was joking.' I smiled as I started picking up plates.

'Ah. Yes. Very good!' He bobbed his head. 'Four thousand and five clauses would be ludicrous! Impossible to keep track of. Suck all the fun out of it.'

Isaac and Arthur made a token gesture of clearing up. Isaac was clearly still miffed, banging and crashing about the kitchen for a few minutes before disappearing with a mumble about how he had to check on the post-wedding clear up. To my alarm, Elliot took a tea-towel out of a drawer and joined Penny, who, as soon as I started running the tap, came and sat beside me, her mouth open in an expectant grin.

'I can show you where things go as I dry them.'

'Oh. Okay. Thanks. I mean, you don't have to. I'm happy to figure it out.'

'I feel like I owe you some decent conversation.' Elliot's mouth flickered in what should have been a smile, if the anxiety behind his eyes hadn't overshadowed it. 'I hate it when that happens. Next time, please interrupt to tell me I'm being rude and boring. It helps me improve.'

'No... I... I'm sorry for making you feel bad about it.' More sorry than he would ever know. 'But you only joined in the conversation with Isaac and Arthur. They don't have any brain injury side-effects to deal with.' I placed a dripping dish on the draining board, taking a peep to gauge whether I'd overstepped.

'That's true.' To my relief, he offered a wry smile. 'Thank goodness you're here. Living with two mega-geeks can't be helping me manage this particular issue.' He opened a cupboard to show where their grand total of two serving dishes were stored. 'It'll be really good to have some broader conversations. For all of us. Might help Arthur get past a first date.'

I turned to him, bubbles dripping off my hand, causing Penny to sneeze. 'Mum mentioned that. Is it as bad as she thinks?'

He shrugged, wiping a pan methodically. 'I don't know what she told you, but behind the bluster, Arthur is growing pretty miserable. It wasn't such a big deal until he met... wait... hang on...' He closed his eyes. 'It's from that Disney film. With the snow. The older sister... Elsa! He met Elsa.'

'Elsa?'

'The new curate at the church. Arthur met her at a funeral a few weeks ago and he's decided she's the one. That's where we were this morning. At church. He's not got another funeral there for a good week and he couldn't bear to go that long without seeing her, so he begged us to be his wingmen.'

'Wow. She must be really something.' I had a pitiful picture in my head of Arthur sitting right in the front row, gazing unnervingly at someone trying to lead the service.

'She's nice. Very smiley and chatty. Energetic.'

'Sounds like a good match for Arthur.' I placed the final pot on the draining board and started randomly wiping down the sink and surrounding worktop. It felt wrong to walk out, but standing so close to Elliot, I needed something to do with my hands.

'I've only met her twice, but she seems quite... well-adjusted. Socially intelligent.'

'Ah.'

'She stopped and chatted to Arthur after the service, and listened patiently to him stammer on about his latest grave hunt, but I couldn't tell if she was doing her job, being polite or was genuinely interested in hearing about a local innkeeper who smuggled stolen art.' Elliot put the last pot away. 'I think he might be heading for another heartbreak.'

He put his hands in his pockets then took them out again. 'Anyway. Um. Thanks for doing the washing up. And sorry again about lunch.'

Then he'd gone before I had time to thank him for staying to have a proper conversation, which in a bizarre twist, had left me able to breathe properly for the first time since walking in the door on Friday evening. Or, if I'm being honest, for a good while prior to that.

I went for a long walk that afternoon. For the first mile or so I stomped out some stress, head whirring and heart clenched. However, it was impossible not to end up drawn into my surroundings. Golden beams of sunlight shimmered between the trees, kissing the verdant bracken beneath. Squirrels scampered, birds chirruped and the air was so crisp and clean it couldn't help but fill my lungs with the promise of a fresh start. I shut down the endless thoughts, shrugged off my hoodie to feel the warmth on my skin, tipped my face towards the thousands of leaves above my head and simply looked and listened for a long moment, then kept on walking, one step in front of the other, which right then seemed like the best plan I'd got for surviving the next few weeks.

Once home, I caught up on some sleep, then showered and changed into my favourite jeans and a pale-grey, cropped cardigan that matched my eyes, before video calling Seb. This consisted of ten minutes of me telling him I was fine over and over again in between him raving about how he'd done three days' work at a music festival in Croatia. It was lovely to see him happy, but after another good cry once we'd hung up, I was more than ready to distract myself from being here, while he was there, with food.

From the sounds of heated discussion coming from the living room, I assumed the others were busy completing another round of the Chimney Cup. I added leftover bacon and tomatoes to a pot of pasta, stirring in a chunk of feta and a sprinkling of herbs, then poured the remaining wine from Friday evening into a glass. Taking my meal outside, I sat in the clean chair and ate watching the shimmering haze of evening sunshine ripple across the fields that sloped up beyond the scruffy hedge, a songbird perched on a tree in one corner keeping me company.

'Hey.' Isaac came to join me a while later. The garden was now a kaleidoscope of shadows, rimmed with the yellow glow from the windows behind us. With the sun now lost below the other side of the hill, there was a distinct nip in the air, and I gratefully accepted the blanket my brother offered, along with a mug of coffee.

'That chair is covered in bird crap,' I said, about half a second too late.

He sighed. 'These jeans need a wash anyway.'

His jeans were fraying at every seam, and not in a fashionable way. They needed tossing out with the cooker.

'I'm kind of surprised,' I said, after taking a moment to enjoy the coffee warming my throat. 'You love things to be all sleek and shiny.

I understand that you didn't choose this old cottage, but, honestly, Isaac, I never expected to find you living like this.'

'I really don't think you're in a position to judge,' he said, with a flick of one eyebrow.

'I'm not judging. You know I've lived in places far worse.' I poked my hand out from under the blanket so I could take hold of his. 'But I know how I ended up there. So that means I can't help but feel a little worried about what caused my neat-freak twin to stop cleaning his multicooker.'

We stared into the shadows while I waited for a reply.

'You worked in your boyfriend's coffee shop?'

'Until it closed. That's why he's gone travelling.'

'So you can imagine how brutal it's been with the lockdowns, all this madness kicking off only a year into a new event business. You'd think that having to cancel so often would have made less work, but it was the opposite. I spent two years hustling, and making rearrangements, while trying not to totally freak out that I'd walked away from a successful career into a catastrophe.'

'I'm sorry.' Every time I uttered those words they sounded hollower and more pointless. 'I should have been there for you.'

He jerked his head, shaking off the memory. 'We all had stuff to deal with. I wouldn't have dumped mine onto you, when you were finally catching a break. If you'd have been there, I'd only have put up a front, and I didn't have the energy for that.'

I knew exactly how that felt.

'Anyway, you're here now, which is awesome, and the Barn survived, so hopefully it'll be worth it. My point is, something had to give. The last thing I felt like doing after yet another gruelling day scrambling to save the business was clean garden chairs. Or cook something that required more than cracking eggs into a pan. And I had it easy compared to Arthur. Can you imagine what being a funeral director is like in a pandemic, when families aren't even allowed a decent goodbye? It crushed him, devastated his family. Losing ourselves in a competition where the biggest loss was points on a scoreboard was literally our way to survive.'

I had no words. Though when I shuffled my chair close enough to wrap my arms around him and press my face against his, the tears spoke for me.

Isaac reached up and placed his hand on mine, where I gripped his shoulder so hard I was fully prepared to never let go. 'I know you're right, though. You and Mum.' He gently bumped his head against mine. 'We've all got sort of stuck here, in survival mode. I'm still giving 80 per cent of my focus and energy to Robin Hood's Barn, 19 to the cup and a measly 1 per cent to everything else. Including that lunch, which was woeful.'

'The hash browns were perfect.'

'They were. It's maybe time, though. Probably well past time, to start redressing the balance. Start caring about not sitting on crap.' He paused. 'I don't know how to let go of it, though. It's as if I've been walking this tightrope, carrying all this baggage for so long that if I try to let any of it go, it'll all come crashing down, bringing me – and Mum and Dad – with it.'

'I know how hard it is to find the courage to make changes, when all you can remember is how to grit your teeth and get through each day. But you'll figure it out. My advice?'

'Wash that cooker?'

'Brother, you know me so well.'

Monday morning, I knocked on the Barn Day Centre office a solid minute before 8 a.m., surprising me almost as much as my parents. When life is spent rebounding between active self-sabotage and pretending not to care about anything, punctuality drops way down the priority list. I'd only avoided getting fired from the coffee shop because the manager had had a massive crush on me.

'Jessie.' Dad beamed, pushing back from his desk. 'You look raring to go!'

I wouldn't go that far, but I was looking forward to the distraction of a new challenge, and determined to give him a genuine reason to be proud of me for once.

'You look perfect.' Mum put down the file in her hand and came to give me a hug.

It hadn't been easy, hunting through my meagre wardrobe for an Activities Coordinator outfit. The ripped jeans and baggy shirts I'd worn to serve coffee and croissants wouldn't cut it for what felt like my first ever grown-up, professional job. In the end, I'd gone for a strappy summer dress with a cream turtleneck underneath, added tights for modesty and a pair of brown brogues. Having hurried the half mile to the Barn on what must have been the hottest April day on record, coupled with a building set to a temperature designed for the frailest of frames to be cosy, I could already feel a trickle of sweat running down my back.

After a celebratory cold drink and doughnut in the office, I had a tour of the building. I'd seen photos on the website, but being here in person, in this amazing space my family had created, took my breath away.

First stop was the main hall, designed to easily convert into the main wedding reception venue on weekends. One wall was entirely made of glass, which, along with several skylights, gave the impression that we were almost outside. It was bright and spacious, and not how I imagined a day centre would be. There was a retracting wall at one end where equipment could be stored out of sight, and a light-up dance floor.

My favourite room was the library. This contained a mix of comfy sofas and orthopaedic recliners in a range of vibrant fabrics, and a huge fireplace. As well as the books, there was a dresser full of board games and even a pool table. A café that opened onto a sunny terrace doubled up as the events bar, and beside this was the enormous kitchen where Wendy and her catering team prepared a range of non-stodgy meals without a single overcooked vegetable in sight.

As well as the main office, there was a modest staff room, although Dad explained that most of the team just took their breaks with the centre members. There was also an art room, again with giant windows and a wall of cupboards containing supplies for more art and crafts than I knew existed. They pointed across the terrace to an out-building that housed all the wedding equipment, including everything from tables to boxes of rose-petal confetti made during a weekday craft activity.

In every room, Dad showed me the discreetly located equipment such as hand rails, ramps and a hoist.

We then took a quick look upstairs, where there were separate rooms for the bride and groom if the wedding party wanted a space to get ready or simply spend time before heading to the church next door. These were more sumptuous than downstairs, with plenty of soft-furnishings and full-length ornamental mirrors as well as two spacious bathrooms. There was also a large office containing an orderly work station in one corner, the other three packed with vision boards, work tables bearing centrepieces and other decorations in various stages of completion and piles of wedding-related clutter such as chalk boards with cutesy phrases scrawled on them.

I smiled, already looking forward to meeting the creative director, who was presumably the person forcing Isaac to tolerate such chaos.

'Now for my favourite place,' Mum said, cheeks rosy with excitement. 'Outside!'

On a different day, when I wasn't on the brink of suffocation thanks to my stupid turtleneck, it would have been my favourite place, too. As well as numerous sets of wooden tables and chairs, the terrace also had garden sofas lining one side. Dotted around the lawn were more seating options, including picnic benches and quirky-looking egg chairs hanging from trees.

There was a vegetable garden, with raised beds and a greenhouse. The large pond had a water feature that I recognised from photos.

'This must be a lovely place to sit and rest.'

Mum scoffed. 'That's if you aren't getting constantly splashed in the face.'

I looked at Dad, confused.

'Some of the members like to go wild swimming.' He shrugged. 'We've tried to stop them, put up a fence and warning signs. It's a health and safety nightmare, but after some of them sneaked in at night for skinny dipping during a *very* exclusive wedding reception, we gave up and decided that at least if it was a scheduled activity—'

'With swimming costumes mandatory,' Mum added.

'—then we could supervise them.'

'This is not at all what I expected.' I looked at the pond, concluding that I was probably the most boring person in this village.

There was a workshop for woodworking, and tucked out of sight around a corner, the bit I decided I loved best of all.

'The secret garden,' Mum whispered, as though someone might overhear, ruining the secret. We walked through a solid gate to a much smaller garden enclosed by a brick wall. There was another wooden table and reclining chairs, a hammock strung between two trees and what appeared to be a giant Wendy house, with two windows framed with shutters and a daffodil yellow front door.

'Our honeymoon suite,' Mum said proudly. 'We call it the Chicken Coop, because once upon a time that's what it was. There's a bedroom at the front, and a dinky shower room and kitchenette behind.'

If I could have afforded Robin Hood's Barn Wedding prices, I'd have asked to move in myself.

'Right. We'd better do the boring admin before the chaos begins.' Dad linked his arm through mine and we ambled back to the main office.

I had enough time to read a couple of key policies and skim the current activities programme, but there was still a huge folder of PDF files to be waded through when Mum opened the front doors at ten.

Dad suggested that I kept at it until twelve-thirty. While there were drinks and snacks available until the centre closed at four, the one compulsory activity was a shared lunch, the perfect time to introduce me to who he called the 'Outlaws'.

'It's what our service users call themselves,' Mum added. 'We tried to stop them, explained it's offensive to those who are well-intentioned, law-abiding citizens, and the rest of them don't need any encouragement to get into trouble. We even held a competition to come up with another name.'

'Everyone entered the same name. They said we had no right to tell them what to call themselves. John Featherby gave a speech about ageism, and patronising them about their chosen identity.'

'To be honest, we failed to come up with anything that suited them better,' Mum said. 'Anyway, you can meet them yourself at lunch.'

I couldn't wait.

\* \* \*

After nearly falling into a stupor wading through what seemed like infinite risk assessments, I finally shut down my laptop with a sigh of relief (even having a work laptop made me feel like some important professional who existed in a different universe to the real me). I appreciated that all this reading was essential, but most of it was nothing new. My parents had started out working in domiciliary care, visiting local residents who were elderly, disabled or otherwise in need of extra support with basic tasks. They loved the work so much that they started their own company. However, they wanted to provide more than a rushed hour or two of practical help. Mum and Dad started to imagine a place where some of these isolated people could come together. Where there was time to really listen and get to know each other, to laugh together even as they shared the struggles of getting older. A place to nurture genuine friendships in beautiful surroundings. So, the day centre dream was born.

In the meantime, Isaac and I spent our school holidays after we turned sixteen working as home carers, so the basics had been ingrained in me for a long time. Over the years, a few jobs in other domiciliary companies had kept up my knowledge, and I'd spent the past couple of weeks redoing online training where needed, so I was more than ready to move on to the fun part of the job, i.e. helping the Outlaws to enjoy themselves. First of all though, I was hoping for a good lunch.

If I'd forgotten where the café was, the noise would have led me to the right place. I'd only ever worked with one or two elderly people at a time. The ruckus drifting down the corridor reminded me more of time spent serving behind a bar.

As I pushed through the glass doors and stepped inside what felt more like a giant furnace than a café, despite the open terrace doors, it seemed as though every one of the one hundred Outlaws on the books had turned up to meet the new activities coordinator. My eyes roamed the throng in vain, hoping a spare chair might appear. Every table was surrounded by people chattering, filling up water glasses, getting up to wave at each other and from what I could see as I stood there trying to gather my bearings, having a whale of a time.

'Well look who it is!' a voice boomed from the table nearest the door. 'Little Jessica Brown!'

I turned to see a tall, broad woman stand up as she waggled her meaty finger in my direction, just in case anyone had failed to notice the new girl hovering in the doorway. Her shaggy bowl-cut was now white, and there was a stoop to her shoulders that hadn't been there ten years ago, but there was no mistaking my primary school headteacher.

I tried not to be too disconcerted that she recognised me. This was an unavoidable fact of village life. Everyone knew everyone, no matter if the last time you'd met you'd been three feet tall. There was nothing you could do about it. Apart from, as in my case up until now, moving away.

'Mrs Goose.' I smiled and nodded hello. She'd been a fabulous teacher, even if she had scared the life out of me. 'How great to see you.'

'Extremely great, I should think,' she boomed, before narrowing her beady eyes. 'Class prefect. Netball team captain. Silver in the school quiz.'

'It was bronze in the quiz, but apart from that, spot on. Clearly retirement has done nothing to dim your memory.'

'If only I could remember what I ate for breakfast and am meant to be doing this afternoon!' She laughed. 'And seeing as I'm retired, please call me Arabella.'

'Jessie!' Dad called, beckoning me to a seat by the terrace. Breathing a sigh of relief, I squeezed through the tables, smiling hello at a few familiar faces, until I saw one that made me stop dead in the middle of the room.

'Madeline.' I could barely speak due to the lump of tenderness welling in my throat. Instead, I ignored the policy about not touching guests without obtaining permission and bent down to enfold her in a hug.

Madeline's frail, skinny arms reached up and patted my shoulders. She probably weighed less than my work bag, but as always there was a strength and a safety inside her embrace that filled my eyes with tears, even as my heart seemed to settle inside my chest.

'How are you, my dear?' she whispered into my ear.

'All the better for seeing you,' I half-laughed, half-sobbed as I gently pulled back to look at her, clasping both hands in mine. Madeline had been someone I'd provided home care to in that dreadful summer after the prom, following complicated surgery.

The truth was, the care she showed me for two hours every Monday, Wednesday and Saturday had got me through it.

The official care plan had included cooking her dinner and household tasks such as changing her bed or emptying the bin. On a good day we managed an unsteady shuffle to the bench at the end of her lane, so she could watch the horses. Other days we played cards, or looked through her photo albums. I never told Madeline that every day felt like stumbling through thick, black fog. That I had no idea how to live with myself any more. She never asked why sometimes I bent double with the force of my sobs as I mopped her floors or sat beside her watching television. Not because she didn't care, but because she saw that what I needed most was a place to take off the suffocating mask of acting as if I was fine and let the tears fall without having to explain.

Instead of questions, she offered me a knobbly hand to hold. A handkerchief embroidered with her late husband's initials. She would tell me stories about her younger life. A father who beat her, and a mother who numbed the pain with whisky. A brother who lied about his age to join up as soon as the war started, his escape route from the hell of home, who then died upon the battlefield.

The soldier who stole her heart at sixteen. The exhilarating elopement followed by the devastation of the baby she lost. Her husband's return, a shell of the man who'd left only a year earlier. The years she spent loving him back to life. Learning to find joy in a marriage so different from the one they'd dreamed of.

I listened to these stories, of love and loss, and learning to love again, and somewhere deep inside I started to wonder if maybe, one day, I could forgive myself. All too often I would go home and hear Isaac's update on how his best friend was still in a coma, or his kidneys had begun to fail, or he'd shown a glimmer of improvement, and I would go to bed, close my eyes and pray that someone would love Elliot back to life again, like Madeline had done for her husband.

Madeline had been a tiny, hunched-up sparrow with a wispy cloud of hair even then. I couldn't believe she was still here, still smiling with those deep, dark eyes that with one look knew exactly what I needed.

'You must be almost ninety by now!' I shook my head in wonder.

'Ninety-three!' She gave my hands a gentle squeeze. 'I don't feel a day over ninety-two. Will you have time to sit with me later? There's a bench in the garden that catches the sun beautifully in the afternoon, although I need a little help getting down the ramp.'

'I will always have time to sit with you, Madeline. You were my lifeline that summer.'

She offered me the softest of smiles. 'And you mine, dear heart. I could burst, seeing your lovely face again. You must eat though; your family are waiting. Come and find me when you can.'

I shouldn't have been surprised that lunch was about as removed from the day centre stereotype as Italian pasta is from tinned spaghetti. Wendy, the head chef, had been hired for her skills in catering high-quality wedding reception dinners. As we sipped mugs of lentil and home-grown vegetable soup served alongside soft rolls and goat's cheese garnished with fresh basil, Mum explained how Wendy loved the challenge of providing nutritious meals that even those with loose teeth and shaky hands couldn't resist.

'She's a genius!' Dad interjected. 'Makes everything from scratch, and the food barely costs us a penny.'

I might have to ask Wendy for some tips on how to cook a meal for a few pennies. I couldn't remember the last time I tried to cook anything from scratch, although I knew it would have been grim.

I was introduced to the other people on our table. One of them turned out to be my old Brown Owl at the Houghton Brownie Pack, so of course she remembered everything about me, including the time I set my hair on fire at Guide camp. Mum and Dad then filled me in on who else I might know, which included a few neighbours, friend's grandparents, two more teachers and our old dentist. It was then time to introduce me to everybody.

Dad stood up, alternating chinking a spoon against his glass with gesturing at the other staff members to please get control of their tables, and eventually the room fell quiet enough to hear him speak.

'Hello, Outlaws!' he bellowed, prompting a cacophony of cheers, whistles and banging of cutlery on the tables.

'I would like to introduce you all to a very special person,' he continued, tugging me up as the whoops died down, and those who'd been a little overenthusiastic stopped coughing. 'Special to me, because she's my daughter, and wonderful in every way.'

I kept my eyes on the wooden tabletop, trying not to think of all the ways I was not at all wonderful.

'However, I know she'll soon become very special to all of you, too. Jessie is going to take the tired, boring, same-old activities programme you're always grumbling about, and turn it into the kind of interesting, lively schedule that will make our insurance company's head spin. She'll be spending the next few days getting to know you all and finding out what kind of bonkers things you want to do, and then she'll see about making it happen. So, can you please raise your glass in welcome to Jessie, the woman who's about to make your dreams come true.'

'To Jessie!' most of them cried, along with a few shouts of Bessie, Tess and Julie. One man then shouted, 'She can make my dreams come true, that's for sure!' prompting a stern reprimand from the staff member sat next to him, and sharp retorts from several of his friends.

'Can we do hang gliding?' a woman wearing a bonnet covered in butterflies asked. 'I've always wanted to fly before I die, and I'm running out of time.'

'Oh, nonsense Enid, you've got years left,' someone else called from another table.

'Poppycock!' Enid replied. 'We've been around long enough to know that you never can tell. Look what happened to Millie, and she was one of the youngest here.'

'What about a bungee jump?' a man in a dinner jacket and tie croaked. 'If you get to fly, then I want to jump off a cliff.'

Various other people then started calling out increasingly outlandish suggestions, causing arguments to break out across the crowded room. Even with the fresh air from the terrace wafting in behind me, sweat broke out around my neckline and my tights felt stuck solid to my thighs.

I threw a glance at Dad sitting back in his chair, who smiled. 'I think this is for the activities coordinator to handle, don't you Pippa?'

Mum grinned. 'Absolutely. They're all yours, Jessie.'

*Right. Okay.*

I gave my head a brief shake, in the mistaken hope that it would kick my brain into action, and glanced at the expectant faces from the rest of the table, which were a mix of encouraging, interested and unashamedly gleeful.

Turning my attention to the room, where a handful of guests had stood up and started waving their arms around or, in one case, jabbing a walking stick in a man's face, I was again reminded of my days working in a bar. Reassuring myself that people were people, whether a load of wasted students or a gathering of elderly villagers who referred to themselves as fugitives, I decided to revert to the tactics I'd picked up in countless minimum wage service roles.

Before I had time to talk myself out of it, I'd climbed onto the table and yelled, 'Quiet!' at the top of my voice, stomping my brogues a few times for good measure. To my relief, gradually everyone stopped to look.

'Is she quite all right?' one person asked.

'Her cheeks are very red,' another answered, in a whisper loud enough for every hearing aid to pick up.

'Let's ask her,' our old neighbour said. 'Are you all right, love? Did you know you're standing on the table?'

'Yes, I did know. It seemed the best way to stop this frankly embarrassing hullaballoo. I'd expect better behaviour from five-year-olds. Do you think I'm going to decide the programme based on the outcome of a brawl?'

Numerous bodies shuffled about on their chairs. A few muttered an apology, while others folded their arms with a huff.

'Anyway, I have noted that what you do at the Barn is clearly very important to you. How you spend your time matters, and I'm so excited to help you make the most of it, doing things that cause your hearts to soar, if not your bodies. As Dad said, I'm going to carefully listen to all of you, but I hear a lot better when you speak one at a time. Now, are there any questions?'

'To be honest, I didn't hear a blummin' word you said,' a woman with a blonde beehive wig chortled. 'But if you can keep this lot under control, you've got my vote.'

'Thanks, Jessie,' Dad said, jumping up quickly. 'Never ask if there's questions,' he whispered. 'We want to get out of here before midnight.'

'Yeah, thanks Jessie!' a few other people shouted.

'Okay, so one final point. Only my family call me Jessie...' I tailed off as Mum sucked in a sharp breath, the exact moment I caught Madeline's twinkling eyes from several feet away. 'So... um... I guess from now on, that includes all of you.'

## 7

After enjoying a martini glass containing lime and mango sorbet, I retreated to the safety of the office, via a quick bathroom detour to peel off my armpit-sodden top and sticky tights. Note taken: practical clothing is far more important than trying to appear professional. There was no way I could cope with the Outlaws while overheating. I suspected some of my conversations during the next few days were going to be heated enough.

At three o'clock I found Madeline in the library, watching a poker game.

'You didn't want to play?' I asked, positioning her walker before helping her up.

'They won't let me any more. Apparently it's boring because I clean them out every time.'

'It's true,' a man with a bushy moustache said. 'If we were allowed to play with real money, she'd have us all bankrupt by now.'

'That still seems unfair, to exclude you just because you're the best player.'

'Phooey!' one of the women snapped, chucking a pile of chips into the middle of the table. 'She's not the best player, simply the best cheat!'

'Ah.'

Madeline shrugged her stooped shoulders. 'I'm not admitting anything.'

I settled her safely on her favourite bench and then fetched us glasses of iced tea from the café. She was right, it was a gorgeous spot, and the sunshine was delicious on my now bare limbs.

Sitting close enough to link arms, Madeline rested her spindly hand on mine, and chatted for a while about what she enjoyed doing at the Barn, and what she wished she could do given the chance.

Initially, she couldn't come up with anything. 'I don't have the energy to do a lot these days, and even if I could, my body won't let me.'

'Is there anything you miss, that you used to enjoy?'

Madeline tried to think.

'We used to go and watch the horses.'

'We did!' Her face lit up. 'Did I tell you that I always wanted to ride?'

'But you never did?'

'Oh, there was never the money for something like that. And look at me now. I can barely manage to get in a chair, let alone on a horse!' She nudged my shoulder with hers. 'I'd love to visit the field again, if that was possible. I can't make the walk from my house any more.'

'I'm sure I can come up with something.' I added it to the list in my notepad, which so far included 'something with music' and 'genealogy?'

'Don't go to any trouble.'

'It's not trouble, it's my job.'

'Honestly, sitting out here with an old friend is more than

enough.' She gave my hand another pat. 'They have these rules now, about physical contact. But being with you, being able to touch another person, and it be completely natural and easy, I have missed that. The last person who hugged me without having to ask permission was my niece, at my birthday party. That's what I miss the most.'

I added that to the list, too, my brain already starting to whir.

We sat for a while longer, watching the butterflies dancing in the flowerbeds, and then I helped Madeline back inside so she could get ready for the minibus that would take her home. Another hour of reading, jotting down notes, pondering and searching through the internet and I'd already decided that this was going to be the best job I'd ever had. For a brief moment I almost wished it could be longer than three months.

'Are you coming back for dinner?' Mum asked, when she and Dad appeared in the office doorway just after five-thirty. 'I've made a chicken pie.'

What I really wanted was a shower, my cotton shorts pyjamas and a good book, the evening breeze wafting the scent of cut grass and barbeques through my tiny attic window. It had been a big day, and I was ready to collapse into a boneless blob on my bed.

But my stomach rumbled at the very thought of Mum's home-made pie. My plan for dinner had been to sneak some lunch left-overs home. Plus, of course, dinner at theirs meant less risk of crossing paths with Elliot.

'You've not seen the new flat,' Mum added. 'It isn't even new any more.'

The glimmer of hope in her eyes was too much. I'd been fobbing them off with excuses for over *ten years*. A whole decade of Mum and Dad gently reminding me that their door was always open, even as against all parental instincts, they stepped back and gave me space to mess up time and time again. Even when rescuing me from the squat, they put no pressure on me to come back.

'Of course, I'd love to.'

Mum flipped around under the pretence of checking the lights were off, but as we walked to join Dad at the front door, a streak of mascara glistened on both cheeks.

We strolled through the village to their flat, in a converted water mill on the banks of the river, cutting through a footpath that led between the tiny primary school and the park. It was strange being back here, watching a whole new generation of children swarming over the play equipment I'd spent so many summer evenings scrambling over and, in my older years, slouching about on. At the sports field beyond, more children were jogging up and down where I used to watch my brother and the boy I'd secretly fallen in love with play football.

My heart jerked in my chest when I spotted a mop of blond hair that for a second I thought was Elliot's. I turned away, annoyed at my memory playing tricks on me, until Dad pointed at the field.

'Elliot's assistant coach for the under nine's this year.'

Twisting my head back far too quickly to appear casual, I saw that it was, in fact, my housemate. In a red tracksuit to match the team shirts, he was jogging alongside them, his grin so wide I could see it all the way over here.

'It's caused a bit of controversy.' Dad stuck his hands in his jean pockets and stopped to watch.

'A raging argument, you mean,' Mum added, tutting in disgust. 'Including the nastiest comments from people I once thought would never discriminate against someone for being slightly less able. As if a children's football team is all about winning matches.'

'Well, it kind of is about that,' Dad said, wincing as one of the children sent a ball rolling off into the bushes.

'No. It isn't,' Mum snorted. 'This isn't the FA cup. They are eight years old. What matters is having fun, making friends and learning new skills. One of which is how to handle losing. Most of the people sticking their noses in, going on about village pride and other nonsense, don't even have children who play. And that so-called manager, Simon Simonson! He's from Brooksby! Can you believe that he had the audacity to demand Houghton Harriers have a *village vote* about it?'

'Wait.' I tore my eyes away from the coaching session and looked at Mum. 'People wanted to vote Elliot off as assistant coach? Because of his disability?'

'No, it's far worse than that. They wanted to introduce trials, and make it so that only village residents could join the club, booting out half of the kids.'

'A Houghton only team? How will that help them win?' The village was so small it would be impossible to find enough eight-year-old children to make a football team.

'Because most of the non-village kids joined this team because Elliot is the only one who will accept them.' Dad's voice was tight with anger.

'Elliot waited until Simonson took a month off to visit New Zealand and then made it known that he welcomes anyone. Of all abilities. And he *really* welcomes them. As long as they can run, and kick a ball.'

'One of the players is registered blind,' Dad said.

'Wow.'

'They started off with a child with one arm, who brought his friend who has a condition that means he falls over a lot. Initially people assumed they'd be allowed to train but during matches stay on the substitute bench, but Elliot insisted they got to play as much as the others. Some of the better players have decided to leave, and Elliot doesn't mind because more kids who've been rejected from other teams are happy to fill up their places. That's when the complaints started, and when Simonson came back it only got worse.'

'They've lost every game since Simonson's holiday. Haven't scored a single goal. But anyone with half a brain cell can see that they're the best in every other way,' Mum exclaimed as we left the park. 'Anyway, here we are.'

We crossed the road and headed down a short gravel drive to a door with buzzers for six apartments.

'The code is nine eight nine four.' Dad winked as he tapped it in. 'Let yourself in any time.'

'Of course it is.' Mine and Isaac's birthday. 'And no, I won't let myself in any time. That's an invasion of your privacy.' My parents were *very* much in love. The Sunday afternoon I phoned and they declared it was perfect timing because they were in bed together was bad enough. There was no way I would risk walking in on anything.

'Anyone else could let themselves in though with a code that obvious.'

'You've forgotten that we live in a village. Everyone knows we aren't worth burgling. What would they take: that vase you made in year two? Besides, there's CCTV in the stairwell, we'd soon figure out who it was.'

Keeping my rational arguments to myself, I followed them up a flight of stairs and through a plain black door into the flat.

'Really?'

They hadn't been joking about the vase. There it sat on a shelf, keeping company with Isaac's clay mug, a framed copy of the poem I'd entered into a writing competition and come second to last, and various other pieces of homemade tat that normal parents gushed over before discreetly tucking into a box.

Not to mention the photos.

Younger versions of Isaac and me covered every wall. A tiny

corner next to the television included the rest of the family – aunties, my grandparents, only one of whom was still alive and living with my auntie in Leicester, plus my four cousins.

I would have wondered where the pictures of my parents were (although they were in a lot of the ones featuring me and Isaac). Then they showed me a quick peep in the bedroom and I stopped wondering.

Mum insisted I sat and 'relaxed' while she heated up the pie and Dad set the table and made us all a cold drink. It wasn't easy to unwind, sitting there, surrounded by my history – not only the photos, but the furniture, the crockery and curtains. I tried focussing on the pre-prom memories, which most of them were, but then I spotted the picture that was like a stab in my guts.

A pair of twins and their best friend, standing in front of a tandem bike. Isaac was laughing as he looked straight at the camera, his expression full of youthful confidence. My face was slightly inclined towards his, I could imagine myself mid-head shake as he guffawed at his own joke. But what made my breath catch in my lungs was Elliot. His dark eyes were completely focussed on me.

He looked exactly the same as when he'd leaned forwards, about to kiss me for the first time.

He looked like a boy hopelessly in love.

I couldn't help glancing at my parents, cheerily bustling about in the kitchen space. Mum must have spotted my reaction to the photo, because a few seconds later she'd come to sit beside me.

'It's one of my favourite pictures,' she said, her voice soft. 'You were all glowing with possibility and promise that night.'

'Yeah. Until we weren't.' It was okay that my voice caught on the words. We all knew the evening ended in tragedy.

Mum waited for a while before she spoke again. 'You know, it's incredible how after getting so hurt that night, despite all the physical and mental limitations, Elliot has been so determined to create the life he wanted, anyway. To be who he wants to be. I'm so proud of him.'

'What's your point?' I asked, unable to hide a trace of bitterness. 'Well done, Elliot, you're so strong and brave and amazing. Unlike Jess, still floundering around in her own failure.'

Mum twitched, visibly shocked. 'No! No, Jessie. What are you talking about? Elliot is strong and brave and amazing, but I wasn't for one second comparing him to you!'

'Well, that's a relief.'

'And my point is,' she said after pausing for Dad to announce that dinner was ready, two red spots appearing on her cheeks the only indication that she was upset, 'that whatever you've been through – and I know something happened that summer; it was more than your friend being in an accident – I want you to take hope from Elliot's story. That however bad things are, how woeful the diagnosis, there is hope that one day, we can get through it. We might never recover completely, but we can be happy, and whole enough, and life can be wonderful again.'

'Some bubbles to celebrate a great first day?' Dad called across the kitchen, eyes gleaming as he held the bottle aloft.

A great first day? I thought about that. About my parents, so determined to look at the best in people, at their successes and not their scars. 'I did manage to avoid a riot at lunchtime.'

'You were magnificent! Maybe take your shoes off before standing on the table next time, but if they're eating out of your hand like that on the first day, before long we won't even need the emergency protocol.'

'The *what*?'

Dad handed me a glass and changed the subject.

## 8

I left a few hours later, Dad dropping me off as it was growing dark. As I went to make myself a cup of tea, I heard the back door open, and Penny burst in, wagging her tail as if finding me there was quite simply the best thing that had ever happened to her.

'Hey.' Elliot paused for a split second when he saw me crouched down, stroking Penny's head.

'Hi.' I stood up, giving him a chance to remember who I was and why I was in his kitchen. He was wearing the short shorts and sleeveless top again. I decided it was best to keep my focus on Penny, nuzzling her head against my waist while he took off his trainers, placed them on the mat and locked the back door exactly as he'd done before.

'How was your first day?' he asked, as Penny trotted over to have her paws wiped.

I looked up, with a flush of surprised pleasure that he'd remembered.

'It was... interesting?'

He grinned. 'I can imagine.'

'From the look on your face I'm guessing you've met some of the Outlaws.'

'My Grandad used to be one of them.'

'And you didn't think to warn me?'

Elliot stood up, running one hand through hair dank from the effort of his run. Penny had sat down, head moving back and forth between us as if this was the most riveting conversation she'd ever witnessed.

'On their own, they're mostly a nice, normal bunch. It's when they gather that they can go a bit...' He stopped, brow furrowing as he hunted for the word.

'Feral? Uncontrollable? Violently mob-like?'

'I was going to say boisterous.' He raised both eyebrows in a gesture so familiar that a spark of ancient chemistry flickered deep down inside. 'You look as though you emerged intact, though. No obvious bruises or open wounds. You must be good at crowd control.'

'I stood on a table and yelled at them to stop acting like five-year-olds.'

'Nice.' He started filling up a glass with water.

'Some of them even apologised.'

His eyebrows flicked up again. *Spark.*

'That's very impressive. Isaac's still waiting for an apology for the time a pack of them broke into the wedding storeroom and had a confetti fight.'

'I think they're getting bored. Mum and Dad are so busy running everything, they haven't changed the activity programme for years. One person told me that during the last 1940s tea party he'd started fantasising about breaking his hip just to liven things up a bit. I'm their only hope; they know they need to stay on my good side.'

'They're going to love you.'

'The feeling's mutual.'

His eyes caught mine for a brief moment before dropping to Penny, who straight away got up and padded across the corridor to his bedroom door opposite the kitchen before turning to look at him.

'You're right. Damn. I must stink.' Elliot hastily put his glass in the dishwasher then followed his dog, looking back at me as he reached the doorway, his movements jerky, face flushed. 'Sorry. I got distracted seeing you here. I should have waited to start a conversation after a shower. More slobbiness from one of your housemates. Sorry.'

Lifting his T-shirt to wipe his face, he realised that this revealed a wide stretch of flat stomach, causing his agitation to increase as he tugged the top back down. 'Next time, just... well. Yeah. I'm... see you later. Shower. Clothes in the wash. Dinner.'

He disappeared into his bedroom too fast for me to say that if he did smell, I'd not noticed. Or that having spent the day broiling in my own perspiration, I probably smelled equally as bad. Or the hundred other thoughts that plagued me after I'd gone to bed that night – that once upon a time I'd happily hung around with him after countless runs or football matches. That the few times he'd celebrated a win or a personal best by hugging me, drenching me in second-hand sweat, I'd been tempted to avoid a shower myself afterwards, so I could carry the scent of him for as long as possible.

I lay in bed, staring at the bumpy ceiling, heart hammering through the vest top of my pyjamas.

I'd expected to feel gut-wrenching shame at seeing Elliot every day. To be swamped in self-loathing and crippled with sadness.

I'd had this picture in my head of how he'd be. His life a wreck. Broken. Lost. *Weak.*

All those things I'd felt the need to be, too, in the years before my therapy.

He was nothing like I feared.

I don't know why I never even contemplated that he'd still be so *Elliot.*

Not for one second had I imagined that the sight of him would bring back these old feelings. Which was somewhat naïve of me, given how fiercely they'd once burned beneath my skin.

To my huge relief, Seb called at one in the morning, bringing me back to reality with a bump as he described his new job hiring out boats on a tiny island I'd never heard of. I was not eighteen-year-old Jessie, hopelessly infatuated. I was twenty-eight-year-old Jess, in a committed relationship and very happy about it.

As I finally flopped down to sleep, grateful that the night brought with it a breeze to dissipate the stuffy attic air, I acknowledged that it was understandable, how coming home and confronting familiar faces would stir up old feelings. Understandable, even if not really acceptable – or in any way helpful. I whispered what had become my nightly prayer since arriving in Chimney Cottage, that my boyfriend would be well enough to come home, soon.

* * *

My second day at work passed in a similar way to the first, except that this time I wore green, calf-length culottes and a white T-shirt with sandals so managed to avoid hovering on the brink of heat-exhaustion. I did some more brain-shrivelling policy reading, spent a lot of time chatting and sat in on the two organised activities for the day, a music quiz and glass painting.

The music quiz, done well, had the potential to be a lot of fun. It didn't quite turn out like that.

Mum was with one of her old home care clients with dementia, who was having a particularly rough day, and Dad was stuck in the kitchen due to the leak having returned with a vengeance. That left Lance standing in as quizmaster.

Lance had been working for my parents since they'd first started the domiciliary care business. I'd paired up with him several times for home visits. He was brilliant at working with older people. I'd seen stubborn grumps melt in response to his unpatronising kindness, and the most anxious, fretful clients laughing at his jokes within moments.

However, it was immediately apparent that Lance was not made for a larger audience. Around fifty people had turned up in the main hall for the quiz, and as each one entered the room he seemed to shrink another inch into the floor. By the time he'd stumbled over the welcome and basic quiz rules, he was a gibbering wreck. The only thing that saved the afternoon was that having done the quiz so many times before, everyone was proficient at organising themselves into teams and passing around the answer sheet and pot of pens.

Unfortunately, they were equally as proficient at remembering the answers.

'We've had this one before!' became the ongoing grumble.

'Let me guess,' called out a man who'd introduced himself to me as Mr Wonka with a tip of his top hat. 'The sixties round. Could the first answer possibly be Marvin Gaye?'

At least they all did well, with the worst score being twenty-seven out of thirty, and four teams scoring full marks. That led to the absolute highlight of the day, when Lance played a clip for the tie-breaker question, only instead of stopping the music after the introduction, like he was supposed to, he couldn't find the right button on the sound system, and 'Dancing in the Street' carried right on playing.

By the time he turned around to ask if I could help, half the room were clapping along, tapping their toes or clicking arthritic fingers. The other half had pushed back their chairs, stood to their feet and starting swaying, twirling or in some cases full-blown boogeying along. The volume rose as more of those with enough breath left starting singing at the tops of their voices and others banged their mugs on the tables, tapped walking sticks on the chair-legs or found whatever way they could to add to the percussion.

It was like a scene from a musical. A wild, joyous, raucously good time.

'Do they always do this?' I asked Lance, having to shout above the chorus.

'Never,' he replied, his face a picture of panic.

'It's fantastic!' I said, laughing as I bopped along.

'We aren't going to get away with any more straight quizzes, are we?'

'I certainly hope not!' I grabbed Lance's hand and spun around, forcing him to join in. 'You're the best care worker I've ever seen, Lance. But if I have to sit through another one of those, I might start rioting myself.'

* * *

The glass painting was, in itself, a perfectly fine activity. For the three women who turned up, that is. We had a nice enough time painting jars for tea-lights and glass coasters. The women who took part were fantastic artists, but the problem seemed to be the same as before. Even as a monthly class, there was only so much glass one person could paint.

'At our age the last thing we want is more clutter,' June told me, adding a streak of turquoise to her jar to complete the striking wave effect. 'We've all run out of family to palm them off on, so nobody can see the point.'

Tracy, leading the session, sniffed. 'The point is that you get to explore your creativity, express yourself artistically while enjoying each other's company. It's not about the end product.'

'I just think that if you don't especially like the end product, there's only so much exploring you can do,' June said.

'It's all right for us,' Hetty added. 'We've got an Etsy shop linked to Robin Hood's Barn Weddings, so we sell them off cheap as wedding favours or decorations, which pays for our extras in the café.'

There was unlimited tea, americano coffee and cordial free of charge in the café, as well as one 'cake of the day' each. Anything else had to be paid for.

'Can I buy some of these off you?' The jars they'd decorated were stunning, and would be one step closer to transforming Chimney Cottage into a home rather than a youth club.

'If you promise to kick some life back into this place, they're yours.'

I helped myself to three, and left the rest for their cake fund.

\* \* \*

Another highlight of the day was meeting Isaac's creative director. She and Isaac usually took Monday and Tuesday off, after working flat out over the weekend, but a particularly tricky client had been bombarding her with messages so she'd nipped in to check a few details.

'Connie's upstairs,' Mum said, bursting into the art room, panting as though she'd sprinted through the Barn to tell me this, which I'd bet my new tea-light holders she had. 'If you're finished in here you could go and say hello.'

'Who's Connie?'

'The perpetual thorn in Isaac's side.'

'Oh – the person who's left all that stuff strewn about their office?' I was smiling already.

'Organised chaos, she calls it. I won't say what Isaac calls it in front of our art class members.'

'A "bloody disaster zone", is what he yelled down the stairs after her last week,' Hetty chortled. 'We love Connie. She's our biggest client!'

'I'll see you next week then?' Tracy asked, stacking the jars and coasters on a shelf.

'Maybe.' June tossed her ash blonde tresses over the shoulder of her mustard pinafore as they got up to go. 'Depends what else might be happening by then.'

'Nothing that'll earn you fifty pence a jar!' Tracy retorted.

Finding the upstairs office door locked, I gave it a tap and it was cautiously opened by a woman with light-brown skin and a mass of shoulder-length corkscrew curls wearing a charcoal, off-the-shoulder top and cream, crocheted shorts revealing endless legs. She was maybe a couple of years younger than me, several inches taller and had a confidence about her that would have intimidated the heck out of me if her face hadn't lit up with such a warm, wide smile.

'Jessie!' She stepped back to let me in. 'Come in, come in! I was hoping to meet you soon. And apologies that you had to knock. I had a terrifying incident with a Bridezilla's mum recently so I keep the door locked if I'm here without Isaac.' She peered at me as I walked past. 'You are so like him, it's uncanny. I knew who you were instantly.'

'I've never figured out if that's a compliment or not,' I said, laughing to show I didn't mind.

'I don't know how to answer that without offending one of you.' She grinned. 'I'm guessing that you're the only one allowed to diss your twin?'

'Well, my mum manages the odd dig.'

'Yes, but Pippa has this way of doing it that's so lovely, she gets away with it.'

'Like, "please be careful that your natural confidence and charm isn't being misinterpreted as arrogant and boorish, Isaac darling".'

If possible, her smile grew even wider. 'Tea, coffee or cold drink?'

'Are you sure you've got time?'

She held up two swatches of fabric, one a pale coral, the other a slightly darker shade of apricot. 'Which one of these says "boho fairy tale" the most?'

'Um... the lighter one?'

'Perfect. Now I've got time.'

She poured us both a pink lemonade from the mini fridge and we settled down on a window bench overlooking the lawn.

'This is an awkward question, but I can't help thinking we've already met. Were you at Brooksby Academy?' I asked, after a minute or two of small talk.

'The year below you,' she said. 'I was in the athletics club, so hung out with Elliot sometimes.'

'Oh, yes!' It fell into place, now. 'Constance Johnson? I'm so sorry I didn't recognise you.'

I remembered a painfully shy girl with cornrows, running races with a ducked head and hunched shoulders as though wishing no one was watching.

'Don't worry about it. I never dared speak when you and your brother were around because I had a major crush on him.'

'Didn't most people?' Isaac wouldn't have looked twice at someone as timid as Connie back then.

'Those who weren't mooning after Elliot Ollerton.' She winked, causing me to shrug, even as I felt my cheeks betray me.

'He was my brother's best friend. Totally off limits.'

'Hmm.' Her arched eyebrow said what she really thought about that. I quickly changed the subject.

'Anyway, what have you been up to since school? Where are you living now?'

'Oh, I took a year out to work as an au pair in Colorado and came home five months later, pregnant. After Wilf was born, I did an events management degree, then worked in a few hotels until this came up. It's literally my dream job. I finally saved enough to get me and Wilf our own place in Houghton – that pale-blue terraced cottage in The Nook? – and I couldn't be happier.'

'Wow.'

'Yeah. Probably the least likely person in school to end up a teenage mother. But my biggest mistake turned out to be my best decision.' She showed me a photograph of a boy on her phone, his beaming smile and apple cheeks making it clear who his mother was. 'Just a shame his dad turned out to be such a loser. He was the pool guy, would you believe it. Such an embarrassing cliché. Him not being interested made the whole situation less complicated though. I don't know how we'd have managed trans-Atlantic co-parenting.'

'That's incredibly impressive. Please don't ask what I've been up to.'

'You forget I work with your twin. I know you've been helping run a coffee shop for the past couple of years in Brighton. Living with your boyfriend a stone's throw from the beach. Sounds pretty good to me.'

'Yeah. It's the mess before that which I'm not proud of.'

'You did just hear how I got pregnant during a crappy fling with a deadbeat? We all get in a mess at some point, Jessie. It's what we do next that matters.'

'What I've done next is rent a tiny room in my brother's frat house and take a pity job from my parents in the hope of one day seeing the grand total of zero pounds in my bank account, rather than a big fat minus sign.'

'There you are then!' Her amber eyes twinkled. 'It's all uphill from here.'

At that moment, the door opened and Isaac strolled in, coming to a sudden stop when he saw us.

'I didn't know you were coming in,' he said, as one of the papers he was carrying slipped off the pile of others onto the floor. He was in even worse casualwear than usual today: sagging jersey shorts and a sleeveless hoodie.

'I could say the same to you.'

Were my eyes deceiving me or was my super-cool brother *flustered*?

'I wanted to get a head-start on sorting the Richmond Higgins debacle.' Isaac shook his head as if disgusted.

'As did I.' Connie nodded at a pile of random clutter on one of the tables before turning her head back to me. 'The wedding is in less than two weeks and yesterday they sent us a barrage of Instagram messages saying they'd decided the Bridgerton theme we agreed a year ago was now passé, they want boho fairy tale – whatever that means, because the images they sent really didn't make it any clearer – including a new colour scheme and décor, menus, entertainment, seating arrangements and forty more guests.'

'Have you spoken to them?' Isaac asked, dumping the papers on his desk and sitting down.

'I've left two messages. I've also emailed, WhatsApped and replied on Insta.'

'Can you try again?' he barked, gaze now fixed on his laptop. 'If you aren't too busy gossiping with my sister?'

'How about you try?' Connie said, her expression a picture of serenity. 'Seeing as I'm taking my first break since coming in at eight *on my day off* to work on these hideous chair flounces?'

Isaac had started furiously tapping away, jaw clenched. I took another sip of lemonade, thoroughly enjoying seeing someone stand up to him. After a few more taps he sat back with a long sigh.

'Once you've finished your break, it would be great if you could spare a few minutes to try them again. I don't want us to waste any more time on this without confirming costs. And...' He cleared his throat, shuffled his chair an inch further under his desk, and to my astonishment started *blushing*. 'You're better at handling them than I am.'

Connie arched one eyebrow.

'And I apologise for taking out my couple-from-hell stress on you,' Isaac half-mumbled. 'I'm aware this is a lot more work for you, too.'

I had to scoop my chin up off the floor. *Was that a genuine apology?*

When, two minutes later, Connie had the couple on speaker-phone, I quickly left them to it. It was no small distraction, however, once I'd returned to my desk. My brother had just been handled.

It may have been a case of one plus one equals a wild guess, but I had a strong suspicion I'd just met Isaac's mystery 'single lady'.

## 9

I went straight home after work, more than ready for a quiet evening with a book and a wedge of leftover quiche from lunch. After hiding upstairs until Elliot and Penny had set out on their eight-on-the-dot run, I decided to risk eating in the garden as they shouldn't be back until after nine.

'Ah, Jessica.' Arthur appeared as soon as I'd taken my first forkful, savouring the gooey ricotta and roasted pepper filling.

'You really don't need to shake my hand every time you see me,' I said, indicating that my hands were full.

'Sorry. Work habit. I shake dozens of different hands a day.'

'All the more reason why I'm happy with a hello.'

'Right. Hello.'

I took another mouthful, finished it, and realised I was going to have to take the lead. 'Have you had a good day?'

'Yes, thank you. A cremation in Mansfield. Slight issue with a misspelled wreath, but who knew that Daisee could be written with two Es?'

'I suppose Daisee's family did.'

'Would have been helpful if they'd told the florist.'

He continued hovering until I couldn't bear it any longer.

'Did you want something? It's a bit weird having you stand there watching me eat.'

'Ah. Yes. Sorry. I forgot. I was wondering if you knew where Isaac was or when he might be back. He's not replying to my messages and the darts quarter final is at nine-thirty.'

'He's working. A Bridgerton wedding's turned boho at the last minute.'

Arthur screwed up his face. 'Ah, I hate it when that happens.'

'Really?'

'When a family feud switched a traditional send-off to the *Greatest Showman* at the last minute, it was a nightmare trying to sort the trapeze.'

I spied a shadow emerge from the distant treeline. 'Right, anyway, I'm going to call my boyfriend.'

'You have a boyfriend?' Arthur's bushy eyebrows shot up in surprise.

'Would you believe it? A very nice one, actually.' I went to remind myself of that, even as Elliot's loping figure drew closer.

\* \* \*

Seb had messaged me an hour ago asking if I could phone after eight. He'd just finished work and was at a bar with the brothers who ran the boat-hire when I called. I waited while he found a quiet spot to talk, my stomach curling up in disquiet. We'd spoken less than twenty-four hours earlier. The only positive reason I could think of for him needing to talk was that he'd decided to come home, and I was holding out no hope of that. Which left the huge list of negative ones my brain had been chewing over.

'Hey, beautiful. How's your second day been?' he asked, which seemed to rule out one of those reasons – surely you wouldn't greet someone you were about to dump with a compliment?'

We chatted for a couple of minutes but I found it impossible to concentrate.

'Did you want to talk about something specific?'

'Oh, yeah. The final energy bill for the flat came through. Turns out we've been underpaying. By quite a lot.'

By *we*, of course he meant *he*.

'How much is it?' My mouth had turned completely dry.

'Eight hundred.'

'*What?*'

'I guess those new hair-straighteners used more energy than we realised.'

'Could it be a mistake? A faulty meter or something?'

'I've spoken to them and there's nothing wrong. There's been those massive price hikes and it's been nearly a year since I sent in a meter reading. But they offered a flexible payment option, two hundred a month. Only...'

Here it came. The hair-straighteners comment had prepared me for it.

'I'm living hand to mouth; there's no way I can pay. Now you've got the new job, are you able to sort it?'

He didn't have to mention that he'd paid all of the rent and most of the bills for three years, while I'd chipped in an occasional token gesture and funded our food and barely-there social life.

Two hundred a month, on top of debt repayments and rent...

Yes, I could sort it, if I did nothing apart from work, sleep and eat scraps from the Barn kitchen for the next few months.

But that would of course obliterate any hope of saving enough to get out of Chimney Cottage to a place where I could rebury the guilt I'd been carrying around since coming back to Houghton.

I ended the call with Seb and spent the next hour pacing up and down my room in a frenzy of rising panic.

I'd been coping with living with Elliot, even managed those couple of conversations. It had helped, seeing that he was okay and the accident hadn't destroyed his life. But the sticky notes, those brief chats and the loping run were reminders that he was doing okay because he'd had to fight and adapt and adopt a thousand different strategies just to get through each day. To compensate for what my stupidity had stolen.

I knew it wasn't about me, that me not being here made no difference to him. But honestly, in that moment, as I wore a path up and down my green rug, I felt terrified that staying here indefinitely could lead to a complete breakdown.

I'd teetered on the edge of that precipice before, and the thought of going back there sent panic tumbling through my insides.

It was late when a thump on my bedroom door interrupted my pacing.

'Jessie?'

'What?' I really didn't want to speak to my brother right then.

'Arthur said you've been stomping about up there for ages. He's got an early start tomorrow. Are you okay?'

'I'm fine.'

'Can I come in then?'

'I'm in my pyjamas.'

'And? It's just me.'

I tried to come up with another excuse but my head was fried.

'Or shall I call Mum and tell her I'm worried about you?'

Sometimes, having a twin was downright infuriating.

I opened the door. 'I said I'm fine.'

'You've been crying.'

'I'm missing Seb.'

Isaac pushed past me and sat on the bed.

'You know I'm just going to bug you until you cave.' He leant back against the wooden headboard, crossing his arms as if settling in for the night.

I did know, and seeing Isaac had reminded me of an idea.

'Seb's just told me that we've got a massive energy bill to pay. I can't afford the instalments.'

'But he's helping?'

I briefly explained why he'd never bothered asking me for rent, and how it was my time to pay my share. I also came clean about the Debt Swamp, because I needed him to know that I was desperate, although I made it sound more like a Debt Puddle, because I needed him to think I wasn't a total disaster.

'I've got loads of waitressing and bar experience. Can I help you out with the weddings?'

'All the event staff work Friday to Sunday, for continuity. The Saturday is a relentless, fourteen-hour day. That's too much on top of your actual job.'

'I can handle it! I've worked all day in a restaurant and then gone straight to a night shift as a carer before.'

Isaac shook his head, although his tone was sympathetic. 'I can't risk hiring people who are going to be dead on their feet a few hours in. Our clients pay top-rate for a flawless service.'

'Please. I really, really need this. All the crap I've waded through the past ten years, until last week I've never asked you for anything.'

He pulled a wry face. 'And now it's a home *and* a job.'

'The room is Elliot's. And I seem to remember you couldn't find anyone else to take it.' I looked him in the eye and waited while he wrestled with knowing how much I needed this.

'You can help set up on Friday, and with the Sunday morning clearing up. Not the Saturday. You need a day off and I need staff trained to Robin Hood's Barn standards. On the condition that

Mum and Dad okay it, you keep up and aren't completely knack-ered on Monday morning.'

'Thank you.' I closed my eyes until the rush of tears had been safely squashed back behind my eyes again. 'I have one condition, too, though.'

'Sis, you aren't in a position to be making demands.'

'No, but I'm in the position where I have to beg for them. If I show you I can hack it, then you let me do some Saturdays. Once a fortnight. The long shift plus tips will make all the difference.'

Seeing his forehead wrinkle in protest, I pushed on.

'I can't bear being stuck in the Debt Swamp. My whole life is stuck there until I get out of it. If I have to work every day for a year the physical toll will be worth the mental relief.'

He took my hand and gave it a squeeze. 'Let's see how this weekend goes, first.'

## 10

The first week in any job is going to be tiring. Throw in a bunch of rebellious Outlaws, my parents clucking about trying to ensure I had the Best Work Week Ever, add to that evenings avoiding a housemate while pretending to Isaac that I was positively brimming with energy and all in all, by Friday morning the temptation to burrow under my duvet and forget the world existed almost won.

Instead, I dragged myself out of bed at seven-thirty, stood under a scalding shower until I could keep both eyes open at the same time, donned jeans and a white T-shirt, sorted my hair, hid my wan face beneath a layer of make-up and hurried downstairs to pour the first of hopefully many coffees down my throat.

I assumed the person I'd heard clattering in the kitchen would be Isaac, but no, Elliot was sitting at the table, with a fresh plate of eggs and a pot of filter coffee.

He looked up from his book as I walked in, a faint glimmer of surprise in his eyes. Penny emerged from underneath the table, tail wagging.

'It's Jess?' I said, past the sudden lump in my throat. 'I'm working with Isaac at a wedding today.'

'Jessie, I can promise you I won't ever forget who you are. I just wasn't expecting you up yet.' He pointed his fork at a sticky note on the filter pot that said,

*Please wake J at 9.15*

'Good to know my brother has such faith in me.'

'He's worried about you.'

I stopped dead, my hand clutching the door of the mug cabinet. 'What's he said?'

'You're taking on a gruelling weekend shift on top of a full-on job. He didn't give details.'

'Well, he's no need to be worried, which is why I'm showing up early, to show him that.' I took out a travel mug. 'Is any of that coffee going spare?'

He nodded. 'There's more eggs in the pan, if you want them.'

I glanced at the clock behind him, debating whether I had time.

'They're a la jam sandwich.'

I jerked my head to look at his plate. Sure enough, poking out from underneath the scrambled eggs was a thick slice of naan bread covered in dark red jam.

'I thought you were supposed to be suffering from memory issues?'

Elliot, Isaac and I had invented eggs a la jam sandwich one morning when Mum and Dad had gone away for a few days and we'd run out of cereal or normal bread. Isaac had hated it, but Elliot and I had found a new breakfast classic.

'Did you make extra especially for me?'

He shrugged, but I caught the glint of a smile. 'I thought it might help you feel at home. You've seemed a bit... on edge, since you got here. I wasn't sure if it was being here, or something else, but I've learned not to underestimate the power of familiar food.'

'I haven't eaten this since I left home. Not so familiar any more.' I found another naan bread on the side by the hob, added a large blob of jam and a dollop of eggs, then grabbed a fork and took a seat opposite Elliot. Penny slid to her belly with a sigh beside me.

'It's my Friday morning staple.'

'You eat this every Friday?' Taking a mouthful, I could understand why.

'All part of the routine. Keep things simple and straightforward. Oh, and in my own separate pan, not Isaac's multicooker.'

We both smiled and shuddered at the same time.

'I'd forgotten how good this is,' I said, enjoying another generous mouthful. Elliot was right. Sat at the same table as the man who'd once meant so much to me, enjoying the weird food unique to our old friendship, in amongst all the strangeness and uncertainty swirling about, it felt somehow easier to push the horror that came between us to one side, as we savoured a shared moment of contented deliciousness.

'Do you want another one?' Elliot asked, once our plates were clean and coffee mugs empty.

'Yes, but I really have to go.' It was nearly eight-thirty and I was determined to show up at least half an hour early.

'Oh. Okay. Are you going out?'

I pointed at the sticky note, which had fallen off the filter jug onto the table.

'Right!' He nodded a few times. 'You're working with Isaac today?'

'Yes.' A thrum of tension hovered over the table before Elliot broke into a grin.

'And that's why I need the notes,' he said, as if reading a punchline, but his eyes didn't get the joke.

'What are your plans?' I asked, loading our plates into the dishwasher as my heart cracked in two all over again.

'Um, it's Friday, so I'll FaceTime my parents, then get ready for the Harriers match tomorrow.' Right on cue, his phone beeped. 'That's my five-minute warning. If I'm late then Mum will start to panic.'

'Okay, well, thanks for breakfast.'

'You're very welcome.' Elliot looked up from his phone. This time his eyes were smiling along with the rest of his face. 'I hope you'll join me again. Eggs a la jam sandwich always tastes better as a shared experience. Breakfast service is at eight.'

I hesitated. The thought of a weekly breakfast with Elliot sent my panic neurones shooting in all directions like a faulty firework. The reality had been a comfortable, relaxing few minutes that I found myself genuinely wanting to repeat. But even if he'd cooked eggs a la bacteria in the multicooker, or if I'd felt hideously awkward, I'd have still said yes. I owed Elliot a lot more than a few Friday breakfasts.

'Thank you. I'd like that.'

It was only to be expected that I'd enjoyed it, I told myself while hurrying down the lane towards the Barn. I'd really liked – *loved* – Elliot once. And while his injury had changed him, he was still the same person in all the ways that mattered. Of course I was going to still like him. Maybe this was going to turn out to be a good idea. Punishing myself hadn't solved anything, as the therapist had helped me to accept. Maybe what I should do – should have been doing all along – was try making it up to Elliot instead.

I could never undo the part I'd played in what happened. I couldn't repair the damage in Elliot's brain, but if I did what I could to help his life be as happy as possible, then it might help both of us to get through however long it took for me to find a new place to live.

The next question was how. Apart from getting up extra early so

I could be the one making the eggs, I had no idea what would make Elliot's life better.

However, way before I'd come up with any answers, I stepped inside the Barn and was instantly sucked into a vortex of frantic activity. All other thoughts were tossed to one side as I spent the next eight hours cleaning, fetching and carrying, setting tables and trying not to tell my bossy brother boss where he could stick his candelabra.

Isaac had paired me up with Avi, who described how after coming along to his cousin's wedding at the Barn he'd left his job as a dentist and emailed Isaac asking if he was looking for new staff. He also worked two days a week in a café, and couldn't be happier. His parents, less so. They'd not spoken since.

'I was here, at this eighty-thousand-pound wedding,' he told me as we laid out sixty wine glasses on the three banqueting tables the wedding couple had requested. 'Suffocating in all the showmanship, being introduced to all these suitable women as a dentist, and when one of them asked what I liked about my chosen career, I thought, "What can I say? I love the squeaky gloves? The drool? Breathing in other people's breath all day? Yanking out small children's rotting teeth while their parents promise more sweets to cheer them up?"'

He repositioned the glass I'd just put down so it lined up a millimetre more perfectly with the cutlery. 'Dentistry was never my chosen career, it was my parents', because they care more about appearing successful than whether their children are happy.'

He handed me a box of water glasses. 'I watched the staff here, working hard, but smiling. The purpose of their job to give people a wonderful day, full of love and joyful memories. When I returned to the concrete surgery where I was destined to spend the next forty years, I found I couldn't do it. I turned around and drove all the way back here from Newcastle. That was one year ago this Monday.'

'And are you happier here, even though your family aren't speaking to you?'

He stopped, a glass in each hand, and looked at me steadily for a long moment. 'I can breathe here. I sing as I walk to work. I met a lovely woman who doesn't want me just because my job can provide her with a flashy car and private schools for our children. I miss my family, of course. I call them every Sunday evening and leave a message. But yes, I am happy here. I love my jobs. I love my tiny flat beside the river. Most of all, I love being free.'

Avi was serious about loving this job. He worked until the back of his shirt was damp with sweat, combining speed with excellence. The plus side of this was me picking up a huge amount of information in a short space of time. The downside was already feeling exhausted by the time Isaac announced it was lunchtime.

I grabbed a pint glass of iced water and a panini from a platter in the kitchen, and went to join the other team members in the garden.

'I absolutely love your centrepieces,' one of the other operational staff said to Connie. 'The sweet peas are gorgeous. How long did it take you to make the mini trellises?'

'Can I remind you that we're on a break?' Isaac said. 'Connie is entitled to thirty minutes without discussing work, just like the rest of us.'

As the young woman he'd reprimanded shrank back into her seat, I had to remind myself that today he was my boss, and I couldn't tell him to stop being a jerk in front of his staff. I could give him a look that conveyed it equally as well, though.

Connie had no such qualms. 'Thank you for attempting to protect my lunchtime, but I'm more than happy to talk about the decorations. And if I wasn't, I'd have no problem explaining that to Gemma.'

Isaac inspected the contents of his brie and cranberry panini.

'Maybe not, but the rest of the staff might not share your assertiveness. I'm maintaining boundaries for everyone's sake.'

'I think the rest of the staff are socially astute enough to pick up when someone doesn't want to chat,' Connie muttered.

Isaac's cheeks had flushed. I watched in fascination.

'Well in that case, I apologise for trying to support wellbeing amongst my staff.' He picked up his plate and stalked inside.

'What is with him lately?' The sous-chef giggled, before a glare from Wendy and a not-so-subtle nod in my direction wiped the smile off his face.

'Sorry Jessie. No offence.'

None taken. I was asking myself the same question. At least being the boss's twin meant I could ask him, too.

## 11

After lunch, Isaac allowed me to stop rushing around after Avi and help with the décor. I sat folding place-cards, and after school Connie's son Wilf joined me, twisting napkins into roses.

'You're really good at that,' I said, watching the pile rapidly grow.

'I know. Most people can't get the edges all lined up the same, but you just need to follow the instructions properly.'

'You're really fast.'

He nodded, eyes fixed on his task, fingers a blur. 'Yes, but can you please stop talking now so I can concentrate.'

'Of course!' I ducked my head to hide my smile and got on with my own task.

Isaac wandered past. 'Hey, great job, dude. I thought you only started that a few minutes ago.'

'One-fourteen,' Wilf replied, stopping to give Isaac a high-five, his face beaming. 'It's now one-thirty-two so it's taken me eighteen minutes to do twenty-nine napkins. If your sister doesn't talk to me again I'll be finished at one-fifty-one.'

'Way to go. At this rate you'll need a pay rise.'

'Hmm.' Wilf looked thoughtful. 'Mum said I can have a burger, fries and coke from the Crooked Arrow after we're finished, which costs fifteen pounds ninety-five in total. How much is this pay rise going to be?'

Isaac grinned, his grumpiness vanished. 'How about an ice-cream from the pudding menu?'

'A rocky road sundae? That costs four pounds seventy-five. It's a... 30 per cent pay rise!'

Isaac gave a mock wince. 'Ooh... okay then, done.'

'*Mum!*' Wilf shouted at Connie, hanging bunting up a few metres away. 'Isaac says I can have a rocky road sundae after my burger!'

'Oh, really, is Isaac paying?' she called back, twisting around while still holding the bunting above her head.

'Well yes of course he is because it's a 30 per cent pay rise for working so fast.'

'Then that's great!' She mirrored her son's exact smirk, arching one eyebrow at Isaac. 'Has he noticed how fast I'm working today, too?'

'Hey, Isaac should come with us,' Wilf said, his face lighting up. 'I *think* the rocky road sundae is four pounds seventy-five, but it might have gone up. Or I might have remembered wrong. He should come just in case.'

'Honey, we both know you have that menu memorised. And Isaac's going to have worked a long day, with an even longer one tomorrow. The last thing he wants is an evening spent at a medieval-themed pub having to answer all your questions about their Cottage Cup.'

'It's the Chimney Cup,' Wilf retorted. 'And you don't mind, do you Isaac? I won't be talking about work, so it's not against the rules.'

Isaac stiffened, no doubt remembering how he'd come across earlier.

'I'm sorry, but I'm sure Isaac's Friday night plans don't include people dressed as serving wenches.' Connie shook her head, smiling. 'Maybe another time.'

Isaac opened and closed his mouth a couple of times. 'I'll check the foyer.'

'Huh.' Wilf pouted as Isaac hurried out the door. 'He forgot my pay rise.'

'I'm sure he'll give it to your mum with the rest of your pay,' I said.

'He already paid me. I get worried he might forget otherwise. Or sometimes I get overwhelmed if there's lots of balloons or other things that squeak and Nana has to pick me up early and then I'm too upset to get my money so he always pays me before.'

Wilf had stopped folding napkins and started to wring his hands. He was blinking furiously, like he had a nervous tick.

'How about I go and ask him for it now?'

'It's rude to ask people for money. What if he gets cross again and decides not to let me have it?'

'Wilf, did you notice that I have the same hair colour as Isaac, the same eyes and freckles?'

He gave a frantic nod, his narrow chest heaving.

'That's because he's my twin. He won't mind at all if I go and explain that he forgot. He understands why you need to get paid in advance, doesn't he?'

Another nod, accompanied with a faint moan.

'Give me two minutes. I promise, Isaac can't say no to me. That's why he let me have this job.'

'I don't understand why he said I could have a pay rise and then he went without giving it to me!'

Connie appeared next to him, face creased in concern.

'Here, look.' I took my purse out of my bag and to my relief was able to count out four pounds eighty in change. 'You take this, and Isaac can pay me back later.'

Wilf looked at the money for a moment, his blinking starting to ease.

'How about I look after it for you?' Connie asked, a picture of soothing calm. 'I can put it with the rest of your pay, here, in my side pocket.'

As Connie continued to reassure her son, I went to find my brother, who it turned out was slumped on a chair in his office, staring at his laptop screensaver.

'Hey, bro. I thought I might find you slaving away up here.'

'Is everything okay?' he asked, sounding as though he really didn't care either way.

'Wilf was upset because you left without giving him his extra money.'

Isaac's face plummeted. 'I forgot. Is he okay? Was Connie able to calm him down?'

'It's fine. You now owe me one rocky road sundae at the Crooked Arrow.'

'Damn. Sorry. He struggles with dysregulation if things don't go as they should. He's autistic.'

'Yeah, I'd gathered as much.'

'Is Connie okay?'

'Do you mean is she mad at you?'

Isaac gave a slight shrug as I carried on.

'Not about you suddenly running off, I don't think, no. I can't say if she's mad or not about all the times you've snapped at her, or said something weirdly unreasonable. What the hell is going on with that?'

He sat up, shrugging his shoulders as if his shirt collar was suddenly too tight. 'You're not used to seeing me as a boss, that's all.

I can't be mates with everyone here. Not when people's big days are at stake.'

'Isaac, I've seen what kind of boss you are during the past four hours. You're great. Approachable and encouraging. Then whenever Connie's around you turn into a total grouch.'

He closed his eyes for a moment, head drooping. I'd genuinely never seen him looking so dejected.

'She's the one you talked about, isn't she? The single lady.'

He gave a grunt of irritation. 'I don't know what's happening to me. It's like I lose control of all my senses when she's there and I can hear these words coming out of my mouth, but I can't seem to stop them.'

'So why the anger?'

'I don't know! I mostly feel angry at myself for wasting years messing about, charming women I didn't really care about, so now I finally meet the one I want to be with, I'm not good enough for her.'

'Have you asked her out?' I pulled a seat across from another table and sat down.

He nodded, miserably. 'A couple of weeks after she started here. I knew by the end of the first day that I was falling for her. It's one reason I suggested we promote her to a director, so I didn't have the issue of being her boss.'

'And she said no?'

'She said yes! I invited her for a meal at mine, because she was still living with her parents, and there was Wilf to think about.'

'Oh dear.'

'Yeah.' If possible, Isaac slumped even further into his fancy office chair. 'I bought this meal for two from the farm shop, which I burnt while reheating. Arthur came in and spent half the meal rambling on about their new range of coffins, you know, just in case she needed one in the near future. I forgot to take down the sticky notes about me.'

'"If a strange woman is here, she's with Isaac"?'

'That and others that I've since thrown in the bin.'

'So, it didn't go well.'

'She was witty, and smart, and ate most of the disgusting tagine. We talked about everything. Politics, films, school.' He pulled an ironic face. 'Work. And when I asked if she wanted to go out again she told me that while she'd had a lovely evening, she wasn't interested in a fling with the village Casanova. She'd agreed to the date because she'd not seen me in years and thought I might have changed.'

'Ouch.'

'I was okay to start with. Took the rejection on the chin, because I knew she was right. I thought we'd stick to being colleagues, no harm done. Then as the weeks and months went by, and I got to know her better... Jessie, I think about her *all the time*. If she's not here, I'm constantly wondering where she is, like the room is empty without her. My life feels empty without her. Only, she doesn't want a washed-up schoolboy player, whose personal life is a shambles. The more I love her, the more I act like this, and the worse it gets.'

'Okay.' He *loved* her? That put a totally different slant on things. I tried to keep cool and collected, like this was not the catastrophe he thought it was. 'On the plus side, your one date shows that she must find something about you attractive, and you got on really well at first. She'll have seen that the weird way you've been acting isn't really you. So, if her problem is that you aren't mature enough for her, then man up. Learn to cook. Turn your house into a nice place for people who don't love gaming to hang out. Show her the kind of partner you'd be if you were in a committed relationship.'

'I've never been in a committed relationship; I haven't a clue how to do that.'

'Isaac, you've been in a committed relationship with me for twenty-eight years. With Elliot for twelve. You're kind. Reliable.

Loyal. Funny. Get out of the mindset of trying to charm some girl you fancy, and think about how you show love to someone.'

He gave a hesitant nod, but was interrupted from saying anything else by his phone ringing.

'Yes?' He stood up quickly. 'I'll be right down.'

'Everything okay?'

'The bride and groom are here to check how it's all going.' He stopped abruptly in the doorway and spun around, causing me to bump into the back of him. 'I'm really glad you're back.'

I followed Isaac downstairs, expecting to find some wannabe influencers or a wealthy businessman on his third wedding. Instead, it was a couple called Bob and Winnie from the day centre.

'We always had a thing for each other, right from school,' Winnie told me after I'd sat them down on the terrace with a glass of champagne each. 'But my father insisted I marry someone who could take on the farm, so I had to settle for James Salterford instead.'

'I was heartbroken,' Bob interjected. 'I'd have knocked his block off if I thought it'd do any good.'

'Instead, he married Doris Jones to make me jealous.'

'It worked, too,' Bob laughed.

'Well, there was nothing to be done then but get on with it, so we did. For forty-nine years. Then last year, James had a stroke the same week Doris passed on.'

'Lung cancer,' Bob said, shaking his head sorrowfully. 'Never smoked a cigarette in her life.'

'And then I bump into Bob at Wood's funeral directors. He's on his way in as I'm on my way out. So, of course, the natural thing to do was offer each other a little comfort.'

'As friends.' Bob gave Winnie a stern look.

'As friends.' Winnie's eyes twinkled. 'Until then it wasn't. Fifty years, and when he kissed me it felt exactly the same.'

'Worth the wait.'

'But we aren't waiting any longer! Thanks to a last-minute cancellation, a month later here we are, about to be newlyweds!'

'First love,' Bob sighed, picking up Winnie's hand and pressing it against his lips. 'Nothing like it.'

With an aching heart, I had to agree.

I was getting ready to haul my weary bones home when I heard the unmistakable sound of my brother about to lose his temper. Connie was at the other end of the room doing a final check of the fairy lights, so it wasn't anything to do with her.

'We'd better see what's going on,' she suggested. I'd have settled for earwigging through the door, but she was sort of my boss so I couldn't refuse.

'According to the checklist you've completed the rooms upstairs,' Isaac said, his voice one decibel below a shout.

'Yeah, I did it after lunch,' Gemma said, hands on her hips, chin jutting out.

'Both the bride and groom's sitting rooms, and the bathrooms?'

'I just said that.'

'Then why is the windowsill covered in dead flies? I found a chocolate truffle squashed into the sofa, and *how did you possibly miss the used condoms in the bathroom bin?*'

'Oops,' Connie whispered.

Gemma's neck was mottled scarlet. Her eyes darted back and forth. 'Well, shouldn't whoever cleaned up after last week's wedding have sorted it? Why aren't you having a go at them?'

Isaac took a deep breath. The struggle to control himself was real. 'Gemma, that was also you.'

'Oh. Right.' Her eyes roamed wildly about the foyer, as if she'd find a decent excuse somewhere in the rafters or the wooden floor. 'I mean. Sorry, I'll give it another once over. But no one needs to freak out over a few flies. It's not like it's one of the important weddings, is it?'

'Oh, girl, that was not the way to play this,' Connie muttered, eyes wide.

'We can't be expected to go to the same effort for the cheap dos as the proper ones. Most of them can't even see if it's dirty or not.'

Isaac's lips were the only part of his body that wasn't completely still. 'You get paid exactly the same.'

'Not in tips, I don't!'

'So, you think only people who give you big tips deserve a wedding venue free of dead insects and condoms?'

'Um...'

'Or is it because they're older, so they don't matter as much?'

'Look, I'm sorry, okay! I said I'll sort it. It's not that big a deal.'

'It is though. For Bob and Winnie this is the biggest deal there is. And I don't want anyone on my wedding team who doesn't think that every person trusting us for the most important day of their life – however long that life has been – deserves the very best we can give them. I'll pay you for today, but please don't come in tomorrow.'

Gemma's mouth dropped open. 'Am I fired?'

'Yes.' Isaac shook his head in disgust. 'For the lousy attitude. I'd have given you a second chance over the shoddy work.' Marching past me, he bent his head and quietly said, 'Still interested in working a Saturday?'

After seeing my quick nod, he was gone. Gemma turned to Connie, her eyes filling with tears.

'Connie, you have to talk to him. It wasn't as bad as it sounded. I've got a cracking hangover so weren't my best today, but I'll not let it happen again, I promise.'

'I'm sorry but I can't help you.' Connie shook her head. She didn't look very sorry.

'Why, though? He always does what you want. You can change his mind, easy.'

'Because, as usual when it comes to running Robin Hood's Barn, I completely agree with him.'

## 12

I kept Friday evening as simple as possible. I ate a pack of fresh pasta from the stash of food Dad had bought me, did a load of washing and then fell asleep watching a cheesy film in bed. Saturday morning followed the same pattern as Friday, only there was no Elliot at the breakfast table. I assured myself that my twinge of disappointment was due to the lack of eggs, not company. Instead I grabbed a banana while Isaac waited impatiently to give me a lift. As much as I was happy to walk, he'd convinced me that my feet would be throbbing stumps of agony by the evening, and I'd be grateful to have avoided half a mile before I even started, never mind not having to walk home afterwards.

I found it no problem to slip into the familiar role of hospitality. The wedding ceremony was at twelve, in the church next door, so we were ready with trays of drinks and canapés by one. The rest of the day was spent in a sweltering swirl in and out of the kitchen, as well as serving behind the bar and repeatedly helping Winnie's bridesmaids remember where they'd put their glasses, slippers and gin and tonics.

My favourite part of the day was the evening, when a local DJ played sixties and seventies classics, and the Outlaw guests showed the younger ones how it was done.

'Do you ever have dancing like this at the day centre?' I asked one woman, as she tottered off the dance floor, dripping with sweat.

'Are you joking?' She rolled her eyes. 'We have tea dances. Or once there was a ceilidh, but someone broke their ankle stripping the willow so we never had another one.'

I made a note in my phone to look into day centre dance sessions.

\* \* \*

Sunday morning, Isaac had told me to be back at the Barn for twelve to help finish clearing up and ready the building for Monday.

To my surprise, the front doors were propped wide open, and when I followed the buzz of chatter through the main hall and into the garden, I found a load of people milling about, sitting down on picnic blankets or standing in small clusters chatting.

Two of the trestle tables from the wedding had been set along one side of the terrace, every spare inch of which was laden with food. After scanning the crowd for a familiar face, I made my way over to where Connie was pouring water into glasses at another table.

'I thought I was here to work,' I said, the confusion clear in my voice.

'Yeah, we've done most of it. Isaac wanted to let you catch up on some sleep. We'll finish the rest after this.'

'What is this?'

She grinned. 'This was me trying to avoid being such a sad, lonely loser when I first moved to Houghton. I had this miserable idea that everyone else my age was meeting friends in cosy pubs for giant roast dinners or out having romantic lunch dates. For some reason Sunday lunch felt like the most depressing meal of the week. Maybe because after long, exhausting Saturdays I then had to drag Wilf out of bed to go back to work again. One week, I decided to bring a picnic to eat on the terrace, to delay going back to our dull little house, and Avi asked if he could join me. A couple of the others on the team noticed, and before we knew it, we almost had a party. Eight months later, it's somehow evolved into this.'

'How many people come?' I was boggled by how many were streaming in through the door. A couple of men had to set up two more tables for the extra food.

'Oh, that's the church rush. A few weeks in we mentioned it to Lara, the minister, and she asked if some of the church could come along. Initially it was people who live alone, single parents like me, or for whatever reason could do with some company. Then the Outlaws got wind of it, and we couldn't stop them turning up if we tried. When they started inviting their friends and families, we decided to make it an open event. There's usually no more than one hundred and fifty. It's a voluntary donation of two pounds, or five for a family, with any profit going to the day centre, but those who can afford it chip in for the ones who can't. Most people bring something to share. The bakery, café and village shop bring unsold stock that would otherwise get wasted, so it works quite well.'

'Works quite well?' I bumped her arm with my elbow before picking up a water glass. 'This is incredible.'

'Okay, did you just nudge me?' Connie asked.

'Um... sorry?'

A strange glint had appeared in her eyes, and I was suddenly terrified I'd crossed some unseen boundary and was on the brink of causing a situation.

'Isaac!' she yelled, to where he was throwing a frisbee with Wilf.

'It was meant to be friendly,' I stammered. Was Connie going to get me fired, along with Gemma?

'Exactly,' she said as Isaac stopped, frisbee in hand, looking like an extra from *High School Musical* in ancient baggy shorts and a basketball top.

'Am I allowed to be friends with my boss's twin?'

'Why are you asking me? I'm not your boss!'

'Yes, boss.' With a wink, she picked up a glass and clinked it against mine. 'Now he can't moan about it later.'

To my surprise, Elliot arrived with the last of the church stragglers. It wasn't that I expected him to live holed up in the cottage feeling sorry for himself, but given how he struggled to remember people's names, or process too much information at once, a large, loud gathering seemed like a lot for him to cope with.

But then I watched him making his way through the crowd. How he smiled, exchanged a couple of sentences here and there, his blond hair glinting in the sunshine, and I remembered how effortlessly he used to talk to people, how he'd always shone in social situations.

I felt a simultaneous wave of pleasure – that he was still able to manage something like this – and heartache, that it must surely be so much more challenging than before.

Arthur was a minute or two behind, scurrying along beside a woman who I knew with one glance must be Elsa, the new curate he'd fallen for. She was tall, with a sturdy frame dressed in an orange playsuit, her hair in blonde plaits which instantly made me think of Vikings. Her strong features created a face that was warm and good-natured, and she was a woman who I suspected more than a few of the single men had noticed.

'Hi Arthur.' I hurried over, deciding the only decent thing to do was interrupt his monologue.

He finished his sentence, which included something about a painting, and then said hello.

I waited a few seconds until realising that Arthur wasn't going to do it, and introduced myself.

'I'm Jessie. Arthur's new housemate.'

'Isaac's twin?' She beamed. 'How amazing to meet the beauty to Isaac's beast!'

She bent her head a little closer. 'Only joking! I think Isaac's charming.' Her face immediately froze. 'Not that I was joking about you being beautiful! I bet you're totally lovely inside and out. I mean, look at your family! Your mum, soooo sweet! And your dad, gorgeous! Not that I think he's gorgeous in that way, of course! I meant personality not looks! No hang on, I don't think he's ugly or anything... just... oh, farts, I totally do not fancy your dad!'

She looked at Arthur for help, face stricken, and to my surprise he actually stepped up.

'Jessica knows what you meant. She grew up with Isaac and is living with Elliot and me, which means by definition she's not easily offended.'

'You must be Elsa?' I asked.

'Yes! Have they mentioned me?' she asked, a pretty pink circle appearing on each cheek. 'I've just started at the church. I'm still finding my feet, really.'

'Elliot mentioned that Arthur was really pleased to be working with you.'

'Oh, that's so nice of him.' Her face switched to delighted as quickly as it had plummeted earlier. I could see what Elliot meant about her energy. Her social intelligence, not so much. 'I'm very happy to be working with Wood's, too.'

'Yes, well, if you don't mind, I was updating Elsa on the progress of my latest grave hunt,' Arthur said, waggling his caterpillar eyebrows in a manner so unsubtle he might as well have simply told me to go away.

Before I was forced to find someone else to talk to, Connie started banging a pan with a metal spoon, declaring the buffet to be open.

'No taking more than one of Pippa's cheese tarts each! Oh, and the cake is from Bob and Winnie. If they can tear themselves away from the Chicken Coop, don't forget to congratulate them. Enjoy!'

Once a mass of children had grabbed plates and started piling them high, I waited another couple of minutes for a queue to form before jumping into the line behind Elliot because I thought he might appreciate a familiar face in amongst the hoards. Plus, he was the only person I knew whose opinion on food I completely trusted, and this was a buffet – choosing wisely was everything.

'Hey,' I said, causing him to turn around. 'It's Jessie.'

He lowered his eyebrows. 'Are you going to introduce yourself every time we have a conversation? Is it because you've forgotten my name and you're hoping I'll introduce myself back?'

'No!' I shuffled about, an awkward smile tugging at the side of my mouth. 'There's a lot of people here. You might have found it harder to place me in a different situation...'

'Jessie, I told you. I won't ever forget who you are.'

'Okay.'

'Okay, then. How was the wedding?'

'Isaac worked me so hard I didn't have time to take in much, but it seemed a lovely day. Everyone was happy. Apart from Winnie's dad, who still considers Bob totally unsuitable to inherit the family farm.'

'Is he?'

'Well, he's seventy-three, which I would think makes running a farm a challenge. But then, Ezra is ninety-two and he's still up with the cows, so what do I know.'

'Okay. I'm sorry... who's Ezra?' The queue had reached the table now, so Elliot handed me a plate and a paper napkin.

'Winnie's dad. Sorry, I hadn't mentioned that.'

Elliot looked at me blankly for second.

'Winnie is the bride.'

'Right. At the wedding yesterday? Did it go well?'

'Yes.' I blinked, hard, and somehow found a smile. 'How are you?'

'I'm good, thanks. Sorry, it's harder for me to keep up when there's a lot of background noise.' There was a *lot* of background noise, thanks to a Beach Boys soundtrack now competing with the conversation and squeals from a cluster of children playing tag. For a split second, Elliot dropped his affable mask and allowed me to see how arduous this was for him.

'Do you come here every week?'

'I came a couple of times at the start, when there were fewer people.'

'So why did you come today, if it's hard?'

He carefully inspected the platters in front of us, before selecting a mini sausage and egg pie, meatball slider and a spoonful of potato salad. I helped myself to the same straight away.

When he answered it was slowly, as if still figuring out the reason while he spoke. 'I think that you moving in has given all of us a fresh perspective. That awful lunch last week...'

'When you could have been here.'

'Isaac and Arthur would have been here, if I'd not suggested we cook something for you.'

'That was your idea?'

He nodded, ruefully.

'Well, thank you. For the thought, at least. Anyway, carry on.'

He hesitated, clearly having lost his thread.

'You were explaining why you came along today.'

'Oh, yes. I thought it might be time to try something new. Mix things up a bit. We've all got stuck in this small, slightly odd rut, not helped by lockdowns. You being here inspired me to take on some new challenges.'

We helped ourselves to a couple more items (honestly, there was enough to feed the whole village) and scanned the garden for a place to sit. 'You know I moved back home out of desperation, nothing inspirational?'

Elliot looked at me. I tried to ignore how his eyes once again sparked a rush of yearnful memories. 'You moved into my house because you were desperate?' His mouth twitched in amusement. 'Makes sense, I suppose.'

We started walking to where Connie waved at me from underneath an apple tree.

'Although I didn't know about the Chimney Cup when I decided to move in. Or the garden. Or the multicooker.'

Elliot let his mouth drop open in faux surprise. 'You're putting the Cup in the same category as the cooker?'

'Hey!' Connie beamed as we reached her. 'For a second there I thought you were going to ditch your new friend to sit with the cool kids.' She nodded at Elliot. 'Nice to see you here, Coach.'

'Coach Simonson?' Wilf almost tipped out of his camping chair as his head shot up. His look of horror morphed into a sigh of relief, and he sprayed out crumbs of pastry as he realised who it was. 'Elliot is the assistant coach, Mum.'

'For now.' Connie arched one eyebrow as she popped a strawberry in her mouth, causing Elliot to frown.

'Speculation like that isn't helpful,' he said, sitting down on another chair. 'It only adds to the instability of the team.'

'Then maybe it'll get so unstable Simonson topples off!' Connie retorted. 'Maybe he'll start listening to the rumours and take the hint. The club can't carry on as it is.'

'Even if he does leave, I won't be taking over from him.'

'Why not?'

'Why not?' Wilf echoed. 'Everyone knows you'd be the best.'

Elliot put the bite-sized pizza he was holding back on his plate. 'Being manager takes a lot of organisation. It isn't just coaching the players, or deciding what positions they're going to play. It's dealing with the club and fees and equipment. My personal limitations mean I'm not great at all that. It wouldn't be fair to the team if I was manager.'

Wilf pursed his lips. 'I read that a manager's most important tool is his team. All you need is someone else to help you do some of those things. And didn't you say that Houghton Harriers under nines are going to push past our so-called limitations, not let them stop us?'

'Well, as far as I know, Coach Simonson has no intention of quitting, and I've no intention of pushing past my limits as his assistant.'

'As far as you know,' Wilf muttered, in such a perfect imitation of his mum I had to hide my smile.

I adjusted my position so that my back was resting against a smooth section of the tree trunk, appreciating how nice it was to be sitting on a blanket, eating a lovely lunch and listening to a dozen conversations blending with the birdsong and background music while the leaf shadows danced on the grass. Much better than clearing up the dregs of a raucous wedding, that's for sure.

## 13

The next thing I knew, Mum was giving me a gentle shake. I found myself curled up on the blanket, with a cardigan draped over my shoulders.

'How long was I asleep?' I sat up slowly, blinking as I took in the near-empty garden.

'It's nearly half past three,' Mum replied, offering a hand to pull me up, which I gratefully accepted.

'Did I miss all the clearing up?' Embarrassment scurried up the skin on my chest and neck.

'Oh, don't worry about that. It doesn't take long when everyone pitches in.'

'Why did no one wake me?'

'You slept through a game of volleyball. We assumed you must need the rest.'

'Ugh. I can't believe I lay there like a big lump, with everyone watching me.'

'No one was watching you! Well, Elliot noticed you looked cold and asked to borrow my cardigan. But really, you aren't that interesting.'

I picked up the blanket and Mum took two corners, helping me fold it up.

'Is there anything else to do?

'Dad's vacuuming the foyer then we're locking up.'

'Where's Isaac?'

'He left a while ago, said he had something important to discuss with his housemates.'

'*I'm* his housemate.'

'Well, yes, I suspect they were discussing you.'

We reached the folding doors leading into the main hall just as Dad pushed the vacuum into the cupboard.

'Jessie! You're awake! We couldn't believe you slept—' He caught Mum's eyes and stopped abruptly. 'Anyway, I hope you enjoyed lunch. Do you want to come to ours for dinner? We've got plenty of leftover cheese.'

I declined the offer, hurrying home as quickly as my sleep-addled limbs would carry me. I'd planned on going straight to the attic to brush my hair, wild with static thanks to sleeping on a blanket, and change out of the old jeans and T-shirt I'd worn to clean in, but only made it half-way up the stairs before Isaac appeared and asked if I could talk.

My heart sank as I reluctantly followed him into the kitchen. I could recall only too well the conditions upon which Isaac had offered me the weekend work, and I didn't want to get fired by my twin. However, to my surprise, Arthur was also there, sitting at the table, while Elliot leant against a worktop, Penny's nose resting on his bare foot.

'Okay... now I'm starting to worry. Have I done something awful without realising? If someone's food has gone missing, or the toilet roll was all used up, it wasn't me.'

'Stop worrying; you've not done anything wrong,' Isaac said, pulling out a chair for me to sit on.

'You're about to find it's precisely the opposite!' Arthur said, with a tentative chortle.

'Do you want tea?' Elliot asked, flicking the kettle on.

'Yes please. But if it's nothing bad then why do you all look so shifty?'

'Shifty?' Isaac repeated, sounding offended. 'I'd say keen to get started.'

'Started with what?'

'Maybe a little nervous?' Arthur asked, rubbing the wisp of hair on his chin.

'How about deeply uncomfortable?' Elliot suggested.

'*Started with what*?' I asked again, feeling increasingly uncomfortable myself.

Isaac slid a plate across the table. 'Tiffin?'

'I really wouldn't,' Elliot said as he placed my tea on the table. 'Finlay McAllister sneezed on that plate earlier.'

'Which sort of proves my point,' Isaac said, getting up and dumping the cakes in the bin.

'What point?' I asked, my voice about an octave higher than usual. 'Will someone tell me what this is about, *now*?'

Arthur and Elliot, who had sat down opposite me, both looked at Isaac.

'It's your idea,' Arthur said.

'One I have massive reservations about,' Elliot added.

'Okay... so we have a proposition,' Isaac said. 'Which solves several problems for all of us.'

'Go on. And speed it up, please,' I said, wishing I had a piece of that tiffin.

'Problem one: you wanted to earn some extra money by working for me, but I'm not going to take you on.'

'Isaac, no. Please. You know how much I need the money. I fell asleep today because it was a warm afternoon; I'd had a really big couple of weeks with moving house and starting at the Barn and—'

'Jessie, at one point a cockapoo licked the crumbs off your bare arm and you didn't wake up.'

'What? Ugh. That's... I think I dreamt something like that was happening...'

'Anyway, I'm not budging on this. We also agreed that Mum and Dad had to give the okay, and they aren't happy with it either.'

'Great. I guess I'll just have to find something else, then. Either that or secretly move into the Barn storeroom.'

'Well, that's not really going to be a secret now, is it?' Arthur said, with a sympathetic frown.

'Problem two,' Isaac continued. 'The three of us have become a bit...'

'Like a bunch of lame losers,' Arthur chipped in, again.

'Insular,' Isaac said, glaring at him. 'In...'

'Inbred,' Elliot finished for him.

'We could really do with an outsider's opinion...'

'An outsider who is cool, capable and, critically, female,' Arthur said. 'One who can get us back up to standard, as it were. Whip us into shape. Teach us where we're going wrong...'

'Get Elsa to change her mind and go grave hunting with Arthur, and Connie to give Isaac a chance,' Elliot clarified.

'What on earth are you talking about?' I was incredulous.

'Oh I don't know,' Isaac mumbled, hunching over his drink. 'Show us some skills. How to cook a nice meal. Help us decorate the games room. Find a social life outside of the Cup.'

'Stop calling it the games room, for a start.'

'Excellent tip, thanks Jessie!' Arthur said. 'Isaac and I would also like some help with conversational techniques, style and things to do on a first date. Oh, and Isaac would like to know how to stop acting like an arse in front of Connie.'

'And Arthur would like to know how to stop acting like a freak in front of everyone,' Isaac snarked back.

'You're talking to the wrong person. Have you tried watching *Queer Eye*?'

'I did tell them,' Elliot sighed.

'And where do you come into all this?' I asked, daring to flick my eyes in Elliot's direction because he seemed like the sanest person there.

'Elliot also needs help with cooking, conversational skills and broadening his interests,' Arthur said. 'He hasn't had a date in a very long time.'

'Because I haven't wanted a date!' Elliot said, his cheeks reddening. 'I don't want any help with anything to do with women. But, well, if you are up for this then I could do with some practical support if I oust Simonson from the Harriers and take over as manager.'

'Dude!' Isaac exclaimed, offering Elliot a high-five which he sheepishly accepted. 'About time!'

'This is all well and good,' I interrupted. 'But what does it have to do with my financial situation? You can't possibly be talking about paying me to be some sort of relationship coach.'

'How does a 50 per cent rent decrease sound?' Isaac said, quickly.

*Oh my goodness. They can't be serious?*

I took a long, slow look at my housemates and concluded that they were deadly serious.

I thought about it.

Took a few sips of tea. Noted that Elliot had added a blob of honey, how I used to drink it before.

Thought about it some more.

Weighed up my horrific financial situation against, what,

teaching them a couple of easy recipes, a shopping trip and redoing the living room so that I actually enjoyed living in it?

I steeled my shoulders, banged my mug on the table a bit too hard and made up my mind.

'Go on then. What's the worst that can happen?'

'Yes!' Arthur stood up and started doing some sort of celebration dance, with thrusting hips and arms pumping either side of his chest.

'Okay, so far that dance is the worst thing. And I'm not formally agreeing unless we establish some ground rules… the first of which is no twerking.'

\* \* \*

A couple of hours later, aided by various carbohydrate-laden leftovers from lunch, we'd scrubbed the past two years' Chimney Cup results off one half of the living room whiteboard and replaced it with a draft contract. This included firm boundaries about what I would, and more importantly would not, be required to do. I insisted upon a list of clear, specified tasks, and an end date of three months from now (by which point I would have almost paid off the energy bill and hopefully whittled away some of my debt, too). There was also an opt-out clause in case Seb arrived back before then, or the whole thing simply proved to be a disaster.

Arthur wanted to include a guarantee that he'd have a date by the end of it. I reminded him that since Elsa had free-will, that wouldn't be possible.

He also insisted on giving it a name. 'How about "Get the Guys a Girl"?'

'The Re-Entry Project?' Isaac suggested.

The others decided that wasn't quite right.

After another few of Arthur's suggestions, all involving him ending up with a girlfriend, I grabbed the marker pen and scrawled:

*The Boys to Men Project*

'What?' Isaac pulled a face. 'That's the worst yet.'

'Maybe so, but it's the most accurate. Not everyone involved is doing this to get themselves a girlfriend.' I nodded at Elliot.

'Elliot?' Isaac asked. 'What do you think?'

Elliot slumped back in his gaming chair, shaking his head in resignation. 'I think that seeing as no one – *no one* – is ever going to find out about this, it makes no difference what we call it. It's nearly eight. Can we sign this thing so Penny and I can go for our run?'

Decision made. The Boys to Men project was all systems go.

Task one: teach them how to cook a simple, three-course meal, this Friday, which they would then each individually replicate for a guest at a later date.

That was the official task one.

It was in reality task two.

Task one was to teach *myself* to cook, well, anything apart from poached eggs and toasties, and then fake that I knew what I was doing when I tried to teach them.

It wasn't modesty that meant I questioned whether I was the most suitable – or in any way suitable whatsoever – to carry out this project. Prior to meeting Seb, I'd spent my entire adult life fumbling along, too often leaving a trail of destruction in my wake. Since meeting him, he'd pretty much taken charge of the adulting, while I managed the fun. This was going to be one long lesson in faking competence, which thankfully I'd had plenty of practice at.

## 14

Monday morning meant heading back to the Barn. While I still had a huge amount to do, and a lot to learn before I could do it, I thoroughly enjoyed the day. Working in such a gorgeous place, spending time chatting to people, plenty of whom were fascinating, being part of what – with a few tweaks to the programme – would be an extraordinarily special community. What was not to love?

I was starting to appreciate why my parents were perpetually cheerful.

After a positive phone conversation with a man about some genealogy sessions, I decided to call it a day.

'Are you coming for dinner?' Mum asked, spotting me packing up my things.

'Not this evening, but thanks for asking.'

'But it's Monday,' Dad said, trying not to sound crestfallen.

'Did we arrange something? I must have forgotten.'

I hadn't forgotten. My social life was still pathetic enough that I'd not forget a momentous occasion like a meal at my parents'.

'Well, no.' Mum looked at Dad. 'We'd sort of assumed, after last time, that it would be a weekly thing. Mondays with Mum.'

'And Dad,' Dad added.

'But you didn't say anything to me. I'm really sorry, I can't come. If you wanted to, though, we could start Mondays with Mum next week.'

'And Dad.'

'Why can't you come?' Mum asked, eyes widening with hope. 'Have you made plans with someone else?'

'Nothing to get excited about, but yes.'

'Too late, I'm already excited!' Dad grinned.

'I'm having dinner with my housemates, that's all.'

'Dinner with your housemates? All four of you?' From Mum's reaction, you'd have thought I was eating with One Direction. 'See!' She turned to Dad, who gave her an enthusiastic fist-bump. 'I *knew* you moving in was what those boys needed! How wonderfully civilised. Is it going to be proper, homecooked food?'

'Isaac's sorting it as he's off today. So I very much hope not.'

To everyone's relief, the chef had gone to Waitrose in Newark, a half-hour drive away, and picked up a fresh pizza, salad and fancy bread that even he couldn't mess up. When we expressed our heartfelt appreciation at his going to all that trouble, he reminded us that it was a lot less trouble than if he'd tried to cook something himself.

We'd set the ground rules for dinner the night before. Everyone had to dress as though they were trying to make a good impression, and bring a topic of conversation that wasn't in any way related to the Chimney Cup.

Once Elliot was back from football training at six-thirty, we convened in the kitchen.

'First things first,' Arthur said, standing bolt upright behind his chair. 'Have we managed to make a good impression?'

'Okaaaay...' I did a quick once over of their outfits. 'Arthur, I appreciate that you've tried, but is that what you wear for funerals?'

He tugged on the black frockcoat. 'It's my most impressive outfit!'

'Yes, but perhaps a bit formal for dinner with a friend? Elsa will be hoping for a fun time, not to feel like she's at a wake.'

'Wakes can be fun.'

'Not very romantic, though, are they?'

He quickly slipped off the coat and pin-striped waistcoat underneath and undid the top button on his white shirt.

'Much better. Maybe next time try a nice pair of jeans.'

'I don't own any jeans.'

'Okay, we can sort that another time. Right. Isaac. Are you taking this seriously?'

'What?' He pulled his chin back, insulted. 'I went out and bought this today, especially. The sales assistant said it was fashionable.'

'Did they happen to be three years old?' I shook my head. 'I thought the whole point of this was that you're showing Connie you've grown up.'

My twenty-eight-year-old managing director brother was wearing a yellow and white striped towelling shirt over huge, baggy shorts in the same fabric.

'There's no need to be offensive.'

'I could say the same about that outfit.'

Aware of my heart starting to tap a little faster, I turned to Elliot, doing my utmost to appear easy-breezy about having to focus my attention on him.

'Not bad.' He wore a pale blue shirt and navy chinos. 'Although, weren't you wearing that shirt yesterday? And most of last week?'

I didn't want to sound as though I'd been taking note of what he wore, but he was paying me for this, so I had to at least try to do a proper job.

'No.' He glanced down. 'That was a different shirt.'

'But the same colour?'

'Yes.'

'And style?'

'Yes.' He looked back up at me. 'I have five matching blue shirts and three pairs of trousers. Five white T-shirts and two pairs of identical jeans. Five sets of running shorts and tops. Oh, and a Harriers kit.'

'Seven pairs of identical boxer shorts,' Arthur added, helpfully.

'Well, they all look very... nice. You can stay at home when the rest of us go shopping.'

'If it's all right with you, I'd like to come. Like I said before, it's time I expanded my world a little and I'd appreciate your opinion. I think we have the same sort of taste and you always look lovely. I really like that shirt you're wearing so, well... time to shut up now, Elliot.'

Oh boy, I did not know how to handle a compliment from Elliot Ollerton. The last time he'd called me lovely, he'd kissed me so passionately I'd forgotten how to breathe. The only thing I could think of to do was bend over and pet Penny, who was wearing a cute blue bow that matched Elliot's shirt.

'You look beautiful, Penny,' I said, wondering how long I could get away with crouching under the table.

'So, who won?' Arthur asked, bending down to find me.

'Won what?'

'The most impressive outfit.'

'Arthur! This is not a round in the Cup. No scores, no points, no first place. The plan is that you'll all emerge winners when you end up more confident and happier with yourselves.'

'Okay. But if there was a first place, who would it be? Definitely not Isaac, right?'

'It would be Penny. Now, time to eat. And talk about your topics.'

The others insisted I led by example.

'Okay. So...um...' I tried to buy myself a bit more time by adjusting the collar on my mint-green, satin blouse. 'Seb was telling me last night he's been offered a job working behind the bar on a river cruise. Have any of you been on a cruise?'

No, no one had, of course, all being twenty-eight-year-old men who barely left their village.

'Right. So, if you could go on a cruise anywhere, where would it be?'

Isaac pulled his eyebrows down as he thought about that, chewing an enormous bite of pizza. I made a discreet gesture to indicate he'd got a string of cheese dangling off his chin, but he refused to take the hint.

'What?' His eyebrows dropped even further as he tapped his chin with one finger. 'What does that mean?'

'It means you have cheese on your face,' Elliot said, prompting Isaac to swipe it off and into his mouth.

'Cheers, sis.'

'Right! Useful tip.' Arthur practised discreetly tapping his finger on his chin, nodding to himself.

'No! Not "cheers". This is supposed to be a civilised meal. Food dangling off your face is gross.'

'I didn't know it was there!'

'Well, if you can't manage to get 100 per cent of the food in your mouth then use a napkin.'

'Alaska,' Elliot said, causing us all to look at him in confusion.

'That's where I'd go on a cruise.'

'Okay, great!' I leant back in my chair. 'An interesting choice. Why there?'

'It seems peaceful. Simple. I think my brain would find it a pleasant change.'

'Nice.' Isaac nodded.

'Day one, leave Southampton,' Arthur said, pointing his pizza slice at me. 'Next stop, Gothenburg, Sweden. Disembark and explore the botanical gardens. The following day, onto Bornholm, Denmark. Time to visit the fourteenth-century fortress Hammershus before taking in a few rock carvings. Possibly a wander into Ronne for some smoked herring. Day four. Or is it five? Hang on...' He started counting off on his fingers.

'Wait!' I barked, perhaps a little too harshly, but I really couldn't bear to go back to day one. 'That's a very detailed itinerary, Arthur. Perhaps keep it a little shorter, so you don't end up monopolising the conversation.'

'Boring your date senseless,' Isaac said.

'I was answering your question.' Arthur's face crumpled with confusion.

'I know. Thank you. But if you asked Elsa that question, would you want to hear all that information, or a shorter answer that you could talk about together?'

Arthur chewed slowly on a piece of bread, his brain processing that revelation.

'Isaac?' I asked. 'Your answer please before we move on to someone else's topic.'

'If I could go on a cruise anywhere, I'd not go.'

'What? Why?'

'Because I'm not an old married couple? I spend enough time surrounded by elderly people and loved up couples as it is. I don't especially want to holiday with them.'

'Not all cruises are like that. The one Seb's working on is for young singles.'

Isaac looked at me. 'Your boyfriend – the one who left you to go and find himself on the other side of the world – is working on a boat with a load of young, single people? Serving them alcohol? And you're okay with that?'

'Yes, that's what I said.' I bristled. 'What's your point?'

'You're the relationship expert here. You figure it out.'

'Or perhaps we'd be better off moving onto your topic?' I retorted, his implication smarting like a slap on my cheek.

'Fine.' Isaac gave me a look that in twin-language told me he'd meant it as a loving warning, and to think about what he'd said. Then thankfully he changed the subject to what became a twenty-minute discussion about the progress he'd made in the garden that day (another task on the Boys to Men project) and possible plans for some serious landscaping.

We then paused to dish out bowls of ice-cream, moving on to Arthur's topic before it got too late.

'So, for my topic I wanted to tell you about Barnabas Brown.'

'Go on,' I said, suspicion twitching like a cat's tail.

'Right, well, Barnabas, or Barney to his good friends, of which he had many, was the Mayor of Sherwood from 1713 to—'

'No,' we all said in unison.

'What?' Arthur asked. 'Are you suggesting I'm incorrect?'

'No, we're suggesting that your next grave hunt is not a valid topic of conversation.'

'Why?' Arthur protested. 'It isn't in the rules. We said no Cup talk.'

'The nature of the task also means no boring talk.' Isaac grimaced.

'Are you saying you find my grave hunts boring?'

'No, but the fact that you've asked Elsa four times if she wants to come and she's politely declined all four times implies she does.'

'The point of the task is a conversation, Arthur,' I interrupted, trying to sound as kind as possible because his face was drooping with dismay. 'Not a lecture. There's not much room for an exchange of information when you're talking about your specialist subject. Can you think of something else? A general question like I asked is great.'

'Can I ask whose grave you'd most like to find and why?'

'No. We've already agreed to avoid the topic of death, at least on the first couple of dates.'

Arthur thought for a painfully long time until he suddenly pulled the ice-cream spoon out of his mouth with a flourish. 'What's your favourite ice-cream?'

'Great!' I sagged back with relief. 'Cookies and cream. What's yours?'

'Raspberry. With real raspberries though, none of that syrupy stuff.'

Arthur then went on to tell us a hilarious story about how his maternal grandparents had grown raspberries on their dairy farm, selling ice-cream from the farmyard all summer, until one day an especially greedy Arthur had ended up tumbling into one of their barrels, up to his neck in cream.

'I smelled of sour milk for days afterwards. The goats wouldn't stop following me about.'

We all sat there, slightly stunned by the sudden upturn in repartee, which prompted Arthur to ask an even better question.

'Anyway, enough about me! What are your best memories of childhood ice creams?'

Before I noticed, it was ten to eight.

'Elliot – I'm so sorry, we've not got onto your topic yet and you need to go on your run.'

'That's okay.' His shoulders stiffened. 'I could always set off a bit later.' He looked more than ready to bolt, now, at the mere thought of it.

'*What*?' Isaac said, stunned.

'We know how important your routine is. Let's reconvene with coffee afterwards,' I suggested, feeling stressed on his behalf.

'Or we've got nine minutes. I can talk fast and get done in time for eight.'

'You'd better go for it, then.'

'Right. I had an interesting training session this evening.'

'Um, I thought we weren't allowed to talk about our specialist subject?' Arthur said. 'Elliot only works part time so the Harriers is basically his job.'

*Elliot works part time*? I felt a jolt of surprise, swiftly followed by embarrassment at being surprised. Why wouldn't he have a job? Just because I'd not been polite or friendly enough to ask him what he did all day.

'Yes, but like I said, this is interesting.'

'Go on, we'll stop you if it turns out not to be,' I said.

'Simonson was yelling at Turner.' He looked at me to clarify. 'Turner's got mild cerebral palsy, and some of the training drills are a real challenge for him. So, anyway, I decided it was time to yell back.'

'Nice one,' Isaac said.

'Only, you know how when I get angry, I can lose control of what I'm saying?'

'We certainly do.' Isaac leant forwards, eager to hear what happened.

'Apparently I called him a disgusting bully who picked on kids to make his own pathetic ego feel better.'

There was a stunned silence around the table.

'So, yeah, well. I'm now the manager and head coach of Houghton Harriers under nines.'

'Awesome!' Arthur cheered.

'What's not so awesome is that Simonson is filing a formal complaint about me, and I can't defend myself because I can't remember most of what I said. He could make up a load of crap, or he could tell the truth and still get me banned from the club.'

'What about the kids?' I asked. 'Did they overhear?'

'Given that I was bellowing my head off, I'd assume so.'

'There you go, then. Wilf will have remembered every word.'

'Like I said, that might be worse.'

'At least you've got an excuse,' Isaac said, shrugging. 'Sounds like Simonson was the one shouting first, and at a child. Most of the people on the club committee can't wait for him to slither back to Brooksby. I really wouldn't worry about it, mate.'

Elliot swallowed hard, his face flushing. 'I will never not worry about losing control of my temper in front of a team of boys who consider me their role model. If anything, them liking me only makes it worse.' He paused, shaking his head. 'I'm really not sure I should do this. It's not only the Saturday matches; Simonson entered them into a tournament, the Sherwood Forest Cup. As far as the boys are concerned, it might as well be the world cup.'

'Do you want to try?' I asked, my heart clenched behind my ribs.

He gave a small, slow nod. 'I do.'

'Then I'll be there to watch your back, next time. If you start screaming and waving your hands about I'll give you a quick poke in the ribs.'

'Thank you.'

I tried not to flush at the thought of touching Elliot's torso.

'Thank *you*. I really need that rent discount.'

Not to mention that helping Elliot to succeed at doing something he cared about, being able to feel good about playing such a positive role in the community, doing such a great thing for these kids? That was priceless.

## 15

The following morning, I prised Wendy out of her kitchen for a chat in the café. The clear blue skies had been replaced with a grey, chilly murk, just in case we'd forgotten that British weather had a mind of its own. So, with only the hardiest Outlaws braving a blanket over their knees on the terrace, the room had a pleasant buzz of people enjoying their tea and cake inside. She plonked a tray bearing two mugs of coffee and three tiny cake squares on our table.

'See what you make of these,' she said, her bright blue eyes like lasers beneath a grey fringe, the only section of her hair that wasn't a buzz cut.

'They all look delicious,' I said, trying not to sound as nervous as I felt. Wendy, like a lot of people who are brilliant at what they do, projected a formidable air of brisk confidence.

'They are. Which one is the best?'

I took three timid nibbles of what turned out to be chewy, gooey, chocolatey flapjacks, washing down each bite with the coffee so it looked as though I was taking the task seriously.

'The coconut one is my favourite, but I love anything coconutty.

This one – hazelnut? – isn't quite sweet enough for my taste. But that's just me, of course!'

'No, you're right. Eli said the same.' She picked up the hazelnut and the other, minty, square and tossed them in the bin a few metres away.

'Um, they were still lovely. I would have finished them.'

'Why settle for less than excellence?' She gave me a piercing stare as if genuinely expecting me to reply to that question.

'Why indeed?' I had several answers to that, all from personal experience. Lack of talent, too busy, too lazy, too poor... but ended up producing an awkward laugh that sounded more like a faulty drain.

'Anyway.' I tried to sound like the competent, capable activities coordinator I planned to be, opening my notebook, now full of random musings, and clicking my pen a few times. 'As you know, I've been brought in to overhaul the weekly programme.'

'I didn't know that. As long as it doesn't affect my kitchen, I don't give a crap what happens out here.'

'Right. Well, what I wanted to talk to you about might involve the kitchen.'

Wendy tipped up her chin, eyes narrowing. I took a quick swallow of coffee and ploughed on.

'You may not be aware that Glenda, who happens to be sat in that corner, used to run a cake business. Seamus, who isn't here today, managed a waffle and doughnut kiosk. Rhianna was a school cook for thirty-seven years. So, in talking to some of the others, and bearing in mind that particularly for those with dementia, using their existing skills can be really positive, I was wondering whether we can hold some sort of Great Barnish Bake-Off.'

Wendy's eyes were now tiny slits.

'It would only be a trial. To start with. To see if it works.'

'Why are you telling me this?'

I took a deep breath and reminded myself that this was simply a friendly chat with a colleague. I wasn't on *Dragon's Den*, and Wendy – whatever she might think – didn't own exclusive rights to the kitchen. 'We would need to use the kitchen.'

I think she may have actually sucked in a tiny hiss.

'If I give you enough notice, I thought you could plan something simple for lunch that day, so it won't take long to clear up, and we could then do the baking in the afternoon. Say, one-thirty until three-thirty, with a half-hour for tasting the results before everyone leaves.'

'That's what you thought?'

'Unless you can come up with a better suggestion for how we do it? The morning would work too.'

'My suggestion is that non-professionals aren't set loose to run wild in my kitchen.'

I would have challenged her use of the term 'run wild', but these were the Outlaws, so I couldn't rule it out.

'I was hoping you'd be our judge.'

'Meaning I'd sample whatever they came up with? Is that supposed to change my mind?'

'Wendy.'

'Chef Wendy.'

'Chef Wendy, one day you're going to retire.'

'I wouldn't be so sure.'

'One day, when your hands start to tremble and your sense of smell and taste wanes, when standing for eight hours straight is agony on your back, and you don't have the arm strength to chop an entire crate of carrots, you will have to call it a day. When that day comes, imagine if you're living by yourself—'

'I live by myself now.'

'Exactly. So most days you've no one to cook for. You could spend time creating exquisite meals at home, but no one else will taste them. Your appetite is so small you can't finish most of what you cook, and you definitely can't afford to waste it. So, instead you keep it simple, leaving the feasts of your past to your imagination. Until, one day, someone offers you the chance to step back into a professional kitchen and show what you can do. Just once, so if it leaves you exhausted and aching for a week, it doesn't matter. You spend hours planning, dreaming, coming up with the perfect show-stopper. Knowing that for one day you won't be that old woman who can't do up the buttons on her cardigan; you'll be an incredible chef again.' I paused for effect. 'Only the new chef says they don't trust you in their kitchen, despite being appropriately supervised, so instead you heat up another tin of soup.'

Wendy sat back in her chair, face blank. I tried not to blurt out my last resort, that I'd get the owners to agree to it whether she liked it or not. That would have not only destroyed my credibility but been akin to declaring a full-on kitchen war.

'Just the once?'

'To start with. If it goes well, I'd like to discuss the possibility of making it a regular event. Every other month or so.'

She gave the briefest, tiniest of nods, but it was enough to give me the courage to ask something else.

'I was also wondering if I could ask your advice about something?'

She took a careful sip of her drink, but didn't say no, so I took that as a sign to continue.

'I need recipes for a three-course meal, something impressive but fairly easy to cook.'

'How can something easy to cook be impressive?'

'Okay, something that *seems* impressive. To a non-professional.'

'How many people?'

'Two.'

She raised one thin eyebrow. 'A date?'

I nodded. 'Not me. I genuinely am asking for a friend.'

'I'd stick with a mezze platter to start with. If you get quality ingredients then all *your friend* needs to do is arrange them on a board.'

She fired off a few suggestions for a main course and dessert, and even offered to send me a couple of recipes. It was all going great until I asked if I could have a practice run in the kitchen.

'I thought this was for a friend?'

'It is. I'm going to teach them how to cook it.'

'Are you a professional cook, Jessie?'

'I've worked in plenty of kitchens.'

'As a chef?'

'Not quite.'

'Washing up?'

I nodded.

Without saying another word, she got up and left.

'I'll take that as a no, then?' I muttered after her.

A couple of hours later, three recipes with minutely detailed instructions pinged through to my phone from an unrecognised number.

# 16

I was still trying to figure out when and where I'd be able to have an urgently needed recipe practice when on Wednesday afternoon, Isaac mentioned that he'd be working late, due to a last-minute meeting with the nightmare Bridgerton-to-Boho couple. I made a casual query in the recently formed Boys to Men WhatsApp group, and Arthur informed me that he was helping Elsa out at the church youth group until nine, and Elliot had football training until seven.

Perfect.

I was out the Barn door at five sharp, making a swift detour to Houghton's tiny supermarket before hurrying home to get cracking. I had ninety minutes to turn two carrier bags of ingredients into culinary magic, clear up any mess and then eat all the evidence.

* * *

I got the fright of my life when a velvety nose bumped into the back of my knee, what felt like an age later.

Whirling around with the electric whisk still in my hand, everything within a two-metre radius ended up splattered with cream, including me and Penny.

'Go and stall him!' I whispered frantically once the whisk was off. The dog licked a blob off her nose and opted to stay where there was more cream. I gave her a gentle nudge. 'Go on! Ten minutes should do it.'

'Ten minutes should do what?' Elliot asked, striding into the kitchen and then coming to an abrupt stop in the middle of the room. His eyes swept over me, the worktops and table before coming to rest on his dog, trying to reach another splash behind her ear. His mouth opened and closed a few times as he took in the carnage.

'Yeah, so it turns out learning to cook is harder than I thought.'

He used a piece of kitchen roll to wipe Penny's head, placed it in the bin and then peered at the baking tray I'd left on top of the hob. 'Apparently so.'

He looked at me then, eyes dancing, mouth twitching at both corners. 'I can't believe you had the nerve to criticise that lunch we made for you.'

'That was sausages and eggs! This is...' I gave up. I'd lost control of what the hell this was a long time ago.

'This is a disaster of spectacular proportions.' He gave in to the enormous grin. 'What happened?'

'You weren't supposed to be back until after seven,' I said, slumping against the worktop.

'It's seven twenty-five.'

'What? This has taken two hours? I'm only on step three of dessert. The chicken is still marinating and I haven't even thought about the salad yet!' I shook my head, aghast. 'How on earth does Wendy do this for eighty people? She said it would be easy!'

'I don't know who Wendy is, but I think she was wrong.'

A solitary tear squeezed out and dribbled down my cheek. I swiped it away, but Elliot had already spotted it.

'Here.' He handed me some kitchen roll. 'I'm sorry for laughing. It's one way of coping with seeing my kitchen in... moderate disarray.'

I nodded, wiping my face and giving my nose an unflattering blow. Elliot held out a couple more sheets.

'No, I'm fine, thank you. I'm just tired and stressed out and feeling like a failure. There are plenty of reasons why a grown woman can't cook properly. All this reminds me that my reasons are because my life has been mostly a complete shambles. Because I *allowed* it to become a shambles. No. That's not true, either. Because I actively made it that way... Oh, for goodness' sake, I'm not going to start crying and I'm definitely not feeling sorry for myself. So, no, I will not be needing any more kitchen roll!'

'Um...' Elliot blinked a few times, still holding it out. 'You've got some cream...'

Contrary to my last statement, I burst into tears. Elliot stepped closer and tentatively started patting at my hair and the smears on my collar and shoulder. As my volume increased, he gave up, wrapping his arms around me and pulling me up against his chest. This manoeuvre only made me howl even harder. How pathetic could I be? Standing here, in the kitchen of the man whose life I helped derail, blubbering with self-pity?

'What we need is a plan,' he said, as I fought to get a grip on myself. 'Breaking it down into straightforward, sequential steps makes everything easier to tackle.'

'I think that's called a recipe.' I sniffed, stepping back, my head ducked to hide my mortification at the whole situation.

'Okay. But we need a recipe that goes beyond the food. Step one, wash up the used pots so we have clean equipment. Um... step two, tidy up the remaining mess and wipe down the countertops so we have a clean, clear space to work.'

'You honestly don't have to help. It's my mess. I'll clean it up and get out of your way.'

'Then what about Friday? How are you going to teach your clients to cook a meal if you've not figured it out yourself?' Elliot leaned up against the fridge, folding his arms. It was such a familiar pose my heart did a tiny stutter.

'I could hand them the recipes, sit at the table with a gin and tonic and bark instructions, swearing and shouting insults if they get it wrong?'

'Or, we could figure it out together, now.'

'If you help then do I forfeit the rent discount?'

Elliot shook his head, his expression a mix of frustration and amusement. 'If we succeed today, will I be able to prepare a three-course meal that I couldn't make before?'

'I suppose so.'

'Then you'll have successfully completed task one.'

'You really don't mind helping me?'

'I would significantly prefer that to walking away and leaving my kitchen like this.'

'Okay.' I offered a hesitant smile. The more time I spent with Elliot, the more naturally we slipped back into the friendship we'd once had. Beneath the shadow of my horrible secret, Elliot and I had once been one of each other's favourite people. It felt increasingly impossible to maintain the distance required for self-preservation.

But that was a problem for another day. Right now I had a kitchen to rescue and a three-course meal to master and for that I needed all the help I could get.

'Can I suggest a slight amendment to step one?'

'Of course.' He gave a serious nod.

'Maybe the pots aren't the only thing needing a wash?'

Elliot looked down at his football kit, eyes widening with horror. 'I gave you a hug while covered in sweat. You probably want a shower too now.'

'It's fine. The hug was worth it.'

'I didn't overstep? I usually stay far enough back to avoid any possibility of crossing any lines. But, I don't know, with you...'

'If you'd have overstepped, believe me I'd have told you. I'll get started on the washing up.'

'Right. You wash, I'll dry?'

I grabbed a sticky note from the pad on the counter and wrote:

1. *SHOWER IMMEDIATELY*
2. *Help Jessie*

I then stuck it on his forehead.

He shook his head, ripping it off and reading it before starting to leave. 'I love you being here, Jessie, but you are totally messing with my head.'

I knew exactly how he felt.

'How come someone who loves food as much as you doesn't know how to cook?' Elliot asked me, half an hour later, as he watched me lower two chicken breasts into a hot pan.

I shrugged. I'd learnt to cook a few basics before I left home. Pasta or curry from a jar, but all that felt like a lifetime ago. 'To cook properly requires stability. I never stayed in one place long enough to acquire things like whisks and casserole dishes. The places I stayed rarely had a working oven. When I worked in pubs I usually ate there. Either that or takeaways and processed crap that I could stick in the microwave. You sort of get used to it.'

'No Sunday omelette?'

Another staple of ours had been mixing all the Sunday roast dinner leftovers into an omelette.

'Not for ten whole years. I mean, things have been different since living with Seb, of course. But he loves cooking, so I leave it to him.'

'Seb?' Elliot asked.

'My boyfriend,' I replied, aware that both of us might need reminding. 'He's gone travelling.'

'Right!' He gave a firm nod. 'Your boyfriend. Of course. I knew that.'

We moved onto the next step in the recipe, chopping the salad. 'How about you? You love food, too. And you've got this amazing kitchen. Why didn't you learn to cook?'

Elliot was quiet for so long that I thought he must have forgotten the question. Then, when he'd carefully sliced up the last beef tomato, he glanced up with a sheepish look. 'I can cook seven meals. Monday, pasta carbonara. Tuesday, Spanish rice. Wednesday, tacos... well, you get the picture.'

'So today should be tacos?'

He nodded. 'I eat a main meal at lunchtime when no one's here. It's easier for me to think, and I don't have your brother trying to guilt-trip me into sharing my food.'

'He would totally do that.'

'It's also easier to run if I haven't just eaten a big meal.'

'Crap, Elliot. Your run!' I checked the clock. Eight-fifteen. 'You're late! Do you want to go now? I can finish the rest off myself.'

Elliot glanced at the recipes. The rest included piping out profiterole pastry and making a salad dressing.

'It's fine. I've been training. I can miss one run.'

Seeing the hunch in his shoulders and neck, I wasn't so sure.

'Elliot, please go on your run. I feel bad enough about you giving up your evening helping me.'

He furrowed his brow. 'Giving up a solo game of *Call of Duty* was hardly a major sacrifice. And I can't run now, I'd feel off setting out late.'

'Okay, but what about Penny?'

Hearing her name, she emerged from under the table, tipping her head to one side as if asking, 'What about my walk, huh?'

Elliot ran a hand through his hair a couple of times.

'Once we're finished here, we could take her for a walk?' He looked at me, a glint of hope in his eyes that made it impossible to do the sensible thing and politely decline. 'It's probably good for her to start learning that a change in routine is nothing to freak out about, too.'

'I'm sorry for disrupting your routine and freaking you out.'

'I'm not freaked out, though.' Elliot shook his head as if baffled at the realisation. 'Or, not much, anyway. Although, I can't see any basil in your ingredients pile.'

'Yes, well, for some reason, the Houghton one-stop shop didn't find room to stock fresh herbs.'

'I guess we'll have to improvise,' Elliot said, trying not to grimace.

'Story of my life.'

\* \* \*

A methodical, step-by-step, slightly improvised hour later we were sitting at the table eating pesto chicken with rainbow salad and sauteed potatoes, a forlorn mound of white chocolate and raspberry profiteroles chilling in the fridge.

'Not bad,' Elliot pronounced. 'But you know what would make it perfect?'

'Mango mayo from Charlie's Chips!' I grinned.

'Precisely.' He got up, opened a cupboard door and handed me a bottle.

'What sweet heaven is this?'

'They started selling bottles a few years ago. It's the main reason I moved back to Houghton.'

As I squirted a giant dollop on the side of my plate, Penny got up and scampered out of the room. Knowing that this meant someone was about to come in the house, I automatically froze.

'What do we do?'

Elliot ate another potato. 'About what?'

'About Isaac or Arthur—'

A hello to Penny from the hallway signalled that it was my brother.

'—discovering that I've been practicing the meal,' I gabbled, panicking. 'He'll know I'm bluffing.'

'Hey.' Elliot nodded to Isaac as he walked in.

Isaac collapsed into the chair next to mine, snatching a potato off my plate.

'That's boy not man behaviour!' I scalded, slapping his hand a second too late.

'Ooh, it's good, though. Any leftovers for a man who's just spent three hours explaining why we can't switch wedding themes for the second time with three days' notice?'

I pointed to where a few charred potatoes sat in a bowl on the side.

Isaac turned his nose up, opting to steal another one of mine.

'Ew!' He grimaced, as soon as he'd stuffed it in whole. 'That's mango mayo! You could have warned me. You two are the only people on the planet who can stomach that evil. Even Charlie Chips loathes it. Sales will double now you're back in the village.'

He got up and opened the fridge. 'What's this? Profiteroles? Did you make this, sis?'

'Um...'

Isaac turned to look at his best friend and sister, sat eating a meal together, a bottle of wine open on the table.

'I was concerned that all three of us learning to cook together on Friday would be too much of an overload for me, so Jessie offered to do a one-on-one session this evening, while the house was quiet.'

'A one-on-one?' Isaac asked, still holding the fridge door open.

'Yes.' Elliot shrugged. 'I didn't do too badly, either. You can try the salad if you want, see what you think.'

'So who are you cooking for when you do it solo?' Isaac asked, with overexaggerated nonchalance. Sheesh. Everyone in this room knew each other far too well to pretend we didn't know where Isaac's imagination had skidded off to.

'Your mum?' Elliot said, picking up his empty plate and dumping it in the sink.

With a nod to his dog, they were out the door and off across the field.

'It was a genuine question,' Isaac said, helping himself to a profiterole. 'This process is as good a time as any for Elliot to start making some friends. Plenty of single mums whose kids play for the Harriers would be ecstatic to have him cook them dinner.'

'What, you mean like Connie?' I said, dumping my plate on top of Elliot's and marching out the other door.

'What's that supposed to mean?' Isaac called, hurrying after me into the hallway. 'Connie and Elliot?'

'Nothing,' I said, already half-way up the stairs.

'Then why would you even say it?'

'I don't know, Isaac. Why would you imply there was something going on with Elliot and *me*?'

'I didn't mean to. I've just always thought there was maybe something...'

*What?*

My heart was hammering so hard it could have cracked a rib.

'Isaac, we share a house. I have a long-term boyfriend, who's planning on proposing to me once he's back. Please don't start being an arse about me and Elliot.'

'I know. Bad day. Bad joke. I'll apologise to Elliot later.'

'You do that.'

'Him and Connie, though?'

'Bad joke,' I yelled back, stomping up the rest of the stairs.

* * *

Elliot returned nearly an hour later, when I'd got over my sibling strop, come back down and almost finished clearing up.

He looked at me, brow wrinkling as his brain tried to locate the relevant information. I resisted the urge to remind him who I was.

'I asked you to come on a walk.'

'It's fine.'

'And then I stormed out, leaving you to tidy the kitchen.'

'I said it's fine. You helped me with the first lot of mess, that I'd made all by myself.'

'I'm sorry. I can't remember why I lost my temper. But it's no excuse.'

He started putting away the few remaining items still on the draining board, face creased with misery.

'Elliot, I said it's fine! Isaac was being extremely irritating. I was equally annoyed, and also stomped off.'

'I hate not being able to remember what he said. What *I* said.'

'Hey, you remembered asking if I wanted to go on a walk; that's something.' I flicked the kettle on, more than ready for some tea.

'I remembered as I walked back into the garden and saw you at the kitchen window.' He took two mugs out of the cupboard and handed them to me.

I spent a flustered minute while the kettle boiled trying to decide how much to tell him. 'Isaac asked who you were going to cook for next week.'

'That seems a reasonable question.' The doubt was clear in Elliot's tone.

'He also implied you and I were having some sort of date.'

'Oh.' He went still for a couple of seconds.

'Don't worry. I reminded him that it was out of order. Especially given I'm with Seb.'

'Seb?'

'My boyfriend.'

'Right!' He shook his head, vigorously, picking up his tea. 'Yeah. Anyway. I've got some stuff to do, so... thanks for the cookery lesson. And for clearing up.'

'Thanks for helping me, and preventing me from fluffing this project manager role before I've even started.'

'Any time.' He offered a tight smile and left the room.

I took my drink upstairs and called Seb.

## 17

On Friday, I had the luxury of a day off. I would have slept until late, but my eyes snapped open at eight with the realisation that I'd promised Elliot I'd have eggs a la jam sandwich with him. I threw on my joggers and a top and found him seconds away from dishing up.

'Morning.' He smiled, offering me a steaming mug of coffee.

'You have far more faith in my ability to be on time than I do.'

'You seem to have conquered your punctuality demons at some point in the past decade.'

I took an invigorating sip of my drink. 'Honestly, it's only started since I came back here. I think it might be because for the first time I really want to get where I'm supposed to be.'

'You're enjoying the job, then?'

I accepted a plate of eggs and sat down, taking a naan bread from the pile already waiting on the table. 'So much. It feels like my years of pick and mix experience are finally slotting together. A job has generally been a means to survive, but I honestly can't think of anywhere I'd rather be most days than with those Outlaws.'

We chatted a bit more, and I finally got around to asking Elliot about his job. He worked from home, a couple of hours a day, as a marketing and admin assistant for a charity that trained up assistance dogs.

'I'm slow and steady, but I'm also free, so they let me get on with it.'

'You work for free?'

He nodded. 'I got enough compensation from the accident to buy this house, and my parents made some good investments with the rest. I'm pretty set.'

'You don't need to work?'

'I don't need to earn any money, but I need to work.'

'Why this charity?'

He bent down and gave Penny a pat. 'They found Penny for me.'

'She's an assistance dog? I hadn't even noticed.'

He shrugged. 'She's more emotional support than practical help these days.'

I tried to keep my voice from cracking alongside my heart. 'I'm so sorry you need emotional support. It's rubbish.'

Elliot looked up in surprise. 'We all need emotional support, Jessie. What's rubbish is having to manage without a dog like Penny. It's everyone else I feel sorry for.'

We spent another half-hour talking about his new role at the football club. Elliot was far better than me at organising things into lists and timetables, writing every stray thought down so that he wouldn't forget it, but I could see that having someone to help him figure out how and when it would all piece together kept him from feeling overwhelmed. He set up various alerts and reminders on his phone – how he'd have managed before smart phones was anyone's guess – and made a checklist for different days of the week.

'Thank you,' he said, once his brain started to tire and we decided to stop. 'I'd never have been able to do this without your help.'

We sorted a few remaining printouts into carefully labelled sections in his new 'Harriers' folder and I stood up to leave. I had a recipe to teach later on and after the teething problems on Wednesday I needed to restock the ingredients.

'Oh, you know I'll do anything for a good breakfast. I'm pleased you felt you could ask me.'

When Elliot looked me in the eyes I could almost pretend the past ten years had never happened. 'While I wouldn't want everyone watching me fumble through a few basic tasks, I've never felt like I had to be anyone but myself with you.'

\* \* \*

The cooking lesson went about as well as I'd expected. Isaac was tired and distracted after a day pandering to more last-minute wedding demands, although to be fair he listened and did his best to get on with it in between fielding yet more messages from the troublesome couple.

Arthur turned up in a white coat.

'I've been doing some research,' he explained. 'The way to become a successful chef is to think of food as a science.'

'I prefer to think of it as an art,' Isaac said, sprinkling pine nuts into a bowl with a flourish.

'Did the research say you needed to wear a lab coat?' I asked, handing him the ingredient list for the starter mezze plate.

'Getting in the zone, Jessica. You know me, I'm not a man who does things by halves.'

'Did you buy it especially?'

'No.' He smiled absently, studying the printed sheet. 'I borrowed it from work.'

'Ew.'

'Don't worry, it's clean.'

Hygiene wasn't what worried me. I tried not to be creeped out by whatever that lab coat might have previously been covered in. I really hoped that working in a church, helping people with all manner of grim challenges, meant Elsa was a lot less squeamish than me.

Once the hard work was over and we were enjoying the results, we discussed who they would do their solo cook for. As the person 'hired' to oversee the project, I strongly suggested they didn't ask the people they really wanted to impress until the project was complete. Isaac was the first to rebel against that idea.

'So, what, I invite another woman to dinner, as part of my plan to prove to Connie that I'm done dating random women? I don't think so.'

'Agreed.' Arthur nodded firmly. I'd insisted he removed the lab coat to eat, but he still had something of the mad scientist look about him. 'I'm not interested in having dinner with anyone but Elsa.'

'You're having dinner with us,' I reminded him. 'It doesn't have to be a date. Elliot ate with me.'

I pointedly ignored Isaac's surreptitious snort.

'What about one of your sisters? Part of the project is improving your social skills before attempting to go out with Elsa. Besides,' I added, helping myself to a couple more slices of potato. 'At this early stage, she could well turn you down again.'

'She hasn't turned me down!' Arthur pulled his chin back, affronted. 'She was busy.'

'All four times?' Isaac asked, gently.

'She's a very busy woman with a full life! That's one of the things I love about her.'

'Arthur, I really think that—'

'Permission to break the no phone at dinner rule for one

message?' he blurted, face turning blotchy. 'It's directly relevant to the task.'

'Is this message asking Elsa to have dinner with you?' Isaac sighed.

'It is!'

'Go on, then,' I agreed. The sooner he asked, the sooner we could move on to other possibilities.

While Arthur started a cycle of typing, deleting and then typing again, all the while muttering under his breath, I turned the conversation back to Isaac.

'How about asking Mum and Dad? All the meals they've cooked you over the years; have you ever reciprocated?'

'This is supposed to be a practice date, Jessie.' Isaac frowned at me, starting to gather the empty plates up. 'I'm not going to learn much spending the evening with Mum. "Ooh, darling, this chicken is raw in the middle, but an evening together is totally worth twenty-four hours of violent sickness and diarrhoea!"'

Arthur's phone chimed, and as soon as he grabbed it, he jumped to his feet, pumping the air with his fist.

'Yessss! A week today, baby!'

Elliot walked in at that point, dressed in his running gear.

'Something to celebrate?' he asked, fetching a glass of water.

'Me and Elsa, next Friday night. Clear the kitchen, people, because we're having pesto chicken and profiteroles!'

'She said yes?' Elliot grinned in surprise as he opened the door to let Penny out. 'Way to go!'

Arthur gave me a smug smirk as Elliot left. 'Oh, ye of little faith. I told you she was busy the other times!'

'Or,' I postulated, carrying the serving bowls over to the dishwasher, 'the other times you were asking her to snoop about in a random graveyard, rather than for dinner.'

'Or,' Isaac said, watching his housemate carefully, before suddenly snatching his phone off him and reading the screen, 'you told her it was a meeting to discuss visiting the Barn for a drop-in session about funeral planning! Dude, you've basically told her Jessie will be there.'

'I'm sure Jessica will be here. Somewhere. It's not like she has anywhere else to be.'

'Rude!' I retorted. 'And that's not really the point, Arthur. You can't lure Elsa here under the pretext of a work meeting then spring a date on her.'

'It isn't a date,' Arthur said, defensively. 'We do need to talk about visiting the Barn. Wood's lead a session twice a year and this time I volunteered. When I spoke to the vicar, Lara, she said it would be a good opportunity for the Outlaws to meet Elsa.'

'You need to tell her it'll only be the two of you. It's creepy to spring that on someone,' Isaac said. 'Trust me, I've been there. It wasn't great.'

'Fine! Permission to use my phone again!'

This time Arthur dictated the message while I fetched dessert. 'To clarify, Jessica may not be able to make it. Are you still happy to proceed if just the two of us?'

'Yes again!' he cried, a second later, jumping up and spinning around before coming to a stop with both fingers pointed at us like pretend guns. 'It's only a matter of time, ladies and gentlemen, before Elsa Larsson falls head over heels in love with me.'

'Great, if that's how we're playing this.' Isaac pulled out his own phone, typing as he spoke. 'Perhaps Connie would like a meeting to discuss lessons learnt from our current wedding fiasco and how we can prevent it happening again. Due to the amount of extra time we've been having to spend at the Barn, I suggest meeting here. We can eat while we talk. My treat.'

We'd finished the profiteroles, the last of a bottle of wine and were on to coffee when Connie replied, right on cue, as the kitchen door opened and a panting Penny and Elliot came in.

'*Yes!*' Isaac jeered. 'Clear the kitchen, people, because Tuesday night Connie's coming around for a mezze plate, pesto chicken, rainbow salad and po-ta-toes! Boom! Second date, baby!'

'Connie, and Wilf,' Elliot added, glancing at the phone over Isaac's shoulder as he grabbed the towel to wipe Penny's paws.

'A work meeting, with her eight-year-old in tow. It's definitely not a date.' I scrunched up my nose in sympathy.

'So, if I remember correctly. For once. Arthur's having Elsa for dinner, and now Isaac is cooking for Connie.' Elliot raised his eyebrows. 'Both your dream women, and you haven't even finished the first task. Huh.'

'One could suggest that this demonstrates we don't need you after all,' Arthur said, turning to me.

'Alternatively, one could *suggest* that after being turned down four times in a row, Jessie gets on board and within a week, Elsa's agreed to dinner. I'd suggest this demonstrates precisely how much you need her.' Elliot moved on to the final part of his post-run kitchen routine: gulping down a pint of water.

'Trust me, if this is going to be anything more than one dinner, you need me,' I agreed.

I don't know where my sudden spurt of confidence had come from, but it might have had something to do with Elliot winking at me as he walked past. 'Great job, coach.'

## 18

---

Now that he had a 'work' dinner set up, Arthur was itching to move on to another task: convert the games room into a proper living room. 'The kind of nice space where a sophisticated woman like Elsa would enjoy stimulating conversation with excellent company.'

Once again, this was a topic in which I had next to no expertise or knowledge. Prior to living with Seb, my interior design experience had consisted of things like scraping black mould off windowsills, re-sticking on tatty flaps of wallpaper with Pritt Stick and covering a manky sofa with a slightly less manky blanket. For a long time, the concept of a 'nice space' had meant my own room – or at least my own mattress – and a shower that spurted a few seconds of warm water. The coffee shop flat had been clean and functional, with white walls and flat-pack furniture. In the three years I'd lived there I'd bought a couple of cushions and a matching duvet cover, and considered that pretty close to paradise.

I suggested Arthur made a start on clearing out the junk and tidying up the items they wanted to keep while I went to watch my first football match in forever.

The Harriers were playing at home against the Ferrington Foxes. I walked over to the recreation ground with Elliot a full hour before kick-off, ensuring plenty of time to get everything ready, handle issues, give the kids a good warm-up and hopefully cool down any parents who weren't happy about the change in manager.

We'd barely set up the smaller, seven-a-side pitch when the first few people arrived.

'I thought you might be here,' one dad grunted, his son standing meekly beside him.

'I've not missed a match all season, so it was a pretty safe bet,' Elliot replied, opening up a net bag full of balls. 'How's it going?' he asked the boy, kicking a ball towards him. 'Do you want to start some practice shots while we wait for the rest?'

'Where's Simonson?' the dad continued, placing a restraining hand on his son's shoulder so the ball simply rolled across the grass.

'As I said in the email, once everyone's here I'll fill you in. In the meantime, I've got a team to manage.'

'The whole thing's a joke,' the man sneered as Elliot turned to welcome a pair of boys. 'This isn't fit to be called a team any more. More like a circus act. And you're the biggest clown in the show.'

Elliot handed the newcomers a ball and pointed them off to one side. He then slowly straightened up and turned towards the dad, every muscle tense, his eyes like lasers. I wondered if I might need to intervene with the promised rib-poke sooner than I'd thought.

'Excuse me?'

'Are you deaf as well as an idiot?'

'Hi, I'm Jessie. What's your name?' I grabbed another ball and held it out towards the man's son, who took the opportunity while his dad was staring down Elliot to duck out of his grasp.

'Olly.'

'Do you want to join the others?'

He nodded vigorously before taking the ball and hurrying off. I ticked Olly's name off the team register and took a subtle couple of steps closer to Elliot, whose neck and cheeks were now a worrying crimson.

'Please don't disrespect the team or the manager in front of the players, Russell,' he ground out through gritted teeth.

'Hey, no disrespect intended.' Russell held up two hands as if in surrender, but his tone dripped with contempt. 'I'm a man who calls it like it is, that's all.'

'Who calls children clowns.'

'I called you a clown. A month in and you're down to four decent players. Another match like last week's and they'll be signing up to Brooksby faster than you can flash a yellow card. By the time we get to the Sherwood Forest Cup we'll be lucky to have half a team left.'

'If they've got the same attitude as their parents then Brooksby are welcome to them.' Elliot shook his head in disgust, but at least his temper still sizzled beneath the surface, for now.

'You want Olly, Jackson, Ibrahim and Wilf to go?' Russell laughed outright at that. 'What is this, reverse discrimination; only specials allowed?'

I grabbed Elliot's arm as it swung back, preparing to launch. 'Stop. Take a breath.' I took a warning glance at the handful of adults now hovering nearby. 'He's trying to provoke you into doing something they can kick you out for.'

Where I might have been unable to make a difference, Penny stepped up and started nudging his stomach. Elliot dropped his head, shoulders heaving with the effort of slowing his breathing.

'Look.' A man with a huge grey beard placed a hand on Russell's shoulder. 'While Russell here expresses himself with the subtlety of a complete twazzock, and I for one have no objections to Ibrahim being in an inclusive team, as long as he's having fun and learning more about the game, Russell does raise a valid point.'

Elliot sucked in another huge lungful of air and looked up. 'Which is?'

'Look mate, we know you love these kids. You're their hero. Never mind an inspirational athlete. Would've put this village on the map, if things'd been different. You can teach this team a thing or two about sport. But honestly, son, how can you coach them from the touchline, when you can't even remember their names?'

Elliot's expression landed somewhere in the grass beneath his boots.

'All I'm saying is, the old setup was perfect. Simonson in charge, you as his right-hand man. Even Cloughie needed Taylor when he took Forest to the European Cup. No one can do this on their own. But you especially. No offence.'

'He's not on his own.' I stopped and looked around as if wondering who'd blurted that out, because surely it couldn't have been me.

'Eh?' a woman asked. 'Who are you?'

'Jessica Brown,' I replied, because it had indeed been me, thanks to my ferocious need to defend Elliot. I held out my hand like a politician on the doorstep, which after a confused couple of seconds the woman accepted with a limp shake. 'Assistant Manager.'

Elliot looked as shocked as everyone else, which was still far less shocked than I felt.

'Do you know much about football?' Russell asked, eyes squinting.

'Yeah, I bet she doesn't even know the offside rule!' someone else chipped in.

'Which wouldn't matter, given that there is no offside rule for under nines,' I replied sweetly, my thumping heart grateful for the hour I'd spent flicking through the youth football regulations that morning. 'Are you seriously assuming I don't know because I'm *female*?'

'She's Pippa and Tom's daughter.' An older version of Connie appeared from behind the mini crowd of onlookers, Wilf alongside her.

'And?' Russell spat. 'How does that give her automatic right to coach our kids?'

'Are you kidding?' the beardy man asked. 'Did you hear how she took control of those Outlaws on her first day? If she can handle that lot, she can coach anyone. Good luck to you my dear. Not that you'll need it.'

'Are you DBS checked?' an anxious looking woman asked me.

'Of course.'

'Fabian has complex needs. He's epileptic, has severe dyspraxia and a learning disability.'

'I'm trained in, amongst many other things, epilepsy, advanced first aid, ASD, learning disability awareness and trips and falls. Oh, and continence. Although I think the only risk of incontinence here is Russell's bigoted blabbering.'

'Okay. Wonderful. I'm off for a coffee then. Good luck! Break a leg, boys!' She gave a cheerful wave before practically running back to her car.

Elliot called the team over and read out a short statement, covering the basic facts about Simon Simonson and reassuring everyone that he would do his very best to ensure every player found the Harriers under nines a fantastic team to be a part of. He also assured them that they'd still be taking part in the Sherwood Forest Cup. Once the boys had stopped cheering and jumping about, he sent them running around the field and asked the adults if they had any questions.

'A nice little speech,' Russell jeered. 'Shame it didn't mention anything about winning. Ending up bottom of the league is hardly "fantastic".'

'Why are you keeping Olly here if you're so unhappy with how the team's run?' Connie's mum asked. 'I heard Bigley Bounders are short on strikers. Why not let your feet do the talking?'

'Yeah, well.' Russell shifted his shoulders. 'Olly wants to play with his friends. He'll soon learn that it stops being fun when you get slaughtered every single match.'

'Same for Jackson.' Someone else nodded. 'So we're stuck here. For now.'

'What a delightful attitude.' Connie's mum tutted.

Elliot's eyes were on fire again. 'Because, by some miracle, you've ended up with amazing kids, they are more than welcome in this team. However.' His voice dropped so low that every adult leaned forwards to catch his next words. 'If I hear you spewing any more filth about them, me, or anybody else here then I will guarantee you a ban from any Houghton Harriers match, training or end of season booze-up. All ages, every team.'

'Doesn't your Karlie play in goal for the youth team, Russell?' someone called out. 'Better keep your gob shut if you want to see them lift the cup this year.'

Without waiting for a reply, Elliot turned and joined the boys, running in a straggly line down the final side of the pitch.

While Elliot oversaw the rest of the warm-up, the Ferrington Foxes arrived in a shiny minibus, their supporters piling out of cars with camping chairs, flasks, snacks and in one case a portable barbeque until the referee insisted they put it back in the car.

At five minutes past two, thanks to a last-minute toilet request, the referee blew the starting whistle.

A few seconds later, Wilf reminded the player standing by the ball that it was up to him to kick it, and they were off.

The next three quarters of an hour were, shall we say, eventful.

A flurry of trips, skids, flailing arms and balls sent rolling in the wrong direction. At one point Fabian even picked it up and ran. There'd have been a lot more of a protest from the Foxes if he hadn't run straight into his own goal.

Elliot kept at least two of the stronger players on the pitch for each of the twenty-minute halves, but overall, every child got equal playing time, much to certain parents' frustration. Russell had been right (about this if nothing else): there were four boys who were clearly stronger, more agile and accurate with the ball than the others. What infuriated some of the spectators, and delighted the rest, was how these boys consistently passed to those who struggled. They called out encouragement, even after giving away yet another goal, and waited patiently for their slower, less able teammates to catch up or stop and gather their bearings before having a go at a kick. Olly spent the majority of the time he was on the pitch helping the partially sighted player, Jan, despite the constant haranguing from his dad.

Goal after goal rolled, blazed and bounced into the Harriers' net. The keeper, Dyson, who wore leg braces, didn't stand a chance at saving most of them. Partly because he was more often than not facing the wrong way, pulling faces at his baby sister.

I would have lost track of the final score, if it weren't for Russell announcing every goal with a sour twist to his mouth. In the final seconds, Ibrahim hit a lucky shot from the half-way line and made it thirteen-one.

The boys exploded in delight, mobbing Ibrahim as if the scores had been reversed. Elliot was equally as euphoric, staging a pitch invasion the moment the final whistle blew, congratulating every player as they jumped and spun and punched the air with glee.

On the other hand, the official winners of the game strolled off with a few pats on the back and a couple of high-fives.

Elliot called the team over for a post-match analysis which

consisted of him whooping for a good half a minute, the players all joining in. He then got serious.

'Boys, we scored our first goal!'

Another round of whoops.

'And our mighty goalkeeper saved three. Two more than last time! A 200 per cent improvement!'

More cheers, high-fives and general jostling.

'Everyone else – could Ibrahim have scored without you?'

'Yes,' came a sarcastic retort from somewhere behind us.

'*No!*' shouted the boys, grinning at their own awesomeness.

'I'm so proud of you!' Elliot went on. 'Your team work was the best yet. Your encouragement blew my mind. Your shooting, passing, dodging, sprinting was miles better than last time.'

Whew. I couldn't imagine what last time must have been like.

'Here's what I loved the most.'

The boys quietened down and stopped shuffling about, waiting to hear.

'Every one of you smiled the whole forty minutes. You all had a far better time than Ferrington. I couldn't be prouder.'

'What about player of the match?' Wilf asked, waving his hand hopefully.

Elliot shook his head. 'As difficult to decide as ever. How about we ask our new assistant manager what she thinks?'

I tried not to choke on my water. 'What?'

'Player of the match, Jessie?'

'Um... I don't think...'

Elliot twisted around so the boys couldn't see his face and pulled a panicked face.

Ah. Okay. He couldn't remember who was who.

'I'm giving it to Olly,' I said after a few seconds' deliberation.

'Well, look at that. One of you has some sense.' Russell nodded.

'The way he helped Jan, always checking to make sure he was in the right position, and knew what was going on, was inspirational. I've watched a lot of sport, and while I won't promise to be a football expert quite yet, I can promise you this: the teams who win in the end are those who play together. And I've never seen a team play so unselfishly, so brilliantly united as you did today. I'm so excited to be part of the team. You guys are special.'

Thankfully, at that point I was surrounded by eleven cheering, bouncing, muddy boys, which prevented me from giving the person who'd just snorted a foul comment about 'being special' either a punch in the face or an uncensored piece of my mind. Either of which would have ended my assistant manager career the day it began.

## 19

Once the team had helped pack the equipment back in the clubhouse, they trooped to the pub garden down the road for the traditional home-game chip butties. Elliot mumbled an excuse about an appointment and left them to it. Sensing that he needed a friend, and thinking that against all odds that friend might be me, I joined him on the short walk back to Chimney Cottage.

'You don't really have an appointment, do you?' I asked, after a stretch of silence.

He shook his head, eyes fixed firmly on the lane ahead. I took the hint and kept quiet for the rest of the way. As soon as the front door closed behind us, Elliot's whole body slumped. He sank onto the bottom stair, shrugging off his trainers with arms that appeared full of wet sand while Penny rested her chin on his knee.

'Tea? Or something stronger?'

He shook his head, eyes creasing with tension. 'I only drink alcohol on special occasions.'

My mind zipped back to our meal on Wednesday. We'd shared a bottle of wine.

'Your first goal as manager? How special can you get?'

There was a loaded silence while Russell's ignorant comments hovered in the space between us.

'I wouldn't have hit him,' Elliot said.

'Really? Some might say he deserves a good thump. Not in front of the kids, though, and not right before a match.' I held out a hand, which to my surprise Elliot accepted, and I disguised the jolt of electricity skittering up my arm by making a big show of hauling him to his feet, dropping his grip the second he was up. 'Maybe we should lure him into the alley by the pub one night and teach him a lesson. I think Connie's mum might be up for joining us.'

We drifted into the kitchen, where I set about making tea. 'There's two ways this could go, and either way both you and the Harriers win. One, he'll move Olly to another club.'

'Meaning Olly doesn't get to play with Jan or his other friends any more.'

'Which isn't the end of the world. Two, he'll stay, and you'll prove Russell wrong.'

Elliot picked up his drink.

'Three, he stays, and I prove him right. The boys grow increasingly demoralised, decide they don't actually love being a bunch of humiliated losers with a clown for a manager, I get fired and they all give up on sport forever, adding to their poor self-worth and feelings of inadequacy.'

'Are you sure you don't want that beer?'

'Trust me, it wouldn't be a good idea.' Elliot collapsed into a chair.

I came and sat opposite him. 'Can you remember their faces? The shouts of glee? Those boys don't care about winning matches. They care about being part of a team. Not the odd one out or the pity player, stuck on the side-lines. What you're doing here is incredible. Most of the parents want to name their next child after you. Don't you dare let Russell and his ignorant cronies get in the way of changing kids' lives for the better.'

'I don't think I can do it.' His face crumpled. 'I can't bear to let them down.'

'You *did* do it. I just watched you. That's all you have to do. Well, apart from the other admin stuff, but we've got folders and phone alerts for that.'

'Every second of that game I was putting on a front. If at any point I came across as in control, or remotely calm, it was a lie. Inside I was in full-on panic mode.'

'Including when Ibrahim hit the back of the net? Because if you were acting then, you're in the wrong career.'

He shook his head, mouth twitching. 'Maybe not then. But as I ran onto the pitch, I opened my mouth to congratulate him and *I couldn't remember his name.* I had to make up some random victory spin so I could see the name on the back of his shirt. And that was his surname. I sounded like some snotty boarding school P.E. teacher. "Super-duper goal, Bashir!" Every time I called out an instruction, I had to direct it at someone with their back to me.'

'So get them new tops. Put their first name on the front.'

'What?' Elliot sat back.

'This is an inclusive team. Start making it inclusive. Get Jan's in braille if that helps. He also said he finds it a lot easier to see the away kit, as it contrasts better with the grass.'

'What else?' Elliot had picked up his pad of sticky notes and started writing.

'I understand why you put Dyson in goal, but he's too easily distracted.'

Elliot furrowed his brow, cogs whirring.

'Dyson has leg braces. Spiky hair.'

'Right, yes. Simonson put him in goal because he's slow.'

'He might be slow outfield, but at least he'll be facing the right direction, and the other boys will be there to help him.'

'It's worth a try. What else?'

'Why isn't Wilf up front? He's a natural striker.'

Elliot sighed. 'He doesn't want to score a goal without Connie watching. If I even suggest it, he starts getting anxious. Last time he pretended he'd injured his toe until I said he could stay as a defender.'

We carried on until Arthur appeared, covered in dust, cobwebs and something sticky on the sleeve of his white coat that I preferred not to identify. I didn't have many tactical insights, being new to the team, but I'd done enough to help convince Elliot that it wasn't time to resign quite yet.

'How did you enjoy your first Harriers match, Jessica?' Arthur asked, helping himself to stewed, cold tea.

'Not quite my first. I watched Isaac more times than I can remember.'

'Of course! So, was it good to be back on the bleachers, as it were?'

'Back on the bleachers?' Elliot smiled. 'She appointed herself assistant manager before we'd had time to warm up.'

'You're not serious?' Arthur's eyes boggled.

'Deadly.' Elliot's face suddenly fell. 'At least. I think I am. I think she has... or did I imagine it? Was it actually a joke?' He darted his eyes to me and then away again. 'I can't believe my defective brain thought you'd offered to be assistant manager.'

'I was going to say!' Arthur chortled. 'You'd be better off asking Isaac. Except that he works on Saturdays... His dad, though. Me!' He laughed so hard it ended in a snort. 'And I haven't kicked a ball since Mr Jenkins banned me from the pitch for all-round incompetence and sent me inside to scrub the changing rooms instead. I hate football even more than cleaning school showers!'

'You didn't imagine it, and it wasn't a joke,' I said, keeping my voice calm to avoid Elliot feeling foolish. 'You wanted my help with this as part of the Boys to Men project. It seemed sensible to make it official. And, with all due respect Arthur, you know nothing about my football experience. For all you know, I've been coaching for years.'

They both looked at me, faces expectant.

'Okay, so I haven't. But I don't hate football and I do know the rules. I've also got pretty good at adapting to new situations.'

I didn't add that I knew more about football than I did cooking, interior design or most of the other project tasks. The longer I could bluff my way through that, the better.

After an excruciatingly rambling apology from Arthur, I went to inspect his progress in the redecorating. Judging by the state of him, I expected a fresh canvas ready for the revamp. What I found was a pile in the middle of the games room that could have fitted inside a waste paper basket.

'What's this?'

Arthur rolled his shoulders. 'Once I started looking, there wasn't much that wasn't worth keeping.'

'Arthur, there's a broken broom handle propped in that corner.'

'We use it for limbo competitions!'

'And you've had how many of those?'

'In the first lockdown... around two.'

I raised one eyebrow.

'Okay, so it was one, but it was really enjoyable and we said we must do it again sometime. It could be a fun activity to do with our dates.'

'No. It wouldn't. And we aren't keeping a broken handle in here just in case. If there's a limbo emergency you can use the actual broom. Right, what else?'

By the time we'd finished, the pile had become a mound. On

the one hand, removing a decent amount of junk improved things (Arthur insisted they needed the labyrinth of wires, even though most of them didn't go anywhere). On the other, it now revealed quite how dingy and dreary the room was beneath the clutter.

'So, what next? Can I see the design?' Arthur asked. 'If we get paint now, we can add the first coat this evening.'

'It's already seven, and we've not eaten yet. It's been a full day; let's wait until tomorrow. Or next weekend, so we aren't leaving things half done all week?'

Or, when I'd actually had time to start thinking about the currently non-existent design and what colour paint to buy?

He jerked his head back. 'Jessica, Elsa is coming this Friday. I know you can't have forgotten. The room needs to be perfect by then.'

'That's not going to happen. I did say not to invite her until we've completed the project.' I started shifting some of the rubbish into a cardboard box.

'Yes, but I ignored you and now she's coming on Friday. *DIY SOS* renovates a whole house in that time.'

'*DIY SOS* has a team of paid experts working around the clock, plus dozens of volunteers.'

'Maybe we could get some volunteers then? This is an SOS situation, after all.'

'I'm not sure anyone else would see it like that.'

'Jessica, this is my future wife we're talking about! My unborn children. The legacy of Wood's funeral directors. An entire family lineage!'

'If we make a start tomorrow then there's still time to get the room to a reasonable standard. If Elsa's worth marrying then she won't allow a half-decorated room to make or break her decision.'

Arthur didn't look convinced.

'If this project is going to work, then you have to trust that I know what I'm doing.'

He sighed. 'You're right. I'm just all in a tizzy because every time I've had dinner with a woman before, she's either outright refused to see me again, moved to Wyoming or been wrongfully incarcerated. And this time it really matters because I happen to be in love with her. But you're right. I trust you implicitly. I know it's going to be brilliant. Sorry for being such a pain.'

I took another look at the scuffed walls, the ugly chairs and not much else, and felt a twinge of panic. While Arthur took the full cardboard boxes to a local recycling centre, I grabbed a cheese sandwich and escaped upstairs to spend the rest of the evening trawling through interior design websites. All that achieved was to bombard my brain with increasingly expensive possibilities, where they jostled for space amongst my growing agitation.

Eventually, I forced myself to stop scrolling, closed my notebook of half-baked ideas and surrendered to another night of staring at my ceiling, wondering what on earth I was doing here, and how I'd had the audacity to ask someone to trust me, when I still couldn't trust myself.

\* \* \*

On Sunday, I did my best to shake off the previous night's pity party and hurried through the rain to the Barn. I was relieved to see that only a few picnickers had braved the weather with umbrellas and waterproof coats. The majority were in the main hall, gathered around the tables and chairs from the previous day's wedding. It was slightly incongruous to see people in their jumpers and jeans sitting in chairs draped with peach covers and gossamer bows decorated with baby's breath. A mass of delicate foliage and fairy lights adorned the three solid walls and ceiling, creating the impression that we were in some sort of fairy glen.

'This is incredible,' I told Connie, slipping into the empty chair beside her, my plate laden with buffet treats. 'Even more so given the last-minute change of plans. I hope the happy couple appreciated it.'

Connie rolled her eyes. 'The lights didn't quite match the apricot napkins, three of the tree-stump centrepieces were too knobbly and I had the audacity to say no to a genuine indoor meadow, but they paid the ever-inflating bill, and Isaac and I have already agreed our migraine bonus. I'm very grateful that next week we've got an eighteenth birthday party, though. That'll be a breeze in comparison.'

'Given your chilled-out week, I was wondering if you could help me with something?'

'Yes!' Connie almost yelped in enthusiasm. 'This will be the perfect way to cement our friendship. What do you need? Advice about a man, in which case I propose face-packs, ice-cream and a pedi-session while we examine the issue from all angles? Ooh – a makeover? Not that you need it, of course!'

'Shall I fill you in, or do you want to keep guessing?' I attempted a laugh, but it quivered with underlying anxiety. 'Wilf, do you want a guess?'

'Um... maybe you've split the back of your trousers and you need Mum to sew them up?'

'Oh!' I pretended to check. 'I don't *think* that's happened. But please let me know if I'm wrong.'

'It happened to Masie in my class and everyone laughed. Not everyone. I didn't. Miss Cooper did, though. I saw her try to hide it with a fake cough. Mum had come in to talk about how I wasn't doing very well and she didn't laugh either; she sewed it up because she's really good at things like that.'

'That's not it, this time. But I do need help with something your mum is really good at.'

Wilf scrunched up his face in concentration. 'Do you want grass growing inside your house?'

'Nope, but getting closer.'

'You want me to help fix the cottage?' Connie asked, eyes lighting up. 'I've been itching to get my hands on that interior disaster ever since your brother invited me for dinner.'

'My brother invited you for dinner?' I already knew this, but it would be interesting to hear her perspective. Purely for project purposes, of course. Nothing to do with general nosiness.

'Oh, ages ago. Just a new colleagues getting to know each other thing.' She flapped her hand as if it was nothing, but I detected a hint of rosy cheek in the not-quite-apricot-enough light. 'Anyway, is that it? You want to harness my creative décor skills to turn the bachelor-sty into a house fit for Jessie Brown?'

'Just the living room, for now.'

'I didn't know they had a living room.'

'Well, the room that they mainly live in. They call it the games room.'

'Ah, yes. Isaac invited me to take a peep in there. I initially mistook it to be a long-forgotten storeroom for an underfunded youth club.'

'That's the one.' We both smiled and rolled our eyes.

'Okay, cool. What did you have in mind?'

I took a deep breath. 'Okay, so it has to fit with the cottage – not too modern. There's still some nice original features hiding beneath the lack of effort. At the same time, it's a primarily male home, so the décor needs to reflect their personal styles, while working with what they use the space for. Just maybe allowing some room for it to be used for other things, too. Also, Elliot needs an environment that's not too busy or cluttered.'

Connie's eyes narrowed in thought. 'What do they use it for apart from their competitions?'

I glanced around while I thought about the question, catching a glimpse of Isaac, sitting with Elliot on one side and Arthur on the other, the three of them guffawing at something or other. It was enough to remind me that this whole thing was supposed to be helping Connie realise Isaac was worth giving a go. Not a man with no life or interests outside of work or mini games with his only two mates.

'Isaac's been getting into gardening recently, and cooking. But neither of those involve the living room, of course.'

'Really?' Connie's eyes were round with surprise.

'Yeah. I should probably say that it was their idea, to decorate. They've all been so busy with their careers that they feel embarrassed at neglecting the cottage. They invited me to come up with some ideas because they want me to feel at home there, too.'

'Right.' Connie took a forkful of feta salad. 'Did Isaac ask you to talk to me?'

'No! Definitely not. Please don't mention it to him. The truth is, Elliot's knocked a bit off my rent in exchange for me redecorating, so I feel like I owe them a really good job, and I didn't want to admit that the only home I've ever decorated was my Barbie Dreamhouse.'

'Don't panic. Either way I'd love to help,' she reassured me. 'It's just that Isaac's been a bit... off with me lately and I wondered if he felt like he couldn't ask me himself.'

'Ah.' I looked down at my plate.

'I'm sorry, you're his sister, I'm not going to drag you into it or ask you to break his confidence. I just thought he and I were friends, you know? I've been trying to ignore it but I'm starting to worry that I've either done something specific to annoy him, or he simply finds me really irritating.'

Oh boy.

'But I'm probably being paranoid. We've had a stressful few weeks. Better to take it out on me than the clients, right?'

I glanced up and Connie's expectant face, then shovelled in a tiny tomato tart, quick. The temptation to blab at least some of the truth was almost too much to bear. I chewed slowly, swallowed, took a drink of water and wrestled those tempting truths back down again.

'He's mentioned that it feels like the past two years are catching up with him,' I said, carefully. 'When he's overtired, or anxious, it can come across as gruff. And you're right, I'd take it as a compliment that he feels comfortable enough to let some of that out with you. Not that it makes it any easier to be on the receiving end, though. Especially when you've both been under the same strain. I'm sorry you've had to put up with it. Although, from what I've seen, you handle him really well.'

Connie nodded, considering my words. 'Thank you. It really helps to know that. I've taken two holidays in the past year while Isaac's only had the odd day off here and there. It's no wonder he's finding it tough. We've got a work meeting at yours on Wednesday. I'll perhaps mention something then.'

'Not that I said anything?'

She leant forwards and rested her hand on mine. 'Woah, I'm not about to break the girl code one week in, Jessie. Besides.' She smiled. 'Not great to reveal to my boss—'

'Colleague of equal status.'

'—To the MD of the company I work for that I've been gossiping about him with his twin.'

She turned to answer Wilf who was asking if he could move to sit with his friends, before whirling back around again.

'I got side-tracked about Isaac and forgot we were talking about decorating. How about I come over a bit earlier on Wednesday and bring some sketches, so you can see what you think? We might have some stuff in the Barn storage that you could use, save a bit of money.'

'That would be amazing, if you're sure? But isn't Wilf coming too? Won't he be bored?'

Connie rolled her eyes. 'If Isaac's there then Wilf will be more than happy. That's why I agreed to an out-of-hours meeting, because I knew Wilf would be over the moon about not only getting to visit his hero's house in person, but eat a meal that he's apparently going to cook – or at least reheat, if the last time is anything to go by.'

I had to smile. 'It is a very strange concept, my brother being idolised by a small child.'

'Tell me about it. And if Elliot's there, even better. I'm highly invested in seeing that house redecorated if for no other reason than my son has decided to make those men his role models.'

We both looked over to where Wilf was now gazing up at Isaac, my housemates apparently being the friends he'd been talking about.

'He could have picked worse, to be fair.' I couldn't resist another chance to big-up my brother. I was starting to really like Connie, and felt a twinkle of hope that against the odds, maybe this bizarre project could work. 'Isaac's successfully building a great company, loves his family. Has been an amazing friend – to Elliot, especially.' I stopped, swallowed, and then decided I couldn't help going for it. 'He also stopped dating around quite a while ago. He's not interested unless there's the potential for a serious relationship.'

Connie's eyes remained fixed on his table. Thankfully, before she could ask anything and I could end up meddling any further, Jackson's mum came over to welcome me onto the Harriers' coaching team.

## 20

I managed to fob Arthur off with a promise that great interior design couldn't be cobbled together overnight, while reassuring him that Elsa would feel more comfortable staying in the kitchen on their first non-date dinner, anyway.

'It'll be worth the wait though?' he asked, looking as antsy as I felt. He'd appeared the second I'd arrived back from helping clear up lunch, fully expecting to find a paint brush already in my hand. Now that my renovation plans had been postponed, I was planning on grabbing a drink and spending the rest of the day holed up in my bedroom preparing for my first formal work meeting. 'And we'll definitely have it done by the next time she comes over?'

'I'd think so. Although, that might not be for a while...'

'On the contrary.' Arthur tugged on a wild tuft of hair. 'I'll be inviting her for a second date immediately. Why hang about when I know she's the one?'

'Um... because she might need some time to draw the same conclusion?'

'Well she's not going to realise it by *not* spending time with me.'

'Okay. Maybe just see how this dinner goes, first?'

'Jessica, I know that compared to me you have a wealth of dating experience, but when it comes to me and Elsa, I'm not sure you understand the power of our connection. What you're saying makes no sense in this situation.'

When I'd agreed to this ridiculous project, I'd accepted that it was going to be a case of fumbling my way through a list of fairly standard tasks that hopefully would help my housemates pick up some useful life skills, and maybe even get past a first date. At no point had I seriously considered that I could end up playing an instrumental part in seeing someone's heart get smashed to smithereens. And the truth was, this felt like so much more than my friend's love life at stake. I realised, with a jolt, as I struggled to find a way to help Arthur see past his lovelorn longing to imagine how Elsa might feel, that the Boys to Men project had become tied up in my redemption.

If I could help three men to see their dreams become a reality, then it would be one small, good thing to counterweight all the bad I'd contributed to so many years earlier.

'Would it make sense to try going somewhere else? Somewhere Elsa enjoys? That way, you can demonstrate that you care about what makes her happy.'

Arthur's eyes nearly popped out of their sockets. 'You are a genius! I take it all back!' he said in wonderment. 'I know she likes God. And churches. She loves running the youth group, but that's probably not a great idea for a date. We would barely hear ourselves think, let alone have a proper conversation. No. It'll have to be a church. Only... hang on, this is perfect! I'm increasingly convinced that Lancelot Limpkin was buried in Southwell Minster. If we locate his grave and then tour the cathedral we can combine both our loves and careers in one date!' He shook his head, eyes shining. 'Honestly, Jessica, only a *fool* would doubt that we are anything less than made for each other!'

\* \* \*

On Monday, I had my first formal progress meeting with my joint bosses.

'Doughnut?' Dad asked. 'I got your favourite, chocolate custard. Fresh this morning.'

'Do they sell these in the new café?' I asked. When I'd lived in Houghton, the nearest place stocking anything more exotic than jam doughnuts was the bakery in Middlebeck, a good few miles away. We would venture there on special occasions for a treat, like the last day of term or our birthday.

'Nope.'

'He was knocking on the Middlebeck bakery door at five to eight,' Mum said, helping herself to an apple and cinnamon doughnut.

I didn't ask what the occasion was, because I suspected it was nothing more than me being here, and as well as making me feel valued, that also triggered the years of guilt I felt for staying away.

'Right, no pressure!' Dad said, opening up his laptop. 'We thought it would be useful to have a quick update on how things are going, and whether a new programme is starting to emerge from all your robust research.'

'I've spoken to over half the Outlaws. They've got a lot of ideas, and some strident opinions about the kind of activities they'd like. I've tried to be clear that this is information gathering, no promises, and we have to factor in overall popularity, alongside practicalities like cost, space and of course health and safety. I think the quote that best sums up their response is, "My health rolled over and died years ago, so I don't give a green banana about safety." I explained that our insurance company do, as do their loved ones and the Barn staff. Some ideas are easy to discard, some need more research, others should be good to go by the end of the month.'

'Excellent!' Mum nodded. 'Have you got a list of the workable options?'

'Hang on,' Dad interjected. 'I'd like to quickly run through the ones you've dismissed as unworkable, first, if you don't mind. The Barn is a place where we like to believe even the most unlikely dreams are possible. If we let things like cost and lack of space hold us back, the Barn would still be a musing in your mother's imagination.'

'Tom, we can trust Jessie to know whether an idea is viable or not,' Mum said, a tiny crease at the top of her nose the only indication that she wasn't pleased.

'I'd like to hear what people are asking for, all the same. You never know!'

'Okay.' I put my half-eaten doughnut down and opened up a spreadsheet. 'A few Outlaws would like us to have pole dancing sessions. Is that a dream you'd like to make possible, Dad?'

'Oh, no,' Mum groaned, the nose crease deepening in distaste. 'Did they mean hiring women to do the dancing, or watching some of our women having a go?'

'I'm not sure which of those is less grim,' Dad said. 'Either way, it's revolting to think men want to demean women in that way on our premises. You'd better give me some names so I can have a word with them about the Barn values of respect.'

'The keenest two were Marjorie Spellman and Hana Shu. They reckon they'd be pretty good at it. Hana has a negligee that she thinks would be perfect.'

Dad looked at Mum.

'I can talk to them, but it won't make any difference,' she muttered.

I scanned my list. 'Other discarded suggestions include setting up a bungee jump, paintballing, elephant rides, strip poker, strip bingo and strippers.'

'The ones that you definitely want to include?' Dad asked, with a resigned shake of his head as he took another doughnut.

'I've spoken to Wendy about the Great Barnish Bake-Off. I think she's followed up with you?'

Dad pointed to a typed list crammed with bullet points. 'Her thoughts on the matter. Don't worry, we've told her it's happening and you're in charge.'

'Great!' I tried to hide my shudder of trepidation. 'Also, a lot of the Outlaws are requesting activities with animals. The group who travel over from the sheltered housing aren't allowed pets, and some of them are heartbroken about having to give up their cats or dogs. I've had a quick chat with the charity Elliot works for, and they'd be happy to provide a petting session with some of their training dogs for a reasonable donation. Animal therapy can work wonders for emotional and mental health, so it seems worth giving a try. On a slightly more ambitious note, some of the Outlaws are used to much larger animals. I'd really love to see if we can get any of them on a horse. Or at the very least, to give one a groom.'

'Bring horses, here?' Mum asked. 'And let people ride them? I wouldn't be surprised if someone jumped the fence and made a break for it.'

'Come on now, Pippa, they're free citizens, not prisoners!' Dad said.

'No, but neither are they free to steal a horse and go gallivanting across the open hills. *That's* what they miss. Not giving a pony's coat a brush.'

'I really don't think Madeline will jump any fences,' I said. 'I'll do all the risk assessments, and make sure there's adequate supervision.'

'Oh, is it Madeline?' Mum's eyes instantly softened. 'In that case, then, yes. Let's see if we can make it work. I don't know what that woman did for you that summer, but I know I'll never be able to repay her.'

I coughed, keeping my gaze firmly on my laptop even as the flush bloomed across my cheeks. I quickly moved on to some of the other ideas, including the genealogy sessions, woodworking and some new, interactive quizzes, all of which my parents gave an enthusiastic green light to. I'd got a few suggestions left.

'Another key theme that came up is how people hate the formality around physical contact.'

Dad grimaced. 'Are we back in the pole dancing arena?'

'Jessie,' Mum added, 'we have safeguarding protocols for a reason. This isn't some 1970s care home where you can manhandle people without a thought for their own dignity.'

'No, but for some of them, the only time anyone touches them is to help them out of a chair or down a step. Arabella Goose said that she sometimes pretends she struggles with her cardigan because when one of the staff help her get it on it's the closest she gets to a hug these days.'

We all paused to absorb that information. Mrs Goose, who had held the hands and wiped the tears of thousands of primary school children in her time. And, yes, hugged them when they needed it, even if that was frowned upon nowadays. This formidable head-teacher, admitting that she faked her own infirmity for a few seconds of human contact.

'It's another reason for the petting sessions, so they get to touch another creature, but I don't think that's a substitute for a person,' I went on once Dad had given his nose a good blow, sneaking the tissue up to his eyes for a discreet dab. 'Especially not for Frannie, who's violently allergic to dog hair. I wondered whether we could bring in some beauty therapists to do massages – even if it's just hands or heads – and manicures, pedis, facials. Hair styling, maybe even some delicate make-up.'

'Jessie, that's brilliant!' Mum said, her voice tight with emotion. 'It's perfectly in line with the whole ethos of the Barn, to make people feel loved, and treasured. How have we never thought of this before?'

'Because we were too busy putting out fires – metaphorical and literal, running a staff team, helping our 20 per cent of clientele who have dementia and the 60 per cent with mobility or other limiting health issues? Making people feel welcome, and keeping them as safe as we can?' Dad suggested. 'That's why we needed Jessie.'

'This doesn't sound cheap, though,' Mum added. 'How does it fit with the budget?'

'Well, I wasn't sure it did, until I spoke to Ada and May.'

'Oh, those two have caused more grief than most of the others put together!' Dad exclaimed. 'They're pure trouble.'

'What they are is intelligent, vivacious women who are bored. And feeling useless.' Talking to Ada and May had been yet another tender tug on my battered heart. They'd won me over the second they'd told me they were twins. Then, Ada had pulled out my pony-tail and deftly retied it in a way that suited me twice as much and looked three times more stylish. 'Did you know they used to run a mobile beauty parlour from a purple VW campervan? They'd visit a different location each day of the week – the Hatherstone camp-site in Sherwood Forest, local markets. They also visited care homes and did hair and nails for free, only stopping a few years ago when the van broke down and May's arthritis meant she couldn't keep up with five days a week.'

'They must be well past seventy by now,' Mum said. 'Although, they do both look amazing. They've got taste, I'll give them that.'

'They're eighty-nine.'

'*What?*' Mum and Dad had been working with older people for nearly three decades; they were as good as it got when it came to estimating age.

'It's the beauty regime, they told me. All natural. But they won't spill their secrets, only share the products.'

'They could be millionaires if they were prepared to bottle it,' Mum exclaimed.

'They aren't interested in selling it. A few of the other women have asked them. Louis Abbot asked if he could buy some for his wife, who according to him would benefit greatly from a new face. They told him that what his wife needs is a new husband. They are, however, prepared to offer one day a fortnight to, as they put it, "provide some much-needed TLC to anyone who wants it, Louis Abbot not included". They also said they'd only charge us enough to cover costs.'

'Absolutely not!' Mum barked, causing me to spill some of my coffee. 'They'll charge us a fair rate, which we will happily pay for. And Arabella Goose will be first in the queue. If there's time, I'll be in the queue, too. Those women defy all reason, looking that good at eighty-nine. Whatever they've got, I want some.'

'Besides,' Dad added. 'It'll save on some grey hairs and worry lines all round if we can keep those twins from getting up to any more of their antics. The day they stole the chainsaw to chop up a fallen tree for a bonfire put years on me.'

'It was a great evening, though,' Mum mused. 'Campfire songs and hot chocolate. And we doused all the rogue flames in time.'

'Right. So, speaking of songs, another must is dancing,' I ploughed on.

'We already have monthly tea dances,' Dad said. 'Although the numbers have dwindled with the warmer weather. They'll pick up in the winter.'

'No, they won't.'

'Excuse me?' Dad looked bewildered that I'd contradicted him on something he clearly knew far more about than me.

'No one likes the dances.'

'Ruby O'Mara loves the dances! She's always begging us to hold them more often.'

'Because Ruby's an attention seeker, and you always let her sing,' Mum scoffed.

'Dad,' I pressed on, 'the average age of the Outlaws is seventy-six. They were eighteen in 1964. They don't yearn to waltz about to war-time tunes from before they were even born. They want to mosh to the Rolling Stones. Boogie on down to Aretha Franklin. We're going to have an afternoon disco, using the light-up dance floor. I'll take requests for the playlist and I can promise you it won't include "The White Cliffs of Dover".'

'Are you also going to call the ambulance when one of them breaks a bone, like at the barn dance?' Dad huffed.

'When Isaac broke his finger playing rugby, no one suggested shutting down the club and making them play tiddlywinks instead. They're grown adults, Dad. Who love rocking out. You're the one who wanted to make their dreams come true.'

'What about karaoke?' Mum suggested. 'They also love to sing.'

'They do, but as previously stated, we've got far too many atten-tion-seeking exhibitionists for that to work. Pit them against each other with a microphone and then there *would* be a risk of broken bones.'

'Fair enough,' Mum said. 'Anything else?'

'I'm wondering about a murder mystery day.'

My parents both sucked in a breath. 'Remember, several of the Outlaws have a degree of confusion or memory loss. Staging a murder could seriously traumatise them,' Mum said.

'And it'll only resurrect the rumours about Millie Mont-gomery.' Dad winced. 'Marco found her in the storeroom covered in blood and imaginations ran wild. It wasn't very helpful for Millie's family when four of the Outlaws staged their own private investigation.'

'Concluding in a citizen's arrest of poor Harrison Smith,' Mum added.

'She'd fainted and hit her head,' Dad said. 'No suspicious circumstances. What none of the self-appointed private detectives knew is that she had epilepsy.'

'Okay, I'll scratch a murder mystery. That only leaves excursions. I was thinking that on Fridays, when the wedding prep is happening, there's no reason why we can't organise some trips out. It would mean paying staff to work an extra day, but we can recoup that in ticket prices.'

This produced an even more adamant response than the murder mystery. I'd never seen them express such a vigorously negative opinion.

'Jessie, I'm really not sure you've taken on what we've told you about this bunch,' Dad said, his voice dripping with dread. 'Don't be fooled by their pleasant exterior when trying to persuade you to build a bungee jump. They are wild. Uncontrollable at times!'

'Fearless and free!' Mum added. 'It's a wonderful combination – I can only hope I've as much spirit in my retirement – but it can be hell to supervise here, let alone setting them loose out there.'

'I understand that some of them will need quite a lot of support. But like I said before, these are grown adults. Plenty of them live independently. They don't need supervision at the theatre or a cricket match. Jed Tetley used to bowl for Nottinghamshire! He already goes to all the test matches. All we're doing is helping them go together.'

Mum's face had turned grey. 'That's what we've been trying to explain, Jessie. It's the together when the trouble starts. One of them has an idea and then another one tries to outdo it, then before we know it they're climbing onto the roof serenading Katherine Lewinski.'

'It seems a shame that everyone misses out because of a select few.'

'Maybe so,' Dad agreed. 'But this new programme will mean some big changes and the older we get, the more challenging some of us find change. And just to be clear, I'm referring to your mum and me, not the Outlaws. Let's get the Monday to Thursday programme up and running, make sure we've smoothed out any snags before we consider Friday trips.'

'But thank you so much, Jessie, and well done!' Mum beamed. 'What an amazing job, in only a couple of weeks. We're so excited to see what a huge difference all these fabulous ideas are going to make. You're our heroine, riding your white steed all the way from Brighton to save the day.'

'Or, I'm simply doing my job.' I picked at the remains of the doughnut, unable to meet their gaze.

'No! No simply about it! What you're doing here is priceless. *Priceless!* And we won't hear any different. Now, it's nearly five thirty. I'd say that's a great time to stop and head home for Monday Mumday!'

'Mum and Dad day,' Dad added. 'I've made lasagne, your favourite. Because you're *our* favourite... daughter.'

'Thanks, Dad. High praise indeed.'

## 21

On Tuesday, I cut short a brutal game of monopoly with Madeline to avoid complete financial annihilation and helped her onto the minibus before heading home myself, reassuring my parents that I'd catch up the lost hour working at home.

'We trust you, Jessie! We know you're a dedicated professional who'd rather resign than be caught shirking or skiving.'

I don't know how they could possibly know that, given the number of times I'd been fired for both shirking and skiving. Sometimes both.

Once home, I followed the sound of exasperated grumbling. Isaac was standing at the kitchen table, his hands covered in sticky dough, a smear of flour in his hair and murder in his eyes.

'How the hell am I supposed to turn this abomination into spheres?'

'Hello, brother. I'm fine, had a good day, thanks for asking. How's yours?'

'How do you think?' he growled.

'Right.' I approached the table, shrugging off my denim jacket and pushing up my sleeves.

'No.' Isaac held up one pastry-laden hand. 'No helping.'

'This is not the time to be proud.' My eyes widened when I got close enough to see the state of the table. 'Connie will be here in an hour.'

'I'm making this dinner by myself. I've built a million-pound company from practically nothing. I can manage a three-course dinner for three people without needing my sister to step in and rescue me.'

'With all due respect, the state of this table suggests otherwise...'

'Are you seriously casting doubt on me now, at my lowest point? I thought you, of all people, believed in me.'

It was good to see that some trace of humour remained beneath all the stains and splatters.

'Oh I do. I believe that you are a man of great accomplishments. Just not when it comes to pastry. I'm not going to interfere with that blob you've made, but you have to let me give you a couple of hints.'

Once Isaac's ego had finished wrestling with his need to impress Connie, he gave a sharp nod. Feeling a surge of pride that I was even in a position to offer cooking tips, I quickly explained where he was going wrong (my disaster last week had proved useful after all). As soon as I'd finished, there was a knock on the front door.

'What the hell?' Isaac spluttered. 'We agreed six.'

'You did, but then I arranged for her to arrive at five.'

'And what, forgot to tell me? Why would you do that?'

'Don't panic! She's here to see me. We've got something to discuss, and Connie thought it made sense to do it when she was already coming over here.'

'Rather than at work, where you spend several hours in the same building two days a week.'

'Wow.' I gave him a stern look. 'I've not even let her in yet and you're already in arse mode. Maybe spend the next hour fixing your attitude along with dessert.'

I ushered Connie and Wilf into the now sparse-looking living/games room. Wilf's eyes widened with wonder at the games table and white board. Connie's? Not so much.

'It's looking better than the last time I was here, which is about the best I can say about it.' She slowly turned around in a circle, taking in the room in all its gaming glory.

Wilf had got a pen and a notepad out of his backpack and was intently copying down the Chimney Cup scoreboard. Thankfully, I'd remembered to take a photo of the Boys to Men contract before erasing it, so Connie didn't get to see that Isaac had hired his own twin as a life coach.

She spent a few minutes inspecting the room more closely, making various scribbles and adjustments on a drawing pad.

'I'd suggest we sit down and take a look, but I'm scared to sit in one of those chairs in case I accidentally press the ejector button,' she said. 'And that beanbag is definitely not for human beans.'

Instead, she rested the pad on the games table, flicking to the first page.

'Connie. This is stunning!'

'Not bad, eh?'

'Not bad, not good, not middling. It's perfect!' I gasped, as she showed me four more pages, all showing different angles of the room with some close-up diagrams.

'You must have spent hours on this. I feel like I should pay you.'

She stared at me, a look of horror on her face. 'Okay, so were you only pretending to be my friend? Because where I come from – which happens to be the village next to you – friends don't pay friends for favours. Besides,' she continued, tenderly stroking a sketch of a shelving unit, 'I loved doing it. My other plans for yesterday included scrubbing the bathroom and washing Wilf's football kit. I should pay *you* for giving me something nice to do instead.'

'Is that how you usually spend your days off?'

She shrugged. 'Single mum life, jam-packed with glitz, glamour and lone evenings watching crap TV.' She stopped then, grabbing my forearm. 'Hey – you should come over one evening. We can... watch crap TV together.'

I pressed my hand on top of hers. 'Connie, I would love to spend an evening watching crap TV with you.'

'Why would you want to do that?' Wilf asked, not bothering to glance up from his notepad. 'You could watch *Droid Defenders* instead. Everyone says it's dead good.'

'Which would mean we'd have to sign up for the subscription package I've been telling you for weeks that we can't afford, and, you get to watch the show you've been going on about. What an excellent plan.' Connie's tone made it clear she was being sarcastic.

'Everybody wins,' he said with a nonchalant shrug.

'Apart from my bank balance.' She gave Wilf a playful nudge.

'You could always watch it here,' I said.

'What?' Wilf sprang to his feet. 'Isaac has the right channel?'

'Are you kidding? You think these guys would miss out on *Droid Defenders*? Besides, they have *every* channel.'

'Can I, Mum?' Wilf looked as though his head was about to pop off. 'Can I, please? Can we ask Isaac now? I could watch it while you talk about the house with Jessie and then I won't get in your way.'

'Or how about an episode after dinner, while Isaac and your mum talk business?' I suggested, before turning to Connie. 'I don't mind sitting with him while I get some work done.'

'Sitting *where*?' Connie asked. Wilf immediately scrambled onto a gaming chair.

'I'll bring in a chair from the kitchen.'

'That would be amazing, thank you so much.'

'Isn't that what friends are for?'

We spent a few more minutes going over her ideas before I snuck into the kitchen on the pretext of fetching glasses of water.

'How's it going?' I asked, bracing myself.

'We're having ice-cream for dessert. Apart from that, I think it's going okay.'

It certainly looked a lot better than forty-five minutes ago.

'We're nearly finished here. Do you want me to keep an eye on anything while you get changed?'

Isaac gave me a sharp glance. 'I am changed.'

I made no attempt to hide my cringe. 'I told you before, that outfit is awful.'

'I like it. It's comfortable.' He tugged on the yellow and white towelling top. 'More to the point, Connie understands fashion and style. She's got excellent taste.'

'That's precisely the problem.'

He opened the oven door and checked the chicken, his way of informing me the conversation was over.

'Isaac, it's not you! If it was, you'd have been wearing pastel stripes years ago. You can't go changing who you are for a woman.'

'But that's exactly what I'm doing. Isn't that why I'm paying a chunk of your rent for the next three months? So I can change. For a woman. Now, I've got a lot still to do, none of which includes arguing with you about what I'm wearing.'

'Okay. If you think it's so cool and stylish, then ask Connie if she likes it.'

'Ask if I like what?' Connie said, suddenly appearing behind me. 'Hey, I came to see if you needed a hand. Oh, hi Isaac. What an... interesting choice of outfit.'

'Hello Isaac. I like your costume!' Wilf said, squeezing past his mum, still hovering in the doorway. 'Is it for the Chimney Cup?'

'Yeah... it was a... thing... Arthur and Elliot... so. I'm going to quickly get changed and then we can eat. Jessie, you are going somewhere else, aren't you?'

'Excuse me?' I said, mouthing the A-word at an angle Connie couldn't see.

'I mean. Um... in case anything confidential comes up in our meeting, would it be okay if you didn't mind, um, not being in the kitchen?'

I offered him my most sugary smile. 'Of course. I had every intention of giving you your space. And feel free to send Wilf through once he's finished eating. There's a television programme we'd like to watch.'

'Actually, I'm not hungry. Can I watch it now?'

'Wilf, Isaac has spent ages cooking us a lovely dinner,' Connie said, a note of warning in her tone.

'We don't know if it's lovely or not. You said that Isaac was a terrible cook and you hoped he'd make the smart move and order a takeaway.'

Isaac, who had been about to leave, stopped and gave Connie a look. One eyebrow raised, the corner of his mouth twitching. It was an expression I'd seen him use on countless women over the years, and it rarely failed to elicit the desired response. Which was, in most cases, for them to fall that little bit deeper for his charm.

Connie froze for a split second before smothering an embarrassed smile as she bent down to ensure Wilf was listening. 'Either way, we're going to sit down politely at the table, eat what's on our plates and say thank you before and afterwards, because that's what polite guests do, isn't it? The sooner you stop arguing and we can start eating, the sooner you can go and watch the droids.'

'Give me two minutes, buddy, okay?' Isaac said.

'Okay, buddy,' Wilf sighed.

I left my brother to his second non-date.

\* \* \*

It was quarter to nine when Connie tumbled into the living room, her face contorted with panic.

'I'm so sorry, I've just seen the time. Wilf should have been in bed ages ago. Come on, get your coat. Here's your shoes.'

Arthur, who had come to join us half-way through episode two, pressed pause on the remote.

'But there's seven minutes left in this episode! I have to find out if R4 makes it out of the crusher! Press play again, Arthur, please. Please just press play, now!'

'You can find out another time,' Connie said.

Wilf gaped at her. 'What other time? This is the only time we've even been to this house. What if we don't get invited again? Then I'll never get to know what happens. Arthur, you have to press play, quickly!'

'Once you've put your coat and shoes on we can ask Isaac when would be a good time to finish it off.'

'Now is a good time!' Wilf started blinking furiously and wringing his hands. 'You were a whole hour late because you're talking to Isaac in the kitchen so why can't I be late for *seven minutes*?'

'I shouldn't have been late, that's why I said sorry. Isaac and I were having a work meeting, which is important.'

'It's not important to me; *Droid Defenders* is important to me. Not worrying about what happens to R4 and the others is important. Why doesn't what's important to me count?'

Wilf was growing increasingly agitated, rocking in the chair as his hands twisted around each other like anxious snakes.

'This is why we need to go now, because you're getting over-tired.' Connie's voice was tight with the strain of trying to keep calm.

'*I'm tired because you made me miss my bedtime! Press play, Arthur; you have to press play!*'

And with that, he toppled into a full-on meltdown.

I'd seen plenty of them before in my caring roles, but this was brutal. Aware that his mum knew best, Arthur slipped out of the room while I stood back and allowed Connie space to crouch beside Wilf, who was now screaming, thrashing and drumming his feet against the floor. When Isaac appeared in the doorway a moment later, Wilf was still lost in his dysregulation.

Isaac opened a drawer in a flimsy cabinet, took out a blanket and gently draped it over Wilf's body. 'Hey, buddy. It's okay. We're here. Take as long as you need.'

'You keep a weighted blanket in your games room?' Connie asked, her voice shaking with unshed tears.

'Elliot's,' Isaac replied softly, taking hold of her hand as he sat on the floor next to her.

Was it my imagination or had Wilf's kicking started to grow less forceful?

'I'm so sorry, I shouldn't have let the meeting go on so long,' Isaac said. 'I'm so sorry Wilf, I know this has messed up your evening.'

'You're sorry?' Connie whispered, choking on a cross between a laugh and a sob. 'This is entirely my fault for rambling on at you about my problems and not watching the time. You probably couldn't have interrupted to tell me how late it was even if you'd known. And you weren't to know that Wilf needs to be home by a certain time.'

'By five minutes past eight, so he can get in the bath for quarter past, pyjamas on and teeth clean ready for story-time at eight-forty-five, lights out at nine?' Isaac quirked up one side of his mouth. 'Of course I knew.'

As Wilf's turmoil began to ease, I quietly left, Connie still gazing at my brother, her mouth open in surprise. I was turning out my bedroom light, much later, when I heard the front door open and the crunch of footsteps on the gravel driveway. Glancing out the window, I saw Isaac's silhouette lowering a sleeping Wilf into Connie's little car, the light from the open door revealing how he gently adjusted the blanket and clicked the seatbelt in place.

Connie stood in the shadow beside him, the strain of the past couple of hours clear in the bow of her back. I couldn't hear what Isaac said, but after a brief moment she slowly leant her head against his shoulders, and he lifted his arms and wrapped them around her, their two bodies blending into a single shape.

I realised, then, what I suppose any sensible person would have known all along. Fancy meals, the right clothes, a tastefully decorated house, even clever conversation – these were not the things that the woman my brother loved needed from him. She'd have appreciated them, sure, but what she needed was a strong and steady heart. A shoulder to rest her weary head on. Not a man with everything sorted, but one prepared to sit with her on a grubby carpet and say, 'It's okay. I'm here. Take as long as you need.'

**22**

_____

Over the next few days, it felt as if my life in Houghton was beginning to take shape. I carried on organising the new programme and attending the current activities at work, went to training with Elliot on Wednesday (he'd been completely understanding about me missing the Monday sessions due to Monday Mumdays – 'How could anyone miss that?'), video-chatted Seb on his cruise when we happened to be both available, messaged him a few times on all the days when we weren't, and kept myself to myself.

I scrutinised my bank account, carefully planned my meals and other measly expenditure, and I hoped and prayed that I'd keep on somehow holding myself together until I was able to leave. To my bemusement, I couldn't help noticing that rather than merely fumbling through each day, I seemed to be surprisingly okay. Of course, that only made me start wondering if I was a terrible person for being able to coexist with Elliot Ollerton without it tearing me to pieces. So then I'd feel decidedly not okay, and all was well again.

Arthur gathered us together on Thursday to discuss the next task on the Boys to Men project, and we reached the clear conclusion that it was going to be impossible to find a chunk of time when we could decorate all together. As the conversation veered closer towards me ending up doing it all, I reminded them that I was the coach and that they were supposed to be the ones transforming, so after more wrangling we decided that if Arthur and I bought the materials on Saturday, Elliot and Isaac would get the room painted on Monday.

Had I deliberately engineered things so that I wasn't spending more time with Elliot?

Absolutely.

Running about a recreation ground, firmly focussed on eleven amazing kids, was one thing. Spending hours in the confines of the living room, with no distractions other than a tin of paint, felt far too cosy. The perfect scenario for the ghosts of the past to come and linger between us.

All the same, was I a tiny, teensy bit disappointed at my own common sense, knowing that a day painting with Elliot would be infinitely preferable to visiting a DIY shop with Arthur?

If I was, then tough. I'd no one to blame but myself.

\* \* \*

To any casual onlooker, the build up to Friday evening might suggest it was going to be the event of the year at Chimney Cottage. I had to remind Arthur, yet again, as he trialled pesto chicken for the third time, that as far as Elsa was concerned, this was a meeting, not a date, using the example of Isaac to demonstrate that there was no guarantee Elsa would be leaving the cottage on Friday with the new status of Arthur Wood's girlfriend.

'Jessica, if you're going to keep checking up on me then I must insist that you stop being so negative.'

It was now three o'clock on Friday, my day off, and I was going to give everything I'd got to help Arthur break his lifetime streak of never making it to a second date.

'All I'm saying is that you don't need to lay everything out there this evening. She doesn't need to know that you've decided you're soulmates. That's a lot to put on someone so soon.'

'What, she'd be better off thinking I'm some sort of Casanova, like Connie does about Isaac?' He snorted, carefully laying a slice of salami on a plate.

'What harm can it do to give her a chance to get to know you, first?'

'Given that my inferno of love for Elsa currently infiltrates my every thought and decision, how can she possibly get to know me without knowing that?'

Fifteen minutes before Elsa was due to arrive, I couldn't resist creeping down the stairs and slipping into the kitchen one last time on the pretext of getting a drink. As soon as I entered, it was clear that my advice to Arthur about making any verbal declarations was going to be irrelevant.

'Do you normally do all this for a date?' I asked, wondering if this was the reason Arthur never made it to a second.

He turned away from the oven door, his expression full-on smug. 'It has been known. You don't have the complete monopoly on dating prowess, you know.'

'Okay, so how about for professional meeting prowess?' I gestured at the worktops, the table, *every single available surface.* 'Does your dad sprinkle rose petals all over the office when you meet with suppliers, or business partners? Does he light candles and turn up the slow-dance playlist?'

'He's a happily married man!' Arthur said, affronted. 'He's not trying to win the heart of his supplier.'

'Plus, it would be completely unprofessional,' I added, aware of the time ticking but working hard to keep my patience. 'I told you

Elsa won't be impressed if she thinks you've tricked her into a romantic dinner.'

'Tricked is a little harsh. I prefer the term, "surprised her with".' Arthur took a bottle of champagne out of the fridge and placed it in a cooler on the table, in between a giant candelabra and a vase full of red roses. It was clear even from where I stood by the door that the cooler was a plastic bucket wrapped in foil and the vase was a plastic drinks bottle with the top chopped off.

'It's only a surprise if it's what she wants,' I said, wincing as he swapped his apron for a jacket. 'And we did chat about the outfit.'

'If it's a work meeting, as you keep insisting, then shouldn't I dress for work?'

'You only wear that dress coat and – no, please not the hat! – for funerals, not meetings.'

'This is a funeral. The death and burial of my single status!' He grinned, turning up the volume of 'Can't Help Falling in Love' on the Bluetooth speaker. 'I don't care what you think, Jessica. I'm not ending this night without a girlfriend. I didn't practice pesto chicken three times for nothing!'

At that point we heard Penny scrabbling down the corridor, signalling that Arthur's unsuspecting guest had arrived.

'Ah. Here we go!' Arthur adjusted his hat, tweaked his cravat until it was no longer straight and brushed off his pin-striped trousers, leaving a smear of flour dust. 'Any last words of advice?'

'So many I don't know where to begin, but you've made it clear you'll ignore them anyway. Just be yourself and I hope it works out like you think.'

I ducked into the living room while he opened the door, feeling that in my role as relationship coach it was my duty to at least earwig on their initial conversation.

'Good evening, Elsa. Please come in.'

'Hi Arthur. Have you just got in from work? You haven't even had time to take your hat off. I hope I'm not too early.'

'I've been on leave this afternoon. The outfit is for you. A woman such as yourself deserves the very best, in my opinion. Whatever others might think.'

I cringed against the door, bracing myself for her reply.

'Well... goodness. That's very flattering. I feel like a right scruff in comparison.'

'*Au contraire*! My finest suit is incomparable to the radiance of your smile, and the brilliance of your eyes.'

Elsa replied with a sound that was difficult to interpret, but when Arthur invited her to follow him into the kitchen she didn't turn and run back down the drive, so it could have been worse.

I tapped on Elliot's bedroom door before retreating upstairs.

'Hi!' he said, confusion creasing his brow. Which was fair enough; it was the first time I'd knocked since moving in.

'Are you running later?' I asked, quietly.

'Yes.' He checked his phone. 'Yes.'

'Elsa's here for her pretend meeting that's really dinner with Arthur, and he's gone a bit... Arthur. Might be worth you checking for signs she's okay when you walk through the kitchen.'

'Right.' He nodded seriously. 'What do I... how do I? What signs?'

'Does she seem uncomfortable, is Arthur respecting her personal space, that kind of thing.'

Elliot blinked a couple of times. 'I... don't know. I'm really not great at reading signals. Why don't you check in on them?'

I shook my head. 'Arthur's already annoyed with me for interfering and, as he put it, "smothering the romantic vibe" with my negativity. I'd need a credible excuse to go in there. But I can't, in all good conscience, leave Elsa to Arthur's "love inferno".'

Elliot thought for a moment, the crease between his eyebrows deepening. 'You could come with me.'

'On your run? I did say a credible excuse.'

'I owe you a walk.'

I looked at him, my turn to be confused.

'Last week, when we cooked together, I invited you to come on a walk that never happened.' He pushed open his bedroom door wider so I could see the note stuck on the inside.

*You owe Jessie a walk.*

'So you do.'

The sight of that note made my throat ache. Sadness, guilt, pleasure that Elliot still wanted to be my friend? I had no idea any more.

'Credible enough?'

'It's perfect.'

\* \* \*

I met Elliot outside the kitchen door a while later, him having set an alarm on his phone so he'd remember to leave half an hour earlier than normal. It was starting to get chilly, so I'd added a denim jacket on top of my playsuit.

'Oh, hi Elsa,' Elliot said as he walked into the room. 'I'd forgotten you were coming over. I hope I'm not disturbing your meeting. Dinner.' He scanned the room, still about 70 per cent flower petals. 'Confetti demonstration?'

'Oh, no, that's fine!' Elsa beamed, putting down her fork. 'Arthur was just talking me through the key stages of preparing someone for a funeral.'

'Hello,' I added, silently praying that the 'someone' he was talking about was the deceased's loved ones, rather than the deceased. Although that would have been bad enough.

'Oh, hey Jessie,' Elsa added. 'I forgot you lived here. Oh – we're not kicking you out of your own kitchen, are we? Please don't feel like you have to stay out of the way. I mean... obviously, this is your kitchen. You don't need my permission to be here. Not that I was trying to grant permission! I just meant that you mustn't feel awkward. Not that you need me to tell you how to feel, of course! Invalidating people's feelings is the worst. Well, not the worst... Accidentally bumping into the coffin while conducting a funeral and it toppling onto the floor was worse...'

Elliot raised one eyebrow at me, as if asking whether Elsa was sending out a signal that she wanted us to stay. Arthur, of course, was about as subtle as ever.

'Actually, while Elsa is trying to be her usual kind self in conveying that you're welcome to join us, it would be a lot easier if you went elsewhere,' he said, the curls on his crown bristling. 'Elsa and I have a private matter to discuss.'

I glanced at Elsa, who was using my trick of bending down to pet Penny so we couldn't see her expression.

'We're actually going a walk,' I replied. 'Unless you'd rather we stayed, Elsa? The more the merrier, and all that.'

She peeked her head back above the table. 'Oh, no. It's fine. We can be merry enough on our own.'

Of course, it was always a merry hoot discussing funerals.

Arthur gave a broad smirk as he shuffled his chair a few inches closer to Elsa's. 'So, the next thing to decide is shoes...'

I was more than glad to be leaving them to it.

\* \* \*

'I know my dating experience is limited, but did you suggest chucking flowers everywhere and that corny playlist?' Elliot said as we climbed the footpath along the edge of the field behind the cottage, Penny whuffling ahead of us, tail wagging in ecstasy. 'If so, I might have to redact your rent discount.'

'The only advice he took from me was to take off the hat.'

'I presume Elsa wasn't finding it excruciating, given that we left them to it? I'd have happily played up on my poor social intelligence and hung around, however much it annoyed Arthur.'

I shrugged. 'She seemed more comfortable with Arthur than she does talking to me.'

We paused to take in the view over the ridge of the hill – the oilseed rape fields gleaming gold, the emerald meadows dotted with livestock. To one side, treetops blended into a hazy kaleidoscope of greens and browns in the distance. The clouds were wispy streaks against a pale-blue canopy. I sucked in a deep breath of sweet, spring air and felt my heart expand. Living by the beach had been great, but I had missed the rolling hills and bountiful woods of home.

Once over the crest, the path veered off towards the forest, and as we wound our way through the trees, we talked for a while about the Harriers. Once again, something about Elliot's company seemed to nudge my angst about our relationship to one side. I couldn't resist indulging in these few, uncomplicated minutes with an old friend, even knowing that it betrayed his trust. If Elliot knew the part I'd played in his accident, we would not be going on companiable walks together, and I would not be staying in his house.

*Ugh.* This was such a mess. I was a mess.

If I kept my distance, acted aloof with no explanation, it would only make Elliot feel like I was rejecting his friendship because of his disability.

*So, what then, Jessie? Are you hanging out with him out of pity?*

I stumbled over a tree root, hidden in the shadows, and as Elliot turned to grab my hand – as his fingers remained wrapped around mine while he guided me along the path he knew better than the lines on his own palm – I knew full well that pity had nothing to do with it.

It took a long, stunned second for my brain to process the sight that greeted us as we stepped through the back door. Usually, upon two people walking in on a couple kissing, the couple would automatically break apart. By the time Elliot and I had hurried past the table and into the hallway, I wasn't sure Elsa and Arthur had noticed we were there.

Like a pair of school kids, we jostled our way into the living room, only bursting into shocked laughter once the door was firmly shut behind us.

'It beats his kiss with Casey Cunningham in year eight,' Elliot said, shaking his head in wonder. 'Looks like you're a better relationship coach than any of us would have guessed.'

'Oh no, apart from the food, that had *nothing* to do with me.'

'Don't sell yourself short,' Elliot said, eyes glinting with mirth. 'If you'd not shown him how to cook, he might never have plucked up the gumption to invite her round.'

'Oh, I really hope this is going somewhere and not a one-time thing.' In lieu of a cushion to squeeze, I tucked my legs up onto the gaming chair and wrapped my arms around my knees. 'Then again, Elsa's a curate. Surely they aren't supposed to go around having one-night stands, even if it is just a kiss?'

'In my extremely limited experience, there's no *just* about that kind of kiss,' Elliot said.

*Woah.*

It was as though his words were a spell, sucking every molecule of oxygen from the room instantly.

We both froze.

Our eyes locked as the memory of those kind of kisses – so fervent and tender – skittered like electricity across every inch of my skin.

*Crap.*

Penny, possibly suspecting something untoward was going on, gave a muted bark, causing Elliot to hastily turn his attention to her.

'Hey girl, you're right. We're not supposed to come in here after going in the woods, are we?'

He stood up, one hand gripping the back of his neck. 'She's going to get stressed if I forget to have a post-run shower. To her, that was still a run.'

'Of course.' I hunched into my knees, still pressed against my chest. 'Thanks for the walk. It's easy to forget how beautiful somewhere is when you've not seen it in so long.'

'Yeah.' Elliot gave a short, sharp shake of his head as he turned to go, his voice soft and deep. 'I know exactly what you mean.'

## 23

When I trudged down the stairs in joggers and a long-sleeved T-shirt on Saturday, I found Arthur and Elliot in the kitchen. The atmosphere was even more serious than Arthur's date preparations as they used homemade paper fans to waft Cheerios along the table and into the cereal packet, strategically positioned on the floor.

At least someone had cleared up from the night before, the only evidence being a few forlorn petals here and there.

'Ah, Jessica! And how are you on this most splendid of mornings?' Arthur asked, twisting his shoulders and sticking his tongue out as he sent several crunchy hoops skidding off the wrong side of the table and into Penny's waiting mouth.

'*Most* splendid?' I shuffled over to the kettle. 'That sounds optimistic. Is Elsa around for breakfast?'

I'd slipped upstairs to bed well before either Elsa or Arthur had exited the kitchen the night before.

'Certainly not!' Arthur shot upright. 'She's a priest!'

'So, what, priests don't eat breakfast?'

'Priests eat their breakfast at the vicarage, where they live with the vicar, the vicar's husband and their cats, and where they slept last night after going straight from this kitchen and out the front door.'

'Okay! No offence intended. It's none of my business what you and Father Elsa get up to.'

'It's Reverend Elsa,' Arthur spluttered, tugging on his baggy checked shirt as if that made things more respectable. 'If she was a father she couldn't get married. And it's actually quite important that no one says anything to besmirch her reputation. She only started here a couple of months ago. It would devastate her to become embroiled in slanderous village gossip.'

'And, strictly speaking, it is your business,' Elliot said.

I glanced over as he sent the remaining three Cheerios into the box with one flick.

'Given that you're his get-a-girlfriend coach,' he added, picking up an old ice-cream carton brimming with milk-sodden cereal and taking a huge mouthful with my new wooden spoon.

'Am I?' I asked, raising one eyebrow at Arthur as I took my mug of tea over to the table and slumped into the seat furthest away from Elliot. 'It looked as though my services might no longer be required.'

'If I'd merely hired you to get me a girlfriend...' Arthur casually ran one hand through his hair, eyes roaming around the ceiling as he deliberately dragged out his answer. 'Then... no! I would be dismissing you henceforth.'

'Wow.'

'However,' he added, before I could pass any more comment on that revelation. 'The plan is not to settle for one goal up at half-time. Until the game is well and truly over, your input is very much required and equally appreciated.'

'And by over you mean...?'

Arthur picked up the Cheerio box, taking a handful and

chewing on them slowly before answering. 'Til death do us part, Jessica.'

'Until one of you are dead?'

'Until we're married!'

'And that's the line from the marriage service you chose to refer to?'

'I told you,' he said, tipping the box straight into his mouth this time, causing a dusting of cereal shavings to coat his face and hair. 'I need your help. I thought we could start with a blow-by-blow of last night.'

'Okay, but anything you say will have to wait until we're shopping later.' I gratefully accepted the brand new, factory fresh hoodie that Elliot slid across the table, opening it up to see JESSIE printed on the front, BROWN on the back. 'I've got a manager to assist.'

'What?' Arthur couldn't believe it. 'After last night's development you're going to ditch me for the Harriers?'

'It's not all about you and Elsa, Arthur. All three of you have hired me.'

'Huh,' he sniffed. 'Elliot doesn't even want to ask anyone out, let alone buy a ring.'

'Be that as it may.'

*Oh I hope that isn't true. Is true. Isn't true...*

'I'll catch up with you later. By then you can have figured out how to cut a "blow-by-blow" down to the pertinent, non-intimate key points. Most crucially, skipping everything between your lips touching Elsa's and then not touching Elsa's again.'

'Honestly, Jessica. Sometimes I wonder what kind of a man you think I am.' Arthur shook his head, sadly, and left us to it.

\* \* \*

The Harrier under nines were playing away this week, in a suburb on the north side of Nottingham. They loved the new tops, especially when Elliot had used a nickname. There couldn't be many football players with 'Wodger' on their shirt. Russell, Olly's dad, of course had his objections.

'Any particular reason why our team is the only one in history who needs this?' he sneered.

'I think it's a great idea,' Connie's mum said, fixing Russell with a gimlet eye. 'It'll be good for team bonding if the new players can quickly learn everyone's names.'

'Yeah. Right. That's why we've wasted a load of club money on giant name badges. What next? Are the kids who can't run getting electric scooters?'

'That would be cool!' Jackson exclaimed. 'Football on scooters!'

'No club money was wasted,' Elliot said. His voice was firm, but I'd spotted the stiffness in his posture. He was nervous, and potentially fighting a twinge of humiliation. 'I paid for these myself.'

'Well Olly isn't wearing it.' Russell placed a large hand on his son's shoulder. 'This team is enough of a laughing stock as it is.'

There was an excruciatingly drawn-out moment while Elliot gritted his teeth and took a couple of long, slow breaths, seemingly in an attempt not to punch the smirk off Russell's face.

'Hey, great shirts!' a man who looked about twenty said, popping the growing tension with an affable grin as he strode up to meet us. 'I'm JK. Manager of the Colts.' He reached out a hand to shake Elliot's.

There was a ripple of excitement in the boys who were hanging around waiting for Elliot to start the warm-up. JK Jennings had been a legend at Nottingham Forest until a knee injury forced him into early retirement. Even I'd heard of him, thanks to his frequent appearances on various reality shows since.

Elliot introduced himself and they chatted for a couple of

minutes, going over the match practicalities. Elliot appeared utterly unperturbed talking to a local celebrity, but then he may not have remembered who it was.

As he turned to leave, JK stopped and looked at Olly, still in his new top. 'Wow! I love your shirt, Olly. Can't help feeling you've got yourselves a bit of an unfair advantage there.'

He offered Olly a wink, gave his dad a clap on the shoulder and strolled off.

There were no more comments about the new kit.

There were, however, plenty of comments when at half-time the Harriers were down seven-nil. A group of the more supportive parents had to literally form a human barrier between Russell and the team so that Elliot could deliver his half-time talk without constant heckling.

'Any other thoughts, Jessie?' he asked, after he'd pointed out how the defenders could tighten up, that the midfielders should try to stop passing the ball to the Colts' fastest player and the strikers could work harder at running in the right direction.

'I think Jan should have a go in goal. Move everyone else up front.'

'Really?' Elliot kept his face open and interested but his eyes were sceptical. Jan was our partially sighted player, and while he had speed and surprising accuracy on the odd occasion the ball was at his feet, he relied on Olly to let him know what was happening if the action moved more than a few metres away.

'You can spot the ball much more easily when it's moving towards you, right?' I asked Jan, who nodded vigorously. 'And if Elliot gives you a shout if it's heading towards the goal, and from what side of the pitch, you can be ready for it.'

He thought about that. 'I guess so.'

'Do you know your left from your right?' Elliot asked him.

Jan nodded again. 'Of course!'

'No of course about it.' Elliot smiled as half the boys held up their hands and formed the 'L' sign to confirm which hand was which. 'I sometimes forget.'

'It's kind of important if you can't see very well,' Jan shrugged.

'So, do you think our assistant coach's idea could work? Are you up for giving it a try?'

'He can hardly do worse than me!' Dyson exclaimed, causing the others to burst out laughing. Elliot hadn't wanted to replace Dyson in goal until he'd figured out who might do better, but an urgent situation called for immediate action, and nobody wanted the boys to face their biggest loss of the season right on the heels of the success of their first goal.

'I'll give it a try as long as no one gets mad at me if I'm rubbish,' Jan said, once the laughter had died down.

'Dude, since when has *anyone* on this team acted like that?' Elliot asked.

'Coach Simonson did,' Wilf chipped in. 'He told Jan he'd be better off listening to sport on the radio.'

Elliot swallowed hard and gripped the ball in his hand a little tighter. 'Anyone who's clever and awesome enough to still be part of the Harriers?'

'No coach,' most of the boys droned, apart from Wilf, who added, 'Olly's dad said he was going to effing lose it himself if we lost one more match. He sounded quite angry, then.'

'Jan, you've already made me proud by being brave enough to try,' Elliot said. 'You guys know there's only one thing I ask of you.'

'To run in the right direction?' Wodger asked.

'Well, that would be helpful, but it wasn't what I meant...'

'Ooh – to help each other out!'

'Whatever you do, enjoy it.'

'Put all the balls in the big bag at the end of training.'

The boys all threw their suggestions into the ring.

'Okay!' Elliot said. 'Maybe more than one thing. But the *most important thing* I ask of you, the one that beats all the rest, is that you give it a go. So.' He held up the ball, nodding to where the referee was calling the teams back on the pitch for the second half. 'What do you reckon? Up for giving it a go?'

The cheers and fist-pumps as fourteen little legs ran, limped and cartwheeled back onto the pitch was the answer that made every failed tackle, missed shot and own goal worth it.

\* \* \*

With Jan our keeper, Olly was now free to fly. Despite the frequency with which he stopped to wait for a teammate to catch up, or help tie their shoelace, the difference was instantaneous. The rest of the boys followed his direction instinctively, and there was no more heading in the wrong direction, even when Dyson's baby sister started chanting for her brother at the top of her voice.

They scored two goals. One each for Olly and Jackson. Wilf would have scored, too, if he'd not sabotaged the shot because of his refusal to score if his mum wouldn't see it.

It might as well have been twenty from the celebrations when the referee blew the final whistle.

Elliot didn't stop grinning the whole way home.

## 24

After announcing the first changes to the Barn's activity programme on Monday lunchtime, we started off gently with an all-new interactive music quiz on Tuesday, giving the competitors the opportunity to sing, hum or mine different songs. Wednesday, we had a fascinating introduction to genealogy, made even more so thanks to various attendees sharing stories about some rather unusual ancestors.

So far, so good.

And then Thursday.

The Lavender Mobile Beauty Parlour came out of retirement and set up shop in the Barn library. There were initial objections from a group who'd been planning a game of Cluedo, but when Ada brazenly assaulted Hetty with a dab of lipstick that added an instant glow to her pallid complexion, they stopped grumbling and joined the queue.

As requested, Lance had set up three of our comfiest chairs in view of the library windows, two for Ada's hair clients and one for May who focussed on face, hands and feet. Two more chairs were reserved for those next in the queue, and everyone else was ushered elsewhere. I'd posted a sign-up chart on Monday, and due to the number of people, both male and female, who had enjoyed pampering and primping from the twin sisters prior to their retirement, it had filled up within minutes. I'd had to persuade the Lavender Ladies to up their sessions to weekly, then print out more sheets for the next few weeks, with strict instructions that no one could sign up for more than once a month unless there happened to be a spare spot, so that everyone could have a turn. That then led to more time figuring out who'd signed up multiple times using false names, as well as my dad uncovering a black-market scheme whereby people sold the use of their names to those desperate for a more frequent blow dry.

As a treat, we allowed the café to provide a waitress service, and the room was soon buzzing with a perfect mix of anticipation, contentment and Ada's outlandish stories about her adventures across several continents. I was so entranced with one tale about a full-moon ball in Florence that I was late for lunch.

It was all going brilliantly, until Vivienne and Veronica Vincent, also sisters although not twins, took their turn. Ada, who did about 90 per cent of the talking between her and May, insisted that I move the schedule so that the sisters could be treated at the same time. Vivienne had requested a head massage and hair styling; Veronica had booked a facial.

'We'll give them both,' Ada had told me. 'They're old friends. Well, ancient friends truth be told, and they both deserve a double treatment. Book them in last and we'll run over time if necessary, so no one else has to miss out.'

After a brief dash to check that the rest of the Barn activities – more glass painting, wood-whittling and a sing-along to *Les Mis* – were all finishing off on time, I popped back to the library just as the two women before the Vincent sisters were finishing their treatments.

'You look exquisite,' I said, delighted at how Enid couldn't stop patting her new layers, a look of absolute wonder on her significantly less angular face, thanks to her new cut. Madeline simply cried.

May, who came across as the dark cloud of tetchiness, balancing out her sister's sunshine, helped Madeline to her frail feet and then wrapped her scrawny arms around her, one hand pressed against the back of Madeline's head like a mother cradling her child. After seeing me hovering with Madeline's walker, May sternly informed me that she would need another few minutes.

While Enid handed the mirror back to Ada and sashayed off, May held Madeline, gently stroking her head.

'Same time next week?' she asked, after eventually moving away and handing her client a tissue that appeared out of thin air.

'Um, actually...' I started, aware of the potential uproar that overriding the booking system could cause.

'Same time next week,' May said, not a hint of question in her tone as she gave Madeline's hand one last squeeze before turning to prepare for the final client of the day.

Who was I to argue? Madeline was ninety-three. Was anyone really going to kick up a fuss about her skipping the queue a few times?

'Ah, the indomitable Vs,' Ada said, clacking her scissors at Veronica and Vivienne, who were still finishing their cappuccinos and coffee cake. 'Your transformation awaits.'

I would have stayed to watch, only Dad asked if I could help some of the less-steady Outlaws safely into their transport. I was on my way back, three steps from the library door when my pleasant thoughts about another good day were interrupted by a chilling scream.

Bursting into the library, I saw Veronica holding Ada's mirror up, face contorted with horror. I say Veronica – that was something of a guess considering how different this woman looked to the one who'd sat in the chair forty-five minutes earlier. The other Vincent sister – recognisable by her dress alone – snatched the mirror and thrust it in front of her own, wretched face.

'*What have you done?*' Vivienne shrieked. Veronica appeared to be rendered temporarily mute, her mouth sagging open in shock.

'You pair of absolute witches!' Vivienne continued. 'I told Veronica we'd be fools to trust you! Put our hair, our faces, our *dignity* in your evil, arthritic hands. We'll sue you for this!' She turned and pointed a trembling finger at me. 'The lot of you! Everyone knows your Pollyanna parents couldn't keep control of a pre-school, let alone manage these vicious old bats, and now we've paid the price. Well. *You're* going to pay for whatever it costs to put this right, plus emotional distress. Look at Veronica! I wouldn't be surprised if you've given her a stroke, you spiteful crones.'

It was hard not to look at Veronica. Where under an hour ago there'd been shoulder length, silver hair, there were now bile-green spikes. Her eyebrows had been dyed the same colour.

Vivienne's roughly hacked mess was scarlet with blue splodges. The same colour as her cheeks, vibrating with rage. One eyebrow was blue, the other red.

'This is assault!' Veronica managed to splutter. 'Forget suing. I'm calling the police!'

'Oh, for goodness' sake,' Ada retorted. 'It's not permanent. Be grateful it's not a tattoo.'

Veronica was right, though. This surely could be classed as assault. Not wanting to leave the room in case either of the victims decided to retaliate, I called Dad. Receiving no answer, I fired off a frantic text telling him that there was an emergency in the library.

'Why would you do this?' Vivienne wailed, grabbing the mirror back. 'Why?'

Ada and May made a point of forbidding their clients to see

themselves until the transformation was complete. In this case, they'd also moved the chairs so that the sisters couldn't have seen each other.

'Since when did these two need a reason to act like cruel bullies?' Veronica spat. 'Thinking they're so much better than everyone else. Well, this time you can explain yourselves to a judge and jury!'

'A minor assault charge would be seen by a magistrate,' May said, calmly packing up. 'We'd have had to snip off your ear for a jury trial.'

'Do feel free to have us arrested, though,' Ada added, not even bothering to hide her smugness. 'May and I would be delighted to explain to an officer of the law precisely why those particular hairstyles suit you perfectly. And you have no grounds on which to sue. You read the small print, signed the form. "I agree to give the Lavender Mobile Beauty Parlour complete creative control".'

'We never agreed to that!' Vivienne was about ready to commit an assault of her own.

May held out the form that every client had to sign. I'd scanned it earlier but took it off her now and re-read the page asking about allergies, basic skin and hair care routines and, in tiny writing that even the best pair of bifocals would struggle to make clear, handing over absolute creative control.

I had no idea how to handle this, apart from trying to stop the situation deteriorating any further until my parents arrived. I sent another, more urgent message to both of them.

'Perhaps it would help if you did explain why you chose such bold styles?' I asked, a tiny part of me still hoping that Ada and May had suffered a momentary lapse in taste, rather than this being a premeditated act of aggression. Thinking about all the others who had waltzed out of the library throughout the day, I was doubtful.

'I already said, because we tailor our work to suit each individual client.' Ada offered a sweet smile, but behind it I caught a glint of steel. 'We went to school with Veronica and Vivienne, so we know them extremely well.'

Glancing over at the sisters, I detected a sudden change in body language. The bristling anger was now tinged with wariness.

'The vomit-green shade reminded Ada of when Veronica repeatedly stuck her head in the school toilet, causing my sister to throw up her lovely lunch,' May said, eyes wide with innocence.

'And the scarlet and blue are an obvious homage to the time we caught Vivienne with May's fiancé, wearing nothing but scarlet knickers. We know you love scarlet, Vivienne. And goodness, your freezing cold breasts were blue!' Ada pointed her scissors in the air for emphasis.

To their credit, the Vincent sisters didn't bother denying it, merely blustered and huffed while Ada and May continued to tidy up, faint smiles dancing at the edge of their identical mouths.

'But all that was decades ago!' Vivienne said, eventually. 'We were silly young girls back then.'

'We've been friends ever since you came back to the forest!' Veronica chimed, accusingly. 'Been on the Robin Hood Festival committee together.'

'All those cricket matches and harvest festivals, and now you do *this*?' her sister said.

Ada and May placed the last couple of items in their suitcases and closed them with a decisive click.

'All we can say is that we're very sorry if you don't like the results, but you did both ask for hair and brows that would suit you. We believe your new looks match your personalities perfectly.'

'What's that supposed to mean?' Veronica asked as Ada and May swept past them, suitcases rolling behind.

May paused in the doorway, lifting one shoulder as she turned back to reply. 'Ugly, absurd and rough as a toilet brush.'

'Sixty-four years I've been waiting for you to apologise for helping yourself to my man!' May called back as she continued down the hallway to the front door. 'We decided we'd waited long enough.'

* * *

'Jessie!' Dad called as he hurtled out of the main hall and towards the library. 'I just saw your message. What's happened?'

Rather than answering, I stepped back and allowed him to skid right into the room, where Veronica and Vivienne had collapsed into chairs. Veronica was sobbing, Vivienne repeatedly muttering about how she'd have to wear a wig to her granddaughter's engagement party.

'Do they even make eyebrow wigs?' she sniffed.

'What on earth?' Dad asked, spinning around to face me and mouthing, 'Who is it?'

'Veronica and Vivienne,' I mouthed back.

If possible, his eyebrows disappeared even further into his fringe. 'Ada and May?' he asked quietly.

'Yes it blinking well was that deranged cow Ada and her evil twin May,' Vivienne shouted. 'What the hell were you thinking, Tom, allowing those two unsupervised with a pair of scissors and a packet of dye? We can understand this poor, naïve child being hoodwinked, but you should know better after what happened with the helium balloons.'

'I take it you aren't happy with the new—'

'*Don't even go there!*' Veronica growled.

'Right. Yes. Of course. It goes without saying that we'll undertake a thorough investigation followed by appropriate action.'

'We're in two minds as to whether to sue,' Vivienne said. 'At the very least, those maniacs need to be barred from the Barn for life!

Do that, and we might consider changing our minds. Providing we are fully compensated for the cost of sorting this disgraceful mess out.'

At that point, I realised that Veronica's shaking shoulders weren't because she was crying.

'Veronica?' her sister asked, having spotted it at the same time.

'I'm sorry,' Veronica wheezed, clutching her wobbling stomach. 'I can't help it. You look so awful!'

Then she opened her mouth as wide as it went and let out a howl of laughter. 'You look like an exotic caterpillar is crawling above each eye.' She paused for another wave of guffaws. 'You've got to hand it to them, they got us good!'

'I suppose it was quite a spectacular revenge,' Vivienne admitted, her own mouth starting to twitch. 'And, blummin' 'eck, Veronica, you've been hiding a grisly looking head underneath that hair.'

'It's hair; it'll grow back,' Veronica giggled. 'It's not like we haven't got more important things to worry about.'

'But they've ruined my chances of getting on *Love Island*!' Vivienne said, full-on laughing along with her sister now. 'Let alone our dream of a modelling contract.'

'To be honest, I've always fancied trying a wig,' Veronica said, as they both heaved themselves up out of the chairs, causing them to collapse back down again in another fit of giggles. 'I might go blonde.'

'And we can figure out how to dye our eyebrows brown again.'

This time they made it all the way up and started walking towards the door, holding each other's arms for support.

'Brown? You mean a nondescript grey, verging on invisible?'

'That's a good point. I should be thanking May – it's the first time anyone's been able to find my eyebrows in years!'

'I'll tell you what, Viv, we'll be getting noticed walking down the street for the first time in a good few decades.'

They paused in the doorway, still chuckling. Vivienne pointed at Dad. 'We're prepared to let this matter drop on one condition. Don't let Ada and May know we're not furious, or who knows what they'll cook up next. This way, they'll think we're even.'

'I will need to speak to them, and if you decide to take things further, you will of course have the Barn's full support.'

'Thank you, Tom, but we we're too old for a war with those two.'

And off they went, their conversation echoing down the corridor.

'It was a rum move, though, boinking her fella.'

'Reckon I did her a favour, finding out what he was like before they'd gone to all the hassle of getting married. Sticking Ada's head down the bog, though. *That* was a rum move.'

Dad and I waited until they were safely out the door and on the way home before we allowed so much as a smile to cross our lips, but I had to admit as I walked home later, I'd not laughed that much in ages.

\* \* \*

The next day was Friday, so I spent breakfast with Elliot, alternately cringing and guiltily giggling as I recounted what had happened the day before.

'I mean, it's an awful thing to do. They honestly looked horrendous. But when Ada and May gave their reasons, I couldn't help empathising.'

Elliot nodded. 'Doing something really awful to someone, then acting like friends when you see them years later, as though it never happened, must be infuriating. I can see why they wanted revenge.'

My throat seized shut and I swallowed, hard, gripping my mug of tea. 'Maybe they should have tried having a conversation first, though. Given Veronica and Vivienne a chance to explain or apologise.'

'I guess some things feel beyond an explanation. And if Veronica and Vivienne were truly sorry, shouldn't they be the ones to bring it up and apologise?'

All I could do was offer a feeble nod.

Ada and May would never forget what had been done to them.

If someone had no recollection of the harm you'd caused them, if you were genuinely sorry, and doing all you could to help them be happy now, should you dredge up the worst time of their life, simply to appease your own guilt with an apology? Or would that person rather not know, if in knowing they lost an old, and rapidly becoming a new, friend?

I was so messed up about the whole thing, I had no idea.

## 25

The others had been working on the living room in their spare time throughout the week. Isaac and Elliot had finished painting the walls a pale grey. They'd ripped up the carpet and found solid floorboards underneath, so on one afternoon Elliot had borrowed a sander and then given them a coat of gleaming varnish. A green sofa and two armchairs were being delivered tomorrow. It had been a long, drawn-out debate whether or not to get rid of the gaming chairs or the games table, but I had insisted there wasn't room for both. In the end, Isaac came up with the suggestion that they club together and buy a summer house to use as a games room, so the chairs went into each of their bedrooms for now, with the promise that the games table would be moving out in due course.

They'd added a rug with a muted stripe, a lampshade instead of a bare bulb and blinds with a green pattern to match the sofa. The next big job was assembling the shelving and storage units. Seeing as they'd done all the rest, I volunteered to give it a go.

Two hours later, I had to admit to a sweaty, exasperated defeat. Eyeing up the various panels of wood and fixings strewn across the room, I retreated to the kitchen for a coffee break.

Elliot was sitting at the table, his laptop open. He wore tortoise shell glasses with a squarish frame that made him look instantly more mature. Like the kind of man who owned a four-bedroom house and worked in marketing while running a football team on the side.

'Sorry, I didn't mean to disturb you.' I grabbed a mug and flicked on the coffee machine.

'No, it's fine. It was too hot for Penny to work in the bedroom today.'

Penny chuffed in agreement from her spot by Elliot's feet. She must have been hot if she couldn't be bothered to get up and give me a hello nose-nudge.

'Do you want a coffee?'

He pushed back from the table, scraping the chair across the tiles before taking off his glasses and wiping his eyes. 'Yeah, go on then. These figures aren't making any more sense the longer I stare at them. I think I might sit in the garden for a few minutes.'

He appeared to notice me then, blinking in surprise. 'Rough morning?'

'You could say that.'

'You look as though you've been wrestling an alligator.'

My hand sprang up and found the mess where my ponytail used to be. Glancing down, I saw a smear of perspiration on my pale green T-shirt. I could only imagine what my overheated face looked like.

'Yeah, but this one is made of wood and comes with a lot of screws and weird bolty things that don't seem to quite fit their holes.'

I handed Elliot his drink and started filling up the second cup.

'I don't suppose you'd have time to help me?' I asked. 'I could take a look at those numbers for you in return.'

*Yes, Jessie. Because engineering even more time with Elliot on top of breakfast today and the match tomorrow is a great idea.*

He looked doubtful. 'If it's following instructions then you'd be better off waiting for Isaac or Arthur. If you can't figure it out, then I've got no chance.'

I shook my head. 'I can understand them fine. What I can't do is hold two large pieces of wood steady at perfect right angles, while simultaneously screwing in a screw that is half a millimetre too big for the hole it needs to go into.'

'Ah, okay.'

'I want you for your brawn, not your brains.'

Elliot jerked his head back.

'I mean... not that I'm saying there's anything wrong with your brain...' I grimaced. 'Crap. I'm sorry. I can't think of a single way to make that comment not completely offensive.'

He grinned, making it my turn to be surprised. 'We both know there's a whole lot wrong with my brain and nothing to gain by pretending otherwise. I wasn't offended. I just can't remember a woman wanting me for my brawn before. Not that that means it hasn't happened, of course. Given my terrible memory, thanks to the brain problem.'

'Are you kidding?' I fumbled about with the coffee machine in a futile attempt to hide my fluster at Elliot's suggestion that I wanted him. While I'd been the one to say it first, it just sounded different – *very* different – coming from him. 'I thought your long-term memory was mostly okay. Half the school were after your runner's brawn once upon a time.'

He furrowed his brow, getting up and indicating that we go outside, where at least the fresh air might dampen the flames of mortification burning across my skin.

'I think you've confused me with your brother.'

'Macy MacDonald? Gaby Stephens?' Feeling utterly ruffled, I threw the names out without even thinking about it.

Elliot shook his head, adopting a baffled grin. 'If you say so.'

He sat down in one of the chairs, which was now fairly clean thanks to Isaac's efforts. 'Anyway, moving on from that disconcerting detour, I'd be happy to provide an extra pair of hands to the furniture building, as long as you can give me clear instructions.'

I sat down on the chair next-door-but-one to his, took an agitated gulp of coffee and flailed about for a change of subject.

'I didn't know you wore glasses.'

Elliot blinked a couple of times while adjusting to the new topic. 'Ever since the accident. They help if I'm focussing on a screen for any length of time.'

'So, most of the time then?' I teased.

'If you're referring to the hours I choose to spend relaxing with a computer game, it's been a lot less in the past few weeks, actually.'

I raised a cynical eyebrow.

'As evidenced by you not having seen me wearing glasses until now,' he added with a hint of triumph. 'Too busy helping phony cookery teachers figure out how to prep chicken and getting roped into gate-crashing my housemate's romantic dinners.'

I shrugged. 'What can I say, you are paying me to help you get a life.'

He burst out laughing. 'Oh, I'm not complaining. It's been my best month in years.'

Those words were a simultaneous salve to my heart and a punch in my guts.

* * *

As soon as the furniture was assembled and positioned in line with Connie's diagram, Elliot went back to work, brushing off my offer of help. I stayed in the living room until I'd neatly arranged the controllers, headsets and other paraphernalia inside the new cupboards, and artfully placed the more attractive items like books and the new photo frames I'd bought on the shelves. I took a quick snap and sent it to Connie, with another message of appreciation, and scurried upstairs to call Seb. Building heavy furniture on such a warm day was a grunty, sticky, physical job. I'd tried my best not to notice Elliot's flexing muscles, athletic strength and sheer *capability*, but it had been harder to ignore the prickle of chemistry that crackled every time we needed to squeeze past each other, or we had to crouch mere millimetres apart while one of us twisted the Allen key as fast as humanly possible so we could move apart again.

I wasn't surprised to see my hair bristling with static after all that electricity in the room.

*Dammit!*

I was trying so hard to be friends with Elliot. To be *normal*.

If I had to start keeping away from him because I couldn't get a grip on my guilt-riddled feelings, then things were going to get even more awkward and complicated.

I *liked* being friends with Elliot! I did my best to grab those stupid, out-of-date emotions and stuff them back in the past where they belonged, before calling my current boyfriend, the one I had real feelings for.

'Hey, Jess. I'm just about to head off for my shift. Are you okay?'

Seb squinted down the camera. He'd let his hair begin to grow out, the floppy strands now tinged blond from the sun. His tanned complexion glowed with health and what I suspected was happiness. I'd never seen my boyfriend look so relaxed.

'Yes, I'm good. I was just, you know, missing you. It's been a while since we had a decent catch-up.'

'Yeah, we should make time for a proper call, soon.'

'So... when would be good? I thought we could make it a like a date. Get some food, take time to really talk.'

'Um, yeah, that sounds amazing. I'm working long shifts for the next three days. Heading out with the boys when we next dock. Maybe... how about... Wednesday? Three o'clock your time?'

'Right. I can do that. I'll be at work, but I can take a late lunch in the staffroom, that's not a problem.'

'Oh, I forgot you'd be at work. No, that's fine. We can rearrange.'

After toing and froing for a few more minutes it was clear that we would struggle to rearrange if we wanted a proper conversation in the next month. In the end I persuaded Seb to go with six on Wednesday, with the promise of plenty of messages in between.

'You know I love you, Jess?' he asked, after saying that he really had to go or he'd be late for work. 'I miss you, every day. But this is helping, being here. I'm starting to feel like Seb again. I promise when I'm back, I'll have been worth waiting for.'

'I know. I understand. Take as long as you need. I'll be here.'

*Just be quick about it. I'm in a total mess, and I need you back.*

\* \* \*

Saturday, I did my best to keep a polite distance from Elliot, while at the same time being supportive when facing snarky comments from the parents who'd come to watch their kids' team play the Harriers at home.

It was a pretty stressful afternoon. Casual friendliness was hard to maintain when both you and your fellow footballing coach were battling the urge to aim a ball at someone's ignorant balls.

I stayed on at the pub for post-match chip butties, feeling that at least one of us should show some solidarity after yet another big loss, and knowing that Elliot wasn't up to it. A glass of wine in the sunshine went some way to easing the inner urge to break something, as did watching the boys messing about on the play equipment, seemingly unscarred by the nastiness of earlier.

When I mentioned how positive the boys' resilience was to Connie's mum, she disagreed.

'The reason they appear unbothered is actually heart-breaking,' she explained. 'They've grown to expect it. This is normal life for some of these children, being mocked for their differences. That's why this team is so important and why we're so glad that you're there for Elliot. These boys need him, and he needs you. This grandma, for one, can't thank you enough. In fact, let me start by buying you a drink...'

It was nearly six by the time I meandered home, having ended up staying until most of the team had left, with only a few dads looking as though they were settling in for the night. I was feeling warm and fuzzy enough that I might have stayed anyway, except when one of them offered to buy me another drink, he stepped into my personal space and winked, reminding me that my days of hanging out with drunk strangers were in the past.

Instead, I found Arthur proudly reclining on the new sofa, Elsa cosied up beside him. The room was unrecognisable from the week before. Seeing Arthur with Elsa was, I had to admit, equally as strange.

'Jessica, come and join us,' Arthur said, to my surprise. 'We've got snacks.'

I was relieved to see that he'd taken on board our conversations about food. Rather than Monster Munch and a packet of iced gems, he'd put out plates of olives, cheese and crackers alongside some chocolate coated strawberries. Admittedly, one of the plates was actually a saucepan lid, but it was a start.

'Are you sure?' I asked, hovering in the doorway. 'I don't want to intrude.'

'Oh, not at all,' Elsa said, hastily wriggling to the other end of the sofa. 'We were just chatting, nothing untoward going on! Not that I was suggesting you have a sordid mind or anything...'

Arthur reached out and placed one hand on her knee, startling her into silence. I settled into one of the new armchairs, infinitely more comfortable than the gaming chairs, and offered Elsa my most reassuring smile.

'I'll get you a plate,' Arthur said, standing up.

I started a brief reply about how I wasn't hungry, but then I realised that it was six o'clock and all I'd eaten since breakfast was a handful of soggy chips wedged between cheap, white bread.

'That would be great, thanks Arthur.' He left the room, and I turned to Elsa. 'Have you had a good day?'

'Yes, thank you.'

I waited for more, but that was the extent of her reply.

'Arthur said you were going to visit Southwell Minster?'

'Yes.'

Another excruciating few seconds of nothing.

'What did you think?'

'Yeah, good. It was lovely.'

'Did Arthur find the grave he was looking for?'

She shook her head. 'No.'

'Okay.'

I left it there. Until, a few seconds later, she blurted out, 'I'm sorry, I don't mean to be rude. I'm trying to stop my mouth rambling on, spewing embarrassing nonsense. It's become this thing, now, where my brain seems to relinquish all control of what I say to you. You must already think I'm a total loon, and I'm trying not to make it any worse. Though now, of course, you think I'm a rude, unfriendly loon instead.'

'Not at all,' I said, though I had to admit, at that point I didn't know what to make of her, and I was also starting to wonder whether Arthur had gone all the way to the shop to fetch me a plate.

'I'm just so nervous,' she said, a weak giggle turning into a worried grimace. 'Arthur thinks so highly of you. He values your opinion so much that I'm terrified you'll decide I'm not good enough for him, and he'll end things before they really get started.' She shook her head. 'So, it's become this self-fulfilling prophecy where I'm so scared I'll act like a fool in front of you, I act more fool-ishly than usual. That only adds to the pressure, and makes it worse.'

'Um...'

'And now I've told you all this,' she babbled on. 'You'll think I'm a total weirdo. Spilling my humiliating secrets to a woman I hardly know. *Isaac's sister*, of all people. One of Elliot's best friends!'

'Okay, can we rewind for a moment?' I asked, my wine-sprin-kled brain attempting to process this cascade of ridiculousness. 'Firstly, Arthur values your opinion far more than mine, and I promise you that nothing I say could change how he feels about you. Secondly, unless I thought you were a genuine danger to Arthur – abusive or controlling or something – I wouldn't say anything critical to him about you. It's none of my business who Arthur chooses to go out with. Thirdly, there is really no question here over whether you're good enough for him, trust me. And lastly, what does being Isaac's sister or Elliot's friend have to do with anything?'

'Well, because you're Jessie! You're a legend to these guys. For weeks before you moved in it was all they could talk about. "Has Jessie called you yet about the room? Why don't you call her? I don't want to scare her off. How about we offer her an irresistible rent discount? Oh, man, imagine us all back together! Dream Team reunited!"'

'What?' I shook my head, as if to shake loose her words, buzzing about like confused bees.

'Arthur missed youth group to stay in and celebrate after you finally agreed to move in.'

'What?'

'They really love you, Jessie.'

Before I could say anything else, Arthur returned. 'I thought you might prefer a bowl,' he said, holding out the plastic mixing bowl I'd bought for the cooking task, a clump of washing-up bubbles still clinging to one side.

I looked at his face, pleading with me to not give away the truth that they only had four plates in the house, all of which were already in use, hence the saucepan lid.

'In my last house, we ended up using paper plates half the time,' Elsa said. 'At the risk of sounding like a cavewoman, I'm impressed you've got baking equipment!'

Arthur tucked his chin into the collar of his *Fortnite* T-shirt. 'Well, you know, profiteroles don't turn up on your doorstep fully formed.'

'They do when you order them from Asda,' Elsa said. 'Honestly, the only baking I've ever done is at school, and I got a D for forgetting the flour. I'm in awe of you guys. Whoever dares call millennials snowflakes needs to meet you four.'

I genuinely had no answer to that. Neither, it seemed, did Arthur. He merely stared at the new rug, blinking in wonder as if he'd just witnessed a miracle.

## 26

On Sunday, I headed back to the Barn to join the picnic. The late May weather was glorious, and it seemed like almost the whole village had turned up to sprawl on blankets, play boules or squeeze chairs around the tables on the terrace. I had spent an immodest amount of time pondering Elsa's revelations about how much my housemates had wanted me to move in, but given how questionable the other views she shared were (starting with worrying about being not good enough for Arthur) I tried not to dwell on it.

Knowing Isaac wanted me at Chimney Cottage was nice, if not a total surprise. Why Arthur would share in that hope was a question to file alongside all the other mysteries about how his brain worked. But knowing that Elliot had wanted me to move into his cottage added yet more feelings to those already sprouting inside me. None of them sensible.

However, I was soon distracted by an even more scandalous topic, zipping around the Barn gardens faster than the frisbee.

'Have you seen it?' Mum asked, nudging me into a corner of the terrace as soon as I'd placed the bowl of coleslaw I'd brought onto the food table.

'I'm presuming not, given that I have no idea what you're talking about.'

'Veronica's scalp!' she said, eyes wide with alarm.

'Well, yes, I saw it on Friday. Didn't Dad tell you I was there?'

'No! Not her actual scalp. Veronica's scalp!'

She yanked her phone out of her red shorts, found the right screen and then thrust it at me.

'Ah.'

I couldn't not smile.

Veronica's Scalp was an Instagram page. It already had a few hundred followers. The close-up pictures of her knobbly, green head covered in spikes showcased it encircled in a bandana, decorated with tiny daisies, wearing back-to-front sunglasses and other pointless, not-particularly-imaginative accessories.

'What's Viv done?'

'Viv's Brows.'

I found the page almost instantly. The snaps of her red and blue eyebrows wearing different googly eyes, stick-on antennae and in one photo tiny moustaches had earned more fans than her sister.

'Everybody's talking about it,' Mum whispered.

'How do they all know?'

'Because Vivienne and Veronica have been telling everyone!' She sighed. 'So much for keeping this quiet. I honestly don't know if our reputation can stand much more.'

'Mum, the Barn is thriving. The Outlaws love it. Who cares what people think?'

'I've had non-stop calls all weekend from family members, residential care home staff, local busybodies pretending to be "concerned neighbours". As if I don't recognise that journalist Joel Robertson's number, all the times he's called sniffing for a scandal for the *Sherwood Times*. If people think we can't keep those we're caring for safe...' She looked at me, eyes shining with tears. 'Your dad thinks we might have to ban Ada and May. At the very least shut down the Lavender Beauty Parlour.'

'Well, if we do then I'm sure I can find a replacement.'

'Oh, I know you can,' she said, voice watery. 'But I'm not at all sure Ada and May will be able to do without the Barn. They'd be lost without us.'

'Right.' The Barn was a family. We couldn't kick two eighty-nine-year-olds out without sending a clear signal to every other community group that they couldn't be trusted.

'It's either their reputation, or ours.'

I pondered this as we walked back to the tables and helped ourselves to cheese and onion pie and tomato salad.

'How about we let the Outlaws decide?' I offered, once we'd found a spare bench near the pond.

'What, take a vote?' Mum frowned. 'Jessie, if we start letting them vote on who gets to stay or go, it'll become all-out war.'

'No, nothing that blatant. Let them vote with their feet. Or rather, feet, hands and hair. The sign-up sheet for this week is still on the noticeboard. I can announce during lunch on Monday that if they no longer want their treatment then they need to cross their name out so someone else can take the slot. If they're still happy to trust Ada and May, then why shouldn't we let them?'

Mum took a thoughtful bite of pie. 'What if everyone cancels? Or, more likely, replaces their names with insulting graffiti?'

'We can cross that bridge if we get to it. Did you see how people walked out of the library last Thursday? I swear that most of them had grown a good three inches, and not only because Ada has a superhuman ability to add body and bounce to the wispiest of hair. Every single one of them glowed. And the only two who didn't have seen the funny side.'

'I don't know.' Mum still looked slightly haunted. 'I'll have to ask Dad.'

'Okay, but whatever you decide, please don't boot them out before I've had a chance to get my turn in the chair.'

'Are you kidding?' Mum smiled at last. 'I'll be fighting you for a spot.'

* * *

I caught up with Connie while we were folding up bunting in the shape of oak leaves ready to be stored away until the next Robin Hood-themed celebration.

'Are things any better with you and Isaac, since the meal at ours?'

She wrinkled her nose. 'Sometimes yes. Sometimes no. Sometimes I overhear him talking to other people, and he still definitely acts differently with me.'

'How is he with you?'

*Apart from utterly smitten...*

'Kind of, I don't know, stiff? All uptight and proper. Almost pompous. I know,' she said, starting to laugh. 'Since when has Isaac Brown been anything close to pompous?'

*Since he fell in love and had no clue what to do about it?* I yelled, disconcertingly loudly, inside my head, while externally nodding and trying to look sympathetically puzzled.

'And then,' she added, face softening. 'There're these moments. Like when we were at yours for dinner. When he's so... *totally lovely*. I think for a moment that we could be friends.' She sighed, tucking the end of the bunting away and placing it into a box. 'Then he barks at me for staying late to finish off some place settings, virtually accusing me of neglecting my child, and I'm back to wondering why I annoy him so much.'

'Connie, you don't annoy him. Trust me.'

She raised her eyebrow, unconvinced.

'He's never cooked anyone dinner before. Not even our parents. And he didn't act like a prig with you then, did he?' I took a deep breath. 'Honestly, I think sometimes he gets nervous and it comes out as surly.'

She gave a confused laugh. 'Why would I make him nervous? We were at school together.'

Before I could get myself into more trouble with my brother, Wilf appeared.

'Hello Assistant Coach Jessie.'

'Hi Wilf, but I'm not on football duty here, you can just call me Jessie.'

'A good coach is always on duty,' he pronounced. 'When can I come and watch the rest of *Droid Defenders*?'

'Wilf,' Connie warned. 'It's rude to invite yourself to someone's house.'

'But you said I could watch the rest another time,' he replied, jaw jutting. 'And you said I can't ask Isaac because he might get grumpy about it, even though Isaac's never grumpy. You didn't say I couldn't ask Assistant Coach Jessie.'

'Well I know, but...'

'How about the bank holiday Monday?' A week on Monday it was half-term and the schools were closed all week. I called across to Isaac, who was busy folding the banqueting tables away with Elliot. 'Hey, bro! You're not busy a week on Monday, are you?'

'No. Why?' His grey eyes narrowed.

'It's half-term, so Wilf and Connie are coming around to watch *Droid Defenders*.'

'What?' He stood there, a giant table propped up against one hand. 'No one wants to waste their school holidays slumped inside watching TV.'

I marched over to him. Wilf was already wringing his hands.

'Why would you ask them that?' Isaac asked, grimacing.

'Connie hardly ever gets a day off with Wilf. She's not going to want to spend it at her grumpy boss's house watching robots shooting each other.'

'I didn't ask them. Wilf asked me. I thought it would be a nice opportunity for you to see Connie again, as *friends*, not offer up more evidence that you don't enjoy her company.' I held up my hands in a 'hello, duh?' gesture. 'Would you rather they watched it with me?'

'Well, no.' He glanced at Connie and Wilf quickly, a sheepish expression creeping across his features. 'But I was going to suggest a day out somewhere.'

'You were?'

He shrugged. 'There's a thing on at Newstead Abbey. A medieval battle re-enactment, with a food market, archery, stuff like that. I thought Wilf might enjoy it.'

I gaped at him. 'Wilf would love it. So why haven't you asked them?'

He shrugged again. 'I wanted to manage a whole day without acting like a jerk before I asked her. She might consider saying yes, then.'

'And what if, by some twist of fate, in a similar fashion to every other day since falling in love with Connie, you don't manage a whole day?' I said, keeping my voice quiet enough so no one else could hear.

'Then I won't ask her. I don't especially fancy being rejected again.'

'Sometimes I think you're the most infuriating twin I've ever had. I am so itching to storm back over there and ask if they want to go and have a fabulous day out with you, then come back to ours for dinner and *Droid Defenders*, but you're paying me to forcibly propel you into manhood, so instead I'm going to watch you confidently yet casually ask them yourself.'

Isaac turned pale. 'I don't know what to say. The last time it was a work meeting. If I ask Connie to spend the day with me, she'll say no.'

Elliot, who'd been methodically continuing with the tables, stopped to clap his best friend on the shoulder. 'Then don't ask her.'

Isaac looked at him, surprised.

'Ask Wilf.'

Isaac rolled his shoulders, frowning. 'Isn't that a bit manipulative?'

'Only if Connie wouldn't otherwise say yes,' I said. 'I'm pretty sure she'd prefer a day out at Newstead Abbey to a day in watching sci-fi.'

Before Isaac could reply, Wilf appeared at his side. 'Are you still talking about whether I can come and watch the rest of the series because I really, really do want to waste the school holiday slumping inside watching TV.' He blinked several times, head twisting between me and Isaac.

'Okay.' Isaac bent down to Wilf's level, keeping his eyes on the ground to avoid the intimacy of eye-contact. 'We can do that.'

'Yes!' Wilf placed his hands on his knees and let out a dramatic sigh of relief.

'But how about *before* that, you and your mum come with me to watch a medieval battle?'

Wilf shot up straight again, eyes gleaming. 'Which battle?'

'The Battle of Stoke Field.'

'The last battle in the War of the Roses,' Wilf said, voice soft with awe. 'And the only official battlefield in Nottinghamshire. So many people died, the river Trent ran red with blood.' His eyes brightened then. 'Do we get to fight?'

'Not this time. But we can hold some swords and shoot arrows at a target.'

'I'd *love* to hold some swords and shoot arrows at a target!' Wilf turned to Connie, who was already walking over. 'Can we go, Mum? Did you hear? Isaac says we can watch a real battle!'

'Well, it's not the real battle, is it?' Connie smiled. 'That happened in fourteen hundred and something.'

'Fourteen eighty-seven.'

'It's a re-enactment, people dressing up and pretending.'

'Yes, I know that, but can we go? We can go, can't we? And then we can watch *Droid Defenders* afterwards!'

Connie looked at Isaac, her eyes asking if he was sure. When he gave a nod, mouth creasing in a coy smile, she took hold of her son's flapping hand. 'Sounds like a great day; let's do it.'

## 27

On Thursday morning, the last thing I needed was a battle with Wendy over kitchen territory. It was the day of the Great Barnish Bake-Off, and tensions were high even before Ada and May set up in the library. Another team member, Alice, had agreed to keep an eye on them after the Outlaws declared their support for the pair by keeping their names on the sign-up sheet. Veronica and Vivienne, who we'd managed to keep away from Ada and May on the one other day they'd both been at the centre, had decided that the perfect spot for enjoying the sunshine was right outside the library windows, causing May to close the blinds with a sharp harumph.

I'd have chosen the library over the kitchen, any day. We'd had thirty-one applications to partake in the bake-off. One of them from Gregory Whistle, who cheerfully informed me he had never baked so much as a potato, but quite fancied being on television. Another from Caroline Jackson, who asked if she could enter something she'd brought from the village café, as cookery wasn't her strong suit but she loved competitions.

In the end, I'd whittled it down to twenty, and split them into two groups of ten, one who would bake in the morning, the other in the afternoon. I was outside with Madeline on her favourite bench when Mum told Wendy, and even Madeline's old ears heard the expletives reverberating through the kitchen windows and across the garden. The offer of a bonus day off, with a local catering company supplying sandwiches instead, was vehemently rebutted. Instead, Wendy slaved away into Wednesday night, long after everyone else had gone home, producing a cold lunch that was, in my varied experience of working in hospitality, far more complex and time-consuming than it needed to be. The first group would bake from ten-thirty until twelve-thirty, giving her an hour to serve up before the second group took over.

A hotchpotch of ten older men and women, who between them were infirm and/or arthritic, short-sighted, partially deaf and ferociously competitive, crammed into a professional kitchen, on a boiling hot day. I was sweating before we'd turned the first oven on.

Two hours later, I was ready for a stiff drink while I typed my resignation letter.

Obviously, with ten contestants and three ovens, some rigorous negotiations had been required. What I hadn't banked on was Seamus setting a tea-towel alight while heating the oil for his doughnuts, then throwing it onto the floor in a panic, where Harris, trying to be the hero who stamped it out, set his polyester slipper on fire.

Thankfully, the steam tooting out of Wendy's ears as she crashed into the kitchen and knocked Glenda onto her bottom helped dampen the flames, which along with Arabella Goose's quick action with a bowl of washing up water negated the use of the fire extinguisher, saving the competition from having to be cancelled half-way through.

I also wasn't expecting Helen to lose her temper, launching a metal ladle across the room that bounced off the back of Angus's head, forcing his retirement from the bake-off before he'd had a chance to prick his Earl Grey shortbread.

Nor for Don to drop his raw cake mix all over the floor, which Hetty then proceeded to slip over on, adding her rhubarb and elderflower trifle to the mess splattering her from head to toe.

At 12.20, by some miracle there were six showstoppers still standing, a sprinkle away from being ready for the judges, waiting in the café.

'Showstoppers? Heartstoppers, more like,' Wendy muttered as she stomped into the kitchen and announced the ten-minute warning. 'I don't care if your bakes are ready. In nine minutes and fifty seconds this kitchen must be cleared of both people and, more importantly, any evidence that anyone other than me and my team were ever in here. Otherwise the first ever Great Barnish Balls-Up will be the last.'

She gave me a look sharper than her best filleting knife, and slammed back out again.

I took one look at the worktops, the hobs and the cupboard doors and grabbed a cloth.

At 12.35, Arabella wiped the last smear off the fridge door and I declared the first heat for group one officially finished.

'Woohoo!' Dad hooted as Seamus wheeled the dessert trolley into the café. 'This all looks spectacular! You've had a busy morning.'

'We certainly have,' Arabella Goose agreed, making the mistake of wiping a trickle of sweat off her brow with one of Wendy's tea-towels.

'Jessie, you must have had a riot in there!' Mum beamed.

'It certainly sounded like it.' Wendy's sous-chef, James, smirked.

'It definitely *looks* like it.' Isaac, who'd ventured downstairs with

Connie to ogle the entries, grinned and wiggled his eyebrows at me. I glanced down at my dishevelled summer dress, covered in splotches, my favourite trainers spattered with cooking fat and a thick, blue plaster on my forearm from an accidental brush with a zester. I didn't need a mirror to picture the tendrils of hair stuck to my clammy cheeks, or the inevitable streak of icing decorating my face instead of a cake.

'And how wonderful that with so many entrants, you get to do it all again this afternoon!' Mum added, positively beside herself with excitement.

I edged my way to the back of the crowd now gathering for lunch, leant against the far wall and closed my eyes, the faint breeze wafting in through an open window the only thing keeping me from either screaming or sobbing. A (far too short) moment later, something prodded my elbow.

'Here.' I opened my eyes to see Madeline, leaning on her walking frame and bumping a silver flask against my elbow. 'You look like you could do with it.'

'Madeline, have you snuck alcohol into the Barn?' I asked in astonishment.

Her dark eyes gleamed with mischief. 'Go on, just a wee nip. I promise it'll make you feel better.'

Scanning the room to ensure everyone's eyes were facing the dessert trolley, I took a wee nip. Of the creamiest, richest, choco-latiest hot chocolate I'd ever tasted. Although I had tasted it, before. Many times, in fact, during that lost summer.

'Oh, I remember this.' I exhaled, as she waved her hand at me to take another sip.

'My mother's recipe never fails to warm the weariest of hearts.'

I took one more sumptuous mouthful before handing it back and helping her to a chair at her favourite table, reaching down to give her shoulders a squeeze before I took the seat next to her.

'Whatever's responsible for those shadows in your eyes, I hope it helped.'

It had, but an old friend noticing that there was more going on than an exasperating morning helped so much more. I did my best to focus on the conversation around the table as we munched through Wendy's lamb pasties and celeriac slaw. However, as the debate flew back and forth about whether the chair of the parish council should resign, my hurt and humiliation were like a bruise, throbbing beneath my skin.

Once the main course was over, the head judge, Wendy – a culinary Simon Cowell if ever there was one – stood up to announce the winners. When she started off by saying that the six entries were, 'not a complete disaster, I suppose, considering they were created by amateurs', it was all I could do to resist throwing my fork at her head, given my fractious state. Instead, I waited for her to announce Glenda's tiramisu cheesecake the winner, left Mum to interject when she attempted to boot Harris from going any further in the competition, and hurried back to the office for a five-minute breather before heading back to the kitchen for round two.

Half-way down the corridor, I bumped into Elliot. The person I probably most and least wanted to see right then.

'Hi.' His face brightened in relief when he saw me.

'Hello.' I automatically tucked my bedraggled hair behind my ears.

'I had a look in the main hall but couldn't find anybody.'

'It's lunchtime, they're all in the café eating dessert.'

'Oh okay, well I've found you, now, so that's saved me from poking around anywhere else.'

I looked at him for a moment, trying to work out quite how confused he was.

'Who were you looking for?'

His smile dimmed a few watts. 'You.'

'Okay.' I waited another couple of seconds, but he didn't elaborate. 'Why?'

'For the meeting.'

'The meeting?'

'Didn't Jane tell you? Her daughter's just had emergency surgery, so I volunteered to step in. She said she'd let you know.'

'Okay. I don't know who Jane is, or what the meeting is about.'

'Jane Burrows. From Good Dogs UK. She was meeting you to talk about bringing some of the training dogs in for a session.' He pulled out his phone, face creasing in a frown. 'It was definitely today. One-thirty, 26 May. Although I am a few minutes early.'

I checked the calendar on my own phone, although I already knew the meeting was next week. 'I've got next Thursday booked in,' I said, gently. 'At half past three.'

He stared at his phone for a long moment. 'Right. My mistake.'

'Maybe not?' I suggested. 'Perhaps she told you the wrong day, if she was feeling worried about her daughter.'

He clicked through his phone. 'No. She sent me the right date. I must have copied it into my calendar wrong.'

'Okay, well these things happen to all of us.'

He looked at me from underneath his eyebrows, showing me without malice the sensitivity of that comment.

'Yeah. I know they happen to you more than most.' I gave his side a playful nudge. 'No need to go on about it.'

'Shall I come back on the second?' he asked, his smile ruefully acknowledging my attempt at lightening the mood.

'If you're sure? It's the special Jubilee bank holiday. The Barn will be open and Jane was happy to pop in then, as she was going to be at a local dog show, but don't feel you have to.'

At that point, Wendy barrelled through the café door. 'Jessie, the next lot of amateurs are preparing to infiltrate my kitchen. The least you can do is be there to supervise them.'

I checked my phone. 'We've got five minutes. I'll be there in three.'

Before she could argue, a group of Outlaws appeared, pushing past her.

'Jessie, we want to make a formal complaint about the results,' one of the women whose name I didn't know called out. 'Angus was clearly the best.'

'Glenda's cheesecake wasn't even baked!' Helen, who'd thrown the ladle earlier, chipped in. 'The clue is in the name. It's a *bake*-off.'

'I think we can allow a cheesecake,' Arabella tutted, strolling past. 'After all, technically the base used pre-baked biscuits.'

'What do the competition rules say?' Helen bristled. 'These things need to be made clear. Could Jackie have entered one of her ice-cream sundaes, if she'd sprinkled a few crumbs on top? What about a salad, with *pre-baked* supermarket croutons? Does it even have to be food? Maybe Ada could have stuck a chocolate finger in someone's hair and entered that?'

'Oh shut up!' Veronica yelled. The hallway was starting to get congested, as more Outlaws who'd finished their lunch came to see what the commotion was about. 'You're just peeved because your boyfriend lost. If Mary Berry beat him you'd still find something to gripe over. How about showing a bit of grace and decorum for once?'

'Decorum?' Helen cried. '*Me?* Me show some decorum?'

'Ruddy Nora, that's what I said. No need to blather on about it.' Veronica flapped her hands in a mean mockery.

'Excuse me!' Nora Montgomery interrupted, her face turning purple. 'Tom and Pippa have already asked you, numerous times, not to use my name as a curse! It's bullying and discrimination and I've had enough of it. Time for the bullied to fight back!'

Before anyone could stop her, she picked up her walking stick and poked Veronica in her rather hefty stomach.

Thankfully, because I was quite honestly not up for dealing with a mass brawl, my parents and Lance appeared. Leaving them to it, I fled into my office, bursting into tears as soon as the door closed behind me.

## 28

A second after I'd hidden in my office, the door opened and Elliot stepped in.

'Oh, Jessie.' He took three strides to where I was leaning against my desk, sobbing angry, frustrated sobs, and wrapped his arms around me.

A small part of my brain wondered for the hundredth time how the more I determined to stay away from Elliot Ollerton, the more I seemed to end up spending time with him.

After a minute or so of uncontrolled crying, I managed to calm down enough to pull away.

'Oh, you've got a...' I pointed to a pale streak on his blue shirt. 'Was that me?'

Elliot reached out a slow hand towards the hair at the side of my face and carefully, as if scooping up a butterfly, wiped a grape-sized blob of cream onto the end of one finger.

'That's been on my hair the whole time,' I said. Standing so close to him, I was suddenly aware of every hot pulsation of blood through my veins.

Elliot's dark eyes fixed on mine, so tender and brimming with concern that it made me want to cry again. We stayed there, looking at each other, him holding his finger up, me not caring at all that I looked a complete wreck, because right then that was exactly how I felt.

The blob of cream plopped off the end of his finger onto the wooden floor.

'Oh, right.' I sprang away, grabbing a clump of tissues out of the box on Mum's desk. 'Sorry.' I bent down to wipe the floor while he brushed at his shirt.

'Here.' He held the tissue out once I'd stood up again. 'You've still got...'

'Right. Yes. Thanks.' I took a fresh tissue and did my best to wipe the remaining mess out of my hair.

'Out there, that was... I don't even know what that was.'

'Savage? Chaos?' I pulled a wry smile.

'Worse than the competitive dads at football, that's for sure.' He frowned. 'Are you okay? I mean, I know you've just been crying, so clearly not. But was this a particularly bad morning, or do they often reduce you to tears?'

'Oh, no. That's not why I was crying,' I said. 'Well, it was the icing on top of the many layered cake, that tipped me into tears. But it's not the main reason.'

'Okay.' Elliot nodded thoughtfully. 'Do you have time to tell me what the main layer is? If you want to, of course. I won't be offended if it's none of my business.'

'Oh no!' I glanced at the clock on the wall. One forty-five. Fifteen minutes into group two's baking time. I tugged my phone out of my pocket; there were two messages from Mum.

Ceasefire holding for now. Dad's in the kitchen keeping an eye. Make yourself and Elliot a drink and take as long as you need.

And don't worry – I've saved you samples of the best round one entries!

I thought about Elliot's offer while making us both tea. Did I want to tell him the main reason I was so emotional? I decided that I did. For different reasons. Some of them better off not thinking about right then.

'I had a call with Seb last night,' I said, handing him a mug.

He squinted one eye at me in apology.

'My boyfriend.' I stopped, as the memory of the conversation we'd had caused my throat to clench up. 'Well, I think he's still my boyfriend.'

'What happened?'

I took a sip of tea, pausing to appreciate the soothing warmth. 'It was supposed to be a video date. We'd agreed to eat together, dress up, have a decent conversation. It's been days since a proper call so I was really looking forward to it.' I blew out a long sigh. 'When he answered his phone, he was in a bar. There was a man and a woman with him. He'd clearly forgotten, although he pretended he hadn't. He was also drunk. I know it's later there, and it was his day off, but he could at least have waited for us to get drunk together. So there I am, in my slinky dress, with a plate of pasta and a glass of wine, and there he is, laughing with some woman in a bikini top, downing shots.'

'Ouch.'

'Yes. But what *really* hurt was after he'd managed to drag himself to a table outside where he could actually hear me, he started rambling on about how hard he was finding it being away from me, and then.' I stopped, swallowed, blinked back the sting of his words before I could repeat them. 'He asked if I'd prefer it if we were non-exclusive. Just until he got back.'

'Ah.'

Elliot took a gulp of his drink. I loved that he didn't jump in with his opinion, calling Seb names or telling me how I ought to feel.

'Given that the topic has never come up, once, since he asked if I'd like to be exclusive three years ago, I could guess what he'd prefer.'

'Did you ask him?'

I shrugged. 'He could tell from my reaction that he'd blindsided me, and not in a good way. He started to backtrack, saying it was just a thought and only because he felt so awful making me wait for him, but it was mostly drunken ramblings. I asked if he could call me when he was sober so we could talk properly, and he got offended. The next thing I knew, bikini woman had appeared with more drinks and he ended the call.'

'I'm really sorry.'

We sat there for a moment, sipping our tea.

'We're supposed to be getting engaged once he comes back,' I said, with a bitter laugh. 'I knew there was a chance, of course, that we'd drift apart. Or crash and burn. But he's always been so keen to reassure me that he loves me and is completely committed.' My voice broke again. 'I'm such a fool.'

'No,' Elliot said, leaning forwards on Dad's chair. 'Trusting the man who's loved you for years doesn't make you a fool.' He paused. 'Could he have said it because he genuinely thought it was the kind thing to do?'

'Or because a half-naked, attractive woman was buying him drinks?' I shook my head. 'Who knows? And how can I find out, when he's all the way over there, and I'm here, and even if he does call me back, sober and sorry, who's to know what the truth is?' I took a deep breath. 'I've been treated like crap by a lot of men. Mostly because I've let them. For all sorts of reasons. I've learned never to trust, to believe. But Seb was different. He's my fresh start.

He's my only hope.' I was crying again now. 'He's my chance to get out of here again.'

'To get out of here?' Elliot sat back. I was too distraught to take much notice.

'You've all paid me to do this ridiculous project, because you see me as some sort of relationship expert. I am. I've had more relationships than the three of you put together. More than I can count. Oh, I am an expert. In dysfunctional, destructive relationships. All of them with liars, cheats and wasters. Including one who kept a pig in his bedroom. And then the *one time* I'm with a good, kind, lovely man, who wants to *marry me*. Me! World class failure me! This happens.' I stopped then, realising how self-pitying I must sound, took a couple of slow, shuddering breaths, and tried to get a grip. 'In fact that's not true. About it being the one time. An age ago, when I was a whole different person, a good, kind man loved me then. I'd give anything to be that Jessie again.'

Elliot reached out and took hold of my hand. 'You are still that Jessie. I knew you then, an age ago, and you are still her, in all the best ways.'

I knew I needed to get back to the kitchen. I'd allowed my personal life to sabotage enough jobs. But once again I found it far too difficult to tear myself away from Elliot's comforting presence.

'It's the same for you,' I said, eventually, placing my empty mug on the desk.

Elliot gave me the look that had become so familiar, telling me he needed more information.

'You said I was still the old Jessie.' I did my best to meet his eye so he knew how much I meant this. 'You're still the old Elliot, too. In all the ways that matter.'

He carefully placed his mug beside mine, ducking his head before glancing up at me. 'And that's a good thing?'

*If only you knew.*

I waited for half a dozen hammering heartbeats before replying.

'You still make a mean egg and jam sandwich.'

'Right. Well, in that case, thank you very much.'

'You're welcome.'

'I'll be back here for the meeting next week. I'm not busy on the bank holiday, so Thursday is fine. Oh, and Jessie.' He paused as he reached the main entrance. 'Whatever you do, don't let anyone treat you like a fool. Them,' he nodded down the corridor, 'or anyone else.'

* * *

Seb messaged me a guilt-wracked apology later that evening. Was it the sorry of a man who'd cheated on his girlfriend? Or simply one who'd messed up what was supposed to be a lovely date?

If he'd bothered to call me, instead of copping out with a message, I might have been able to work that out. Instead, I decided to shove it to join all the other emotional debris squatting in the back of my mind. The sorry truth was that even if he'd done something with another woman, it was a blip I was prepared to forgive and forget if it meant he came back to me.

* * *

Saturday was the penultimate match of the Harriers' season. The boys were away again, up against a team from another local village. Ibrahim and Jackson, two of our best players, couldn't make it, but the remaining nine were raring to go as they started their warm-up.

'Okay, boys,' Elliot called them together for a pre-match talk. 'The Rangers are a pretty good side. In the tournaments last season, they won every game.'

'Well they're about to find out what it's like to lose!' Wodger stuck his hands on his hips defiantly.

'That's a great attitude,' Elliot went on. 'I hope you boys play to win. But at the same time, don't be too disheartened if they manage to slip some goals in. They're fast, and strong, and have been playing together for twice as long as you.'

He spent a few minutes going over the extremely simple tactics we'd chatted about at breakfast the day before, then asked if there were any questions.

'Yes.' Jan waved his hand in the air. 'How are we going to score any goals if Ibrahim and Jackson aren't here?'

Some of the boys started arguing against that question, while others chimed in their agreement. Spotting that Elliot was overwhelmed by all the talking at once, I stepped forwards, holding up my hands.

'Hey!' I repeated myself a couple of times until I had everyone's attention. 'You've scored three goals this post-Christmas season, am I right? In how many games?'

'Thirteen,' Wilf answered.

'So in eleven games, you didn't score a goal. But have you had fun, playing together?'

There was a general murmur of assent.

'Have you bonded as a team, got fitter and learned absolutely loads about football, improving with every match?'

Another yes.

'So, what makes this time any different? Get out there, play your best, encourage each other, enjoy yourselves and if we win, we win. If we score, we score. If we lose a million-nil, that's okay. Either way we'll have learned something, and be one step closer to winning our first match.'

'Winning the Sherwood Forest Cup!' Dyson yelled.

'Winning the FA Cup!'

'The *World* Cup!'

'That's more like it! Now get out there and show them what makes the Houghton Harriers under nines so brilliant.'

As the opposing team swaggered onto the pitch, they eyed up the Harriers with growing grins of contempt.

'What's that metal thing on his leg?' one of them sneered, pointing at Fabian.

'Woah! That one only has one hand!' another gasped. 'I hope he does the throw-ins.'

'Settle down, boys.' The referee, an eighteen-year-old girl who'd only recently qualified, glared.

Those boys were not going to settle down.

By half-time, I'd lost count of how many goals had smashed into the back of the Harriers' goal. Jan, starting to wilt after number nine, had been swapped with Dyson and then Wilf, to no avail. Almost all the team had retreated into defence, but it made no difference. The other side gleefully knocked our less steady boys over, tackled them mercilessly on the rare occasions we managed to get close to the ball, and – worst of all – celebrated every goal with a spiteful superiority that started to wear on even Wodger.

'Come on, now.' Elliot gathered them into a half-time huddle. 'It's not all bad. You've done some great passing – Olly, Jan, you held them at bay for a good couple of minutes. Dyson, I think that's the most shots at goal you've ever saved.'

'Yeah,' a boy called Timmo droned in reply. 'Because it's about a hundred times as many as usual.'

'Can't we just end the game now?' Jan asked.

'Yeah,' another boy added. 'They keep laughing at us.'

'One of them called me a stupid dumbhead,' Fabian said, causing Elliot's face to set like concrete.

'He said what?'

'They all keep saying things.' Wilf folded his arms. 'Every time they get close to us, they whisper something horrible.'

'They're nasty bullies, and we don't want to play with bullies!' Jan said.

'I don't mind losing, but I don't like being called names.' Fabian sounded close to tears.

'You're right.' I'd never seen Elliot look so grim. 'Wait here with Jessie, please.'

And before I could stop him, he'd marched over to the other team, lounging about drinking out of matching, branded water bottles.

'Are you aware of this?' Elliot ground out, coming to a stop about a foot away from the Rangers manager's nose.

'Do you want to take a few steps back?' he replied, folding his arms.

'Not really. I want you to talk to your team about showing respect for the boys they're playing against. You know, sportsmanship?'

'Respect, against that lot?' The coach grinned, turning away in dismissal.

Oh boy. I quickly told the Harriers to stay where they were, and hurried over. Elliot looked like a volcano ready to blow. Just as I reached him he grabbed the manager's arm and spun him back around.

'Pretty clear where your team gets their code of conduct from,' he snapped.

'Yeah? It's just as clear where yours get their complete lack of ability.' He turned away again, only this time he muttered a word under his breath that I prayed none of his team had used on the pitch earlier.

'What?'

I tried to move in front of Elliot, but the Rangers manager side-stepped me.

'I said, you're a bunch of—'

'Shut up.' Elliot gave him a rough shove in the chest, causing him to stagger back several paces before righting himself, lowering one shoulder as he prepared to charge.

Suddenly, as if out of nowhere, Olly's dad smacked into the side of the manager, knocking him to the ground with a yell.

Then all hell broke loose.

Some of the Rangers team clustered around the two men, now rolling about on the ground with their arms around each other's necks. A couple of them burst into noisy tears. A few more hurtled over to the Harriers, uttering a war cry that made my hair stand on end. Various parents from both sides started yelling as they ran towards their children. In the chaos I spotted several more shoves and at least three punches being thrown. One mum threw her coffee over the pair still wrestling on the grass. The referee sprinted up, but the poor girl had no idea how to handle the pandemonium.

I tried to elbow my way through to Elliot, to help him move to somewhere quieter, where he could calm down, but it was impossible to reach past the adults either shouting in his face or attempting to drag him away. As they shepherded him towards the club house in a big clump, I caught one glimpse of his face.

Distorted with anguish and confusion, his expression said it all.

*I knew I couldn't do this. It's all my fault.*

I went to go with him, but he jerked his head at the Harriers, who were mostly now huddled with a few parents and supporters. Giving him as reassuring a nod as I could manage, I went to assist the Harriers' manager in the best way I could: by taking care of his team.

## 29

On Sunday evening, the Boys to Men project members convened at the kitchen table for a progress update. It was about the last thing I felt like doing, after such a rough week, but as Arthur pointed out, they were paying me.

'Ta-da!' Arthur waved a proud hand at a plate of caramel short-bread in the middle of the table, with a pot of tea and four mugs.

'Very nice.' I picked up one of the crumbly golden slices. 'Nicked some leftovers from the picnic, I see.'

'Well, yeah.' Isaac was sitting beside Arthur. 'But it shows we put thought into obtaining snacks in advance. And we got an actual teapot, with matching mugs. Come on, sis, this is genuine progress.'

'You're right.' I glanced at Elliot, at the end of the table, opposite me. Back straight, face neutral. In the depth of his eyes a raging hurricane. 'Even if it doesn't always seem like it, you've all come a long way.'

'So, what's next?' Arthur asked, handing me a mug that he'd poured tea into with a flourish. 'One month down, two to go.'

I couldn't help smiling. 'Arthur, you've seen Elsa, what, three times this past week?'

Arthur went pink with pleasure. 'Well, yes, but one of those was youth group.'

'And the two hours after youth group that you sat in the garden snogging?'

'We were talking!' He wriggled about on the wonky stool in protest. 'Mostly talking.'

'Anyway. You have the girl of your dreams, it's going great. What more could you want?'

'This. Obviously.' Arthur stood up, rummaged in the pocket of his giant cotton shorts and gingerly placed a ring box on the table.

'Bro.' Isaac stared at the box, a slow grin of disbelief spreading across his face.

Arthur nodded his head slowly as his gaze travelled around each of us. 'Time for the game to hit the second half, baby. And this boy needs to become a man damn quick because he ain't chancing a last-minute own goal.'

I took a few sips of tea, hoping that one of Arthur's friends would step in to address this madness.

'Jessie?' Isaac turned his delight in my direction. 'Thoughts?'

'Okay.' I took another sip, stalling for time. 'You already told me about the ring. Can we safely say that this is going to wait until the end of the second half? You aren't planning on proposing any time soon?'

'Of course not!' Arthur guffawed, causing a momentary flood of relief. 'An Elsa-worthy proposal takes time to prepare. I will resist the urge to declare the true extent of my feelings until the party.'

'What party?'

'The engagement party, of course! It would be ungentlemanly to propose until I've met her family and asked for their blessing. They're travelling up from Hampshire, so I had a stroke of brilliance and decided to combine the meeting and the proposal into one event. From there, the obvious thing to do was to make it into a party.'

'An engagement party?'

'Yes. Did I not make that clear?'

'Arthur, people have an engagement party after the proposal, to celebrate getting engaged. What's not clear is that you seem to be hoping to propose to Elsa at the party itself.'

'Incorrect!'

'Oh, thank goodness for that.'

'No hoping about it! I *am* most definitely, 100 per cent going to propose at the party.'

'Okay, so when is this party?' I asked, clinging to the fact that Arthur had said it wouldn't be any time soon.

'Like I said, there's a lot to do so I'm not rushing it, despite the torment of having to wait. I've booked the Barn for Sunday, 17 July. Everyone I know will be invited, but you need to keep it quiet. She thinks it's just going to be a normal Sunday picnic.'

I could feel the blood draining into my feet. Isaac, the git, was still grinning. Elliot, on the other hand, had done no more than twitch one eyebrow during this whole conversation.

'That's two months away.'

'Correctamundo, Jessica.'

'You've been going out for two weeks.'

'Your point being?'

I took a couple of slow, steadying breaths. 'Arthur, I know that you've decided Elsa is the one for you, and she seems to like you back, which is great.'

'Love,' Arthur interrupted. 'She *loves* me back.'

'Has she told you that?'

'She doesn't need to,' he huffed.

'Okay, well however you both feel, if you're going to do something as huge as proposing, the first time you've even met her family, then at the very least do it in private so that she can give you an honest answer without feeling any pressure. It'll be awful for both of you if the answer isn't yes.'

Once again, Arthur shook his head at my foolishness. 'She's going to say yes. That'll be her honest answer. Why would there be any pressure?'

'Arthur, you've known her a couple of months! You'll have been dating for...'

'Ten weeks,' Elliot said, causing me to jerk my head in surprise.

'I'm not saying that she'll give you a straight-out no.' I tried to make my exasperation sound more like friendly concern. 'But she might want some time to think about it. It's a bit of a bolt from the blue. And it'll be much easier and less awkward all round if you give her a chance to say that away from your family and friends.'

'So what you're saying is that I should ask her first, before the party?' Arthur screwed up his face. 'I hate that idea.'

'What I'm strongly advising, as your relationship coach, who's been 100 per cent successful so far, is that you enjoy the picnic, and then think about proposing once Elsa's family have had a chance to get to know you. It's a lot to ask for their blessing when you've only just met.'

'Yes, but Elsa's told them all about me. She tells her mum everything.'

'What if they don't give their blessing? If they ask you to wait?'

'That's a completely pointless question.' Arthur was growing more belligerent the longer this conversation went on. 'Elsa's family wouldn't stand in the way of her happiness!'

'Isaac, Elliot?' I asked, desperate for some backup. 'What do you think?'

Isaac shrugged. 'I'm hardly an expert, here. I've no idea what Connie thinks about me. But I do know it took me about three seconds to be sure I wanted to spend the rest of my life with her. I say go for it, if that's what your heart's telling you. What's the worst that can happen?'

'Um, he humiliates his girlfriend, and himself, in front of all their friends and family, irreparably damaging their relationship? She freaks out and breaks up with him because she thinks he's being reckless about something so important, which is a massive red flag? Arthur loses the woman he loves and spends the rest of his life alone, mourning her?'

'I agree with Isaac.' Elliot glanced up from under his brow. 'Arthur, it's your life. Only you know how you feel. Don't let anyone' – his eyes flashed at me for a nanosecond – 'convince you to do something that you know in your gut isn't right for you. You'll only regret it.' He stood up and dumped his mug in the sink, Penny crawling out from under the table to join him. 'If we're done here, I'm going for a run.'

* * *

'He doesn't mean it,' Isaac said, with uncharacteristic sympathy once Elliot had disappeared out the back door.

'You think?' Prior to this meeting, I'd seen Elliot once since we'd driven home from the match in silence, and that was only as I'd entered the kitchen and he'd immediately walked out. He'd forfeited the final round of Chimney Cup darts against Arthur on Saturday evening, and skipped the Sunday picnic.

A full report would be made to both Houghton Harriers Football Club, the youth league that the teams belonged to, as well as being gossiped about to everyone who knew anyone who'd been there. Which meant by Sunday the whole village knew that either Elliot was a hero who'd defended his team with valour, or a liability who'd brought disgrace to the club and the village.

Initially the Rangers manager had threatened to press charges for assault on both Elliot and Russell, but when multiple witnesses pointed out that they'd seen him squeezing both hands around Russell's neck, as well as heard him call a team of young boys the kind of word that meant instant disqualification from the league, he settled for a torrent of yet more abusive language and booting the Harriers' lucky ball, signed by various Nottingham Forest players, over the hedge.

Connie had messaged as soon as I'd got home from the Barn. Elliot had clearly delayed his announcement to the team WhatsApp group until after the picnic.

Elliot's withdrawing the team from the tournament! Did he speak to you about this?

He hasn't spoken to me at all since it happened

The boys'll be devastated!! You have to change his mind

Seeing their faces on Saturday, I'm not sure any of them will want to play football ever again

Are you joking? That's not what Elliot taught them. They're more determined than ever to show what they're made of. Wilf spent three hours in Mum and Dad's garden yesterday afternoon practicing. THEY HAVE TO PLAY FOR THE SHERWOOD FOREST CUP

Before I'd had a chance to reply, she'd sent another message.

For Elliot's sake as much as the boys, he has to do this.

* * *

'Any chance you could talk to him for me?' I asked my brother, once we'd all helped ourselves to another piece of calorie-laden comfort food. 'The boys'll be gutted if they don't get to play in the tournament.'

'Connie's already messaged me. I can try, but in twelve years I've not found a way to change Elliot's mind once it's made up.'

'Speaking of Connie, can we get back to the next task in the project?' Arthur asked.

'Speaking of not being able to change a mind once it's made up, is there any point when you've already planned the big proposal and have no interest in my advice?'

'I am very interested in your advice,' Arthur retorted. 'I just reserve the right to reject it. I already acknowledged that I need to step it up before the party. I'm not hiring you to tell me *what* to do, Jessica. Your job is to get me ready to do it.'

'Okay.' I gave up. I had too much going on to spare any more energy fighting Arthur. 'How about we tackle the makeovers next?'

'Excellent!' Arthur nodded, eyes glistening with anticipation. 'I've been wondering about a statement outfit like Isaac's yellow number. Perhaps in green? Green is a great colour for redheads.'

I stood up. 'Before we go any further, would anyone else like a glass of wine?'

* * *

On Monday, I came home from dinner with my parents to find Connie and Isaac on the new sofa, Wilf squashed in between them, all eyes glued to two droids speeding through a desert dodging laser beams.

'Hey, how was your day?' I asked, presuming it wasn't terrible judging by the relaxed atmosphere and the glasses of gin and tonic on the new coffee table.

'It was the best day ever, but I don't want to talk about it now,' Wilf said, speaking so fast all the words blended into one.

'No problem,' I whispered, backing straight out again.

'So, was Wilf's assessment of the day accurate?' I'd left my garden chair and gone to interrogate Isaac as soon as I heard him come into the kitchen a few minutes later.

Isaac stuck his hands in the pockets of his favourite shorts, bought in a ramshackle market on a family trip to London when we were both seventeen. I counted at least three holes, but we could deal with that on Friday's shopping trip. He wrestled with how to answer for a few seconds. 'It was a good day.'

'I sense a but coming?'

He blew out a sigh as he flicked on the kettle. 'I think I managed to avoid being an arse. When I focus on Wilf, it's far easier to be myself. I mean' – he pulled a wry smile – 'to be the okay version of myself, not the immature, idiot one.'

'The Mum and Dad version,' I added.

'Exactly! Anyway, we had a good day. I'm glad we went. I think it even helped Connie having me there.'

He made the drinks and picked them up, ready to go.

'You forgot the but.'

'The what?' Isaac looked behind him, confused.

'You didn't tell me what the but was.'

'Oh. Right.' He frowned. 'I think, for the first time ever, I've found myself smack bang in the middle of the friend zone.'

'Ah.'

'With no clue how to get out of it.'

I waltzed over to the back door, where my book and tea were waiting. 'Good job you've hired someone who does, then, isn't it?'

Isaac put down the mugs and walked over to me, pulling me into a hug. 'I'm so glad you're home, sis. I know this is terrible, but every time Arthur drags me to church I pray that Seb is really, really crap at finding himself so you can stay longer.'

I thought about my shaky relationship. And then I thought about work, hanging out with new friends at Sunday picnics, cheering on a team of the best boys ever, Monday Mum and Dad days, and for the first time since arriving back, I wondered if Seb taking his time might not be the worst thing ever.

Then Elliot appeared, heading out for his evening run, and I remembered that I had a very good reason for Seb to come home as soon as possible.

## 30

I turned up to the promised girls' night at Connie's with a bottle of rhubarb gin, a tub of peanut butter ice-cream and only the tiniest agenda about nudging Isaac out of the friend zone, should the conversation meander in that direction at any point.

Irrespective of the Boys to Men project, did my loyalties tip slightly more towards the man with whom I'd shared a womb, rather than the woman who I'd known for a few weeks?

Absolutely.

Not only that, but I loved Wilf and I really liked Connie and I happened to agree that they'd make a great couple.

Not that I was going to bring it up, of course. But if *she* happened to bring it up... well, aren't friends meant to be honest?

But to my dismay, she took that topic in a completely unexpected direction.

Connie lived in a tiny Victorian terrace that she'd renovated into a gorgeous home, making ingenious use of every nook and cranny so that rather than feeling cramped, it was delightfully cosy. The downstairs consisted of two rooms, one behind the other, but we took our drinks and snacks outside to the small square of lawn. It was the first day of June, and the air was heady with summer. The evening sunshine lit pots of peonies with a hazy glow. The scent of sizzling burgers wafted over the fence, and we could hear sheep bleating in the field beyond.

After taking a moment to savour the surroundings, closing her eyes and taking in a couple of slow breaths, Connie ditched the small talk and got straight to it.

'I don't know what the general rules are; you'll have done far more girlie nights than me. What do you think about setting a limit on time spent talking about men?' Connie continued.

'Um, yeah, okay.'

'I get that we're two young women, we're bound to end up mentioning your boyfriend, my complete lack of a boyfriend, blah blah blah, but there are so many other, fascinating, things to talk about, aren't there?'

'Absolutely.'

'I'm guessing you get to discuss other things with your house-mates. Politics, current affairs, culture.' She took a giant handful of popcorn. 'When I come home from work, it's either droids, football or medieval battles. Preferably droids playing football then fighting a medieval battle. You know?'

'To be honest, that's not too different from Chimney Cottage. You've met my housemates?'

She smiled. 'So you're up for some sophisticated conversation this evening, then?' She smoothed out a crease in her emerald jumpsuit.

'I certainly am.' I didn't dare look down at my flared jeans and baggy shirt.

Leaning forwards, we chinked glasses.

'Perfect. Only before that, I need, ooh, fifteen minutes to grill you on the elusive Sebastian?' Connie waggled her eyebrows. 'Then I might have some half-decent gossip about me.'

I filled her in on what had been happening, finishing with the stilted video chat we'd managed the previous evening. Connie sat back in her chair, eyes narrowed in thought.

'You've been together, what, more than three years? Has he ever acted like this before?'

I shook my head. 'But he's never been off travelling the world without me before.'

'How do you feel about what he said?'

'About it being okay to see other people?' My shoulders automatically hunched. 'If he was here, I'd hate it. After being committed for so long, how could it mean anything other than, "I'm bored of you"? But with him being away, as a temporary thing, what if it's the only way to make it work?'

'If it is, are you okay with that?' She frowned. 'I know we're all different when it comes to these things, but I couldn't just pick up where we left off knowing he'd been out there doing who knows what.'

'But is it better to be honest about it, or wonder if he's simply doing it anyway, behind my back?'

'Jessie, if you've been clear that you hate the idea, then he shouldn't want to do it either with your permission or in secret. Maybe the question here is do you trust him to put how you feel above some holiday fling with bikini girl?'

'Maybe I have to prioritise how *he* feels, for now.' I tried to ignore the faint look of pity creeping onto Connie's face. 'Maybe that's the only way we can stay together.'

She was quiet for a moment. 'Is it worth staying together, if it means making yourself miserable?'

I shrugged. 'Breaking up will make me feel worse.'

She waited for me to elaborate.

'It's hard to explain quite how bad life was before Seb. I was like this dented pinball, ricocheting about from one disaster to another.

Seb steadied me. He gave me the stability of a job, a home. Security. I'm honestly terrified at the thought of how bad my life would end up if I had to go it alone.'

Connie gently took my drink out of my hand and placed it on the wicker table. She firmly took both my hands in hers and looked me right in the eye.

'Jessie, *this* is where you are. You have a great job. A home. A busy social life. Friends and family who love you. You are *thriving* without him.'

Before I could process that bombshell, a figure in a fabric suit of armour popped up beside Connie's chair, causing both of us to jump an inch off our seats.

'Wilf,' Connie said with a resigned tone. 'Why aren't you in bed?'

'I can't sleep.'

'Okay, but can you remember that we agreed you'd read for a bit if that happened, so I can talk to Jessie?'

His lips flattened into a stubborn line. 'I want to talk to Jessie; she's my friend too.'

'You can talk to her another time. It's past your bedtime, and you're coming to the Barn with me tomorrow. You don't want to be too tired to help Isaac, do you?'

'No I don't want to be too tired but I can't get to sleep!' Wilf's voice rose in agitation.

'That's why I said you could read.'

'But that won't help because I have a question and when I've stopped reading I'll just start thinking about the question again so I'll *never* be able to sleep, ever again! And then I'll be so tired at the Barn, Isaac will get cross with me and not want to be my friend any more. And then—'

Connie deftly took hold of his hands to stop them jerking, and spoke slowly and calmly enough to interrupt his panicked torrent. 'What's the question?'

He stopped. 'What?'

'What is the question that's stopping you getting to sleep?'

'Oh! Why didn't Tendro use his freeze spray to stop the megalorian from ripping off the chain-thingies that were keeping the tentacles from getting out of his mouth?'

'Right.' Connie nodded. 'I didn't spot that. Any ideas, Jessie?'

Wilf turned to me, hope burning in his eyes.

'I'm going to be honest with you; I never made it past episode two.'

'What?' Wilf looked aghast. 'But you have both entire series *at your house*! You could watch it any time you want.'

'Yeah. I've been quite busy lately.'

'Too busy to watch *Droid Defenders*?' Wilf shook his head. 'You need to get your priorities straight, Jessie.'

'You're probably right, thanks Wilf.'

'Okay.' Connie was reading her phone. 'Tendro couldn't use his freeze spray because the megalorian is so hot it would turn to steam as soon as it touched his scales. It happened in season one, episode five when they were cornered in the dungeon.'

'Oh!' Wilf jumped up and down, a miniature knight in polyester armour. 'I remember, I remember. When that big bird with the round thing in its beak came and swooped Tendro up at the last second before his head snapped off! *Yes*! That's why! Phew! I'm glad he didn't try; that freeze spray runs out really quickly. Thanks, Mum.'

And before we could say goodnight, he'd gone.

'Thanks, Isaac,' Connie said, her mouth curling up in a gentle smile as another message pinged through.

'Always there when you need him,' I couldn't resist saying.

'You know,' she said, putting the phone down. 'He really has been there a lot, lately. That day at Newstead Abbey was brilliant. It's just... so stress free when Isaac's there. Like, rather than finding Wilf a complication, or something to be managed, he steps in and helps. Sometimes before I've even noticed that Wilf needs it. When Wilf started getting nervous about a horse coming too close, without causing a fuss, Isaac just quietly asked him if he wanted to move to a different section where he could see better.'

She went to take another handful of popcorn, before noticing it had all gone. 'I guess all that tension between us must have been work stress. If he invited us out for the day, he can't find me that annoying. Unless he's got a secret passion for local history and couldn't think of anyone else to ask.'

'I can promise that he doesn't find you annoying. And he really likes Wilf.' I took another sip of gin to congratulate myself on resisting a comment about Isaac's true secret passion.

'Ugh.' She sat back, releasing a noisy sigh. 'It makes such a difference when we hang out with someone who gets my son. Ooh!' She sat up again, quickly, eyes lighting up. 'Can you bear to talk about men for a few more minutes, because if I don't get this out there, I'll burst. I have literally no one else to tell this to apart from Mum, and as far as she's concerned I can't go near a man without getting pregnant, so I already know what she'll say.'

'Okay?' I braced myself, determined that however I responded to this, it would be as a great friend, and an even better twin.

'Someone asked me out.' She stopped, one hand pressed against her chest. 'And I think I'm going to say yes!'

* * *

Thursday was the first of the special bank holidays celebrating the Queen's Jubilee. Enough of the Barn's regulars were royal fans that instead of closing, we'd planned a celebration. As well as decorating every inch of the ground floor with purple and silver bunting, thanks to the new embroidery group, we'd opened the Barn up to family members for the afternoon, and set up games in the garden including croquet, giant Jenga and boules. There was even a small bouncy castle in one corner. Mum had tried to insist only children could bounce, but their grand and great-grandparents were having none of it. A few of the Outlaws had dug out their instruments and formed a brass-band, now tootling away in the shade of a tree.

'Isn't this marvellous!' one woman exclaimed. 'It's the first time in years my Gerry's had his trombone out.'

'We can tell,' Arabella Goose declared. 'It's the first time in years I've been grateful for the deterioration in hearing in my right ear. At least I can position myself so it's no more than a background fart.'

'How very rude.'

'Rude, but true,' someone added to a chorus of nods.

Wendy had come up with an afternoon tea fit for the monarchy, including delicate sandwiches and lavender scones spread with thick, clotted cream and blackberry jam. There were miniature quiches and vol-au-vents stuffed with coronation chicken or herby cheese filling, and seemingly endless sweet treats to go alongside the pots of tea or homemade lemonade.

It was all very charming until Veronica and Vivienne Vincent whipped out their water pistols.

'Death to the monarchy!' Viv shouted, aiming a squirt at Hetty, who'd made the mistake of dressing up as the Queen.

'Power to the people!' her sister roared, shooting a blast of freezing water straight up, that promptly came down and soaked her green bristly head.

'How dare you insult Her Royal Highness!' a woman called Natalia screeched, jumping up from her seat beside Hetty and throwing her glass of water at Viv's face. Whether she meant her friend or the actual Queen was anybody's guess, and immediately irrelevant as chairs were pushed back, water receptacles were snatched up and the peace and gentility of the Barn garden erupted into all-out war.

'I counted at least eight water guns,' Lance panted, a few minutes later as we sheltered behind a tree. 'This was a premeditated attack.'

'Thank goodness the jugs are plastic.' I winced as a man staggered past in sodden wet trousers, closely followed by another one carrying a water bomb.

'Shut the doors!' Dad cried, as he attempted to shield Olive, one of our oldest Outlaws who was in wheelchair, with his body. 'Cut them off from the source!'

'Oh, stop blathering and get out of the way!' Olive cried, leaning past him brandishing a pistol that was at least half as big as her. 'I had a perfect shot at Freddie Woodthorpe. He was a fiend to babysit.'

'Babysit?' Dad tried to gently get hold of her weapon, but she was waving it about too much. 'He's eighty-seven! Surely it's time to let that one go.'

'He didn't let go when his tiny little teeth were clamped around my wrist! I've still got a scar.'

Meanwhile, a couple of the other staff members had ducked and dodged their way through the melee and were now guarding the terrace doors, only allowing in those seeking refuge, once they'd been frisked for weapons. Poor Mum was still trying to persuade people to stand down, even as she glanced tearfully at the soggy remains of the afternoon tea.

'We should blockade the outside tap,' Lance said.

'Where is it?'

'A standpipe by the chicken coop wall.' He nodded to where a queue was forming. 'With no access to the main building, they'll soon run out of ammunition once we shut that down.'

I nodded, taking in the sight of a lawn full of older people, ducking and shooting and chucking bowls of water at each other with howls of glee, while their grandchildren capered about in the wet grass, the droplets on their bare skin glistening in the sunshine.

Madeline was perched on her favourite bench, gripping her sides as she wept with laughter.

I shook a strand of sopping wet hair off my face. 'Maybe give them a few more minutes?'

## 31

Once aching legs began to tire and stiff backs seize up, we guarded the outside tap while Mum and Dad negotiated a ceasefire. Before anyone came up with any more mischief, I took the opportunity to shoo them inside the main hall for the final entertainment of the day. The one I'd been looking forward to the most.

'Okay, everyone. We couldn't have a Queen's Jubilee party without a tea dance, could we?'

I ignored the collective groan as people sank into the chairs positioned around the edge of the room. 'I expect everyone who can to get their booties on the dancefloor, and for those who can't, I'm coming to get you anyway.'

Lance and another staff member whipped the curtains closed, plunging the room into semi-darkness. At the same time, the disco balls usually saved for wedding receptions flicked on, sending hundreds of tiny lights spinning across the shocked and delighted faces. Most importantly, loud enough for even Bertie's broken hearing aid to pick up, the room was filled with the 'Hippy Hippy Shake'.

The dancefloor was shaking before we got to the second verse.

* * *

This was where Elliot found me, oblivious to the time ticking, one arm supporting Madeline as she leant on her walker, the other hand gripping Ada's as we na-na-naahed our hearts out to 'Hey Jude'.

I spotted him standing in the doorway into the foyer, hands in his pockets, mouth slightly open as he took in the mass of sweaty, dishevelled bodies having the time of their lives.

Letting go of Madeline, I held up a finger to indicate that I'd be with him in a minute, prompting the first smile I'd seen from him all week as he nodded, settling up against the door frame to wait for me. That smile made my breath tighten in my chest. Seeing Elliot so low had reawakened the grimy accusations that I'd done so well at burying since we'd re-established our friendship.

*This is your fault.*

I knew that wasn't true.

*Doesn't matter if you didn't mean it. If you were young. If it was ages ago. Still your fault.*

It was a very different experience, singing along while aware that someone – someone I'd once been in love with, and certainly still loved – was watching. Those nahs felt as though they were never going to end. Once the song had faded out, I asked Mum to help Madeline back to a comfortable chair to catch her breath and with an apologetic glance at the clock, hurried through the crowd to the doorway.

'Sorry, sorry, I totally lost track of the time.' We'd agreed a three-thirty meeting, and it was now almost four.

'You're a lot closer to the correct time than I was, so I suppose I can let it slide,' Elliot said as we started walking towards the office. 'Besides, I wouldn't have wanted to miss that sight for anything.'

He grinned. After almost a week of bleak, distant glances, this made my heart ache. 'I can't remember the last time you looked so...'

'Embarrassing? Sticky?'

'Alive.' He paused to let me enter the office first. 'You looked completely, unashamedly alive.'

'You should have seen me at the water fight, earlier. Ron Potter chucking a mug of freezing cold water down the back of my neck certainly woke me up.'

It was worth it to see the delight spread across his face. 'A water fight?'

We spent a few minutes chatting about the day while I made us both a drink, and then got down to business. Or rather, we tried. We seemed to end up on one tangent after another, until Mum poked her head in and told me that they were going in five minutes, and if I wanted to stay any longer I'd have to lock up. Spurred on to race through the final arrangements, we met Mum and Dad jangling their keys by the front door, making no attempt to hide their smirks.

'Well done today. You put together a phenomenal celebration,' Dad said, before turning to Elliot. 'She did the Queen proud.'

Mum gave Elliot a playful nudge. 'Who'd have thought the monarchy could be so contentious among the older generation? But Jessie, you did an incredible job distracting them with your disco. You made today so special, you really deserve a celebration of your own, now.' She paused, quite possibly due to being unable to say anything else thanks to the huge, impish grin taking up most of her face. 'Maybe Elliot could join you? I mean, we'd love to, but we've got to file a report on the water fight. Helen slipped over and bruised her hip and her son is up in arms about it. Despite it being while she tried to turn the table cloth into a water slide. Anyway.' She gave a not-at-all-sorry sigh. 'These things must be done so I'm afraid it will be just the two of you.'

With that, she somehow managed to herd us out of the door and disappear.

I kept my eyes on the path ahead as we started walking home. 'Don't worry, after today the only celebration I'm up for is a mug of tea, and the one piece of cake I managed to salvage from the battlefield.'

'Yeah. I'm not really in the mood for celebrating either at the moment.'

'Elliot, you can't let one slip up—'

'It's not one, though. This was just the worst one since you've been around.'

My heart gave an agonising twist. 'That man was hideous. What he said was disgusting. A lot of people reckon that a shove was the least he deserved. And what about all the parents who joined in? Your reaction was mild in comparison.'

'Really?' Elliot stopped to look at me as we waited for a tractor to chug past, before crossing the road. 'Can you honestly tell me it was in any way okay for me to behave like that? Because I'm pretty sure the league won't see it that way.'

'Fine.' I tried to keep my voice steady. 'It wasn't okay. It was a bad example to the boys. You lowered yourself to his level, and all those other things you've told yourself since it happened.'

I ran an exasperated hand through my tangled mess of hair. 'But is *this* a good example, what you're doing now? Pulling out of the tournament, moping around, refusing to forgive yourself? Is that what you've been trying to teach them – mess up and that's it, you'd better give up?'

The storm that had persisted in Elliot's eyes all week tossed and turned. 'That is not what I'm doing.' He started walking again, long, angry strides that I had to practically jog to keep up with.

'I was very clear that I couldn't do this. I would fail them. Now I have. And the last thing...' He stopped, voice breaking. 'The *last thing* that those brilliant boys need or deserve is me for their coach.'

'I generally agree with about 99 per cent of what you say, Elliot, but that is a load of crap.'

'Don't push me on this, Jessie. Please.'

'Why? I'm not worried that you'll shove me back.'

'No.' He shook his head, which looked as though it bore ten years of struggle. 'But if you of all people push me right now, I might just break.'

\* \* \*

I was looking forward to Friday about as much as I would relish having Wendy over for dinner. The plan was that we'd all head into Nottingham together, then Isaac would be the first to undergo a makeover before he headed back to oversee the preparations for this Saturday's wedding. I knew about as much about men's fashion as I did women's – i.e. virtually nothing. Seb had worn black T-shirts and jeans to work, and blue, grey or white T-shirts with the same jeans on his rare days off. He had one 'going out shirt' and that was about it.

I'd never given much attention to what was in my wardrobe. There'd been times my 'wardrobe' had been nothing more than a couple of carrier bags, and I genuinely hadn't cared enough to spend serious time and effort on my appearance.

Nevertheless, here we were. Me with a list of supposedly stylish men's clothing shops, and far too many images of male models on my phone. Arthur with his red hair standing straight up from where he had been continually tugging on it in his excitement. Isaac shifting about, arms crossed defensively over his body. Elliot, always two steps behind them, wearing a careful expression to match his neatly ironed blue shirt, that was so perfectly Elliot even a professional stylist couldn't find anything more suitable for him to wear.

'Well, hello!' A shop assistant who looked about nineteen jumped out from behind a stack of jumpers the second we walked into the first shop.

'This is quite a crowd! Let me guess.' He stuck one finger on his chin. 'A wedding party? Which of you lucky guys is the groom?'

Arthur raised his hand. 'Guilty!'

'Congratulations!' He gave Arthur a quick once over. 'We've got some brand new, hot off the catwalk jackets that will be *fabulous* against your skin tone.'

'Perfect!' Arthur said, bouncing up and down on his toes.

'When's the big day?' The man led us towards a rack of jackets. 'Oh, I'm Cillian, by the way. And you are...?'

'Not actually getting married, yet,' Isaac interrupted. 'Though you can call him Arthur.'

The man whipped around to look at Isaac, mouth open in confusion.

'Sorry, but I haven't got much time and we aren't here to buy wedding suits.'

'Okaaaay...?' Cillian paused, clearly preferring to know the names of the random people he was serving.

'Isaac.'

'Isaac, perfect. So, if you aren't here to buy suits, how can I help you?'

'I need an outfit for my engagement party,' Arthur said.

'Oh, so you're engaged! Right. Perfect. The wedding togs will come later, then.'

'No,' Arthur said, with an oblivious grin. 'Not engaged yet, either.'

'They're looking for a couple of outfits each,' I said, before Arthur got around to mentioning the Boys to Men project and making us sound even sadder than we were. 'Smart casual, something to wear for an evening out with friends, or—'

'Basically, whatever you've got that will make it impossible for women to resist us, we want those,' Arthur added.

It was going to be a long day.

## 32

In the end, we only made it to the first few shops on my list. I'd bumbled on about a capsule wardrobe, statement pieces and other waffle regurgitated from the websites I'd scoured, and then spent two hours trying to coax them away from one extreme (a lavender boiler suit) or another (a virtually identical blue shirt to the five Elliot already owned). Arthur was more than happy to allow the shop assistants to treat him like their dress-up doll, with mixed results. Isaac ended up mostly sticking with me, despite objecting to most of my suggestions, which I knew from lifelong experience was mostly due to pure stubbornness, not because 'only creepy midlife crisis men wear patterned shirts'.

Elliot, on the other hand, preferred to browse alone, occasionally venturing into a changing room with a look of determination on his face, before leaving again seconds later, his expression one of faint disgust. For now, though, I had to focus on my brother. Elliot's time would come.

'So,' Isaac began, with a casual tone that I knew indicated he felt anything but. 'You were round at Connie's the other night.'

'I popped over for a couple of hours,' I murmured, mirroring his nonchalant tone as only a twin can do.

'Had a good time?'

'We did, thanks.' I pulled a lightweight jumper off a rack that I knew would make his eyes look amazing, and held it up. A completely futile attempt to get him off this topic.

He pretended to consider it, even going as far as fondling the fabric. 'What did you do?'

'We drank rhubarb gin and tonics and ate snacks in her garden.'

'So mostly talking, then.' He shook his head, no, to the sweater. I added it to the 'maybe' pile in my arms. 'She... happen to mention me?'

'She messaged you while I was there to ask about that ten-droid thing. So yes, your name came up.'

'And?' He stopped, grabbing a pair of purple leather trousers that looked skinny enough to fit Wilf and thrusting them at me. 'Don't make me sweat here, sis. You know what I'm asking.'

'Yes, and *you* know that it's not fair to ask me to blab about what my friend and I discussed in private.' I accepted the trousers then put them straight back on the shelf.

'Come on, I'll buy the sweater. I'll buy everything you recommend. The twin code says blabbing is obligatory under these circumstances.'

'You won't buy anything until you've tried it on first.' He had me with the twin code, though. I blew out a long sigh. 'Okay. I will say this. She really enjoyed the day at Newstead. She likes you, and most importantly she really likes how you are with Wilf.'

Isaac dropped his head in relief.

'However.'

'No,' he groaned. 'Leave it at she likes me.'

'Okay.' I started flicking through some T-shirts.

'I didn't mean that.' He bent so close that his breath tickled my ear, which he knew made me shiver in revulsion. 'I won't sleep, eat, or stop annoying you until I know the however.'

I stepped back, taking a couple of seconds to formulate an answer that would betray neither my brother nor my friend. 'You were right about being in the friend zone. But, honestly, I think for now that's a good place to be. Connie is deadly serious about who she's going to let into her and Wilf's life. Keep being there for her, showing her that you're a decent guy, without putting any expectations on her, and when it's the right time, she'll know that you're worth the risk.'

What I didn't tell my brother was that I was hoping Connie would soon realise Isaac's worth, because she was about to go on a date with Wodger's dad, who was, in my utterly biased opinion, nowhere near as good a match for her as my brother. Plus, he had a nervous giggle that made my innards clench.

By the time we were ready to leave the first shop, Isaac had agreed on a few basics that at least were free of holes or slogans that stopped being funny a decade ago. Arthur, however, had splurged on two suits, his first ever pair of jeans, several tops that could be worn with either, and a pair of green Converse. I had to hand it to Cillian; he knew his stuff. If you ignored Arthur from the eyebrows up, his vintage-style checked suit matched with a brightly coloured T-shirt looked a perfect combination of fun, quirky and even a tiny bit cool.

I think all of us had a lump in our throat. Cillian had to grab a pocket square from one of the mannequins to blot his eyes.

Isaac left for work, Arthur had an appointment for his first ever professional haircut (his mum and sister usually gave him a trim using their funeral parlour skills). That left Elliot.

'How are you getting on?' I asked, as we browsed the third shop, having made a swift exit from the second once we'd seen the four-figure price tags.

'I've got this.' He held up a white T-shirt.

'That's the same as the white T-shirt you already have.'

'No.' He frowned. 'Mine has a rounder collar. Look.'

'No, I won't look.' I grabbed it off him and shoved it back in a wrinkled pile on the table. 'I've said, several times, that you need this makeover the least. Your clothes are fine; they work for you. If you want white T-shirts and blue shirts then don't waste your money on new ones. If you want to try something different, that has to mean *different*.'

'A checked suit?'

'A checked *shirt*?'

Elliot appeared to be in pain. The shop assistant, this time a much older man, jumped in. 'Can I help at all?'

'No thanks, I prefer to trust my personal stylist,' Elliot said, in the kind of dismissive tone that I imagined men who take personal stylists shopping with them might adopt.

I waited for the man to wander off again. 'Okay, you've admitted that you trust me. From now on I get to decide what you take into the changing room.'

Nearly two hours and two shops later we had a non-blue shirt, a jumper and a multi-pack of socks.

I didn't mind. The truth was, there was very little I wanted to change about Elliot Ollerton.

* * *

Arthur had arranged to go to the cinema with Elsa that evening, and asked if she could pick him up. The rest of us huddled in anticipation in the living room, having insisted Arthur, practically unrecognisable with his new haircut and jeans, wait for her in prime position by the bookcase.

We all held our breath once I'd ushered her into the room.

'Hi.' She nodded, before going over and giving Arthur a peck on the cheek. 'Have you had a good day?'

'Yes,' Arthur replied, somewhat ominously.

'What did you get up to?' Elsa shifted her bag up higher on her shoulder, starting to realise something was up, but, to my astonishment, seemingly not sure what that was.

'Well, this!' Arthur said, holding out his hands.

'Um... what?'

'You don't notice anything different about him?' I asked.

Elsa took a few steps back for a proper look, forehead creasing as she inspected Arthur from top to bottom. The truth was, he appeared about a decade older, several inches taller and a whole lot fitter in his jeans and slim-fit shirt. The hairstylist had even plucked his eyebrows.

'Oh!' she blurted, eventually. 'Have you had your hair cut?'

'Yes!' Arthur beamed.

'Elsa, he's had a whole wardrobe makeover,' Isaac said. 'His sister called round earlier and it took her a full thirty seconds to recognise him.'

'Oh!' she repeated, face turning crimson. 'I guess... I suppose I just don't really notice what he wears. I'm really sorry,' she said, taking Arthur's hand. 'You always look lovely, to me.'

If things carried on like this, I'd be the one paying Arthur to sort *my* life out.

* * *

On Saturday, there was no football match due to it being the Jubilee weekend. Isaac was working and Arthur was out with Elsa, so after faffing around until almost lunchtime, I plucked up my courage and asked Elliot if he wanted to come on a walk with me.

'No. Thank you.' He kept his eyes on the video game, jerking the controller as he shot at some baddies. There was barely a trace of the man who'd been shopping with me the day before.

'Are you going to play this all day?'

'Probably.'

'You don't want any lunch, or a drink or...'

He swore, dropping the controller into his lap in frustration at the game.

'Or some company, at all? I know how to control a joystick.'

'I'm fine.'

He immediately started playing again.

'Really?' I took a deep breath. I wasn't about to give up. 'Because you've been in that chair for nearly five hours, so I'm wondering if you've lost track of time, or forgotten to set a reminder on your phone to stop and eat. You didn't get up to make Friday breakfast yesterday...'

'I'm very sorry I had a lie in, and you didn't get your breakfast.' More beeps and blasts as Elliot continued staring at the screen.

'That's not what I'm saying! I'm worried because I don't think you *are* fine. This isn't about me.'

'Really? This isn't part of the fix-Elliot project? Because I don't need you trying to fix me, Jessie. If you hadn't realised yet, I'm unfixable. I certainly don't need you monitoring whether I've eaten or not.'

I fled the room before he could hear me burst into tears.

\* \* \*

Sunday, at the picnic, I asked Isaac if he thought Elliot was okay.

'Of course he's not okay. Have you heard that some of the parents have started a petition to get him kicked off the team?'

'How do we help him?'

'I don't know.' Isaac shrugged. 'Nothing much we can do until the club committee make a decision. You have to admit, the team wasn't going that well. Maybe it's best to let it go.'

'The team was going brilliantly!' I shook my head in annoyance. 'The difference it made to those boys can't be measured in goals or matches.'

'Maybe not.' Isaac looked apologetic. 'But in the real world, it's results that matter.'

'So, if they won a match, that would count in Elliot's favour?'

'Jessie, if by some miracle they didn't *lose* a match, that would be a start.'

So, I had a new mission. Firstly, I needed to get Elliot to agree to re-enter the Harriers in the Sherwood Forest Cup in a month's time, where twelve local teams would play two matches each in the first round, the winners then progressing to the quarterfinals. Secondly, the Houghton Harriers under nines needed to draw one of those matches.

I wasn't sure which of those tasks would be harder.

I initiated the first stage of my plan the very next day. It was the trial animals' day at the Barn, and I was confident that it couldn't fail to lift even Elliot's spirits. We had six puppies in the morning, all of whom were undergoing training to be various types of support dog, along with their owners, who were more than happy to sit about in the sunshine while other people petted and played with their animals. Penny was also there, making a point of saying hello to every single person in turn, in between checking that Elliot was coping with the noise and busyness.

Initially I felt as concerned as his dog about his stiff shoulders, the tight smile, but once Mum had shooed him to a quiet corner, beside an older man nodding off with a Yorkshire Terrier in his lap, he eventually sat back and started to ease into himself again.

While the puppies were being rounded up ready for home, I made my move, approaching Mum as she double checked that none of the dogs had left an unpleasant surprise behind in the grass.

'I was wondering if you should ask Elliot over for Monday Mumday this evening, as a thank you for today?'

I'd barely finished the sentence before she'd raced off to find him.

I then spent a surprisingly peaceful afternoon with Eddie and his horse, Duchess, who belonged to a local riding for the disabled charity. Duchess graciously permitted a dozen strangers to brush her coat, stroke her nose and feed her a carrot or three, while Eddie listened with interest to their stories about the horses they'd owned, or ridden.

Madeline, who this whole day was really for, waited until last. Tottering to her feet, she leant against Duchess, closed her eyes and allowed a beatific smile to spread across her wrinkles. Once she was too tired to stand any more, she sat in a chair and brushed the small patch of coat she could reach until it gleamed.

At four o'clock she was still sitting there.

I placed a gentle hand on her shoulder. 'You're going to miss the minibus.'

'Oh, what a shame. I couldn't have a few more minutes?' She pressed her head up against Duchess's flank.

'Everybody's already on board. We shouldn't keep them waiting.'

'Will she come again?' Madeline asked. 'Before too long? I'd love to see her while I still can.'

'Of course. If that's okay with you?' I asked Eddie.

'I've got an even better idea,' Eddie said, his eyes glinting. 'Do you live in the village?'

She nodded. 'Cooks Lane.'

'Then how about Duchess takes you home?'

'Um, excuse me?' I asked. Had Eddie not noticed that Madeline was about as brittle as a dead twig and struggled to get into an armchair, let alone up on a horse?

'Trust me, love. My nan rode until well into her eighties.'

'Madeline is ninety-three.'

He gave a long whistle. 'Looking good for it, if you don't mind me saying!' He winked.

'I really don't think that's a wise idea.' I glanced about the garden, but all the other staff were helping see everybody off. 'She's never ridden before.'

'Well, it's about time she started then, isn't it?' he said with a wink. 'How about a couple of laps of the garden? What do you reckon, Mads, are you up for it? I brought our accessible equipment, just in case.'

Madeline looked at me, a gleam of fire in her eyes. 'Yes. I am.'

So, thanks to some sturdy steps, a specially adapted side-saddle, a lot of careful manoeuvring from Eddie and a woman who was determined to get on that horse or die trying, Madeline's lifelong dream came true. She managed four laps of the garden, before her muscles began to tremble and even Eddie could see she'd reached her limit.

But, oh. Those few minutes. I don't think Madeline had such straight posture even when I'd first met her, ten years ago. Head about as high as it could go, she laughed her way around the first lap, wept the second, and then adopted a stately air of jubilant pride as the staff who were still there whooped and clapped her around the final two.

'Do you wish you'd tried it when you were younger?' I asked, as I accompanied her home in a taxi, afterwards.

'I've not got enough time left to spend it regretting what I did or didn't do. Wishing it had been different. All I can do now is make the most of here and now, like today.' She rested her papery hand on mine. 'You should try it sometime.'

'I'm trying, believe me.' I swallowed, hard. 'I'm glad you enjoyed it, though.'

'Oh, Jessie. It was the best day. I can't thank you enough.'

'You're welcome. I'll book Duchess in for another visit, soon. As long as you promise not to tell anyone you got to ride her, or they'll all be wanting a go.'

'My lips are sealed! But, ooh, to not be the smallest, slowest person for once. To look down on all of you! I try not to wallow, but I spend so much time feeling so very helpless and *old*.' She closed her eyes, still holding onto my hand. 'Now, I can simply shut my eyes and be back in that magical moment!' She opened them again, and flashed a mischievous smile. 'I didn't mind that lovely man's hand on my bottom, either!'

It was in that moment that I decided I would work at the Barn for as long as my parents would have me.

* * *

Elliot arrived at my parents' a few minutes after me. Dad busied himself stirring a risotto while Mum poured us drinks, gushing about how much everyone had enjoyed the day.

'Well, not everyone. Frannie grumbled that a dog hair must have found its way inside, because she sneezed a few times, but personally I think she was putting it on because she felt left out.'

'That woman will tell us she's allergic to oxygen, next,' Dad said. 'Remember when she decided she was intolerant to Martha's "natural odour"?'

'Coincidentally the same week that Hugh, who she'd had an eye on for ages, asked Martha to sit next to him at lunch.' Mum rolled her eyes. 'We should have become primary school teachers; it would have been easier.'

'And a lot less messy,' Dad chuckled.

Just as I'd hoped, as soon as we started eating, Mum asked Elliot about the Harriers. 'It must be so difficult waiting to find out if the club are going to do anything about what happened.'

Elliot shook his head, his face tight. 'Not really. It won't make any difference to the outcome.' He ate a large forkful of rice, as if hoping that would end the conversation. A futile hope, which he should have known given that this was my parents.

'Elliot's quit,' I said, keeping my tone casual. 'He's also pulled the team out of the Sherwood Forest Cup.'

Mum dropped her fork onto her plate with a clatter.

'*Quit?*' She glanced at all of us in disbelief. 'Are you that sure they'll rule against you? Agatha's son is on the committee and she said most of them love how you've managed the team. You really don't need to give up hope.'

'I've not resigned because I think it's hopeless.' He shrugged, awkwardly. 'It's the right thing to do.'

'Why on earth would you think that?' Dad asked.

'Because I'm not capable of being the role model the team needs. Even if with Jessie's help I can handle all the logistics, I'm a liability. Those kids have got enough to deal with without me behaving like a thug and causing all this drama. They're better off without me.'

'What,' Mum scoffed. 'With Simon Simonson? Where will that leave Wilf, and Wodger? Who is Fabian going to be better off with than you?'

'I don't know.' Elliot was trying to remain calm and logical, but the strain was clear in his voice. 'It's not up to me to decide that.'

'No.' Mum banged her fork down. 'Nope. You don't get to do that, I'm afraid. You started this... this... wonderful, inspirational, *life-changing* team. *You* did, because you understand what it's like to face the kind of challenges those boys deal with every day. In believing in them you dared them to believe in themselves. And now, because the very disability that makes you so perfect for this role happened to impact a horrible situation, you decide you can walk away? That's it? You aren't like everyone else after all, so you'd better quit?'

'Pippa, I allowed myself to lose control and shove someone. I'd have done a lot worse if Russell hadn't stepped in and done it first.'

'You allowed yourself to lose control?' Dad asked, gently. 'You say that like you made a mistake, a bad judgement call.'

Elliot lifted his head for the first time. 'Well what would you call it? You can't agree with those who think that guy deserved it. There's no excuse for violence.'

'Son, you didn't allow yourself to do anything. Any more than Wilf allows himself to become dysregulated, or someone with Tourette's makes a mistake when they tic. You have a brain injury. In extreme situations, your brain is sometimes unable to remain calm. It isn't an excuse, it's a reason.'

'But that's even more reason to quit; knowing I can't control it means I can't do anything to stop it happening again.' His face twisted up in distress. 'I'm not safe to be running a football team. I'm not safe to be around those boys.'

'What a load of rubbish!' Mum said. 'In ten years, how many people have you actually hurt?'

Elliot shrank back, as though trying to disappear inside himself. 'Three.'

'Isaac told us about them. Two insisted on picking a fight with you. The third one had just assaulted a young woman.'

'Plus all the people who've had to put up with my rudeness, bad temper and inappropriate comments.'

Mum made a dismissive noise. 'They can get over it.'

'How many times have you been rude to the Harrier boys?' Dad pressed on. 'Lost your temper with one of them, or made an inappropriate comment?'

Elliot was quiet for a moment. 'I once told Dyson that he ran like a penguin.'

I hid my smile behind a forkful of risotto. Dyson ran exactly like a penguin.

'Connie said Simon Simonson told Wilf that he'd not got the mental capability to play sport, and he was dragging down the team,' Mum said.

'Is there a point to this?' Elliot asked, a sheen of perspiration on his forehead.

'The point is that the boys are the complete opposite of being unsafe with you,' I said, fearing that my parents might drag the point on forever, otherwise. 'You understand them. You care about them. They don't simply feel safe with you; they feel invincible. The one time they felt threatened and bullied – *unsafe* – you stood up for them, with no thought for what it might cost you.'

Elliot looked at me, his eyebrows furrowed.

'And you giving up after one, completely understandable, incident tells them that it's not okay to have a brain – or a body – that might not always fit within the margins that society has deemed acceptable.' Dad kept his voice soft, but the authority behind it was clear.

'You're saying that if they experience a tricky situation, their hero thinks they should run away, listen to the haters,' Mum added. 'Isn't that the exact opposite of what this team is all about?'

'Never mind that they really, really enjoy it,' I said. 'It's a few hours a week where they have fun with great friends and feel positive about themselves. Please don't take that away from them.'

'I'm not taking it away from them!' Elliot said, but his tone wavered. 'I'm taking me away from it, so they can keep on being a part of an amazing team.'

'But don't you see?' Dad asked, his eyes crinkled with compassion. 'Without you, this team would never be the same.'

Instinctively sensing that Elliot had heard enough, Mum moved the conversation onto other topics, including catching Isaac admiring his new clothes in a Barn mirror, and whether either of us knew if he was trying to impress anyone in particular, and how lovely the cottage had looked when she'd called in a few days ago...

Elliot remained almost silent throughout dessert and coffee, but every time I took a peek at his face, his expression remained intent, but no longer in turmoil.

I'd have bet my new bedroom on the most positive people in the world being able to change his mind, and I felt a twinge of hope that they'd succeeded.

\* \* \*

As soon as I walked into work the next day, Mum handed me a doughnut and a mug of tea and dragged me into the empty library.

'How are you, darling?'

'You only saw me last night. Not that different since then.'

'Okay.' She leant a few inches closer towards me in her chair. 'What I really mean is, is everything all right with you and Seb? When I asked about him, you were a bit vague.'

'Oh, you know, we've not been able to spend much time together lately. He's busy, I'm busy. Different time zones... It's not easy.'

She studied me for a moment. 'Okay. You don't have to tell me if you don't want to. But you know I'm always here if you need to talk about it?'

She sat and watched me pretend to be confused until I gave up.

'We had an argument. Not even an argument. A disagreement. We tried to put it behind us, but it's not easy to move on through a laptop screen.' I chewed on a mouthful of jam doughnut. 'I'm starting to wonder whether it's going to work out, to be honest.'

'Oh, darling. I'm sorry to hear that. I know you care about him.'

She frowned at my lacklustre shrug. 'Just make sure you don't settle for less than you deserve. Which, if I haven't said it enough, is someone so in love with you he can't stop marvelling at how blessed he is to have you, and treats you accordingly.'

I took another bite as if stuffing my face would stuff back all the sorry feelings. How did Mum always know what I needed to hear, even when it hurt? 'While my head might almost dare to believe that, my heart's not sure yet.' I gave her a watery smile. 'Every day I spend back here is helping me get there, though.'

Before she could answer me, Phil, the minibus driver, poked his head in the room.

'Sorry to bother you, ladies, but Madeline wasn't on the wall this morning.'

'The wall?'

Mum was instantly alert. 'There's a spot on her garden wall where she sits to wait for Phil every morning.' She put her mug on a side table. 'Did you knock?'

''Course.' He grimaced, clearly worried. 'I tried the back, looked in all the windows, but there was no sign of her. No answer when I called her phone, either.'

'Just a home phone?'

He nodded. Madeline had never bothered with a mobile.

'What about her carer?'

Phil shrugged. 'I don't know any more, sorry. She's last on my round and I didn't want to keep the others waiting.'

'Of course. Thanks, Phil.'

I hurried after Mum into the office, where she clicked open Madeline's file.

As she tried phoning her again, then followed up with a call to her carer, apprehension began gathering momentum as it pulsed through my arteries.

'Her carer left at eight. She was fine, then. A little tired from yesterday's adventure, she said, but nothing out of the ordinary. Phil would have been there around nine-fifty.' Mum pursed her lips. 'Her next of kin is a niece in Scarborough. It seems a bit premature to call her just yet.'

'I'll go,' I said. Mum nodded. She knew that nothing on earth could have stopped me.

## 34

Wheezing from the exertion of sprinting the whole way there, I peered through Madeline's windows and rapped on both doors in time to the thundering in my chest. For a second I wondered about finding a blunt object to smash a window and climb in, but if it came to that, the carer had a key, and there was no real reason to be overly concerned yet. Maybe Madeline simply decided to give the Barn a miss and have a snooze instead.

The churning inside me was screeching something different.

I tried her neighbour.

'She was just leaving when I saw the kids off to school. A bit earlier than usual, but she seemed her normal self.'

Okay, so she'd gone out. The question was, where had she gone, and should I be worried about it?

*Think, Jessie.*

I tried to get my frantic brain to think, but the truth was she could have gone anywhere.

She could have popped to the shops, not wanting to wait for her supermarket delivery. Or decided to treat herself to breakfast at the café. Except that the carer had given her breakfast. She could have simply decided to go for a walk. It was a beautiful spring day. Perhaps she fancied a quiet day rather than the drama of the Barn for once...

And then I knew, with utter certainty, where she would be.

I hurried to the end of the road and around the corner. The bench was set back from the road, on a wide verge, and at this time of the year it was partially hidden from view by the bushes growing beside it, but spying a glimpse of what looked like Madeline's walker through the greenery propelled me to a jog.

*She'll be fine,* I panted inside my head. *She's just gone to see the horses. She'll be fine.*

I found my friend, sitting upright on the bench.

She was not fine.

\* \* \*

The initial blow was so fierce I squeezed my eyes closed for a few seconds, praying with every cell in my body that when I opened them, I'd see something different. Her twinkling at me. Nodding her head in sleep. Even slumped unconscious was something I could handle. But not this. Not now. Not Madeline.

After a couple of shaky breaths I sat beside her on the bench and gently cradled her hand in mine for one last time while I called my mother.

\* \* \*

Isaac had wanted to stay at home with me for the rest of the day, but I knew he'd offered to drive Connie and Wilf to a paediatrician's appointment in Nottingham, so I shooed him away, insisting that I preferred to be on my own.

Which was true, until twelve-thirty, when Penny came and found me in a heartbroken huddle on the sofa.

'Jessie,' Elliot said, when he followed her in a moment later. 'I didn't realise you were off today.'

'I'm not. I mean, I wasn't.' I shook my head as if trying to jostle the right words into place. I only needed two: 'Madeline died.'

Then three more, after he'd come to sit beside me, my face buried in his new shirt as I sobbed. 'I found her.'

'I'll make some tea,' Elliot said once I'd composed myself enough to prise myself away from him and pat down my dungarees pockets until I found a tissue. 'I think Isaac has chocolate biscuits in his cupboard.'

'You were going to make lunch,' I said, realising the time. 'I've messed up your schedule again.' I shook my head. 'I *really* need to stop doing that.'

Elliot stood up, a look on his face that I was too overwrought to interpret. 'I'd rather you didn't. You messing up my schedule is the best thing that's happened to me in years.'

'I couldn't tell. I didn't notice anything different about her,' I said, croaky from crying. 'Should I have spotted it? I took a taxi home with her after riding Duchess.'

'She rode the horse?'

'Oh my goodness. She rode a great big, massive horse!' I pressed one hand against my forehead, wishing for the millionth time that I'd held my ground the day before. 'I was there. I let her, even though I knew it was probably dangerous. I gave in because it was Madeline. If it had been Veronica, or Rusty, I've had said no way. What if me giving in was what... what made her...'

'No.' Elliot's voice was tender as he bent his head to meet my eyes, which were brimming with tears again. 'The guy with the horse, he's qualified in this stuff, isn't he? Riding for the disabled? It was up to him to authorise it. And Madeline was perfectly capable of making her own decision. She wanted to do it.'

'Jim wanted to pet lions instead of puppies, but I said no.' I sniffed.

Elliot smiled. 'Not quite the same.' He adjusted his position to face me. 'Think of it this way. The day before she died, you made her dream come true.'

I nodded, remembering our last conversation. 'She said it was the best day.'

'There you go, then.'

'It's not a terrible way to die, either,' he said a minute or two later. 'Sitting on her favourite bench, watching the horses.'

'She...' I stopped, took another shaky breath, waited until the lump in my throat had eased enough for me to speak. 'She was smiling.'

Elliot nodded. 'Feel sad, Jessie. Mourn your friend. Miss her. But promise me you won't feel one second of blame for how she died.'

'But if I'd not left her... if I'd only...'

He took my hand in his and I wanted to hang onto it forever.

'Looking back with what ifs and if onlys: those kind of regrets will only hurt you. They can't change anything for the better. Trust me, I learnt that the hard way.'

I could only nod. I'd learnt that the hard way, too.

\* \* \*

Two weeks later, nearly two hundred people crammed into Houghton church dressed in their brightest and best outfits. As per Madeline's written instructions, the funeral service followed an earlier cremation attended by family and close friends. Arthur greeted us with sympathetic smiles and reassuring handshakes as he pointed out empty seats and reminded us that we were all invited to the Barn for drinks and refreshments afterwards.

Elsa led the service with a warmth and sincerity that showed how she'd taken the time to get to know Madeline in the few months they'd been part of the same church. She put an arm around Madeline's niece when she choked up half-way through her eulogy, and made the perfect, gentlest of jokes when a four-year-old boy asked, 'Where's Madeline gone?'

In between squeezing some air past the rock of grief in my chest, I thought I'd better at least try to be a comforting presence to her friends from the Barn. As we sat in the garden with plates of Wendy's sandwiches and cakes, it soon became apparent that they were the ones offering comfort to me. These men and women had experienced loss countless times between them, and their pragmatic honesty, their ability to laugh and cry as they embraced the sadness, while at the same time celebrating a wonderful human being who'd lived a long life full of love, was a lesson I'd never forget. I caught glimpses of Arthur – often with Elsa – and his family, gliding through the mass of mourners as they ensured a seamless farewell, and for the first time I understood what his job really meant.

'You were amazing today,' I told him that evening, when we all gathered to sample Isaac's first attempt at homemade meatballs around a new garden table. My housemates were pretending it was a coincidence that everyone was there, including Elsa and Connie, but I recognised a show of solidarity after my emotional day.

'Oh, well, not really,' he said, helping himself to another piece of garlic bread. 'Madeline left clear, detailed instructions so it was straightforward enough. Nothing overly complicated.'

'No, I mean it. I hadn't appreciated until now how important it is, making sure a family and friends get to have a proper goodbye. What you do – I used to think it was a bit morbid. Like, something to hide from prospective dates in case they were creeped out. But your family get alongside people at their most painful, difficult times, and make it as lovely as you can. That's incredible work and I owe you a massive apology for ever thinking it was anything other than that. You should wear that suit and hat with pride whenever you feel like it. Oh, and if I die any time soon, you'd better be the one arranging my send-off. Both of you,' I added, looking at Elsa.

'With all due respect, Jessica, and thank you for your insights, but I did already know all that,' Arthur said, with a smile that was only as condescending as I deserved. 'As did Elsa, hence her not being creeped out at all by my job. But I'm glad you thought today went well.'

'Feel free to fire me,' I said. 'I did try to tell you I don't really know anything.'

'Fire her?' Elsa asked, a meatball half-way to her mouth. 'Has Jessie been moonlighting for Wood's?'

'Um, no,' I said, quickly. 'He just asked me for some advice a couple of times... you know, a woman's perspective on what outfit to wear... we had a couple of conversations about colours for the living room...'

'It wasn't just me!' Arthur blurted, face starting to glow. 'Isaac and Elliot wanted advice, too.'

'But it's not a job?' Connie asked, eyebrow raised with a hint of amusement. 'You didn't pay Jessie for advice?'

There was a long, lingering moment before Elliot broke the silence. 'We didn't give Jessie any money, no.'

'Phew!' Elsa exclaimed. 'Paying your housemate, sister and friend to tell you how to dress? Now that *would* be creepy!'

'How's Seb getting on?' Isaac asked, in a blatant attempt to steer the conversation away from potential humiliation all round. 'Still renting out boats?'

My cheeks began to flush before I sternly reminded myself that this was nothing to be ashamed of. 'I wouldn't know. We broke up.'

I couldn't resist sneaking a peek at Elliot, sat on the far corner of the table to me. His eyes, wide with surprise, sent a ripple of electricity across my skin.

'What?' Isaac sat back, looking almost as astonished as his best friend. 'Why didn't you tell me?'

'It only happened a couple of days ago. I've had other things on my mind.'

'That insensitive git,' Isaac went on. 'He could have at least waited until after the funeral.'

'Oh, no.' I couldn't look at Elliot this time, sure he would notice my heart pounding through my tea dress. 'I ended it, not him.'

'Wow.' I tried not to be offended that this seemed an even bigger shock to my twin.

'Well done you,' Connie said, holding her glass up to chink against mine. 'I knew you'd make the right decision.'

'Is there something going on here that I don't know about?' Isaac asked, growing increasingly miffed.

'Either way, now's probably not the time and place to be asking Jessie about it,' Connie said, patting his arm in a way that bore a startling resemblance to my parents.

I took a large swig of wine.

'He's having a great time wherever he is this week, and I realised, contrary to my expectations, I enjoy being here. If that doesn't sound insensitive, given I went to a good friend's funeral today.' I sighed, trying to find the right words. 'I suppose that home is starting to feel like home again. And I'm thinking I might like to stay here, more than I'd like to be wherever Seb ends up. So, yeah.' I shrugged. 'It felt like the right thing to do.'

'Cheers to Jessie coming home!' Arthur cried, holding his glass up, and seeing my new friends smiling as they toasted my decision was the loveliest end to a heart-breaking fortnight.

Only one friend wasn't laughing. His smile was small but deadly serious, as his dark eyes fixed on mine from across the table, with a question behind them that I suspected the answer to would thrill and terrify me at the same time.

The truth was, I had admitted to myself before calling Seb a couple of days earlier, Seb's suggestion to stop being exclusive was the major reason we needed to break up. Not because I was upset about it, as I had been initially, but because thoughts about being non-exclusive had started popping into my head at random moments. For example, when walking back from my parents with Elliot, or when he brought me a coffee and a piece of cake and asked how I was feeling, or left a bunch of cow parsley he'd picked on his evening run on the table with a sticky note saying that he was here if I wanted to talk. Increasingly, in those moments, I started to wonder what it would be like if I was free to hold Elliot's hand or eat dinner with him on a real date. To rest my head on his shoulder when we both ended up on the sofa watching a film. And when I found myself imagining what it would be like if he tilted his head towards me and pressed his lips against mine, I knew that I had to be honest with myself, and then with Seb.

Nothing could ever happen with Elliot; these were sentimental feelings about a first love, who could never be anything more than that because of one terrible night. But, if I was having these kinds of feelings about anyone other than the man I'd been living with for three years, who was clearly moving on, then it was time to accept that I was moving on too.

Was I sad about breaking up with Seb? Of course. Did I miss him? At times, with an ache that burned in my guts. But entangled in the sadness was a tiny shoot of joy that I was not only surviving without him, but starting to thrive again. It felt like a whole new stage in my recovery, and one that it felt right and proper to continue alone.

Alone. That was, until I remembered the look on Elliot's face when he'd heard I was now single.

## 35

When Elliot excused himself for his run, I too thanked everyone for the meal and the company, but I was going on a walk, and no, I didn't want anyone to come with me.

It took twenty minutes to make my way through the village. We were now in the heart of June, and even this late in the day, heat lingered in the air along with the scent of blistering pavements and sun-scorched lawns. I'd set off with the intention of wandering along with my thoughts, but wasn't at all surprised to find that my feet had taken me back to the bench.

The lane was empty, so I sat down, the sense of my missing friend so strong that I felt sure if I turned to the side I'd find her sitting beside me, gazing dreamily at the horses in the field across the road.

It wasn't long, or eloquent, what I needed to say to her, but here seemed like a far better place than at the church, or the crematorium.

'Thank you.'

I watched a couple of butterflies dancing past and thought about how someone could be in your life for a relatively short time, yet their impact be so profound that it echoed for years afterwards. I'd shared homes with people for far longer than the summer I'd spent getting to know Madeline, and I couldn't even remember some of their names.

As yet another tear rolled on down my face, I thought about Madeline's life, about the tragedies she'd faced. The man she'd loved, and almost lost to the horrors of the war, and then found the strength and the courage to love again.

And I wondered.

I wondered if the best way that I could honour my friend was to pledge to do the same. To dare to love a man again, even though it would mean finding the courage to face my deepest regrets and darkest shame.

\* \* \*

For the next week or so, I listened to my parents' advice about grief and tried to keep life as gentle as possible. I worked in the garden with Isaac, finding the simple, mindless repetition of digging up weeds and turning over the newly exposed soil a balm to my heart. Arthur brought us a couple of sub-standard, rectangular coffins to plant vegetables in, and amongst that strange juxtaposition of life and death, I found comfort and a contentment that I'd not felt since the carefree innocence of childhood.

I pressed down the clumps of seedlings into rich, crumbly compost and knew in my bones that, like them, it was time to stretch my fragile roots down into the earth here. To settle, to stay.

Connie and Wilf joined us on a couple of mild evenings, as well as on Sunday after the picnic. Those days I found other things to do, such as tidying my sock drawer or flopping on my bed wondering if Connie would ask me to be a bridesmaid, while I tried not to earwig on their conversation through my bedroom window.

One evening Connie left Wilf with Isaac and we met Elsa at the pub for an early meal, full of raucous laughter and earnest conversation.

I gathered yet more feedback at the Barn, and had meetings with my parents to debate which of the new activities would become a regular part of the programme, and what plans we might come up with for the autumn. I ripped up my temporary contract and signed a fresh, shiny permanent one. As we celebrated afterwards with champagne and doughnuts, all of us cried, even me.

I de-escalated arguments, foiled mutinies and broke up three fist and two food fights.

Most days I arrived home exhausted but with a sense of fulfilment that meant even as I collapsed into bed, I couldn't wait to get back to start all over again the next day.

I sat with my housemates as they insisted upon more practice 'dates', and made the momentous, unanimous vote to reduce the number of Chimney Cup events from twenty down to eight. For another task they all came up with a suitable present for a girlfriend. Arthur bought a book on local history. Isaac a voucher for a spa day.

Elliot handed me a photograph frame painted with forget-me-nots, my favourite flowers. It displayed an image from the prom night, only unlike my parents' picture, this time Isaac was already seated on the tandem, Elliot beside him with one hand outstretched, tugging me towards the bike. All of us laughing. Carefree. Radiant.

'The present is supposed to be for the girl you want to date,' I said, trying to control the quiver in my voice as I rested the picture on the kitchen table.

Elliot blinked, once, before lifting his eyes to meet mine with a slow burn that sparked a fire in my belly.

'Yeah, but Elliot's not met anyone yet, has he?' Arthur said. 'Makes sense for him to choose something you'd like, instead.'

'Oh, man. This is awesome.' Isaac swivelled it around for a closer look, wearing the exact same grin as in the picture.

'Doesn't it bother you?' I asked, my words barely a whisper. 'The reminder of that night...'

Isaac frowned, answering before Elliot could reply. 'He can't remember it, so it's not really a reminder.'

After a second or two, Isaac flipped back to the grin. 'Probably nice to have a record of the one and only time you looked half-decent, isn't it?'

'Well, thank you. It's... it's perfect.'

\* \* \*

The first Saturday in July, I was yanking out the weeds in the raised bed coffins when the doorbell rang. By the time I'd reached the hallway, Elliot had already answered it.

'Coach Elliot. I've come to give you this.'

Peeping past him, I saw Ibrahim holding out an A4 envelope.

'It's just Elliot now, but thank you.'

Ibrahim stuck his hands on his hips. 'I'm sorry, Coach, but you don't get out of it that easily.'

'Oh?'

'The Harriers need you. Not next season, when you've stopped feeling sorry for yourself. We don't have time for that! The Sherwood Cup is next Saturday and we've been looking forward to it all season. You said that if we worked hard and kept trying then we could play in the tournament. We kept our end of the bargain, now it's time for you to keep yours.'

'Ibrahim...' Elliot's voice was a rough croak. 'That's not going to happen. The best thing you can do is follow Olly and Jackson and find another team. One where you stand a chance of actually winning.'

'You must be joking!' Ibrahim practically shouted. 'I'm a Houghton Harrier. Harriers 'til I die! Is that really what you think: that if a team loses some matches then everyone should quit and go somewhere better?'

'Well no, but at the moment there is no Houghton Harriers under nine's team. If you want to keep playing – and you're a great player, you really should – then you have to find another team.'

'Not happening!'

I crept closer. Ibrahim's arms were folded, chest puffed out in defiance.

'I'll never kick a ball again if it can't be with the Harriers. Well.' He stopped then, squinting upwards. 'Apart from at school. Or at the park with my friends. But not in a team! So, you have to come back or else I'll never get to play for Nottingham Forest.'

'I hear what you're saying, but it's a lot more complicated than that.'

'No it isn't. You promised. Are you a man who keeps his promises or not?' Ibrahim stuck his hands back on his hips. 'I'll tell my mother to expect a message on the group chat by the end of the day.'

With that, he marched off. Eventually, I reached past Elliot, still standing there clutching the envelope, and closed the front door.

'Do you want a cup of tea?' I asked, giving him a gentle nudge. 'We can talk about it?'

Elliot turned his head towards me, but it was tilted too far down to meet my eyes. 'No. Thank you.'

'Okay, well I'm here if you change your mind.'

* * *

A couple of hours later, when I'd moved on from weeding to lounging in a chair with a book, Elliot appeared, holding two mugs.

'I changed my mind. Is now a good time?'

'Of course.'

I tried to ignore my heart accelerating when his fingers grazed mine as he handed me a mug.

I'd felt certain there'd been another shift between Elliot and me since I'd broken up with Seb. What I wasn't sure about, was whether the shift was just in me. Without the protective shield of a boyfriend, I found it harder to ignore the prickle of chemistry, the heat of memories that clouded my senses when our eyes caught or he brushed past me in the kitchen. With Arthur spending so much time with Elsa, and Isaac either working or in the garden, as well as increasingly meeting up with Connie and Wilf, I found myself alone with Elliot more often than felt sensible.

On the surface, we ate eggs and jam, chatted about work and watched television in a silence more comfortable than it had any right to be.

Beneath that, my feelings towards Elliot were digging in like the roots of Isaac's cucumber plants.

I knew that I was orchestrating excuses to be sitting in the garden when he finished his run, coincidentally deciding I wanted a drink at the same time he'd be preparing his evening meal, causing us to somehow end up eating together. It was impossible to accidentally bump into a man who ran such a rigid schedule, especially when any variants were usually displayed on prominent notes on the kettle or the front door.

Night after night, as I lay in my attic bedroom, I vowed to stop playing with fire, to for goodness' sake manage just once to avoid sabotaging a perfectly good situation.

But then he'd look at me. Burst out laughing at the same joke on the television. Get out his phone to find where he'd made a note of something that had happened earlier that day that he'd thought I'd find interesting and therefore wanted to remember.

How could *anyone* stay away from a man who feels like home?

'I was wondering if you're free next Saturday?'

I gripped the mug a little tighter.

'Um... yes?'

His shoulders drooped with relief. 'Excellent. Great. I was terrified at the thought of having to do it without you.'

'Is this what I think it is?'

He kept his gaze on the distant hillside. 'I thought we might have a go at winning the Sherwood Forest Cup.'

'Elliot!' I beamed, knowing that this was about so much more than a football tournament. 'Did you speak to the club?'

His own smile wavered. 'The chairman phoned a few days ago, and asked me to reconsider. Officially, they were willing to offer me what he likened to a yellow card. Unofficially, most of them wished I'd smacked the Rangers manager in his nasty mouth.' He paused to swallow. 'I have their full support, if I decide to keep the team going.'

'That's amazing.'

'It seems a lot of people whose opinion I respect think I made a mistake. And then Ibrahim turned up, with this.'

He handed me a homemade card. On the front was a picture of a man with yellow hair and a red top and shorts, his giant hands planted on another person whose face was mostly huge, angry teeth. Written in childish bubble writing across the top was 'SUPERHERO'. Inside were nine messages, thanking Elliot for standing up to the bully and imploring him to come back.

'"We don't want a different manager, we want you because you're the best and we like how you make us all see how good we are only in different ways".' I read out, squeezing the words past a giant lump in my throat. '"Before I joined the Harriers I had only one friend and now I have loads. Please come back because I really, really like having friends".'

I shook my head. 'How could you possibly say no to that?'

'Well, clearly I couldn't. So. Will you please come back and be my assistant manager?'

'I wouldn't miss it for the world.'

## 36

The following Monday, Wilf was with Isaac when I arrived home from work, learning how to play pool on the table now set up under a gazebo in the garden.

'Is your mum not here?' I asked, once they'd paused for an ice-cream break, and I'd decided it would be rude not to join them considering I'd spent over an hour that day umpiring an argument about whether someone cheated in a village cricket match. The match had been played in 1967.

'She's out with a friend,' Isaac added. 'So we're having fish and chips here.'

'Oh?' I asked, feeling not the slightest prick of jealousy that Connie was out with an unknown friend and I hadn't been invited. 'Who's that?'

Then Wilf spoke up, and suddenly I wasn't the one feeling jealous.

'Wodger's dad,' he said, after a careful lick of his cone. 'Only now he's Mum's friend, I'm supposed to call him Martin.'

Isaac's ice-cream came to a screeching stop half-way to his mouth.

'Martin Bradgate?' he choked out. 'The shrimpy guy with long hair?'

'He doesn't have hair any more.' Wilf frowned.

'Shame.'

'I don't know what a shrimpy guy is. I didn't see any fish or anything.'

'He means that Martin is quite small,' I said, with a glare at my brother. 'Which he is, yes.'

'And Connie is now... *friends* with him? As in, going out for dinner friends?'

'They've gone to the Rocking Horse. I thought they should go to the Crooked Arrow. That's way more fun and definitely where I would go if I had tea with a friend, but Mum said it didn't need to be anything fancy.'

'Right.' Isaac stared at his ice-cream for a long moment. A trickle of vanilla started dribbling down his thumb. 'Did she look fancy?'

Wilf shrugged, stuffing in the last of his cone and clearly bored with the topic. 'Not really. Can we play more pool now?'

I gave Isaac a nudge.

'Oh, yeah. Of course. You go and rack up while I have a quick word with Jessie.'

I tried to slip past, but he snagged the back of my T-shirt as I reached the doorway.

'Spill.'

'Excuse me?' I adopted my most innocent face.

'You knew about this.'

'About what?' There was no way Isaac was falling for my act, but I could at least stall for time while I tried to work out what and how much spilling was required.

'I can't believe you didn't tell me Connie was going on a date. With *Martin Bradgate*. He's a total... nerk!'

'He seems okay.' I shrugged. I'd seen him at football matches and a couple of practices, and the best description I could come up with was 'nice enough'.

'And you think "okay" is good enough for Connie?' He tugged at his hair in exasperation. 'Nothing about this is okay!'

'Isaac, you need to chill. This isn't some grand romance. He asked and she thought he would be a safe person to dip her toe back into dating with. It's an early bird special at the Rocking Horse.'

'Yes, but... why him? Isn't he still working at the scrapyard? His wife left him for an insurance salesman. They've got *nothing* in common.'

'They're both single parents raising eight-year-old boys with additional needs.'

'Oh, well that's great!' Isaac grabbed a glass from the shelf then turned on the tap so hard it sprayed water all over his T-shirt. 'She wants the one thing I can't compete with.'

'Isaac?' Wilf appeared at the kitchen door. 'I've racked up. You've had time for quite a lot of quick words.'

'Okay, buddy. I was just getting a drink. Do you want one?'

'No, thank you. I have my water bottle.'

'She doesn't want anything from Martin,' I whispered, once Wilf had disappeared back outside. 'Apart from a nice evening out. Have you considered that she chose him because there's no chance of her or Wilf getting hurt, precisely because that's all she wants?'

He narrowed his eyes. 'She doesn't really like him that much?'

'I honestly don't know. But I know that she's starting to really like you. The non-arse Isaac who's understanding about her situation, and there for her when she needs it, no pressure, no rush. The kind of man who won't let his wounded emotions allow him to revert back to behaving like a petty old grouch.'

'Screw that.' Isaac slammed the glass back on the countertop. 'I love you, sis, but as of now, you're fired as my relationship coach. Nice, kind, patient Isaac has got me nowhere but babysitting while she's out *dipping her toe* with a nerk!'

\* \* \*

I made a point of being closest to the front door when it rang at quarter to eight, managing a quick 'How did it go?' before Wilf came hurtling out of the kitchen and down the corridor.

'Good,' Connie whispered, grabbing onto her son before momentum carried him out into the front garden.

'Good? *Good* good, or nothing especially bad, good?' I muttered out one side of my mouth as Wilf wriggled for freedom.

'I don't know. Fine, good.'

'Good, as in good enough for a second date good?'

She gave a coy shrug as Isaac appeared. I gave him a quick glance, feeling a flood of relief at his expression.

'Nice evening with your friend?' he asked, with a cheery smile that only a twin would detect concealed a heart twisted in torment.

'Yes, thanks. And thanks again for watching Wilf; I'm honestly so grateful.'

'Not at all. You know I love spending time with him.' He held out Wilf's rucksack. 'Well, apart from when he thrashes me at pool.'

'You beat Isaac at pool?' Connie helped Wilf shrug his rucksack on.

'I did! I was stripes, and first I shot at the yellow and white ball but I missed it, so then Isaac went for the blue one...'

She began shepherding him down the drive, turning at the last second to mouth another thanks as Wilf continued his post-match commentary. Isaac waved, grinned and then closed the door, slumping his back against it, eyes closed and jaw flexing with tension.

'Well done,' I offered, meaning it.

After a few seconds he opened his eyes again, and rather than the anguish that had been hiding in them earlier, I was surprised to see solid granite.

'Did you see that?' he asked, as we walked back towards the kitchen. 'Connie, I mean?'

'I didn't notice anything different to normal, no.'

'Exactly.' He opened the fridge and pulled out a bottle of beer. 'No sparkling eyes, glowing cheeks. She didn't float down the path lost in a dreamy haze.'

'Okay.'

He popped the cap on the bottle and then pointed it at me. 'Once Connie's been on a date with me, there'll be no mistaking it.'

\* \* \*

For the rest of the week, I couldn't resist ducking to the Barn's upstairs office more often than usual, under the pretext of a question about Arthur's party plans (with less than a fortnight to go, my anxiety was increasing in direct proportion to his excitement), offering them a leftover chunk of cake from round two of the Great Barnish Bake-Off or borrowing a stapler.

'She's at the wholesalers,' Isaac said on Thursday, not bothering to glance up from his computer screen. 'You'll have to spy on us another time.'

'Fair enough,' I said, with an indifferent shrug. 'I'll see you both later.'

'Wait!'

I hovered in the doorway, my back to him.

'Would you like a coffee while you're here?'

I slowly swivelled around. 'Ooh, I'm not sure. I only popped in because Arthur wanted me to check whether Connie had found the banner he wanted.'

'Despite Arthur having called to ask her that exact thing yesterday?' He gave me a pointed look. 'If you're going to keep slinking up here to check on me, the least you can do is fill me in.'

I cleared some bunting off a chair and sat down while he poured us both a drink.

'Well?'

Taking a couple of sips, I considered whether there was any point in trying to dodge the question. Isaac narrowed his eyes, confirming that there was no point whatsoever.

'I'm actually quite impressed. I thought you'd be mooching around here like some scorned Victorian poet. Either that or back to snappy and stroppy.'

'I was never stroppy! You make me sound like a moody teenager.'

'You said it, brother. Anyway, as I was saying, you're doing an admirable job of pretending you aren't seething with envy or walking about with broken chunks of heart rattling about in your ribcage. I'm pretty sure Connie suspects nothing.'

Isaac puffed up his chest like the woodpigeons currently courting their mates in the Barn garden.

'Although, I am wondering if you're acting a bit *too* Mr Reasonable, Friendly Nice Guy.'

'Too reasonable? Is this how you earn your expert relationship fee, by giving your clients directly contradictory advice so they can't complain if whichever one they follow doesn't work?'

'Well.' I shifted in my chair. 'If she is starting to like you, she might secretly hope that you don't love her dating someone else.'

'It was one date.' Isaac was very still. 'Wasn't it?'

I hesitated about whether answering that was betraying my friend's confidence, before realising that what Connie did in a public place was hardly a secret. 'She stayed for training on Wednesday and a bottle of lemonade and packet of fancy crisps might have been shared on the side-lines.'

'Shared between who?' Isaac gripped his coffee mug so tightly I feared the handle would snap off. 'Just the two of them?'

I nodded. 'I mean, it's hardly a date, but...'

'But what?'

'But he offered to save her a seat at the picnic on Sunday.'

'Dammit!' Isaac pushed his chair back and sprang to his feet. 'Right.' He started pacing up and down, in between the boxes, piles of fabric swatches and vases of dried flowers peppering the office floor. 'I was going to play it cool, give her a couple of weeks so she didn't feel bombarded, but if she thinks I can sit there at the picnic and watch them... *sharing fancy crisps* together, laughing at all the single parent in-jokes, then she's sorely mistaken.'

My phone beeped with a message from Mum.

Terry Messina is trying to catch frogspawn using Yusuf's toupee on the end of Layla's walking stick. Please assist immediately!

'I have to go. But, Isaac, promise me that you won't—'

'Jessie.' He came to a stop in front of me, the glimmer of a smile creasing the corners of his eyes. 'I am utterly in love with this woman. I intend to spend the rest of my life with her. Trust me, I'm not going to mess it up.'

## 37

On Saturday morning it took a moment to remember that the nerves jangling in my stomach were because today was the Big Day. The day that the Houghton Harriers would hopefully, possibly, miraculously Not Lose a match when they competed in the Sherwood Forest Cup.

Elliot and I had spent hours during the past week planning, dreaming, doing our best to support the boys' football skills. We'd considered going for a defensive approach, simply aiming for a draw, but that had jarred against the burgeoning sense of optimism since Elliot's return. Every time we tried to talk tactics, the team were adamant. They were going for the win. And not only one of the two matches in the first round of the tournament. They were going to win the whole cup.

In the end we decided it was pointless trying to coach them any differently. We had to work with what we had, which in this case was a team of boys bursting with exuberant self-belief. We had three practices that week, and I didn't make it through any of them without having to pretend that a fly had coincidentally flown in both eyes, at the same time.

\* \* \*

The sports ground was buzzing. Elliot stiffened beside me as he walked through the main entrance, Penny automatically moving closer to his side in response. Twelve teams of under-nine children raring to go made a lot of noise, even when surrounded by miles of empty forest on three sides, wide open fields on the other. The vast array of supporters were even worse. It was ten in the morning and already cans of bitter were being cracked open, chairs and picnic tables set up and portable speakers blaring out competing genres of music. Smaller children ran about chasing balls and each other, with accompanying shrieks and squeals, and someone boomed and crackled indecipherable announcements through a loud-speaker.

'Okay?' I asked, as we identified ourselves at the sign-in desk, the name of the team causing a few interested glances and outright stares.

'I will be.' Elliot gave me a pinched look. 'It's not about me. I'll manage.'

'That's why you're here, after all,' I said, bumping against his shoulder. Having the tournament to focus on had helped ease the simmering new *something* between us, but there had still been enough moments when it was impossible for me to ignore how when Elliot looked at me, it stirred up a heat deep inside that no longer relied on old memories to keep smouldering.

We herded the boys over to the pitch assigned for their first match, thankfully positioned on the side nearest the fields where it was a decibel or two quieter, and started warming up.

Before they'd completed a jog around the pitch, a middle-aged man with a blue and white tracksuit stretched across his paunch sauntered up.

'Well, well, the rebel returns from the wilderness of disgrace.'

He smirked. 'I hadn't realised there'd be a sideshow providing extra entertainment.'

Penny gave a warning chuff, before turning her nose away in disdain. I watched Elliot carefully, hoping he could do the same.

'So busy forcing a takeover at Brooksby that you've forgotten the youth league code of conduct?' Elliot replied calmly.

The man narrowed his beady eyes. 'I'm not the one with memory problems.'

'Great.' Elliot gave a polite smile. 'Then I'll look forward to you and your players treating mine, and their manager, with respect. It would be a shame if anyone had to be disqualified for breaching the code that you know so well.'

'As if anyone here needs to resort to cheating to beat you.' The other coach shook his head, openly grinning now. 'Might as well give us a free pass to the quarter finals. Save our legs.'

'I guess we'll find out in fifteen minutes. I heard you lost to the girls' team a couple of weeks ago. Used to be your worst insult, playing like a girl.'

The man clenched his fists. 'You're out of date. Nowadays the worst insult is playing like a Harrier.'

To my huge relief, Elliot turned his back and started calling out encouragement to the boys, running so much better than they had even a month ago.

'Let me guess, Simon Simonson?' I asked once the man had left, standing close enough to see Elliot's pulse, pounding in his neck.

'We're playing Brooksby second.' Elliot gave a smile and a wave of encouragement as the boys started jogging back towards us. 'Even the thought of it makes me want to get straight back on the minibus and keep on driving until we run out of petrol.'

Penny stood up, pressing her nose into his midriff. I resisted the temptation to join her.

'Hopefully Olly and Jackson being on their team will stop it becoming nasty,' I said. 'Boys listen to them. And aren't there others, who left earlier in the season?'

Elliot rolled his shoulders back. 'Some of those lads weren't exactly friendly. And even for those who were, pit competitive boys hungry for a win against each other and past friendships are meaningless.'

'Surely after what happened with the Rangers, the adults will behave themselves? In which case, what's the worst that can happen to our brave boys?'

He looked at me, one of those looks that made me want to reach out and somehow wipe away everything that had ever hurt him. Even as I still ached with the knowledge that most of those things were, however tenuously, linked to me.

* * *

Forty-five minutes later, I had the answer to my question. Watching a bedraggled bunch of boys limping off the pitch, doing their best to shrug off a seven-nil loss, a knot of dread tightened in my stomach at the thought of the second match.

After a drink and a breakfast butty, Elliot regathered the boys for their second pre-match talk.

'Come on, now, where's that fighting spirit gone?'

'Maybe it quit like Olly and Jackson and went to join Brooksby,' Turner said, his shoulders slumping.

'It's hopeless without them,' Fabian groaned. 'I don't want to play Brooksby. Can't we play at the funfair instead?'

Elliot's jaw set firm. 'No. We can't. A week ago, I felt just like you. Worse, because I'd already given up. Decided that us doing something amazing together, showing all those haters what a true team is made of, wasn't worth the disappointment if we lost.'

'Turns out you were right, Coach,' Wodger said, dejectedly.

'No, I wasn't right! I was completely wrong. Everything worth doing takes effort. You boys know that more than anyone. It takes guts, and grit, and sometimes risking every damn thing you've got.'

'My mum says damn is a bad word,' Jan said.

'She's right, I apologise,' Elliot carried on without pausing for breath. 'But you lot, every one of you, showed me that this team is worth fighting for. What you boys have achieved in these past few months is more than those other teams can even imagine. This is something we'll remember forever. Not whether we win, draw or lose a hundred-nil. But that we gave it our all and most importantly, we did not quit. We are going to walk onto that pitch, heads held high, look Brooksby in the eye and dare them to beat that.' He shook his head, a tear flying off and landing on Penny's nose. 'Whatever happens out there, you boys are champions. Heroes. It's time to act like it.'

There was a stunned silence, until Wilf hissed a muted, 'Yessssss!', instantly followed by Wodger letting out a war cry so loud that people all across the sports ground looked around to see who was being murdered.

'*Yeeeeeeaaaaaaaah!*' One by one, the other boys starting yelling, jumping up and down and waving their arms about. After a second or two I figured I'd better join them. Even Penny howled along.

'Right.' Elliot beckoned them into a huddle so he could finish the speech. 'You all know what to do. Block Olly as often as you can, he'll be their fastest player. Keep pushing down the left side – that's the side of your shirt the badge is on – and, most importantly, play your great, big, giant hearts out.'

The Houghton Harriers did not block Olly, or remember to push down the left side. However, none of the spectators could deny that they played their giant hearts out.

Olly and Ibrahim met for the coin toss. Ibrahim standing tall, chin up, shoulders back. Olly, looking as though he was facing the best friend he'd betrayed two weeks earlier.

Elliot and I braced ourselves for disaster.

We'd not taken into account the power of a united, positive team up against a stressed-out shambles where half the team were trying to steal the glory, the other half too nervous not to let them.

'They're a mess,' Elliot murmured to me in astonishment, when three minutes in a Brooksby striker tackled the ball off Jackson, his teammate, causing enough confusion to allow Wilf to steal it away.

'It's pretty obvious why,' I replied, over the sound of Simonson and various Brooksby parents screaming different instructions as their team scrambled to reclaim possession.

Every time a Brooksby player touched the ball they were instantly bombarded with aggressive hollers, mostly parents demanding that it was passed to their son. Every time they lost the ball, the shouting turned to 'not again!' and 'how could you fluff an easy shot like that?'

In contrast, the Harriers' supporters provided nothing but cheers of encouragement. Our boys started to make increasingly confident passes, runs and tackles. As the minutes ticked by, the Brooksby team began to crumble.

Nevertheless, we were a bunch of inexperienced boys with numerous challenges, keenly feeling the loss of our two best players, competing against a team of natural athletes. At half-time, Elliot and I kept our game faces on as we handed out drinks and orange wedges, heaping nothing but praise on the team for their spirit and skill, but at three-nil down, our dream of not losing felt like a fading fantasy.

That is, until precisely two minutes and twenty-four seconds into the second half. I know, because I was watching the clock like the lives of those boys depended on it.

After one boy on the other team slipped over while trying to dodge past Wodger, who'd been doing a great job of getting in everyone's way, there was an outcry of disgust from the Brooksby side-line.

'For goodness' sake!' someone shouted. 'Stop being so pathetic and *hold on to the damn ball!*'

Ibrahim, who'd neatly intercepted the ball as it sailed past Wodger, came to a sudden stop. 'Excuse me, referee, but that's a swear word,' he pointed out. 'Swearing is against tournament rules.'

The referee turned to the crowd of onlookers. 'Let's keep it clean, people.'

'That's all you're going to say?' Olly asked. 'Billy's dad called Ryder pathetic.'

'Oh for goodness' sake!' Simonson called out, as Ryder, who'd understandably had enough of being bawled at by his own team's supporters, burst into tears. 'Ryder? *Cryder*, more like!'

'Right that's it!' Olly said, as the referee tried to move the game along. He wrestled off his yellow shirt and flung it on the ground.

'Any spare tops over there, Coach?' he called to Elliot. 'I've decided to switch back. If that's okay. And sorry for quitting in the first place, Dad made me do it.'

Before Elliot had time to reply, Jackson had joined him.

Elliot didn't have any spare tops, and the referee soon confirmed that players weren't allowed to swap teams half-way through a game, but if anything that only made it worse. When Simonson tried to replace the defectors, the boys on the subs bench refused, declaring that they didn't want anyone to shout and swear at them, either.

So, there was nothing to be done but continue the match with two Brooksby players now shirtless and refusing to move.

As soon as Ibrahim passed the ball to Turner, who easily rolled it into the back of the net thanks to more of Wodger's blocking tactics, Elliot asked the referee if he could speak to Olly and Jackson. Short on any other ideas, he waved Elliot over. Of course, I hurried after him.

'Boys, what you're doing is admirable,' Elliot began, once they'd given him an enthusiastic fist-bump, 'but you need to start playing.'

'We're on strike! We don't want to play for Brooksby any more. Harriers until we die!' Jackson said, sticking out his chin.

'Okay, but you made a commitment to Brooksby for this cup, and you need to see it through. Plus, this is actually the best chance the Harriers have had. If you keep this strike up, then if we score another goal – or even two, and get our first draw! – everyone will say it was because it wasn't a fair game. Now, I want you to put your shirts back on and show the Harriers that you respect them as opponents.'

Olly and Jackson exchanged glances. 'Can we come back to your team as soon as it's finished?'

Elliot grinned, shaking his head. 'No.'

The boys looked stunned.

'You can come back to *your* team. Now get back out there and give us a decent challenge.'

Despite this talk, it was clear where Olly and Jackson's loyalties lay as they jogged up and down, looking continuously on the brink of settling down for a nap. However, the goal was yet more fuel on the fire in the Harrier bellies, and there was no stopping them.

When Ryder, still bawling his eyes out as he struggled on, knocked into a teammate, somehow they both ended up fumbling the ball into their own net, leaving the score at three-two.

The crowd, most of whom had wandered over as rumour had spread that it was a match worth watching, went wild.

'They could only bleedin' well go and draw!' an older man cried in delight.

'We could,' Elliot whispered, his face an equal blend of joy and fear. 'They could get a bleedin' draw.'

Thirty seconds later, they did just that. Ibrahim took the advantage of a team reeling from their own goal, and dribbled the ball from the half-way line straight into the net.

The boys raced down the pitch to where Jan was waiting near the other goal, throwing themselves into a mass pile-up of sheer, unbridled triumph, Olly and Jackson ditching all pretence and joining them. It took Elliot running onto the pitch to remind them that they still had four minutes left before they started disentangling themselves and getting back into position.

'I can't believe this.' Elliot's eyes shone as he jogged back over. 'We are actually going to not lose. Come on boys, three minutes and fifty-six seconds. All you need to do is keep the ball out of the net and we've done it.'

'Um, that's not quite true,' I said, with an apologetic grimace.

'What?' Elliot flipped around to look at me.

'In the first round of a tournament, if the match ends in a draw then it goes to penalties. Five each.'

Elliot's face fell. 'We've not got five boys capable of scoring from the penalty spot.' He ran a hand over his face.

'Before this game they couldn't,' I said, trying to sound encouraging. 'Who knows what they can do now.'

'Our only hope would be that Brooksby are all so terrified they miss.'

'Not impossible, then.'

'You think?'

I slipped my arm through the crook in his elbow. 'About as impossible as us drawing with Brooksby FC in the first place. Whatever happens, it's been a brilliant day.'

But in the end, it didn't get to penalties. When a frantic Brooksby player, having been yelled at for being a wimp, threw himself at Dyson, knocking him to the ground with mere seconds to spare, the referee had no choice but to award a penalty to the Harriers. This having never been envisaged, there was a hasty scramble to decide who would take it.

'Let the boys choose,' I said, in a blatant copout because my heart was so high in my throat I couldn't think straight.

'Who wants to take it?' Elliot called to where they huddled in trembling anticipation.

'Dyson should,' Wilf said. 'It was him who got pushed over.'

'No thank you!' Dyson said, with a vigorous shake of his head. 'Being encouraging and giving us all a fair chance is fine most of the time, but we could win if we score this! It's, like, the most important kick ever!'

'Okay, who wants to take our most important kick ever?' Elliot asked, only to be greeted by a lot more shaking heads as the boys started to back away. 'Come on, someone has to take it.'

For the first time, none of them had anything to say.

'Wilf?' I asked, knowing that in all fairness he was our best shot.

Wilf blinked a few times. 'I would, only I promised Mum she'd see my first goal and she's not here yet.'

I checked my watch. I knew Connie was ducking out of work to come along, and should have arrived ten minutes ago. 'How about we film it?'

'But she promised to be here.' Wilf's hands gave a warning twitch. 'I said I won't score if she's not here. That's why she promised.'

I whipped out my phone and dialled her number.

'Jessie, hey. Traffic's terrible but I'm seven minutes away. Have I missed it?'

'If you really put your foot down and dodge around the side of the barrier, then sprint across to the right-hand corner where the big crowd is, you'll be just in time to see Wilf win us our first match.'

'*What?*'

'We need him to take a penalty but he won't unless you're here.'

'Right. Stuff the speed cameras. I'll be there.'

The referee came over, impatient to get the match over with, and when Elliot pleaded for more time, the response was a firm no.

'I won't do it without her. Ibrahim will have to take it instead.'

Ibrahim responded to that by throwing up on his boots.

'Your mum's a couple of minutes away,' I reassured Wilf, as Ibrahim's parents rushed over. 'Start getting ready and she'll be here.'

Wilf gave me a slow nod. Half-way towards the penalty spot he suddenly discovered a stone in his shoe. After painstakingly undoing his lace, hunting for the non-existent stone and taking what felt like forever to wrestle his foot back in before doing the lace up again, ensuring the ends were precisely the same length, a bug then flew in his eye. When the referee ordered us to use someone else, he fortunately blinked it away and slowly took his place on the spot.

'I think there's something wrong with the ball...'

'Either take this penalty in the next twenty seconds or you forfeit the match.' The referee was purple with exasperation.

'But my mum!' Wilf's face began to crease up in panic.

'She's here!' I yelled, adrenaline surging at the sight of her red car skidding past the barrier and screeching to a stop. 'Wilf, it's okay. She's here!'

Wilf wasn't okay. His gaze flicked from me, to Elliot, to the referee, to a thousand other points, seeing none of them as his body began to tremble and the crowd began a restless murmur. Just as I was about to run over and rescue him, Connie burst through the crowd.

'Wilf!' she called, waving frantically. 'I'm here! Give it your best shot, babe!'

But it was only when Isaac appeared, two steps behind her, that

Wilf began to focus. Ignoring the rules and regulations, Isaac sprinted across the pitch, bending down so his face was level with Wilf's, taking his hands and pressing them gently together as he'd learned from Connie. He spoke too quietly for any of us to hear what he said – other than telling the referee to 'do one' when he tried to speed things up – but it was enough to cause Wilf to take some much-needed deep breaths, turn and give his team a double thumbs up and fire the ball into the back of the net before the Brooksby goalkeeper had time to stop picking his nose.

The cheers still roared across the ground when the final whistle blew three minutes later.

Not a single parent, nor the manager, assistant manager and half of the strangers could contain their tears.

The boys, on the other hand, laughed, yelled, jumped on each other and took the time to shake every hand of the Brooksby team. When they heard that they'd been knocked out of the tournament thanks to goal difference, it did nothing to curb their celebrations.

'Even better!' Jan shouted. 'Now the last match we played is a win!'

'Well, you never know!' Wodger said. 'I reckon we could have beaten the Colts in the quarter finals, now Olly and Jackson are back.'

'There's always next year.' Elliot grinned, as he tried to herd them away from the pitch.

'So you're definitely going to manage us next season?' Wilf asked. 'Jessie, are you staying for next season, too?'

I gaped at him, not sure if I could form a coherent answer. My brain was scrambled.

The second Wilf scored, Elliot had turned to me, and we'd flung our arms around each other in jubilation. So far, so normal for a manager and his assistant under the circumstances.

What was perhaps more unusual, was when he pulled far

enough away to look me deep in the eyes, and then before I'd had a chance to blink, kissed me.

So, to answer Wilf's question, right then I didn't know what the heck I was going to be doing next season. A very large part of me wanted to say yes, of course, I'd be in whichever corner of the planet Elliot was going to be, because he was my home and I loved him and I wouldn't ever be happy anywhere else.

The smaller, wiser, more weathered part?

That part needed a stiff drink and a friend.

## 38

'Oh my days!' Connie handed me a glass of wine. 'You kissed Elliot Ollerton.'

'Shhhh!' I said, glancing around the Rocking Horse. 'Keep your voice down.'

'Doesn't matter how quietly I say it, it still happened.' She grinned, taking a seat next to me. After several hours of letting off steam in the pub garden, the boys had finally started to flag, and been taken home to bed. Connie had nipped to the Barn to check that the transition to the evening wedding reception had gone smoothly, and ducked out just after nine to kiss her sleeping penalty shooter goodnight before leaving him with his grandparents and meeting me in the pub.

'Has he gone home?'

I nodded. 'Hours ago. It was a big day for him.'

I would have gone home too, except that every time our eyes caught or Elliot and I happened to end up within more than a couple of metres of each other, I turned to mush again. It had been several hours and my cheeks were still flaming. There was no way I was going home until I knew he'd be in bed. Which I also knew was ten-thirty, on the dot.

'It most certainly was!'

I took a gulp of wine. I'd stuck to soft drinks all afternoon, and the accompanying fuzz of alcohol was more than welcome.

'Well?' Connie asked, with an exasperated smile.

'Well, what?'

'Well, tell me everything! And you can't deny it, because I saw it with my own two eyes.'

'If you saw it, then you already know everything. Wilf scored, we hugged. Then *Elliot* kissed *me*.'

'Did you kiss him back, though?'

'I can't really remember. It was over before I realised it was happening.'

'Hmm. But if it hadn't have been, would you have kissed him back?'

I scrunched my face up. 'Not really relevant. It wasn't that type of a kiss.'

'Nonsense.' She arched her eyebrow. 'That was not a nothing-much kiss. You don't get to pass it off as no big deal.'

'It was a carried-away-in-the-moment kiss. If you'd been standing there, he would have kissed you, instead.'

Even as I said the words, I knew they weren't true.

'If he'd kissed me like that, he'd have found a knee in his crotch,' Connie replied, wryly. 'Which leads me to draw the conclusion that, given he wasn't rolling around in agony, you were down for kissing him back.'

'Okay, I didn't hate the kiss. But—'

'No!' Connie cried. 'No but!'

'*But*,' I repeated, with emphasis. 'I live with Elliot. He's my twin's best friend. We have a whole load of complicated history. However nice that kiss might have been, it can't happen again. And, as my friend, you have to promise not to tell anyone. Even Isaac. *Especially* Isaac.'

Connie grudgingly agreed.

'Now, while we're on the topic, what about you and Martin Wodger? Any kisses been going on there?'

*     *     *

I was fully expecting the next few days to be torture, Elliot and I skulking around each other avoiding any mention of what had happened, as per the Jessica Brown standard guide to dealing with awkward moments. However, I'd forgotten that Elliot had his own guide, based on an inability to be anything other than honest and open.

He found me the next day, at the picnic, while I was lurking about near Connie and Martin. Isaac was currently dealing with an unusually nasty mess in the bride's bathroom, but my twin senses were tingling and I knew he was planning something.

'Jessie, could we have a quick conversation about what happened yesterday?'

My stomach flipped right over.

'I wanted to apologise. For... for kissing you. It was completely unacceptable and I feel terrible. I could explain how it was the elation of the moment, poor impulse control, blah, blah, blah, but that's no excuse. If you want to... report me. Find somewhere else to live. Whatever you think is best.' He dared a quick glance, and the misery in those eyes that always told me everything, convinced me that I had to be honest. With myself, as well as him.

'Elliot, it wasn't just you kissing me. I kissed you, too.'

'Really?' He looked properly at me then, eyes round with shock.

'Yes. Really. So, I'm also sorry. It was inappropriate and almost certainly against tournament rules and it won't happen again.'

'Right.' Elliot nodded. He swallowed, hard. The air shifted between us, growing heavy with expectation, like the atmosphere right before a storm.

'Just to clarify,' he asked, carefully. 'Do you mean it won't happen again in an inappropriate, football-related situation, but could potentially happen if circumstances were different?' He stopped to clear his throat. 'Or, would you prefer it not to happen again, ever?'

It felt as though every last whisp of oxygen in the garden had evaporated.

'I... that would... it doesn't just depend on...' Then I stopped, frozen in horror, as over Elliot's shoulder I saw Isaac stride right up to where Connie and Martin were sitting a few metres away, with a face that made my heart screech to a stop.

'Connie.'

Elliot, noticing my stricken expression, turned to see what was happening.

'Isaac, hi.' Connie sat up straighter, clearly disconcerted by his demeanour. 'This is Martin, Wodger's dad. Wodger plays for the Harriers.'

'Yes, hello. I know Martin. We were in the same scout pack. If you don't mind, Martin, I need to talk to Connie.'

Before Martin mumbled a reply, Isaac barrelled on.

'Given that you've decided you're dating people, I would like to take you to the party next week. As my date. A long time ago, you told me that you aren't interested in a fling. The truth is, that's the last thing I want. I know I've made some bad decisions in the past, but I wouldn't have gone out with any of those women if I'd known you. I understand that you need to be careful, and take things slowly. I'm not asking for more than a date, right now, but you probably ought to know, Connie – you're it for me. I'm fully intending you to be the last woman I ever go out with. I am completely, utterly in love with you. Can I please take you to the surprise party next week?'

Everyone within hearing distance held their breath. That is, apart from Martin, who shuffled in his chair and muttered something about how this wasn't really on.

Connie had been looking straight up at Isaac the whole time, her face serious. She glanced at Wilf now, who was quivering with anticipation on a blanket near her feet, before smoothing down her skirt as the hint of a smile began to crease the corners of her eyes.

'You can. Thank you for asking.'

Isaac's whole body flinched in surprise, he crossed and uncrossed his arms a couple of times, unsure of what to do until Wilf sprang up and offered him a high-five.

'On the understanding that this is one date. There's no pressure or expectation for anything more.'

'Of course,' he breathed in relief.

There was an awkward silence for a moment.

'Um, is it okay if I pull up a chair?'

'No worries, mate,' Martin said, hauling himself up like a man defeated. 'You might as well have mine.'

* * *

The following Sunday, all Arthur's preparation was about to come to fruition. We'd spent several evenings together, as he insisted on going over his proposal plans numerous times. It was hard to offer advice, given my concerns about the whole idea, but he wasn't backing out, so I decided the only option was to support him as best I could.

Elliot and Isaac had joined us for a last-minute meeting of the Boys to Men project, where we'd gone over suitable topics of conversation when meeting Elsa's family, and Isaac had asked for our opinion on a date outfit.

'How about you, Elliot?' Arthur asked, when he'd eventually covered every possible aspect of the engagement party. 'This'll be my last meeting, and maybe Isaac's. Has the Boys to Men project hit the target from your perspective?'

'He's still as solidly single as ever, so I'm guessing that would be a hard no,' Isaac said. 'There's only so much Jessie can do with a man who refuses to be moved.'

It took every last drop of willpower to keep my eyes firmly on my tea mug. I'd spent another week avoiding Elliot wherever I could, including staying late at work, hanging out with Connie and hiding in my bedroom.

'If you remember, my target wasn't about dating. I asked Jessie if she'd help me with the Harriers. We won our first match, and have two new players joining us next season, so from my perspective, it's already a resounding success. I've beaten you boys to it.'

'Only thing you will be beating us in this year.' Isaac grinned. 'Shame your Chimney Cup performance isn't as successful.'

'The football result wasn't anything to do with the project, though, was it?' Arthur said. 'Your new clothes, the new recipes you've been trying out. You still don't feel ready to open yourself up to the wonderful world of women?'

'And this, ladies and gentlemen, is how Arthur Wood talks about dating *after* he's had weeks of relationship coaching.' Isaac grimaced.

'My relationship coach knows where I stand on that,' Elliot said, his voice a deep rumble that vibrated through my insides. 'I'm still waiting for her opinion before I take it any further.'

*Oh my goodness.*

Cue various whoops and probing interrogation from the others, while I tried not to boil in my own embarrassment.

'Jessie?' Arthur asked, after Elliot refused to go into any more detail. 'What are your thoughts? Have you met this mystery woman?'

'I...' I wrenched my eyes up to find Elliot's burning into me across the table. I sat there, with my brother and his best friends, and realised that I'd done it again. I'd let things get completely out of hand, and now someone – everyone – was going to end up hurt and having to deal with the consequences. 'I suddenly remembered I have to do something...'

It wasn't a lie. I scrambled up the stairs, flung myself on the bed and called my mum.

## 39

When I bumped my bags down the stairs half an hour later, my housemates were waiting in the hallway.

'What's going on?' Isaac asked, face creased in concern.

'I'm going to stay with Mum and Dad for a bit,' I said, failing to blink back the tears.

'What? Why? I thought we were finally becoming half-decent housemates. Have we done something to upset you?'

'No surprises that it's me,' Elliot said, his face hidden in shadow. 'Jessie, I'm sure if we talked about it...'

'No,' I answered, needing to move things on before my courage scuttled back off to where it usually hid. 'It's not you. It's me.' I took a deep breath. 'I can't keep living here with this secret. I never would have moved in, only I didn't realise it was Elliot's house. Then I tried to come up with a plan to leave, but then there was the energy bill and I started to really love my job and, honestly, I love living with you guys. I feel safe here. Happy. I feel like *me* for the first time in forever. My therapist said I should put the past behind me. But I've tried and I can't. Then Elliot and I kissed so I need to tell you the truth. I'm so, so sorry that I didn't before.'

'Jessie.' Isaac moved forwards to put his arm around me, but I stepped back.

'No. Let me do this.' I looked straight at Elliot as I carried on. 'I was with you at the prom. When you were walking home, we were messing about and then I distracted you and you got hit. So. All of it. Everything you have to live with. Nearly dying. The times you wished you had. None of it would have happened if it wasn't for me. In answer to your question last Sunday, I would *love* to kiss you again, Elliot. I have wanted it since I saw you walk into the kitchen the day I moved in, and every day since. So, that's why I have to go, because now you've heard what I've done, I know the last person you'll want to kiss is me. All I can say is that I'm sorry. I'm sorry it happened and I'm sorry I never told you and I'm sorry if me trying to put it behind me has only ended up hurting you again.'

Then I turned, and did what I always do – I ran. Right into Dad's car, waiting at the end of the drive.

\* \* \*

For the next couple of days I hid, of all places, in the Chicken Coop honeymoon suite at the Barn. There was no one booked in that week, and the couple getting married on Saturday had chosen an expensive hotel in Nottingham for their wedding night. I turned off my phone, tried to eat the food Mum pilfered from Wendy's fridge, lay under the luxury bamboo duvet or curled up in the hammock, and wondered what on earth I was going to do now.

Telling Elliot hadn't miraculously made everything feel better. It still didn't change what I'd done, or who I'd been ever since. But, I thought that somewhere deep inside, a tiny version of me had begun to open her eyes and stir. The me who I would have been if none of this had happened. The me who didn't feel the need to keep ruining her life, to pay for ruining his.

For the first time since the night of the prom, I felt a glimmer of genuine hope.

\* \* \*

On Sunday afternoon, after failing to convince me to join Arthur's party, the sounds of which had started drifting over the hedge, Mum blabbed to Isaac.

'I've been sent to fetch you to the party.' He came and sat on the spare lounger, holding out a tissue when I immediately started crying again.

'Not happening,' I hiccupped, after he'd given me a long, twinly hug.

'Come on, can we skip you listing all the reasons why you don't want to, and me explaining why you need to come anyway, and you eventually giving in and agreeing to come for half an hour, just while Arthur makes his speech, and you just come now? I'm on a *date*. With *Connie*. And it's actually going okay. I don't want to waste it arguing with you.'

'Then go,' I said, half-annoyed, half-laughing through my tears. 'I didn't ask you to come.'

'No, but now I'm here you know I can't go back without you.'

'Is he there?' I asked, my voice quavering.

'Of course he's there. Most of the village are there. But you really need to talk to him, sis.'

'I can't,' I said. 'Not yet.'

He stood up, the heartbreak scrawled across his face. 'Okay. But will you talk to me? Not today, but soon? It kills me that you kept this from me.'

'I couldn't bear you blaming me,' I sobbed. 'I couldn't take the look in your eyes when I told you.'

'And you think I've been able to bear the look in your eyes ever since it happened?'

* * *

He left a couple of minutes later and I crept back inside and folded myself into one corner of the bed, trying to convince myself that Arthur wouldn't mind me missing his big moment. Isaac started sending me photos, of the gravestone chair covers and urns stuffed with flowers.

Elsa's arriving with her family in fifteen minutes. At the very least you could spy through a hole in the fence.

I was contemplating this while standing in my flip-flops in the doorway when the gate opened again. Expecting my parents checking up on me, I'd not moved when the figure stepped through, a slight list to the left as he closed the gate behind him.

'Isaac told you,' I mumbled, when he'd come to a stop a couple of metres in front of me.

'We agreed there'd been enough secrets for now.'

'I'm sorry. I don't know what else to say.'

It turned out no other words were necessary. Without saying anything, Elliot took two steps closer, wrapped his arms around me, and held me as I sobbed. It wasn't long before I realised he was crying, too.

'You shouldn't be comforting me,' I wept. 'You should hate me.'

'Never,' he breathed into the top of my head. 'There's nothing you could do to make me hate you.'

'I ruined your life!'

'No more than I did, being an idiot trying to impress you. Or the driver, speeding after smoking weed all night. It was a horrible accident. We were kids. The worst thing that could happen is for that to spoil what we have now. Jessie, I really care about you. I know I'm not good at picking up this stuff, but I think you feel the same way about me.'

'But how can you ever forgive me? You might think you have, or that it doesn't matter any more, but then you'll forget something important or lose your temper again, and instead of being angry at yourself, you'll blame me.'

'I won't blame you, Jessie. I promise.'

'How can you promise? You don't know!'

'I do know.' He pulled away, wiping the matt of hair from my cheek with a trembling hand. 'I know because I never blamed you. I never hated you. If you had any part to play in what happened, I forgave you for it a long time ago.'

I rubbed a hand over my face, trying to process what he'd said. 'But you didn't know. You couldn't remember.'

'I already told you. When it comes to you, I remember everything.'

Fearing my legs had turned to water, I crumpled onto a lounger. 'What?'

'I didn't, at first. But it came back, in pieces, over time.'

'You remember the accident?'

He came to kneel in front of me, forehead resting against mine as our tears mingled together. 'I remember that whole night.'

Both hands instinctively reached out and clutched his shirt, needing to hold on to something. To *him*.

'I remember talking to you. Sitting with you on the golf course. My heart thumping harder than the bass of the music behind us.'

As he spoke, he inched his face closer to mine. 'I remember kissing you.'

With another tiny movement forwards, he softly pressed his lips against mine. 'Like that.'

I smiled, closing my eyes as I gave a tiny shake of my head, whispering, 'You remembered it wrong. It wasn't like that.'

'Oh?'

Reaching forwards, I resumed the kiss. A little firmer this time. 'More like this.'

'I've replayed those kisses a million times. They were definitely something more like this.'

This time, the kiss was long and deep. Sweet and strong. Just like I remembered.

'Are you sure? That memory of yours isn't confusing me with someone else?'

He laughed. 'Jessie, there hasn't been anyone else to confuse you with.'

'What?' I sat back, stunned.

'You may have noticed I've got some issues. And then years had gone by, just me, and I hadn't a clue how to be with anybody apart from my dog and uncivilised housemates. In the end I paid this woman to be my relationship coach. I thought I'd get some clues about what she wanted in a man. So I could be that for her.'

'When all she ever wanted was you.'

We kissed again, and then some more, until Arthur rang Elliot to say that Elsa had turned up, his float had punctured, he was freaking out and needed his wingmen.

'Maybe don't go?' I said, resting my head against his chest. 'Maybe freaking out about a public proposal two months in is an appropriate response, and the best thing that can happen is no one talks him into it. Elsa and her family can go home none the wiser.'

'It'd be kind of hard to explain the party, let alone the banner, if he did chicken out.'

'And if he goes through with it, and she doesn't say yes, he's going to need his friends,' I added.

Elliot stood up, holding out one hand. 'You're coming with me, though?'

'Well, seeing as the only reason I was here was to hide from you, I suppose I am.'

* * *

The Barn garden looked even worse – better? – than I'd imagined. Connie had gone to town, stringing up church bell shaped bunting between the trees. There were plastic plinths displaying photos of Arthur and Elsa's brief courtship all over the place, masses of church candles, and Isaac's photos hadn't done those gravestone chairs any justice.

Mum spotted us across the grass, bouncing up and down with glee, but I was spared from her sprinting over as at that point some classical music started blaring, and everyone's attention was soon caught by an almighty splashing over in the pond.

For an excruciating twelve minutes, Arthur sploshed and crashed his way through the algae-infested, freezing cold water. He had a turquoise float under one arm, which kept propelling him around in a semi-circle before he realised and did a course correction by swapping it to the other arm.

The whole scenario was an attempt to recreate the iconic scene from the *Pride and Prejudice* film. Unfortunately, unlike Mr Darcy, Arthur was not only unable to swim very well; he had also decided to keep on his waistcoat and best funeral suit. As he staggered out of the water, chest heaving, dripping with mud and a strand of pondweed caught in his hair, he appeared more like an extra from a horror film than a romantic hero.

As Isaac solemnly handed him his top hat and cane, Elsa gave a round of rapturous applause, crying out 'bravo!' as her boyfriend squelched towards her and took her hand to kiss.

Climbing unsteadily onto a chair, water still streaming off him, he'd certainly got everyone's attention.

'Firstly, thank you everyone for coming on this most special occasion,' he said, his voice cracking like a pubescent boy until he stopped to wipe his forehead with a purple handkerchief, and took a few deep breaths. 'Right. Where was I? Oh yes, I was about to offer sincere thanks to my beloved, Elsa, and her delightful family, who I have the pleasure of meeting for the first time today. They are as splendid as I'd have imagined the people who conceived, birthed and raised Elsa to be.'

'I told him not to mention conceiving,' I whispered to Elliot, my trepidation growing.

'As most of you know, I've never had much luck with the fairer sex. That is, until the wonderful Jessica Brown re-entered my life.' Arthur tipped his hat at me across the lawn.

I resisted the urge to bury my head in my hands, as a tall, blonde woman who looked the image of Elsa turned around, frowning.

'She helped me see that the best way to win the heart of the woman I loved was to be myself.'

'That's *so* not how it went,' Elliot murmured.

'And here I am! Arthur Wood, of Wood and Sons. Funeral director, runner up in the Chimney Cup, grave-hunter and novice cook. A man no longer in possession of his own heart, because I gave it to Elsa Larsson the moment she said, "Would you all please stand for our first hymn".'

A tiny snort escaped, as I battled to contain my nervous laughter.

'After so many years of waiting, I've got no reason to wait any longer, because I know I couldn't find a better woman if I kept on looking for the rest of my life.'

He hopped down from the chair, top hat falling off as he stumbled into a man I presumed to be Elsa's dad, before righting himself and going down on one knee.

'Elsa, I want you so much it's given me indigestion. Will you marry me? Preferably as soon as possible?'

Crunch time. Elsa was at an angle to me, so I'd not been able to gauge her reaction so far. I prayed she wouldn't break his heart, but if the answer was no – or at least, not yet – she'd find a gentle way to say it.

Her opening words made me prepare for the worst. 'Arthur Wood, we've only known each other for fifteen weeks! It's ridiculous to decide that quickly whether you want to spend the rest of your life with someone! I'm twenty-six! That's a lot more weeks I'd be stuck with you.'

'Around 2,500, if we survive until the current life expectancy,' Arthur chipped in.

'But, the truth is, that from the moment you offered to show me Elspeth Tickle's grave, I knew you were the man for me. A billion weeks isn't long enough. I've spent the past month wondering whether I was going to have to give up waiting and ask you myself!'

'For the benefit of my blood pressure, and our gathered family and friends, would you mind answering the question, please?'

Elsa twisted around, jolting slightly as she took in the hundred or so guests waiting with bated breath.

'Well, yes! Of course. I mean, not yes I mind, no I don't mind but yes to the question.' She stopped, held up her hands. 'Yes, Arthur Wood. I would like nothing more than to marry you. As soon as possible.'

**40**

----------

The midsummer sun was nestling against the Barn rooftop when Elliot and I finally slipped away from the party. As usual, there'd been numerous hands to assist with the final stages of clearing up and reorganising ready for the day centre tomorrow, so we felt no guilt in ducking back through the Chicken Coop gate and clambering into the hammock where we gently swung, my head resting against Elliot's chest as we watched the birds swooping across the cornflower sky and Penny nosing about in the flowerbeds lining the garden wall.

For now, it was enough to be together, with many things not yet spoken, but no shameful secrets towering between us. The talking and the figuring out could wait.

Besides, Elliot had missed out on a decade of kisses. I felt it my duty to help him catch up.

That is, until the gate creaked open again and my brother wandered through, Connie a couple of steps behind him.

My initial irritation at being disturbed was soon appeased by the blankets they'd brought, along with a cool bag containing a stash of leftovers. Arthur and Elsa also appeared with a bottle of Prosecco and six glasses.

We lit the Chicken Coop fire pit and cooked the juiciest burgers made from Wendy's secret recipe, topping them with cheese before squashing them into fluffy brioche buns along with thick slices of beef tomato and fried onions from the Barn vegetable patch.

'Is Wilf with your parents?' I asked Connie, once we'd filled our glasses and toasted the newly engaged couple, the newly dating couple and whatever me and Elliot now were.

Connie shifted on the blanket, appearing uncomfortable for the first time since I'd met her.

'He's at a sleepover. The school holidays start this week.'

'At Wodger's house,' Isaac added, 'which isn't at all awkward.'

'It's totally awkward!' Connie blushed. 'Martin came round a few days ago with a bunch of flowers. Said he wanted to make his intentions clear, seeing as he now had competition.'

'What did you say?' Elsa asked, leaning forwards in interest.

'I said thank you very much, I'd enjoyed our dates and really appreciated his friendship, but I wasn't prepared to commit to anything more.'

'Competition,' Isaac snorted, producing a glare from me and an arched eyebrow from Connie. 'I mean,' he backtracked, realising the mistake. 'This isn't medieval times. You aren't some prize to be won.'

'Thank you for the clarification.' Arthur looked pensive. 'I'd assumed you were making a blatant remark about your superiority to Martin Bradgate.'

Isaac looked smug. 'I'm sure Martin is the perfect match for someone out there. Just not Connie.'

'Oh what, and you are?' Connie asked.

His wink had Connie burying her nose in her wine glass.

'Will he cope with a strange house?' I asked, hoping to spare her further embarrassment.

'He slept there a couple of weeks ago, when we were over for dinner, so he should be okay. I went to help settle him in and Martin will call if there's a problem.'

The lingering smugness on Isaac's face vanished at the reminder that this was a first date, with no promise of any commitment following it.

'Did your parents enjoy the party?' I asked Elsa, although it was obvious that I was really asking what they thought about the engagement.

'They did.' She beamed, her blissful gaze drifting between Arthur and her antique diamond ring. 'Apart from me getting engaged to a man they'd only just met. They were pretty horrified at that bit.'

'Oh dear.' I winced.

'Don't worry,' Arthur said, wrapping his arm around her. 'I soon won them around. There's not a human being on the planet who can resist the charms of me dancing to eighties' soft rock.'

'It's true!' Elsa retorted with a giggle, when we all broke into incredulous laughter. 'My man has some smooth moves.' She paused, eyes twinkling. 'And he had cleaned up and changed into a dry shirt and jeans by then. That pond water reeked. It was understandable my parents weren't convinced.'

'Don't worry, my beloved,' Arthur said. 'We've got until the end of the year to win them around.'

'New Year's Eve,' Elsa added. 'Save the date!'

She then burst into happy sobs, and despite thinking I'd surely run out of tears for one day, it was impossible not to join her.

'I propose a toast!' Arthur said, once he'd blotted Elsa's cheeks with a claret handkerchief. 'To the six of us, and the official completion of the Boys to Men project!'

Isaac went rigid, his glass frozen half-way to his mouth.

'The what?' Connie asked. 'Please tell me you aren't starting a tribute act, because if you are, that's really not the band to go for.'

'I love "End of the Road"!' Elsa said. 'You could perform at our wedding?'

'We aren't forming a band,' Arthur chuckled, although his mirth dried up when he saw Isaac's granite glare. 'I'll explain later, my sweet.'

'Will you explain later?' Connie asked Isaac.

'Of course.' He downed the rest of his Prosecco. 'Once we're engaged.'

'Oh yes!' Elsa waved her hand at me. 'That was the whole point of coming to find you. I wanted to say thanks for everything you did to help Arthur put all this together. He told me you helped, a lot. It's honestly been the best day of my life, so thanks, Jessie.'

'You're very welcome. Although, to be honest I was nervous that Arthur was rushing things a bit, and you'd not be ready to say yes.'

'I told you,' Arthur replied. 'Once you've found the one you've been waiting for, why wait any longer?'

'I agree completely,' Elliot said, reaching for my hand. 'It's been more than long enough for me and Jessie. I'm very relieved the waiting is over.'

'*What?*' Elsa screeched, jerking so abruptly half her drink landed in the fire pit. 'You and Jessie are engaged, too?'

'No!' I exclaimed, at exactly the same time as Elliot.

'Oh, I'm so sorry,' she blurted back. 'Of course not. Of course you aren't. That would be ridiculous. You'd have told us. And you aren't wearing a ring. That wasn't at all what you meant. Unless. Oh my goodness. Was that it? Were you about to propose and I just interrupted and ruined it all with my stupid, blabber mouth? Arthur will you please shut me up before I wreck things any further?'

As Arthur planted his mouth on Elsa's, as effective a way to stop her talking as any, Elliot turned to me, his face stricken.

'I didn't mean... I didn't just propose to you, did I? Because that wasn't what I meant.' He stopped, ran a hand over his hair, searched the fire for the right words. 'Is that okay? Are we still okay?'

'Yes. That's more than okay.' I gave his hand an affectionate tug.

'Whew. That's a relief. Not that I'm saying I don't want to. One day, I mean. Probably not in fifteen weeks' time. But for now... this is okay, isn't it?'

'Just okay?' I gave him a sideways look.

Elliot leant closer to me, ducking his head so that no one else could hear.

'No. It's not okay. This is... It's perfect.'

I glanced across the crackling flames at my brother, his grey eyes dancing as he chatted with Connie. At Arthur and Elsa, pressed tightly together as they inspected her ring for the billionth time. At the streaks of amber, gold and rose across the sky above the Barn, signifying a place and people I'd grown to love like my own family. At the sign hanging in the Chicken Coop window:

*Welcome to your beautiful new adventure*

The unmistakable words of my mother, who I now got to see smiling across the office at me every workday.

I turned back to Elliot, the boy who I had fallen in love with a lifetime ago. The man who had offered me the grace of forgiveness. Whose patient, unyielding love would, I trusted, enable me in time to forgive myself.

For me, in that moment, as always, I agreed with Elliot Ollerton.

It was absolutely perfect.

# ACKNOWLEDGMENTS

I'm writing this at the end of 2022, the most incredible year for me as a writer, and I'm as always full of admiration and gratitude for the fabulous team at Boldwood Books. There are too many names to mention them all, but particular thanks go to Nia Beynon, Jenna Houston and Claire Fenby. My editor, Sarah Ritherdon, is unfailingly brilliant and such a pleasure to work with. Amanda Ridout has created a publishers that I'm proud to be a part of. Enormous thanks to my agent, Kiran Kataria, whose input and advice remains as invaluable as ever. I must also mention Candida Bradford, whose copyedits were so encouraging. A massive thank you to Sam Wightman, for sharing so openly with me. I hope I did your courage, compassion and ingenuity some justice. Thanks also to Lorna Carlin, for your helpful insights. To all those who have read, borrowed, reviewed or told their friend about my books – thank you for helping my author dreams come true. And to those who've contacted me to say you enjoyed one of my stories – it makes such a difference to know you're out there! Ciara, Joseph and Dominic – seeing your stories unfold is my greatest joy. And George, thank you for remaining my biggest fan.

# MORE FROM BETH MORAN

We hope you enjoyed reading *Always On My Mind*. If you did, please leave a review.

If you'd like to gift a copy, this book is also available as an ebook, hardback, large print, digital audio download and audiobook CD.

Sign up to Beth Moran's mailing list for news, competitions and updates on future books.

http://bit.ly/BethMoranNewsletter

Explore more heartfelt, uplifting novels from Beth Moran.

# ABOUT THE AUTHOR

**Beth Moran** is the award winning author of ten contemporary fiction novels, including the number one bestselling *Let It Snow*. Her books are set in and around Sherwood Forest, where she can be found most mornings walking with her spaniel Murphy. She has the privilege of also being a foster carer to teenagers, and enjoys nothing better than curling up with a pot of tea and a good story.

Visit Beth's website: https://bethmoranauthor.com/

Follow Beth on social media:

facebook.com/bethmoranauthor

twitter.com/bethcmoran

instagram.com/bethmoranauthor

bookbub.com/authors/beth-moran

# Boldwood

Boldwood Books is an award-winning fiction publishing company seeking out the best stories from around the world.

Find out more at www.boldwoodbooks.com

Join our reader community for brilliant books, competitions and offers!

Follow us
@BoldwoodBooks
@BookandTonic

Sign up to our weekly deals newsletter

https://bit.ly/BoldwoodBNewsletter